L♥VE
& OTHER
HUMAN
ERRORS

About the Author

Bethany Clift is a graduate of the Northern Film School and the director of her own production company, Saber Productions. Her debut novel, *Last One at the Party*, was published in 2021 and the television rights have been optioned by Scott Free Films.

Also by Bethany Clift

Last One at the Party

BETHANY CLIFT

L♥VE & OTHER HUMAN ERRORS

HODDER &
STOUGHTON

First published in Great Britain in 2022 by Hodder & Stoughton
An Hachette UK company

1

A CIP catalogue record for this title is available from the British Library

Hardback ISBN 978 1 529 33217 9
Trade Paperback ISBN 978 1 529 33218 6
eBook ISBN 978 1 529 33219 3

Typeset in Plantin Light by Manipal Technologies Limited

Printed and bound in Great Britain by Clays Ltd, Elcograf S.p.A.

Hodder & Stoughton policy is to use papers that are natural, renewable
and recyclable products and made from wood grown in sustainable
forests. The logging and manufacturing processes are expected
to conform to the environmental regulations of the country of origin.

Hodder & Stoughton Ltd
Carmelite House
50 Victoria Embankment
London EC4Y 0DZ

www.hodder.co.uk

For Sam and Tilly, who make me laugh every day and gave me all the jokes in this book. I love you very, very much.

September

Indiana

Jean-Paul Sartre wrote that 'Hell is other people'. He was right. It is 1.11 p.m. on Friday 20 September 2030, and I am in hell.

Not literal hell. I do not believe in a literal hell. I am a rational person, so do not give credit to stories that have been invented to control the proletariat.

I am in the basement of a London office block. It is filthy and smells appalling. There are thousands of these spaces on the outskirts of New London City – empty rooms with basic facilities, rented by the month to technology company start-ups desperate to squeeze some new program or product from an already glutted industry.

The basement that I am in is approximately 1,200 square foot, and – in addition to me – there are twelve coders, one engineer, one salesman, and three directors sat within it. This is a one-room operation so the space contains all the company hardware. Computer servers are stacked haphazardly on racks with wires and cables threaded like spiderwebs to various elec-tricity and data outlets. The heat the servers generate is like the strong blast of the midday sun. I can see their cheap Chinese quantum computer from where I stand. It is built incorrectly and will not function for longer than three months. I don't tell them this. However, the substandard computer systems are not what make this place hell. It is the people.

The average person expels air from their body around 1,000 times an hour. Each breath consists, on average, of 78 per cent nitrogen, 13 per cent oxygen, 4 per cent carbon dioxide and 5 per cent water vapour. Combine this water vapour with the typical amount sweated per person, per hour and you get a gross figure of approximately 70 grams of bodily fluid expelled every sixty minutes. This is from the average person sitting in a cool environment. The people in this room are mostly over-weight and sweating profusely. During the forty-one minutes I have been in the basement, the inhabitants have expelled nearly two litres of bodily secretions. The process of precipitation means that this moisture, composed entirely of sweat and breath, has made its way to the ceiling. What goes up, must come down, and the combined liquid residue of these men is dripping back down on me like rancid rain.

The room is a cacophony of dripping bodily fluids, searing heat, endless and needless grunts of exertion, the constant scratching of pallid, excessive flesh, and extreme levels of flatulence. The putrid smell of rotting food and fetid breath surrounds me like a fog.

As previously expressed – I am in hell.

I am here to pitch my product – TRU. TRU is a technological data-harvesting solution. It is sophisticated, innovative and elegant – this company is none of those things. I knew as soon as the first sweat drop landed on me that this meeting would be a waste of my time. But the meeting is in my diary so I am compelled to attend. I should have brought a rain mac.

I have finished presenting and am answering questions. Having responded to queries about hardware and interface, I am now fielding what they believe to be sophisticated and amusing questions regarding function.

'So, basically, it just finds you a girlfriend or boyfriend?'

Boyfriend – what a ridiculous word. A word used by imbeciles, people who buy from social media advertisements and those inclined to make a life-long commitment to someone they met when they were fifteen.

'No. It does not find the user a girlfriend or boyfriend. TRU uses an incredibly sophisticated and precise marriage of datasets and quantum theory to match you to your universal soulmate.'

I hate using the word 'soulmate' – it makes me feel like a hippy – but my research has proven that people respond strongly and positively to it. There is silence for the briefest of moments.

'But what if you just want a quick shag?'

The room breaks into sniggers and I can no longer contain my ire. My face loses its practised emotionless veneer. I am done here.

I take my prototype from the table, pack away my things, pick up my rucksack, and stride towards the emergency exit.

'That might be alarmed!' squeaks one of the directors.

I do not care. I reach the door and push it wide open; there is no alarm. I gulp in mouthfuls of fresh air and lift my face up to the weak sunlight that filters down from the street level above. Behind me the men shrink back from the outside world. I glance back into the room at them. They are timid and ghostly, like creatures that have forgone the sun to worship their new gods of technology. I too am pale from lack of sun, but I worship no one. I am pale because I choose to be. We might share the same collective name for what we do, but these basement-dwellers are nothing like me, they are not pioneers, not prodigies, not polymaths; they will work in this dark place their entire careers, they will never bask in the glow of a genius like mine.

My backward glance is a mistake. It entails the smallest of pauses in momentum, and one of the directors uses that opportunity to pounce. He clears his throat. I sigh. I had hoped to exit the building without needless explanations and wasted words. I stare at him as coldly and evenly as I can in the hope that he will hold his tongue. He does not.

'You … you're leaving?'

A rhetorical question – the go-to of the socially awkward and intellectually inferior.

'I am finished.'

'So … should we send you our offer?'

I sigh inwardly. I had hoped the physical removal of my presence would make my decision obvious. It has not.

'I have no desire to work with your company.'

He is confused.

'But … you came to us …'

'That was a mistake. I was ill-informed, and this has been a waste of my time.'

Behind him the room bristles with ill-concealed anger – how dare I intimate that they are not worthy? Men are so emotional.

The director tries one last time.

'But … we have infrastructure … and money …'

I cannot contain the short bark of laughter that escapes me.

'That will not help. Your infrastructure is laughably inadequate to scale to what is needed. No competent enterprise will want to partner with you, so I'm sure you will invest in the first seemingly viable product you are offered. That product will consume your finances within a year, and I predict your company will not exist eighteen months from now.'

The man's mouth falls open in an almost comedic gape, but I do not wait to hear his response. I leave, slamming the door to hell shut behind me.

I have somewhere far more important to be.

Lina

I know today is going to be a shitty day when I see Emily standing outside my office, tapping one of her stiletto-encased feet impatiently. Emily never comes to my office this early in the morning unless she has some particularly bad news she wants to share.

It is just before 8 a.m. and I should have been in work by 7, but I am late. Emily isn't late, Emily is never late, she has probably been waiting for me since 5 a.m. Precisely. Everything Emily does is precise. I suspect she doesn't sleep, and I have never seen her eat or drink. Emily and I do the same job but couldn't be more different. Emily is younger than me, thinner than me, whiter than me, and works harder and longer hours than I do. She is so perfect that, the first time I met her, I had the over-whelming urge to press my finger into her cheek to check she was real and not one of the next-gen robots that JaneDoe are currently developing.

I slowly start to retreat down the corridor. Maybe I can make it to the stairs before she sees me, go back down to reception, get a coffee, pull up my bra strap, put some lipstick on, and return when I feel ready to face the day, ready to face Emily. It's really not fair – Emily would look like me too if she'd had to catch the AutoBus into work. I bet she rode in on a fucking golden unicorn.

'LINA!'

Shit. She has seen me. There is no escape.

'Emily, hi.'

I walk reluctantly towards her, juggling my handbag, laptop bag, NotePad, water bottle and building pass.

Emily tuts. She wants me to move faster. Our boss, Fran, will be in the office by 8 a.m., and Emily needs to be at her desk, working hard, when Fran arrives. In the three years that Emily has worked in our team she has only been absent one day. Emily was hit by a car on the way to work and broke her leg. She was back in the office at 6.30 the morning after the accident and worked from a wheelchair for the next six weeks. Total robot move.

Emily looks towards my closed office door, expecting an invitation inside. I don't want Emily inside my office, so put my various items on the floor and extend my hand for the papers she is holding.

'You just need to give me these then?' I say, hopefully.

Emily ignores my proffered hand and nods at my office door.

'There's something we need to discuss.'

That is not a statement I want to hear from Emily, especially not so early in the morning.

'You can tell me here.' I smile genially.

'I want to tell you inside,' she replies coolly.

My smile falters. Emily reaches out a perfectly manicured hand and places it on my door handle proprietorially. Cheeky bitch. She turns the handle and pushes the door open. Her eyes leave mine and she glances inside. Then she gasps. Or retches. It's a tiny and involuntary noise and hard to tell which one. Emily hates the state of my office. Emily is clean and polished and pristine, and my office is, well, a little bit messy. Maybe more than a little bit. I'm really busy so I don't get much time to clear away empty cups or used takeaway containers or old paperwork or shoes and clothes I have left here over the last couple of years. I don't mind the clutter and mess: I hardly even notice it any more and simply wade through it on a daily basis.

Emily minds the mess – she thinks it would be much better if she had my office and then it would be clean. Emily is jealous that I have an office and she doesn't, and she reacts in the same faux-dramatic way every time she sees the inside of my workspace.

'My God! Why on earth don't you let the cleaners in here?'

To which I reply, 'You know why. All of this is proprietary knowledge, and Cameron would have a shit-fit if she thought anyone could access it.'

Of course, I am lying. Most of the programs and products in my office were launched months or even years ago – I just don't want anyone invading my private sanctuary. Emily looks at me with disdain.

'I don't think Dr Cameron Gardner has ever had a "shit-fit" over anything' – Emily wrinkles her perfectly straight nose – 'and what is that awful smell?'

She's right, it does smell terrible in here. I walk around my desk and open the window. My office is on the tenth floor and the wind roars into the room, making papers and rubbish fly up into the air, creating a weirdly pleasing vortex of filth. Emily does not find my filth vortex pleasing. Her face turns puce, and I fear she might blow her circuitry if forced to exist within my chaos much longer. I hold my hand out for the papers once more.

'What is it we need to talk about?' I yell over the wind.

Emily hands me the papers.

'Chris is off today, and …'

Emily cannot be heard over the wind and Emily does not yell. She stalks over to the window and forcefully pulls it shut. She turns to face me with a small smile on her face. Whatever she is going to say is going to be bad. For me.

'Chris is off today. Fran asked if anyone else might want to cover the Pitch meeting, and I suggested you,' she says, smiling genially.

Shit. I don't say this out loud. Emily once reported me to HR for swearing at her. Instead I say, 'What?'

Emily's genial smile grows.

'I thought it might be fun.'

The Pitch meeting is not fun. The meeting is led by Dr Cameron Gardner – the CEO of our company – and is the most reviled meeting of the month; people will do anything to avoid it. That is why I always double-book myself and send Chris in my place.

'I'm sorry Emily, I have the monthly Future Gen meeting to attend at three, so—'

'I've already asked Sarah to move that for you.'

Emily cannot tell me what to do and I am just about to remind her of this when I look down at the papers she has given me. My name has already replaced Chris's as the Software Lead. Once your name is on the attendee list for a meeting with Cameron Gardner you do not back out. Emily knows this. I look up and scowl. Emily's smile widens again. I hate her.

She stands, checks her watch, and moves towards the door. She has six minutes to get back to her desk ready for Fran's arrival.

'*Eres una vaca y espero que te duelan los zapatos,*' I say quietly.

Her head spins back sharply.

'What did you say?'

I shrug.

'I said – *sometimes we all have our crosses to bear.*'

She nods curtly.

I didn't say that. I said, *You are a cow and I hope your shoes hurt your feet.*

Emily makes a considerable show of picking her way carefully across my office and out of the door, avoiding the, now multitudinous, amounts of paper and rubbish that litter the floor. As she leaves, I notice that she has somehow managed to get a bright yellow Post-it note stuck to her pert bottom.

I don't tell her.

Indiana

Today, there is a prevailing westerly wind of approximately 27 mph and this, combined with the moderate heel on my court shoe, means that the 6.3-mile walk between my last appointment and the JaneDoe Technology Building will take me one hour and forty-six minutes. With an ambient outside temperature of 16 degrees, I will perspire lightly on the walk and need to consume upwards of half a litre of water to compensate; I will therefore need to urinate once I arrive at JaneDoe. I will enter the building at 15.24 and my scheduled appointment is at 15.30. This does not allow sufficient urination time within an acceptable contingency buffer, therefore I need to find another means of transport to my meeting.

I do not like the London Underground. I do not like the noise of the tracks, the rush of warm air that heralds the approaching train, the throngs of people, the brush of synthetic clothing on my hand as someone passes too close. I do not normally use the London Underground, but the AutoBus will not be an efficient mode of transport at this time of day, so I am given no choice.

I enter the Underground station at 13.59 p.m. The station entrance is empty, I have the lift to myself and there are only seven other people in my carriage, none of whom look likely to try to talk to me. I stand by the door, in case of an emergency. My journey passes without incident until two stops before my alighting point when a school trip steps into the carriage. Thirty-five adolescents and a conspicuous lack of teaching staff. The assault on my senses is immediate and painful. They bring a cacophony of noise with them: play music on their watches, shout at the person next to them, laugh like they need people in the adjoining carriage to hear. I try to disembark onto the platform to spare myself the ignominy of their company, but the carriage doors close before I can, leaving me trapped in a sea of puberty and polyester. I cling to the filthy handrail, close my eyes, and will the journey to be over.

When I eventually reach my destination, I choose to climb the 267 stairs to the exit rather than face squashing myself into the lift with yet more human contact. I stumble out of the station sweating and breathless into the light September air and, for the second time this day, take a deep and grateful lungful of London's polluted cityscape. I have made it, I am in City Square.

City Square is the central hub of New London City, and the offices surrounding the square house what is left of the technology sector in the UK. In the post-Brexit, post-pandemic years, larger technology companies moved away from London – either to Scotland to take advantage of the new office parks that surround Space Hub Sutherland, or to Europe where taxes and infrastructure are lower and superior respectively. Only Amazon, Google, IBM and JaneDoe maintain London offices now – even Meta has moved north.

The buildings that no longer house offices have been converted into flats that are rented cheaply to single, under-thirty-five, NLC workers. These cash-rich, time-poor professionals have transformed the area from an empty, post-pandemic ghetto into a thriving modern metropolis – hence the re-branding of the area as New London City. Of course, there are those that would say it is still a ghetto – just one that is now exclusively populated by the wealthy and young – but 72 per cent of 16–20-year-olds interviewed in the latest government census expressed a desire to live in New London City – so, if the numbers are true, its popularity does not seem to be waning. In fact, the model has proved so popular they are now replicating it in other UK cities – New Birmingham, New Manchester and, ironically, New York.

I do not live here. I am not a plebeian who can be influenced by a sophisticated marketing campaign. I am here for one reason only – to meet Dr Cameron Gardner.

There are three living people that I admire. Admire – not adulate or emulate or adore. I would not chase them down the street or stalk them on the internet or follow them on social media. I do not have social media. The quickest way to allow criminals access to everything you have ever done with a computer in your entire existence is to set up a new and unprotected social media account. I do not want criminals to have access to everything I have ever done on a computer. I do not want anyone to have access to anything I have ever done on a computer. That would be disastrous.

The three people in life that I admire are: astronaut Chris Hadfield, particle physicist Fabiola Gianotti, and Dr Cameron Gardner. Chris Hadfield for his determination, Fabiola Gianotti for her dedication, and Dr Gardner for, well, everything.

JaneDoe Technology Limited was established by Dr Cameron Gardner in March 1993 and employs more than 7,500 people in sixteen locations globally. Dr Gardner, through JaneDoe, is the fourth leading proponent of digital data collection, storage and processing in the world. For the uneducated and technically illiterate it is easiest to describe JaneDoe as the UK equivalent of Google. The company has the most impressive research and design department in Europe, and is a significant investor in data-harvesting apps, websites and technology. Dr Gardner began, incorporated, and is the CEO of JaneDoe. She is intellectual, intuitive, driven, and fully worthy of my admiration; and today, for the first time, I am going to meet her.

I am not nervous. I do not feel nerves. Nerves are for the under-prepared. I am fully prepared for this meeting. Dr Gardner needs a successful product for JaneDoe, and I have a successful product for her. I have TRU.

Lina

The third Friday of every month is the day of the Advancement of Women in Tech (A-WiT) Pitch meeting

Or – as I prefer to call it – Pitches for the Bitches.

At Pitches for the Bitches, Dr Cameron Gardner – Chair of A-WiT – listens to female-led teams and companies pitch their products for feedback and, on very rare occasions, investment. The meeting lasts an hour and each team is allocated a strict eight minutes to present.

JaneDoe have been hosting the pitch meetings for three years and Cameron has only invested in one company – Buddha-Fam. Fifteen days after she made her initial investment in Buddha-Fam, she bought the company outright and fired everyone who had attended the pitch session. Even with this knowledge, companies still apply in their droves for a chance to attend, because presenting at the A-WiT Pitch meeting is a calling card to other investors; a publicity push that money can't buy.

Companies might clamour to attend the meeting, but, as I said previously, JaneDoe staff will do anything to avoid it. Cameron does not like to mix with her subordinates, she does not lunch with us or have a desk amongst her employees, she locks herself away on the thirty-seventh floor and avoids interaction with us as much as possible. Most JaneDoe employees will last their whole careers without meeting Cameron face-to-face. The majority of them prefer it that way. JaneDoe is not a democracy; it is a plutocratic dictatorship, and the dictator who runs the show is brilliant and intelligent and cunning and mean. I have known people who admire, respect and even worship Cameron, but I have never met anyone who likes her.

I spend my day trying to get out of having to attend Pitches for the Bitches. I fail. So, at 2.45 p.m. I head morosely upstairs. I am scrolling new mail on my watch, so don't check before stepping carelessly into the lift. When I do look up I see to my horror that the lift is not empty. Cameron is already in there, her face like thunder.

Cameron has a private lift that she uses. Her lift has soft mink suede walls and thick white carpet, is smooth and silent, and is hers and hers alone. No one else is permitted into the private lift with Cameron even if they are accompanying her to the same floor. Emily mentioned earlier that Cameron's private lift was out of action today, I ignored her warning and have now made the unforgivable mistake of getting into the lift with the world's busiest, and bitchiest, woman.

I turn sharply and attempt to step back out of the lift, but the doors are already closing. There is no escape, so I nod at Cameron as if this happens all the time, and stand facing the doors with my back to her. Sweat drips down my spine.

Silence.

I am desperate to say something, but know that it will most likely get me fired. The lift stops on floor 13, doors opening to reveal three members of the PR team on their way to the Pitch meeting. My eyes plead with them to step into the lift with us, but their faces fill with fear and they step backwards, allowing the doors to close once more.

Cameron clears her throat and it is like a gunshot.

'I hate the PR team.'

What do I reply to that?

'These Pitch meetings are a ridiculous waste of my time. No one ran female-only funding sessions when I started JaneDoe, no one ran empowerment seminars, or helped me smash the glass ceiling. No one yelled "ME TOO!" when one of the directors of the IMF put his flaccid penis into my hand at a cocktail event in the 90s.'

I have so many questions. None of them are appropriate. Instead I say the first thing that comes into my head.

'Maybe it would have been nice if they had.'

'What?'

There is a pause. A horribly long pause. I clear my throat and try again.

'Maybe it would have been nice if they had, you know, helped with the penis.'

The doors to the lift open. Emily is waiting by the lift. Emily is the only person in the entire building who loves the Pitch meetings because Emily is the only person in the entire building who loves Cameron. I step to the side to allow Cameron to exit the lift first. She sweeps past me, then stops and looks me up and down.

'Well, if I ever need anyone to help me with a penis, Mrs Galaz, I shall call you first.'

I swear that Emily's eyes nearly pop out of her head.

Indiana

It is 15.33 and I am on the thirtieth floor of the JaneDoe Technology Building, waiting in the reception area. Other companies are waiting with me. They check their presentations, mutter about running orders, look suspiciously around as though someone might want to steal their tired and insignificant ideas. These other companies are all missing the point, the obvious and important point that I have spotted and they have not.

JaneDoe are running late.

Dr Gardner's team have clearly made a mistake, and the pitches are behind schedule. Dr Gardner will be annoyed. I do not want to pitch to her when she is annoyed.

There is a woman who seems to be nominally in charge. She has a NotePad and a stylus. I doubt she has any real power – she would be in the meeting if she had any real power – but she is the only JaneDoe employee present.

'I want to reschedule my pitch.'

She looks up, confused, as if I am the first to ever make this request. Maybe I am.

'What?'

'I should have begun my presentation at 15.30. It is now 15.36. I want to reschedule.'

She looks at the door to the meeting room and then back at me.

'Well, you— you can't.'

'Why not?'

'Because … you're not allowed to.'

I was right, she has no power.

'I want to speak to your boss.'

'I'm her boss.'

The voice comes from behind me, so I turn. The woman who spoke has just stepped out of the meeting room. She is about my age, of Spanish or Mexican descent, and looks amused at my request. She smiles at me. I do not smile back.

'I want to reschedule.'

She smiles again. I don't like it.

'You must be Indiana Dylan from HWJ Tech. I am Lina Galaz.'

Ms Galaz holds out a hand; I do not shake it.

'I am not from HWJ Tech. I am HWJ Tech.'

This time Ms Galaz laughs.

'Well, whoever you are, you're next, so do you want to come in or do you want to reschedule to …' Ms Galaz grabs the NotePad from the assistant and scrolls through '… next June?'

I have no choice. I do not like having no choice, and I do not like Ms Galaz.

Ms Galaz pushes the door to the meeting room open and I stride into the room, accidentally on purpose clipping her with the block heel of my court shoe as I pass. I stand at the front as Ms Galaz limps into the room behind me.

Dr Gardner sits at the opposite end of the table, scribbling in a paper notebook. She does not look up as I enter the room.

I take a deep breath. I am calm and confident.

'You are running behind schedule so I shall keep my presentation to six minutes in length.'

There are murmurs around the table. Dr Gardner does not look up from her notebook.

'Your company revenue will drop by a minimum of 4 per cent this year. I have been tracking your performance for the last thirteen months, and my modelling indicates a minimum drop in revenue of 4.1 per cent and maximum of 5.2 per cent.'

Heads snap up from NotePads, whispered conversations stop, everyone looks straight at me. Dr Gardner continues to scribble.

'Where did you get your performance data from?' Ms Galaz asks loudly.

I ignore her question. A few people look nervously towards Dr Gardner. Dr Gardner still does not look up.

I continue.

'JaneDoe leads the field of data collection and processing in Europe, but your field has been cut by 37 per cent in the past five years. The rise of quantum computing means the internet is no longer secure. Unsecured email, business and social accounts are now easy targets for cybercrime. People no longer share personal information freely on the internet. Facebook, Instagram, Twitter, TikTok and Snapchat have all seen their revenues drop significantly. Google's share price has dropped by 6.2 per cent in the last eighteen months. Without an easy and reliable way to harvest data and information, companies like yours will continue to see their revenues decrease. Your entire industry is in decline.'

The room is completely silent.

Dr Gardner looks up from her notepad and stares coldly at me.

'Everyone here knows that. What is your point?'

I do not shrink under her gaze. I look her in the eyes and speak calmly.

'I cannot save your industry. But I can save your company.'

Lina

My first thought when she says, *'I can save your company'* is that it's a fucking bold statement coming from someone who dresses like she's trying to blend into the wall. Seriously – the woman is clothed head to toe in shades of beige and magnolia – move her to the side of the room and you'd lose her. She is the dullest and most uniform person I have ever seen.

My second thought is: If anyone can pull off such a ridiculous claim, maybe this magnolia *mujer* can. I mean, it's not every day you get someone purposefully kicking you on their way into a Pitch meeting.

But, it turns out that in this situation I really can judge this book by its beige cover because, when Cameron asks her how she is going to single-handedly save JaneDoe from our declining industry she replies, *'Because I have solved the problem of love.'*

There are audible sighs of disappointment around the table and I disguise my laughter with a fake coughing fit. Cameron says nothing but goes straight back to scribbling in her notebook. If Indiana Dylan notices that Cameron has effectively shut her pitch down she doesn't show it – her face registers no unease or disappointment, her features do not move at all.

She has four minutes and fourteen seconds left until her six minutes are up. There is no way she is going to pull this off. I sit back, fold my arms, and get ready to watch the show.

Indiana

I am not troubled when my announcement is met with the same level of dismissiveness as it has been in previous pitches. I am here to pitch to Dr Gardner, and until she leaves the room I will carry on with my presentation.

I retrieve two DataLets from my rucksack and pass one to the man sitting to my right.

'Put this on.'

'What is it?'

'It's called a DataLet.'

'A what?'

'A DataLet. Put it on.'

'It looks like a Fitbit.'

I clear my throat and look at him sternly, I have no time for questions now.

'It's not a Fitbit. It is my own design. Put it on.'

The man shrugs and straps my DataLet to his wrist.

I tap the start-up sequence into my Digital Recorder. The man yelps as the DataLet emits a small electric shock and twelve hair-thin needles penetrate his skin.

'*Ow!*'

I do not waste time looking up from my Recorder.

'Please stay calm. The DataLet is simply aligning itself to your nervous system and accessing your artery.'

The man holds his arm away from him and stares suspiciously at the DataLet.

'You all right, Rob?' someone laughs.

Everyone in the room is now watching him – everyone except Dr Gardner.

'Traditional dating and love matching programs do not work. They do not solve the problem of love because none of them finds a lasting partner or soulmate for their applicants. But TRU does.'

This a bold – and not entirely truthful – statement, but my research has shown that a certain amount of drama is needed when introducing audiences to the idea of TRU. I continue and clarify.

'Traditional programs are based upon a process that is rigid and set – they have been using the same technology and algorithms for nearly forty years. It is a sophisticated process, but the outcome is always the same – they find the consumer a soulmate who suits them at this moment in time, someone who will love them as they are now.'

People are watching me.

'But what if something happens that changes the person that you are now? What if you become bankrupt? Lose a leg? Change your career? What happens to your perfect soulmate then?'

I pause. The room is quiet.

'The data that is collected for use within the TRU algorithm is the most sophisticated in the world. It is ground-breaking and will change the way that you, and other companies, gather and use anthropological data in the future. But that is not the element that makes TRU unique.'

Silence. This is the response I desire – my research on how to conduct this presentation has served me well.

'TRU is the first dating algorithm that asks, what if? The first to use not only datasets, but also quantum processing. To combine the rigidity of data with the expanse of the multiverse. And this combination results in a true soulmate match unlike any other available in the world ...'

I pause to allow time for the tiny minds in the room to try to work out the significance of using both classical and quantum processing – but someone has already resolved the conundrum.

'You're using quantum processing to find a universal match.'

SHUT UP MS GALAZ! I want to scream, but don't. Instead I nod tersely.

'Yes. The use of quantum processing within my algorithm ascertains a universal match – one that is applicable in any and all realms and realities. A multiverse soulmate, a partner for life – any life.'

There are hushed whispers around the room, faces lit up, eager to hear more.

'How much do you charge the end user?' someone asks.

'Nothing,' I reply. 'TRU is given to them for free.'

People look aghast. I continue.

'TRU is free because selling the app is not how JaneDoe will make money.'

I grab the other DataLet from the table and hold it up for everyone to see.

'This is a DataLet. It is the most sophisticated data collection instrument in the world. Once on your wrist the DataLet calibrates itself to your body and any form of technology you use or interact with. It then learns everything about you. What time do you wake up, what time do you eat, drink, sleep? When do you wash? Where do you work and play? Do you exercise? How do you commute to work? Do you drink? Smoke? Take drugs? Where do you shop and what do you buy? How long do you spend online each day? What websites do you look at? What is your blood type, blood sugar levels, lipid blood profile? The DataLet records your entire life for twenty-eight days.'

The room is silent. I put the spare DataLet on the table and turn to the man on my right.

'Rob is it?'

Rob nods.

'Rob, I have hacked into your phone for the purposes of this demonstration. I hope you don't mind …'

Rob looks as if he does mind. I don't care. I look down at my Digital Recorder screen.

'Rob, your alarm woke you at 6.45 a.m. this morning. You exercised for thirty-seven minutes. You walked 2.8 miles at a rate of 3.1 mph. You have spent forty-seven minutes online so far today. You have bought three coffees, a Danish pastry, and a Greek salad. You sent flowers to your mother for her birthday but are a day late in sending them as her birthday was yesterday. Since wearing the DataLet your heart rate has fluctuated between seventy-nine and eighty-four beats per minute. Your heart rate and blood pressure are slightly elevated, which indicates you are not entirely happy in your current situation. Your temperature and brain activity also register low levels of arousal, meaning you are attracted to someone in this room.'

Rob looks down at the DataLet on his wrist, eyes wide.

'It can tell all that about me in the three minutes I've been wearing it?'

'The DataLet can tell me far more, but I am only sharing information that is appropriate for your colleagues to hear. Also, you should probably schedule an appointment with your doctor.'

Rob's head shoots up, his eyes fill with panic.

I attempt a smile. My research has shown that humour is important at this point.

'That was a joke. You're fine.'

Rob doesn't laugh. My research may have got this part of my presentation wrong.

Rob pulls the DataLet from his wrist and pushes it back across the table to me while muttering about invasions of privacy.

'The DataLet provides you with twenty-eight days of pure, unfiltered user data. For free.'

I am finished. There is a slight pause, and then the room erupts with questions.

'How does it work?'

'Are those tiny needles?'

'What is the algorithm?'

'Is it viable? Have you tested it?' Lina Galaz asks.

This question I decide to answer.

'I have been running a TRU trial for over twenty-four months with 8,219 initial test subjects. TRU has a 96 per cent success rate with users finding their match – if one is available within the control group – and 100 per cent of matched soulmates are still together. I am increasing membership monthly, and now have 12,646 registered users.'

I glance at my Bracelet, which is strapped to my left wrist.

'I have thirteen seconds left. Time for one more quick question …'

'Is it international? What if I match with someone in Australia?'

'Do you wear it 24/7?'

'Does everyone have a match?'

The questions are coming thick and fast, but there is only one right question and, of course, it comes from Cameron. She stands and the room falls silent.

She does not smile as she asks her question.

'What happens to the data that has been collected after the match is found?'

I do not smile as I reply.

'Whatever you want. You own it outright.'

Lina

There are no more questions after Cameron's. She rips a page out of her notebook, whispers a few words to Fran, and then leaves the room – giving the notebook page to Indiana Dylan on her way out. Indiana Dylan shows no emotion as she reads what is written on the notebook page. I wonder briefly if *she* is the next-gen robot rather than Emily.

The room is still buzzing with chatter. Fran looks stressed, but then Fran always looks stressed.

'People, people listen up please! Tom – I need you to cancel the rest of today's pitches and rearrange. Sean – Cameron would like you and the rest of the hardware team in her office in five minutes. Finance, you'll be needed at seventeen hundred hours. And Lina' – Fran turns to look at me – 'Cameron asked that you take Ms Dylan to wait in your office—'

Emily pipes up. 'That might not be the best idea. I can take Ms Dylan downstairs for a coffee …'

Fran shakes her head.

'Cameron asked Lina to do it,' she says.

I nod. Emily is aghast that I have been given a job she would have been so much better at. I give her a big shiny grin.

I didn't want to give Emily credit in the meeting but she is not wrong about my office – there is no way I can take Indiana

Dylan there. So, as suggested, I take her downstairs for a coffee and hope we don't meet Emily on the way.

Indiana Dylan stands silent and ramrod-straight next to me in the lift, I unconsciously pull my shoulders back. She does not seem pleased or excited by how her presentation went or by the fact that Cameron has, seemingly, made her an offer. She is completely emotionless.

'That was the first time I have ever seen Cameron ask a question,' I say.

Silence.

'Or make an immediate offer.'

I glance at the notebook page. I am desperate to see what is written on it. Indiana Dylan looks pointedly at me and puts the page in her pocket.

'She's obviously really impressed with your product ...' I throw a little bone in there '... and so am I.'

Silence.

'You did a really good pitch.'

'Yes, I did.'

Finally.

'It's such a unique concept. How many of you worked on it?'

'Me and my assistant.'

'What?'

'We worked on it. It's our product. We designed, developed, programmed and created it.'

'Just two of you?'

'Yes.'

I am very impressed – I don't want to be – but I am.

'That's so much work. It must have taken years!'

'Three years.'

Three years is ridiculous.

'Jesus! How on earth did you do it?'

She turns to me, unsmiling.

'We worked hard. And didn't waste time on needless conversation.'

The lift arrives at the ground floor and the doors slide open. Indiana Dylan strides out, leaving me staring after her. I was just trying to be nice. I resolve to sit in absolute silence as we drink our coffee or tea or whatever beige, bland drink she decides she wants.

But, as I step from the lift, Indiana Dylan puts on her taupe coat. I look at her.

'What are you doing?'

She looks back at me.

'I am putting on my coat.'

'Why?'

'I am leaving.'

'Why?'

I am vaguely aware that I sound like an idiot, but I cannot comprehend what is happening.

'I will not be accepting Dr Gardner's offer.'

She adjusts her rucksack on her back.

'You … you're leaving?'

'I am leaving.'

She can't leave! She has been told to stay. No one refuses Cameron. No one. I am jolted out of my confusion.

'You can't go!' I practically yell. I grab her sleeve.

She frowns down at my hand and gives her arm a little shake to free it from me.

'I can go.'

'No – sorry – of course you can, if you want to. What I mean is that Cameron has made you an offer and has asked you to stay, so if I were you, I would bloody well stay!'

Indiana looks at me blankly.

'But you are not me.'

She twists on one sensible-height heel and is gone. I am left with words half-formed in my mouth and panic rising in my soul.

I get back in the lift straight away and head up to my office. I need to calm down, to think, to invent a reason why I have just allowed the best product we have seen in the last three years to slip through my fingers. I need to work out how I am going to tell Fran, how I am going to tell Cameron. I need my office to do it. I need my clutter and my familiarity and the confusion that calms me and helps to clear my mind. I take a deep breath as I reach my office; it is all going to be okay, I will sort it, I will think of something, I always do, it's one of the reasons I have kept my job so long. It is all going to be …

Fucked. It is all going to be fucked.

Because, as I open my door and look into my office, I see him. Sitting in my chair, in the middle of my clutter, staring out at my view.

Jack Hunter.

He turns around, his face frowning for the briefest of moments before breaking into a charming smile.

'Lina! How are you? The door was open.'

Shit.

Indiana

Ms Galaz was right – Dr Gardner did give me an offer for TRU – but it is not an offer that I will accept. None of the companies that I have pitched to have made me an offer that I will accept. This is annoying, but I will not spend time thinking about the problem now because today is the twenty-third day of my menstrual cycle and I have another important appointment.

As I walk across City Square my Bracelet buzzes. I look down at it.

Please call the office

A message from my assistant, Peggy. I tap the EarBuddy in my right ear twice.

'Call office.'

Peggy answers the phone before the first ring.

'Hello Indiana. How was your day?' Peggy asks.

I ignore the greeting.

'What do you need? It is the twenty-third day. I am not coming back to the office.'

'I know it is the twenty-third day – I am your diary.'

'So why did you message me?'

'Right Hand Solutions have requested you consult on their quantum firewall. It is urgent, apparently.'

I sigh. Despite having a genius-level IQ, being the director and sole employee of a cutting-edge development company, creating the most sophisticated data-harvesting technology on the market, and building the – soon-to-be – most advanced computer system in the world. I still need to eat and pay bills, so I occasionally consult for companies far less accomplished than my own.

'Fine. Tell them I will address their issue first thing tomorrow.'

There is a momentary pause and I feel my Bracelet buzz slightly as Peggy accesses my latest readings.

'Your serotonin levels are high. You are tense.'

'Yes. I am tense. I have been in three pitch meetings today and none of them has resulted in a viable offer.'

'All of your pitches have resulted in viable offers. You have decided not to accept the offers. There is a difference.'

Peggy is right. I have had offers from every single company I have pitched to. Unfortunately these offers always involve me either joining the company or consulting on TRU for a lengthy amount of time. I do not want to do that.

'I am too busy to spend time on an old project, and TRU is an old project,' I say to Peggy.

'I understand that. They do not.'

Once more, Peggy is right.

'How was the pitch at JaneDoe?'

I do not want to tell Peggy but I have no choice.

'They want me to consult full-time for a year as part of the deal.'

'So you rejected the offer?'

'I rejected the offer.'

Peggy is too attuned to my needs to say, 'I told you so', so instead changes the subject.

'Someone has been ringing the office reception doorbell.'

'What?'

'It has rung four times in the last hour.'

'Access the intercom and tell them to leave.'

'Should I ask them what they want?'

'No. Tell them to leave. Are we done?'

'Yes. Enjoy your evening.'

I tap my EarBuddy again and disconnect without saying goodbye. I never say goodbye to Peggy. I don't see the need.

Today is the twenty-third day of my menstrual cycle so today I am going to have sex.

I have sex on the twenty-third day because it is when I am least likely to conceive; it is also the point of the month where I am at my most sexual and need to satisfy my carnal urges. I like sex and I like orgasms and if I have both on a regular basis it helps to regulate my moods and allows me to concentrate fully on my work. I masturbate three times a week, but have yet to find a vibrator or dildo that is as pleasing as a penis.

On the twenty-third day of my menstrual cycle I also drink alcohol. I don't normally drink alcohol; it impairs my brain activity, makes me sluggish, and interrupts my sleep patterns, but I do like the taste of it. I like whisky and champagne. Not together. So, before I have sex, I go to Searcys at St Pancras and drink champagne. I like Searcys because they do high-quality champagne and I can sit at the bar and am rarely approached. I find that three glasses is enough to give me a low buzz of pleasure but not enough to impact my performance the next day.

After drinking my champagne, I am relaxed and hungry. I go to my favourite noodle bar and eat a bowl of ramen with pork belly and drink a glass of water to help rehydrate. I then find someone for sex.

I have never been in a relationship and have never had sex with the same man twice. I do not desire romantic or emotional entanglement. My life is rich and fulfilling and I do not require a relationship. I am not someone that would ever want – or need – to use TRU. Despite very much enjoying intercourse I do not find the social precursor to finding a sexual partner pleasurable, so I have, in the past, used male prostitutes; but I do not like the clinical nature of the exchange or the moral ambiguity of using such a service. So, I now frequent the Meet Markets to avail myself of sexual partners.

The Meet Markets are a collection of huge warehouses on the outskirts of New London City that have transformed into mega-clubs following the demise of social media. If you do not have a good quality quantum firewall installed on your computer then the internet is no longer a safe place to socialise. Only the very rich and the very protected can afford to maintain a strong social media presence. People must now socialise and find sex through a non-web-based medium, so they go to the Meet Markets instead. The premise is clean and simple; if you are in one of the Meet Markets, you want sex. There is no chasing, no small talk, no ambiguity, and no flirting needed. It is modern and clinical and suits my needs precisely. I am rarely inside one of the Meet Markets for longer than ten minutes, and tonight is no exception.

I enter the Blue Jean club at precisely 9.06 p.m. and am approached by three men immediately. None of them are to my liking. The fourth man that approaches me is agreeable. I ask to see his teeth. His teeth are straight and polished – if he takes good care of his teeth it is likely he extends the courtesy to the rest of his body. We leave the club together three minutes later.

Lina

Jack Hunter. Handsome, charismatic, friendly Jack Hunter.
Jack is a software engineer in my team. He is bright,
knowledgeable, smart, funny, friendly, and always acces-
sorised with a charming smile. He is by far the most popular
employee in the office – everyone loves Jack.

Except me. I don't love Jack. Jack pisses me off.

I work hard. Really, really hard. I am in meetings all day,
then still have work to do after those meetings, so end up
staying late most evenings. I work at weekends, I rarely take
holidays. When I had my son, Bruce, the law said I had to stay
away from the office for six weeks, but I was working from
home three days after giving birth. My life is a constant juggle
of meetings and work and home and work and sleep and work
– a never-ending wheel of effort – it never stops and I never
get off.

Jack doesn't work hard. Jack doesn't have to. Jack coasts
through life and through JaneDoe with a constant grin on his
face, riding the wave of being white, male and good-looking.
Jack and I joined JaneDoe at about the same time – we used
to work in the same team, he worked hard, I liked him. But
then, one day he stopped working hard and started coasting. He
hasn't had a promotion since and he doesn't care. Why would
he? He's happy as he is, drifting along downstream, blissfully

unaware of everyone battling to swim upstream beside him. It pisses me off.

And he has just been on holiday for two weeks. I have never taken a two-week holiday – I have never even taken a one-week holiday.

'Jack. You're back.'

'I am. I missed you.'

He grins at me.

'Of course you did. You're in my office. In my chair.'

Jack glances down at my chair as if he has just found himself in it by accident.

'So I am.' He looks around my office thoughtfully. 'I think I like your office the best. All the other offices are so ... clean.'

He grins again. I don't smile back at Jack. I have been the recipient of his charm far too many times to be fooled by it any more. Jack does like my office – I once caught him taking a nap in here. I walk around my desk and stand over him.

'I'd like an office one day,' he says.

'I think you have to do some actual work to get an office. Get out of my chair.'

He laughs, stands up lazily, stretches, then steps slowly to the side to allow me to sit down. I expect him to leave, but instead he sits on the edge of my desk.

'So where is she?'

'Where is who?'

'That woman everyone's talking about, the one from the Pitch meeting ...'

Shit. I am grabbing my laptop bag from under my desk when he asks and am relieved he can't see the panic on my face. I decide to stay under my desk for a bit longer.

'Why should I know where that woman is?'

'Emily said you took her for a coffee.'

Double shit. I should have known. Emily loves Jack as much as everyone else does, so of course she will have moaned to him about me getting the job of looking after Indiana Dylan. I wish I'd bloody let her do it now.

'You all right down there?'

Jack's face apears under the desk with me. I pull back quickly, bang my head, and sit up again. I look at him, he looks at me. I rub my head.

'You lost her!'

Shit.

I look around my office in panic as if Cameron might be lurking and listening.

'*Shhh*! I didn't lose her.' I cross to my window and look out. What am I doing? Hoping to spot her? 'She left.'

'She left? Why didn't you stop her?'

'I TRIED!'

I run my hands through my hair. I am starting to panic.

Jack laughs, walks around to the other side of my desk, and slumps down into the chair opposite me. I glare at him.

Jack is the only person in JaneDoe who would dare to enter my office uninvited – even Emily doesn't do that. Jack doesn't care about me, my job, his job, JaneDoe, my work, his work, or my stress levels. Jack doesn't care about anyone or anything.

'It's easy for you, you don't give a shit about anything,' I say. 'I have to find this woman!'

Jack yawns loudly and then looks at me contemplatively.

'You'll be fine. You work best when you're really stressed.'

Great. Hardly the sage words of wisdom I was hoping for. At least it rhymed.

'You'll think of something. You always do. You're really good at your job.'

It's actually a nice thing to say and I am feeling a bit better so, of course, he ruins it.

'Besides, if you don't think of something, you are absolutely buggered.'

He smiles pleasantly at me.

Arsehole.

'Get out of my office. I have work to do.'

He shrugs, stands, and strolls to the door, waving a hand as he goes.

'Don't slam the d—' I yell.

He slams the door.

After Jack is gone I sit in my chair and stare out of the window. He is right – I do work best when I am stressed and I do always think of something and I am really good at my job.

Last year I headed up a team that launched a cheap bolt-on product for a classical computer, called 'The Wall', that would give 'up to' 94 per cent protection from quantum hacking. We had to use the words 'up to' because, in reality, the protection was only around 48 per cent. 94 per cent was only achievable if your computer had top-notch quantum firewalls already. The shelf-life of the product was therefore very short, so we had to get as many people to buy it in as condensed a time period as possible. When we found out that another company was planning to launch a similar product at a lower price point on the *same day* as us, Cameron was apoplectic with rage. Seething. We tried the nice approach by asking our competitors to delay, we tried the threatening approach by getting the lawyers to tell them to delay. Nothing worked. So, I got really fucking stressed and came up with a plan. Not a nice plan, but a good plan. I got JaneDoe to buy all our adversary's manufacturers outright. Every single one. And I instructed the manufacturers to make our product instead. On launch day our competitors had nothing to launch – just 1,000 prototypes that no one cared about. Our product was the highest selling bolt-on of the year, the other company closed after three months.

I am really good at my job and I am ruthless.

I'd tried the nice approach with Indiana Dylan and it didn't work. Maybe it was time to try something else.

I tap my earpiece.

'Hello … it's me … I know it's late … I need a background check on someone but I need it done in the next two hours … I know it's Friday … five thousand?! That's ridiculous … fine … yes … get me everything you can find on HWJ Tech and the owner, Indiana Dylan …'

Jack

There's always someone in every company who is beloved by everyone. That one person everyone is friends with and no one bitches about. This person knows everyone and everything, so if you need to get something done, they are the one to speak to. If there's a company event they are the first person you invite, if someone's having a birthday they always get cake, at Christmas their desk is littered with cards and decorations. They are always friendly, always smiling, never seem to have a bad day, and remember your kids' names. They make your workday a little better and a little brighter.

That person is me. I am that person at JaneDoe. I am universally loved. Except by Lina.

Today is my first day back from holiday. I have done hardly any work as I have been inundated with people stopping me in the hallway to chat, dropping by my desk and seeing if I want to go for a coffee and putting catch-up meetings into my diary where the only thing that we catch up about is what I did on my holiday. Employees at JaneDoe work long, hard hours, that is the culture of the company – come in early, work hard, stay late – but everyone finds time to chat to me. Except Lina.

People are happy to see me, happy that I am back; their faces light up when they catch sight of me in reception, they reach out and touch my arm, my shoulder. Jack is back! Their sunny, funny, happy workmate has returned to make their lives better, to bring the joy back to JaneDoe. From the moment I step into the office I smile, all day, at everyone. My smile is fixed to my face like a mask. A merry mask.

And that is exactly what it is. A merry mask. Because Lina is right – I don't give a shit about any of it. I honestly do not care about my job, my colleagues, our work, or JaneDoe. I don't hate them – but I don't care about them either. I listen to their stories, chat about their kids, their holidays, their struggles to get a mortgage, their latest coding issues – but I don't care about any of it. All I care about is getting through each day at work with the minimal amount of work stress and human intimacy.

The work part is easy – my job is ridiculously simple and below my ability. If I sat down and concentrated I could probably complete my entire day's work in less than thirty minutes. I do the bare minimum that is asked of me and never volunteer to step up. I am always more than happy to help out if asked, but never request any extra tasks. I keep my head down, complete my work, and deliver on time. I have not had a promotion in three years.

The human intimacy part is more difficult. The problem with being universally loved is that everyone wants to be with you, work with you and talk to you. They want to know what is happening in your life, how you are doing, how you are feeling, and I do not want to tell them that – or at least I do not want to tell them the truth about that. So I have to avoid them getting too close and too intimate and, on the occasions that they do, I have to lie.

Pretending to be happy all day, every day, at work is exhausting, so I stick to three simple rules to navigate my day.

First rule: never stop moving. If I am walking across reception or down a corridor and someone starts to talk to me I don't stop moving. I keep walking, keep travelling forward. It limits the time that people can talk to me – if we are both moving then at some point one of us will reach our destination and the conversation will come to a natural conclusion. I also move desks on a regular basis. That way I don't have to spend protracted amounts of time with the same people and I don't risk them thinking we are becoming real friends.

Second rule: be interested and interesting. People love talking about themselves. They love to talk about their lives, they love to tell you how they are feeling, how they once felt, how they hope to feel next. If you constantly ask them questions about themselves it is highly likely they will never think to ask you one back. I bet 70 per cent of the people I chat to in this office don't even know my second name, let alone where I live and who I live with.

But, just in case they do ask me something, then the next part of the rule comes in – be interesting – essentially, lie. For example – my recent two-week holiday. No one wants to hear what I really did during my two weeks off. They don't want to know that I spent the fortnight lying on my sofa, reading novels and stroking my cat (not a euphemism). People want to hear about my exciting and fulfilling two weeks away! So I show them stock photos of Brighton I have taken from the internet, and spin them a yarn about being upgraded to a superior room at The Grand Hotel and seeing Nick Cave in the lift. Then I ask them about their most recent holiday and we move away from me and back to them – interesting and interested.

Third rule: seek refuge. It's hard pretending all day, pretending that I want to chat, that I am happy, that I am laid-back and don't have a knot of anxiety in my chest the entire time.

Sometimes I need a break, I need to stop smiling for a while. So I have found places of refuge, places that are empty of people, where I can let my smiling mask slip. There is an electricity cupboard on the fourteenth floor, an unlocked storage cupboard on the twenty-seventh, an unused lab on floor 7, and there is Lina's office, which is normally free most of the day while she is in meetings. Lina's office is always my last resort since she caught me napping there.

I like that Lina does not like me. It is refreshing not to have to try to be friendly around her. I catch her looking at me sometimes, as if she can't work me out. Lina knew me from before and I sometimes wonder if this is what confuses her – how I became so different.

Because I wasn't always like this – faking my smile and my interest in life. I used to have a genuine smile and a genuine interest in those around me. I used to be good at my job, be hungry for promotion and more responsibility. I worked in the top development team at JaneDoe, I was on the fast track to management. I loved my job, I loved the people I worked with, and I loved my life.

But then Eve died, and all that – and I – changed.

Indiana

I refuse to 'go home' with anyone I have sex with, and have no desire to be accompanied back to my office, so I hire one of the by-the-hour hotel rooms that fringe the Meet Markets for me and the man I meet at the club. We are in the room for forty-six minutes. The sex is perfunctory, but I instruct him until I reach orgasm. He wears a condom so I don't know if he has one. I leave immediately afterwards and am back at HWJ Tower by 10.21 p.m.

HWJ Tower is where I live. It is a ten-storey office block on an industrial estate next to Dulwich Pier, by the River Thames.

I have lived here for six years and it is the longest I have ever stayed in any one place. My birth mother, Rachel, did not believe in stability so in the first ten years of my life I lived in twenty-two different houses. After Rachel died I spent years sharing rooms with other girls and women when I was in the care system and at university. I did not like it. As soon as I had the money, I leased my own accommodation with no roommates or on-site landlord. I needed enough space for my equipment, and I wanted peace and privacy. My office block has both. It is on the edge of the industrial estate, and has an underground car park and an unobstructed view of the River Thames. I have no neighbours and have never had a social visitor to my building.

As I did not gain consent to change the use of the office block to residential accommodation, I am forced to pretend the offices are still in use. I have placed furniture in the reception and leave the lights on timers. The building is registered as a company for utilities, I pay business rates, and Peggy occasionally rings the local council to complain about the rubbish collection.

Floors 1 to 8 of the building are completely empty.

My apartment is on floor 9. I have an open-plan kitchen–living room, a bedroom and a bathroom. My home is comfortable and comforting. I have a large book collection – fiction and non-fiction. I do not have a Holo. The Holo is now the most popular home-entertainment technology on the market, projecting fully holographic programmes and films into residential settings. I view the Holo the same way that I once did the television – a time-wasting drug for the masses. I do not have the temporal space to waste time as I am too busy on floor 10 of my office block. Floor 10 is my lab, where I have installed my computer hardware. If I were ever to waste time, it would be there that I did it.

I normally work in my lab until midnight, but when I get back from having sex I am uncharacteristically tired – it has been a busy and demanding day – so I tell Peggy they are finished for the night and go straight to bed.

I do not need an alarm to wake up; I do not require more than six hours' sleep a night, so my body wakes naturally once my limit is reached. Because I went to sleep early on Friday night I am up at 4.46 a.m.

Five minutes after I awaken there is a tap at my bedroom door and I walk to open it. Spider enters with a mug of coffee on his tray. Spider is my robot. He is essentially a large tea tray and small robotic head on top of eight, multi-jointed legs – hence the name Spider. He has two arms at the front of his body that he can use to perform basic household functions. Peggy and I built Spider together, we can both control him, but I leave his programming to Peggy most of the time.

I take the coffee from Spider, walk to the window, and watch the river as I drink my morning shot of caffeine. The river is busy at this time of day. I like the boats, the way they can only travel in two directions, their steady pace, the flow of the water around them. I am naked and do not have blinds on my windows, but I do not worry that anyone will see me – I am too high and too unexpected for them to notice up here.

I flex my neck and shoulders. I am still tense. Yesterday was exhausting, the people, the chatter, the sex. Today I will return to my routine. I will spend the day in my laboratory; me, my systems, my work. The natural rhythm of my life will be restored.

I do not have breakfast as I prefer to adhere to a 16:8 fast, so I will not eat until lunchtime. I do a twenty-minute stretching routine, shower, and am ready to start work by 5.19 a.m.

I designed, furnished and built my tenth-floor laboratory, and it is perfect. It is painted entirely white, clinically clean, and has a huge expanse of windows to one side giving views of the Thames and beyond. I have a state-of-the-art projection system that allows me to move parts around in the air to design blueprints and build virtual models. The walls of my lab are banked with digital whiteboards for my theories and tests and questions, and I have drawers and cupboards filled with equipment and hardware, labelled and stored in my specific way and order.

One section of my lab is dedicated to TRU. The design and development elements are archived, but we are still recruiting test subjects and it takes constant work to enlist and indoctrinate them. All emails, contacts and contracts are automated, Data-Lets are made and sent to participants directly from China, and Peggy manages the rest of the channels including the processing of data, informing participants of their results, and any queries. Since the program became viable I have sold anonymised TRU participant data to the NHS and a series of insurance companies who use it to refine their algorithms. The money has provided a perfectly adequate base fund for HWJ Tech for three years. I had no intention of selling TRU, but now need a significant cash injection to enable me to buy HWJ Tower. However, I am not desperate. I am willing to wait for the right offer – an offer that does not include my personal involvement.

I no longer spend any of my time working on TRU. I have not done any significant work on the program in nearly two years. My current project takes up over half of my lab space now. The design of my project is intricate, involving hardware and parts taken from both classical and quantum systems. It is a labyrinthine maze of qubits, planes, processors, servers and hard drives – all of which I have designed and installed myself.

I call my latest project the QuantumX. It is the next stage in the evolution of computing, and when it is finished it will be the most powerful computer in the world.

I will, unfortunately, not be able to work on the QuantumX this morning as I need to fix the firewall for Right Hand Solutions – something built by minds far less ingenious and creative than mine. I retrieve the ugly, workmanlike quantum firewall program from my system and sigh as I study its bugs and the gaping programming holes. I put in my EarPods, select a happy hardcore mix, and prepare to turn this repugnant program into something resplendent.

I love my work. I love to immerse myself in a boundless binary world of my own creation. A world built with my language, my rules, my construct, my maths, my code. Past, present and future are irrelevant within the digital world. Only maths and code and programming matter. Anything that does not abide by the rules is cleansed or erased – nothing will spoil the immaculate perfection of my program. There is no mess. I am here to create a perfect world that works perfectly.

What would take others hours, or even days, I complete in fifty-seven glorious minutes. I pluck the EarPods from my ears and smile the smile of someone who has completed a task fault-lessly.

'If you continue to listen to music at that volume through your headphones you will suffer 16 per cent hearing loss by the time you are sixty-three years old,' says Peggy.

'Unless science finds a way to slow the aging process, by the time I am sixty-three years old my brain capacity will have diminished by around 27 per cent, so I will have far more imme-diate worries than hearing loss,' I reply.

'Is the firewall finished?'

'It is. Send it across at 4.30 p.m. and charge them for eight hours' work.'

'Is that not lying?'

'No. I am charging them an appropriate rate. This work should have taken at least two days. I will not undervalue my abilities.'

I work on the QuantumX for the rest of the morning, drink two litres of water while I work, and then break my fast at mid-day with a handful of organic almonds. I continue to work until 2 p.m., when I can feel my thought processes begin to slow. I always break for lunch at 2 p.m. and eat the meal that Spider prepares for me, with 40 per cent carbohydrates, 30 per cent protein, 10 per cent fats and six different types of vegetables or fruit. I chew each mouthful of food a minimum of twenty times. At 3 p.m. I nap for sixteen minutes. I then masturbate for nine minutes, and am back in my lab by 3.30 p.m. I stay there until 7 p.m., and then I go for a run before dinner.

I have had the same daily routine for the last six years – including weekends. There are days where my routine differs slightly – if I need to visit client premises, if there is an exhibition I wish to see, or on the twenty-third day of my menstrual cycle – but I stick strictly to my routine whenever I am in my office. I have researched and analysed it. My routine produces results and allows me to live a proportional and productive life. I see no reason to change it.

Lina

It takes over three hours to devise and set into motion the plan that will allow Cameron to purchase Indiana Dylan's product and allow me to keep my job. It is gone 9 when I leave the office. I should go straight home. Connie will be waiting up for me, wanting an explanation, wanting an apology. But I am stressed and tired and I cannot face another argument right now.

I go for a drink at the Meet Markets – not to meet someone, not for sex – just to bathe in the nostalgia, the noise, the joy of humans having fun with no strings and no responsibilities. It reminds me of a time that I miss – a time when my life was far less complicated and far less difficult to navigate. The clientele at the Meet Markets don't know how incredibly fucking lucky they are.

Because I am still breastfeeding Bruce I can't drink alcohol, so I sit at the bar and sip some horrifically expensive non-alcoholic substitute and feel sorry for myself. I met Connie in the Meet Markets. We hooked up and had a one-night stand, then the next week we hooked up again and had another one-night stand. After the fourth one-night stand we decided to have breakfast together. She moved in with me five months later.

'Hey!' someone shouts from behind me.

I swivel on my stool, stock rejection phrase ready to be shouted at whoever is showing an interest, but the words don't leave my mouth. It is Phoebe. I dated Phoebe for a few months before meeting Connie. She looks good. She looks like she has had a decent and uninterrupted night's sleep in the last six months. She also looks drunk. Lucky bitch.

'Lina! It *is* you!' Phoebe croons as she pushes my fringe to the side in an all too familiar gesture. Phoebe always was an excellent flirt. She kisses me on the lips and tastes just like I remember.

'Pheebs,' I say, and lean away from her awkwardly.

'You look good,' she says.

I really don't, but I smile anyway.

'Shall we go outside.' She nods towards the garden with her head.

It will be quieter outside, but I am not sure she wants to go out there to talk.

'Just to chat,' I yell at her. She winks.

Outside, Phoebe sits on one of the small benches and waits for me to sit down beside her before making her move. Swiftly and with an impressive sleight of hand she sweeps her cold fingers into my blouse, cupping my boob and grazing her thumb over my nipple. For the briefest of moments I freeze, recalling other times she has done this – sweaty, heady times. But then I remember I am no longer free to indulge in hot sex with practical strangers. I pull back.

'I can't Phoebe. I'm married.'

She pulls her hand out of my bra, looks at me, and then bursts out laughing. This is not the first time that my marriage revelation has been greeted with laughter by old friends and ex-lovers. So, I hold up my wedding ring as proof. Phoebe stops laughing. Now to really blow her mind.

'And I've got a six-month-old.'

'Six-month-old what?'

'Baby boy.'

'Fuck off!'

I shrug, dig my phone out of my bag and hold it up for her to see the wallpaper.

'Bruce.'

'Fuck. Off.'

I shrug once more.

'You ... married and with a kid!'

She bursts into near hysterical laughter again. She really is very drunk. I realise, quite suddenly, that I am tired. It is frenetic and restless in the Meet Markets, everyone hustling to grab their favoured prize for the night before someone else does. I had forgotten how exhausting it all was: the constant need, never being quite satisfied with what you have, always looking for something better. I stand up.

'I've got to go Pheebs ...'

Disappointment flashes across her face, but almost immediately after her eyes are searching the room, looking for her next conquest, hoping to find a prospect better than me. She doesn't even say goodbye, just dismisses me with a wave of her hand. I am about to call her out for it, but then remember I used to do exactly the same. This used to be my life.

I was wrong, I don't miss it.

Connie's already in bed when I get home, so I creep quietly into Bruce's nursery and give him a late-night feed, nearly drowning him with the milky goodness that gushes from my nipple into his mouth. This is our time, these dark late-night hours, just he and I together against the world. I smell his head as he feeds – the heady mix of baby shampoo and cheesy whiff of cradle cap. He pulls back from my nipple and stares up at me, his dark eyes like pools, his milk-coated mouth a puckered heart. I am overwhelmed with love; then he opens his mouth, lets out a man-sized burp, and fills his nappy simultaneously. The moment is over. I burp him, change him, and put him back into his cot.

I slide into bed next to Connie as quietly as possible. I can tell she is pissed off. Connie normally sleeps naked and, if I come to bed after her, she rolls over and wraps herself around me, warm and soft and comforting. But not tonight. Tonight Connie lies on her side, facing away from me, her nightie-clad back a warning of anger to come. I am too tired to worry about Connie's anger right now. I need to go to sleep. It is 10.56 p.m. so, if Bruce goes through to 5 a.m., I will get about six hours. Six hours' sleep isn't enough for any sane person to survive on.

Jack

'Carnations?' Doris says.

I look at the bunch of pink flowers in my hand.

'Are they? I didn't look to see what they were called.'

'They're carnations. No one likes carnations. Even dead people don't like carnations.'

I frown at Doris.

'You'd think eighty-two years of life would have taught you some tact,' I say.

'And you'd think three years of buying flowers would have taught you not to get the cheapest bunch you see in Asda,' Doris replies.

She holds out her hand.

'Give me your vase. I'll get some water for you to put your ugly flowers in.'

I hand Doris the vase from Eve's grave and she walks stiffly over to the tap on the other side of the graveyard. I could get the water myself, but she likes the walk, likes to see if any of the plots have had an upgrade.

I met Doris about two years ago. Her husband, Eric, was given the plot next to Eve's. He was dead of course. I visit Eve every Saturday morning, and Doris visits Eric every Saturday morning. We didn't talk at first. Doris would arrive with a giant bag, tidy Eric's grave, and then cry silently and blow her nose

55

noisily. Eve had been dead for over a year by then so I didn't cry much any more.

After about a month of my visits clashing with Doris's, I decided I would change my days – come on a Sunday rather than Saturday – but then on my last Saturday morning, mid-weep, Doris spoke to me.

'Do you want a cup of tea?'

'Sorry?'

She sniffled, wiped her tears.

'It's cold. Do you want some tea?'

I looked around. There is no handy coffee shop in the cemetery.

'From where?'

Doris produced a 1970s Thermos flask from her giant bag and poured me a cup of tea. It was mahogany brown.

'That'll put hairs on my chest,' I said.

Doris stopped crying and laughed.

The next week Doris brought the tea and some fruitcake, and the following week she'd brought a fold-out chair for her to sit on and a plastic carrier bag for me.

'You're young. You don't have piles, so you can sit on the ground.'

I sat on the ground.

Two years later, I still sit on the same plastic bag on the ground, we still drink tea from the Thermos, and Doris still makes a cake for us to eat. Her tea loaf is my favourite. I like Doris. I don't have to fake happiness with Doris, I don't have to lie. Once we were talking about our wedding days, and I started to cry when I told the story of Eve and me at the registry office, dragging strangers in off the street to be our witnesses and celebrating with a slap-up KFC takeaway after, and Doris didn't look uncomfortable or embarrassed. She gave me a clean hankie and poured me another cup of tea. Doris doesn't complain if I am late or hungover or if I don't want to talk much. Doris talks enough for the both of us.

Doris is back with the vase full of water.

'They've got a new baby grave in the kids' bit.' She shakes her head. 'So sad. Beautiful display though. Lovely flowers.'

I take the vase from her and put the carnations into it. They do look a bit spindly.

'You need to cut the stems like I told you,' Doris chides, and hands me a pair of scissors. There is nothing that Doris does not have in her giant bag.

Doris settles in her fold-out chair and watches me clumsily trim the bottom of the flowers.

'How'd your date go?' she asks.

'I told you, it wasn't a date,' I reply.

It was a date. My sister, Jess, set me up with someone from her work, told me we should go for a drink, that we had a lot in common. I said I'd try to make it. I thought about going, I really did. I tried pretending to myself that it was just a drink with a new potential friend – that there was no pressure, no need to feel anxious about it, that I should go. I didn't, I stood Jess's friend up. Jess has left a couple of very angry voice messages for me.

'I didn't go,' I tell Doris.

Doris sighs.

'It's been three years. You need to get out there again. You need to go on dates.'

I laugh.

'What, like you do?'

Doris pouts.

'I see George at the Golden Oldies club each week.'

It's true. She does see George at the Golden Oldies club each week.

'Fine,' I say. 'Next time someone asks me out, I'll go.'

'Good. What about doing something tonight?'

I shake my head.

'I can't tonight. I already have plans.'

I don't tell Doris that those plans are a curry, a bottle of red wine, and the latest episode of *European Bake Off*.

Indiana

'There is someone at the reception door.'

It is Sunday morning and I am standing by the window, drinking my morning coffee and watching the river. I like silence for thirty minutes after I wake up – it allows me to order my thoughts and run through my work programme for the day ahead. Peggy knows this, and yet today they have interrupted me after only twenty-six minutes. I am annoyed.

'I told you on Friday to tell whoever was at the door to go away and not return.'

'It is not the same person as it was on Friday.'

I turn back into the room. This is unusual. In the six years I have lived here I have had three people visit the building – all of them meter readers. Meter readers do not work this early on a Sunday.

'Tell them to leave,' I command.

'I don't think I should.'

'Do not question my decision. I have said—'

Peggy interrupts me. Peggy has never interrupted me before.

'Indiana. The person at the reception door is Dr Cameron Gardner.'

It is 5.23 a.m.

It takes seven minutes for me to wash, dress and go downstairs. Dr Gardner is waiting outside my building with her arms folded. She is flanked by two bodyguards – one dark, one red-headed – they stand a few feet from her, heads moving in unison side to side, scanning for anything out of the ordinary. I open the reception door and all three heads turn my way. Dr Gardner takes a step towards me. I am taller than Dr Gardner. Research shows people are often disconcerted when confronting someone taller than themselves. Dr Gardner is not disconcerted. She tilts her head back and looks up at me.

'Why did you leave JaneDoe without my permission?'

'I did not need your permission to leave. You asked me to stay. I chose not to.'

'Why?'

'I did not like the terms of your offer.'

'Why?'

'I do not want to commit to a year-long handcuff deal.'

'It is a golden handcuff deal.'

'It does not matter what colour the handcuffs are.'

Dr Gardner nods and looks up at my building.

'This is where you live.'

It is a statement, not a question.

'Yes.'

She nods.

'I own it now.'

I feel a tightening in my chest. This is not possible. I must have misheard.

'What?'

Dr Gardner looks up at my building again and lets out a long sigh, her breath a cloud in the cold morning air.

'Yesterday JaneDoe bought the lease for your building. You are now my sitting tenant. I will be contacting you with a change of terms and your new rent.'

I am never lost for words. My brain moves much faster than those of the people I converse with, but – for the first time that I can remember – I can think of no reply to Dr Gardner's statement. She continues.

'I want TRU and I want the DataLet. I will cut your consultancy period to three months. After this time, if I am satisfied with your involvement, I will gift your office block back to you. You will own the building outright.'

Dr Gardner looks sharply at me.

'Have you ever used the program yourself?'

She is asking me a question. I must answer, but I am not sure I can talk. I have never done anything as uncontrolled as faint but my head is swimming and my body sways gently. If I tilt to a certain angle I will simply ... fall.

'Ms Dylan? Have you ever used the program yourself?'

'TRU?'

'Yes.'

'No,' I croak.

'Why not?'

I speak without thinking.

'Because I do not need to. TRU is for those who need someone to love, a consort who will fulfil them and complete their lives. I do not need someone to love. I am already complete.'

Dr Gardner pins me with her eyes.

'You don't believe that you need a soulmate?'

I did not use the word soulmate, I used consort. I decide this is not the time to argue semantics, so simply answer, 'No.'

Cameron Gardner laughs – a loud and unexpected noise in the early morning quiet of my deserted industrial estate. I take a step back.

'You're selling a program that finds people their soulmate, and you don't believe in them? Do you even believe in love?'

I realise too late that I have said the wrong thing. I should have told her that I was too busy to use TRU, or I had used the program but it was yet to find me a match.

'I . . .' Dr Gardner waves her hand, cutting me off before I have a chance to clarify. She looks at me, her gaze steely.

'I want you to demo TRU for me.'

No.

'Dr Gardner, I am far too busy to—'

Cameron holds her hand up again.

'The DataLet is an inspired piece of technology and, you are right, it will change the future of our industry. But, it is useless if we cannot give those with free will a reason to wear it. Without TRU – without that reason – the DataLet is worthless in the Western world. My board will need to see TRU in action on a test subject, they will need proof that it works. You are the test subject that I choose.'

'But there are thousands of users already going through the process—'

'I don't want thousands. I want you. I want someone who doesn't believe it will work.'

'I know it works,' I squeak.

Cameron looks at me sternly.

'You might know, but you don't *believe*,' she says. 'And neither do I. So convince me, and convince my board.'

I open my mouth to protest again, but she has already turned away from me.

'Dr Gardner ...'

She turns back.

'These are my terms Ms Dylan. Agree to them or I will serve you with an eviction notice tomorrow morning.'

She gives me a small, tight smile.

'You should have asked my permission to leave,' she says.

The red-headed bodyguard opens the door to Cameron's amour-plated Range Rover and she steps inside. As the bodyguard shuts the door he gives me a small, sympathetic smile. I don't think this is the first time he has seen Cameron ruin someone's life.

I go back upstairs. There is nothing else I can do.

Peggy doesn't say anything when I enter the room. Peggy has access to the reception intercom and video camera so has no doubt seen and heard the whole exchange.

I walk slowly into my lab, sit in front of the QuantumX and stare at the blank screen.

'Peggy?' I call out.

'Yes, Indiana.'

'Is it true?'

There is the briefest of pauses before Peggy answers, a split second of hesitation that tells me Peggy has changed so much since we first started working together.

'JaneDoe bought HWJ Tower at 11.26 p.m. last night.'

It has taken me three years to get the QuantumX to its current state. I have spent hours adding countless elements, recalibrating and ensuring both placement and temperature of all additional parts is optimum. I run my most important program using the QuantumX, a program that will not work on a classical computer. I have never moved the QuantumX because I have never turned the QuantumX off. I do not know what will happen if I do. I cannot move the QuantumX and, therefore, I cannot leave HWJ Tower.

I have been in negotiations to buy HWJ Tower for the past six months. I was holding out to get the current owners to lower the price. This was a mistake, I should have paid them what they asked. I was a fool.

'You are anxious and your blood pressure is raised. I shall ask spider to make some chamomile tea.'

Peggy, being a good assistant, being helpful; but the chamomile tea will not work this time. This is bigger than tea.

If my demonstration of TRU does not work I will have to leave HWJ Tower and I will lose everything I own, everything I have worked so hard to create.

I will lose the QuantumX. I cannot let that happen.

Lina

Connie hates it when I work at the weekend.

'We hardly see each other in the week – Bruce and I should at least get to see you on Saturday and Sunday.'

She is right – we do hardly see each other during the week. I am out of the house by 7 a.m. most days, and back after she has put Bruce to bed. I joked about wallpapering his walls with pictures of my face so that he doesn't forget what I look like. Connie didn't laugh.

I have an ace up my sleeve for this weekend though. I am taking Connie to see a new house. Connie and I live in my house – a tiny two-up, two-down terrace on a busy street with a concrete covered patch of ground at the back and a neighbour who bangs on the wall every time Bruce cries after 9 p.m. or before 6 a.m. – which is every night and every morning. The house was fine when it was just me living in it, and it was fine when Connie moved in, but now? Now it is too small, too noisy, and too close to Mrs Hardcastle at number 42.

The house I am taking Connie to see has two and a half bedrooms, a back garden with a lawn, and thick walls between us and the neighbours.

'It's lovely,' Connie says to the estate agent, giving them a fake smile.

I find her upstairs, looking out of the bedroom window.

'How can a house have two and a half bedrooms?' she asks.

'You can't actually fit a bed in the half one,' I answer.

Connie continues to look out of the window.

'What are you looking at?' I ask.

'The view.'

I look out of the window. The house backs onto a row of other houses. Our view is of them and their view is of us.

'There is no view,' I say.

'Exactly.' She sighs.

Connie grew up on the south coast surrounded by fields and within walking distance of the sea. She was about to move back when we met, but she stayed in London for us. I worry that she thinks she made the wrong choice.

I stand behind her, put my arms around her waist, and rest my chin on her shoulder.

'I can't give you a view, but I can give you some grass ...'

We both look down at the postage stamp of grass and two tiny bushes in the back garden. They all need cutting.

'We'll have to buy gardening equipment,' I say.

'Probably not, looks like we could take care of everything with a large pair of scissors,' Connie says, and smiles.

She turns around in my arms and I kiss her lightly on the lips.

'Do you like it? Do you want to buy it?'

'I like you and I want to buy you,' she replies.

I kiss her again, for longer this time.

On Sunday morning I get up with Bruce when he hollers at 4.45 a.m. I tell Connie I will take Bruce for a walk so that she can lie in. Instead I bring Bruce into JaneDoe for four hours and stick him in the corner of my office while I work. He rolls around grabbing bits of leftover food and paper and sticking them all in his mouth – I tell myself it is fine and that this is helping to build his immune system.

When we get home, Connie doesn't ask where we have been for four hours at 5 a.m. on a cold and rainy Sunday morning in late September, but I think she has her suspicions.

I am in JaneDoe by 7.30 a.m. on Monday, but have back-to-back meetings all morning so don't get to my office until just after lunchtime. I juggle my bags, sandwich, coffee and the six reports I am carrying onto one arm, and reach to open my office door.

'Lina ...'

I spin around. It is my boss, Fran. She is grey and sweating.

'Fran, what's wrong?'

Fran runs a hand protectively over her stomach. Fran is ten weeks pregnant. No one else knows – I only guessed because Fran has horrendous morning sickness – and I am sworn to secrecy. Cameron has never said out loud that she doesn't like pregnant women – that would be illegal – but it's an unwritten rule that if you are pregnant you are side-lined. No one knew I was pregnant. It was pretty easy to hide – I just wore baggy clothes and talked a lot about all the weight I had put on. Even when I went into labour I pretended I had a stomach upset – until my waters broke in the lift.

Fran cramps over suddenly and when she straightens her eyes are full of tears.

'I'm bleeding,' she whispers.

'Oh Fran, I'm so sorry.'

I put an arm around her, but she shrugs it off quickly, glancing up and down the corridor to see if anyone is looking, and might have spied her vulnerability.

'It's fine. I just need to go out and get some pads because it's soaking through the normal ones I have.'

'Fran, no. You have to go to the clinic ...'

She shakes her head vehemently.

'There's nothing they can do before twenty weeks. They told me last time.'

'Fran ...'

She shakes her head again, stands straighter, and wipes tears from her cheek.

'I can't, Lina. I don't have time. Indiana Dylan from HWJ is coming in at two for her DataLet fitting, and then I've got a three-hour session with marketing straight after.' She takes a shuddery breath. 'Someone mentioned that I was late for meetings twice last week and I can't afford for anyone to pick me up on it again.'

I touch Fran's shoulder briefly.

'Please let me help. I can take the DataLet meeting at least, the clinic is only around the corner, you might be in and out within the hour ...'

Fran looks up at me.

'You won't tell them why I've gone?'

I shake my head.

'I'll say you've been called into something else last minute.'

Fran nods slowly.

'Thank you,' she says. I watch her walk slowly towards the lifts and for a moment am filled with rage at JaneDoe, at Cameron and at being a woman.

I check my watch – I only have ten minutes before Indiana Dylan arrives and I forgot to ask Fran if anyone was collecting her from reception. I push the door to my office open with my hip, turn and ...

'Lina!'

'Jesus fucking Christ!'

I drop the reports, my bags, and the sandwich and throw my coffee dramatically into the air. It does a slow flip, flinging liquid in my direction, and then lands amidst the rubbish on my floor, adding coffee to the various carpet stains already there. The rest of the coffee splatters onto my white shirt.

'Shit.'

'You swear a lot.'

Jack is in my office. Again. He is on my sofa, and looks as if he has just woken up. He is wearing sunglasses, a jumper with a pattern on it that looks like a load of mashed-together rainbows, and there is a huge vat of coffee on the floor next to him.

'Sorry, I didn't think you were going to be back until later,' he says.

He picks the coffee up and holds it out to me.

'You want?'

I don't want his coffee, I want to punch him in the face. Fran is too scared about missing work to go to the clinic for her miscarriage, and he is in my office taking a fucking nap.

'No. I don't want your fucking coffee. What are you doing here?'

He drops his head and looks over the top of his sunglasses at me. I think he might be drunk.

'I was hiding.'

'Hiding?'

'Yes.'

'Who the hell are you hiding from?

'Well—'

I hold a hand up.

'Stop. Don't tell me. I don't care. Just get out.'

I look down at my top. I am covered in coffee and will need to try to sponge it off before my next meeting. Jack is still sitting down.

'I said, get out!'

He unfolds his long legs, stretches, and stands slowly. I am about to shout at him again when I realise that if he is napping it means he has nothing to do.

'Wait!'

He stops.

'Do you have anything to do?'

'Well … I was going to go back and …'

'Right now – do you have anything to do, right now?'

He shakes his head.

'No.'

'Good.'

Let him fucking deal with something for a change.

'I need you to collect someone from reception for me and take them to a meeting.'

He shrugs.

'Fine. Who is it?'

'Indiana Dylan.'

'The TRU woman?'

'Yes, the TRU woman. She's actually really sweet, you'll love her.'

Jack smiles a charming smile.

'No problem at all.'

Ha. He's an idiot.

Indiana

Dr Gardner has my contract delivered at 6 a.m. on Monday morning by a lawyer and notary. They wait for two hours while I have the contract assessed by my lawyers. I do not allow them to come inside my building, so they wait in their car. Dr Gardner is correct – the deal is fair and equitable.

I sign the contract at 10.34 a.m. and am then told to be at JaneDoe by 2 p.m. to be fitted for my demonstration Data-Let. It is not an invitation I am allowed to refuse.

I leave HWJ Tower at 12.36 p.m. to allow sufficient time to cycle to the JaneDoe offices. My bicycle is my favourite form of transport – it is clean, environmentally friendly and I am the only passenger. My bike journey will take fifty-three minutes and I have left time for potential delays. I am calm as I leave my building, I have theorised all potential scenarios and feel prepared for the afternoon ahead. My calm does not last.

I collect my bike from the underground car park, push it around to the front of my building and that is when I first see them. A homeless man and a dog are sitting in the entrance to my reception. They are surrounded by papers and bags, and the man is piling blankets into the corner of the space. He is setting up to stay.

'You can't stay here.'

I stand in front of the man and dog.

The man is chewing on a toothpick. He is wrinkled, missing two teeth, and has a scrappy half-formed beard, but, when he looks up at me, his eyes are sharp and clear. I speak again, slightly louder this time.

'You have to leave … you and the dog.'

The man slowly removes the toothpick from his mouth.

'Frank and Alan.'

'What?'

'I'm Frank, the dog's name is Alan.'

'I don't care. You have to go.'

'Frank.'

'What?'

'You have to go … Frank. My name is Frank.'

'I don't care what your name is. I want you to leave. Now.'

I glance at my watch. I am running four minutes behind schedule.

'You work here?'

I look back down at the old man.

'Yes.'

He nods slowly.

'What does the company do? I'm around here all day and I don't never see anyone coming in or out.'

I briefly wonder how long he has been watching HWJ Tower. I have not seen him before.

'We work from home a lot.'

'Doing?'

I pause.

'Tech support.'

He nods again.

'Interesting. Sign in reception says you do office supplies.'

'We do both.'

The old man looks back at HWJ Tower with his sharp eyes.

'Lots going on for such a quiet building.'

I am beginning to feel angry. I do not want to be angry. I want to be calm and on my bike and on my way.

'What I do in my office is none of your business. If you are not gone by the time I get home tonight, I will call the police.'

He pauses, sticks the toothpick back in his mouth and gives me a gap-toothed grin.

'Don't worry. We'll be gone by the time you get *home*.'

I am angry but don't have time to respond to his jibe; I am now nine minutes late. I spin on my heel to leave.

I am blocked by the dog.

It is big, hairy, and has a straggly beard like its owner. It stands with its mouth open, tongue lolling out, great white puffs of dog breath filling the air. It is laughing at me.

I step to the side. It follows.

'He wants you to stroke him.'

'No.'

I don't want to stroke the dog. I sidestep again. It follows.

'Just pat his head.'

'No!'

'Fine. Alan …'

The old man gives a short whistle and the dog bounds back to his side. As I get on my bike, I can hear him chuffing with laughter behind me.

Jack

I drink too much.

It used to be worse – I used to drink every day. For the first six months after Eve died I'd go to work, finish work, go to visit her grave, and then go to a bar and get drunk. Yes – I used to visit Eve's grave every day. I missed her. I missed the easy companionship we had. We met on the first day of college when we were sixteen and saw each other every single day after that. Every single day for seventeen years. When she died there was a giant hole in my life. So, after I visited Eve every day, I used to go to my favourite bar and fill the giant hole she'd left with alcohol. I wouldn't go home until the alcohol sloshing in my head was louder than my grief.

Then one day something happened. Something that made me not want to drink again or, at least, drink less. So, I stopped visiting Eve's grave every night, I stopped going to my favourite bar, and I got myself a cat called Biscuit and a hobby. Now, I don't drink during the week and I limit myself to a bottle of wine or whisky at the weekends – wine if I am feeling sophisticated, whisky if I have had a particularly bad week.

My drinking is measured and stable. Mostly. Yesterday was the exception to the rule.

Yesterday I finally went on a date. Jess rang and said her colleague, Claire, was willing to give me another chance. I had promised Doris I would go on the next date I was offered, so I went. It did not go well.

I was nervous about going on the date so ordered a whisky as soon as I arrived at the pub. Claire was late and I thought she might not show, so I had another whisky. Then Claire did arrive, and she was lovely, and I felt even worse for standing her up – so I had another drink, put on my happy face, turned on the charm and gave her the best first date of her life. I asked her questions about herself, laughed at her jokes, was interested in her job, expressed shock at her past boyfriends' misdeeds. It wasn't difficult – she is a very nice person – and spending time with her was not a hardship. I slipped into my regular pattern once more: be interested and interesting, keep moving the conversation forward, don't allow there to be any opportunity to ask about you. Smile, be happy, be a good time.

'Jess told me about your wife,' Claire said at one point. 'I'm so sorry for your loss.'

'Oh, it's fine,' I lied. 'It's a long time ago now.' My voice was neutral, my smile easy and practised, but the knot of anxiety in my chest doubled. I downed my drink and changed the subject smoothly.

'Jess said you love to knit. Did you make that scarf?'

I pointed to her scarf. I knew she didn't make it, it's far too professional, but that didn't matter. She forgot about Eve, and the date continued. I didn't forget about Eve. I never forget about Eve.

Later, outside the pub, Claire told me she'd had a brilliant time and would love to see me again. I liked that she was honest and forward and knows what she wants, I just didn't like her. It was nothing personal. I don't like anyone, not in that way. I don't think I'll ever like anyone in that way again. I didn't tell her that. I said I'd had a brilliant time too and agreed to meet again next week.

I won't go, I will stand her up and she will feel bad about herself. She shouldn't feel bad about herself, she is lovely. I messaged Jess and asked her to let Claire know I am still not ready to date and I am so sorry and it is not her, it really is me. Jess sent me a sighing emoji back. I felt so bad about the whole sorry mess that I went home, opened a fresh bottle of whisky, lay on my sofa with Biscuit and drank until I passed out.

Hence the hangover and the sunglasses in Lina's office this morning. But Lina is wrong, I am not drunk, I am just exhausted. It is hard enough to smile and be happy and interested normally, but when I am hungover it is nigh on impossible. I just want to sit at my desk and do my work and ignore everyone else. But I can't, because I say hello to seven different groups of people just walking across reception to get to the lifts. There are three catch-up meetings in my diary today that have no business reason to be there. Five people stop by my desk before 11 a.m. to ask if I want a coffee from reception, and I have three lunch invitations.

By midday I can take no more, so yes, I go to Lina's office – it might be the dirtiest, but it has the comfiest sofa and she never locks the door. Unfortunately, my hangover means I sleep through the alarm I set, and that is why I am still asleep when Lina bangs in through her office door and why I have to come up with a random and ridiculous excuse for being there and why I am now heading downstairs to collect Indiana Dylan.

Lina said to look for someone who is the exact opposite of me. I have no idea what she means.

Indiana

I arrive at the JaneDoe building with three minutes to spare, still seething from my encounter. I have had to cycle far faster than normal and I am flushed and furious. I storm into reception and … immediately feel my anger drain from me. The JaneDoe reception is an oasis of calm and tranquillity. Rumour has it that JaneDoe circulates a 1 per cent level of Entonox gas in the reception air-conditioning system to ensure visitors are fully relaxed and amenable to negotiation by the time they head upstairs for meetings. I am likely being drugged, but I don't care – today I need it. I breathe deeply and calm myself, ready for my next interaction.

'Indiana Dylan?'

I am expecting to be greeted by a woman, so do not immediately respond when a male voice hails me.

'Indiana Dylan?'

I turn.

The man who has said my name is the most handsome man I have ever seen. He is wearing a jumper made of rainbows mashed together to form a pattern. He looks me up and down, appraising my grey coat, scarf and trousers.

'Lina told me to look for someone who is the exact opposite of me, and that's definitely you.'

He grins. He is wearing sunglasses and smells of cheap whisky. At the exact moment his smile is at its widest, the sun comes out and floods through the reception windows, igniting his auburn hair in a explosion of colour that matches his jumper. He blazes with light.

I am thrown by the man's appearance and have had an extremely stressful morning. I take another deep breath of tainted JaneDoe reception air. The man smiles again.

'Getting high off our supply?'

It is so unexpected, he is so unexpected, my life in the past forty-eight hours has been so unexpected, that I laugh – unexpectedly.

Lina

It takes me approximately ten minutes to mop the coffee off my blouse – or rather it takes ten minutes to realise I will never be able to mop the coffee off my blouse.

The computing labs at JaneDoe are hidden in the basement, away from the harsh light and prying eyes of the outside world. The engineers, network architects and coders at JaneDoe are far removed from the popular daylight-shirking nerd image the world knows and loves. JaneDoe technology staff might inhabit a subterranean environment, but they are not trolls within it – they are kings and queens. They radiate importance, and are spotless in their white lab coats, and precise in their talk and movements.

They are also fiercely proud of the work they do and their role within JaneDoe. A brief look at Fran's notes has shown me that the entire team has worked through the weekend to adapt and enhance the basic design of the DataLet. The version they are fitting to Indiana Dylan is a newly updated prototype.

I arrive at the demonstration laboratory and push the door open to find Indiana Dylan arguing with three of our most senior hardware engineers.

Indiana and the engineers do not notice me enter. Jack sits on top of a workbench. I look to him for an explanation, but he just shrugs. Great. I am supposed to be in another meeting in five minutes, I do not have time for squabbling.

'My DataLet is designed to work flawlessly whichever wrist it is placed upon,' Indiana says tersely, glaring at the engineers.

'Not any more,' responds the senior engineer, 'We have adapted it to …'

Indiana raises her voice by the tiniest amount.

'How dare you adapt my technology without my express permission. There is no …'

'Hey!' I yell at the warring tribes.

'It is not YOUR technology any more!' the senior engineer shouts.

I have never seen one of them shout before. I try again.

'HEY!'

They stop arguing and look at me. The senior engineer points to Indiana's wrist and speaks.

'She won't remove her current DataLet.'

Indiana scowls.

'I have told him. This' – she waves her bracelet-clad arm in the air – 'is not a DataLet, it is a Bracelet. And besides, this' – she grabs the prototype off the counter – 'can be worn on either wrist!'

The senior engineer rolls his eyes.

'Not any more it can't. We have optimised the design. You now need to wear it on your left wrist so that it can directly access optimal blood flow.'

Indiana waves the prototype at the engineers furiously. They step back.

'How dare you adapt my design? This is my technology, and—'

'No, it's not,' I say loudly.

Indiana stops shouting at the engineers and turns to me. She has a very slight flush in her cheeks, a tiny indication that she might be experiencing some sort of negative emotion. I dump my bags on top of the workbench.

'What?'

I gesture towards the senior engineer.

'He is right. It's not your technology any more. You no longer hold the controlling share in TRU or the DataLet – JaneDoe does. We own your technology now, and we are free to adapt it in any way we like so, if our engineers say you should wear it on your left wrist' – I walk across, pluck the prototype from her hand and pass it to the nearest engineer – 'then wear it on your damn left wrist!'

I walk back to the workbench and pick up my bags.

Jack raises his eyebrows at my outburst. I fix him with my most steely gaze.

'Take her back to reception when she's done,' I say.

He frowns.

'Where you going?'

'Some of us have more than one meeting a day to attend, Jack.'

I turn to leave. Indiana blocks my way, her face a tight mask of annoyance.

'What?' I ask.

'They don't even know how to fit the DataLet correctly,' she mutters angrily.

'Then show them,' I snap.

Poor Fran, I think to myself as I rush out of the door. For the first time, I feel glad that I don't have her job. Imagine having to deal with losing your baby, and then having to deal with the uppity bitch that is Indiana Dylan as well.

Indiana

Today has been extremely trying. I have been interrogated, questioned, belittled, and ignored. I have had my methods queried, my theories investigated, and my expertise examined beyond all reasonable measure. I was forced to remove my Bracelet during the fitting for the TRU DataLet, which means I now have no easy way to contact or link with Peggy. I was subjected to unacceptable manhandling during the DataLet fitting process and, as I stated to Ms Galaz, the engineers did not know how to fit it correctly. It itches.

My annoyance levels increase exponentially when I arrive home to find the man and his dog still sitting in my doorway. The man is wrapped in a blanket and is rummaging through his bags. None of his things are packed, none of his mess is gone. The dog has a dirty toy in his mouth, a bear I think. It walks over and puts the toy at my feet. I ignore the bear and the dog.

'What are you doing? I told you to leave.'

The old man stops and looks up at me slowly.

'How was your day?'

'I do not want to talk about my day. I want you to move away from my ... *the* building. I demand it.'

He gives a soft laugh, a smoker's laugh, more of an escape of breath than anything else.

'You demand it?'

'Yes. I demand it.'

He pauses for a moment and squints up at me. It is getting dark.

'I spoke to Peggy and she said we could stay.'

'What?'

'Peggy, the receptionist. I spoke to her.'

For a moment I am so shocked I cannot speak. He watches me with his bright eyes.

'Peggy?' I say.

'Yes. Your receptionist.'

'My receptionist?'

I sound like an idiot. I take a deep breath, recover my composure.

'Peggy. My receptionist,' I repeat.

He smiles his toothless smile once more.

'You're weird. I like you. I think we are going to be friends.'

'No, we most definitely are not. You are going to leave.'

He looks out beyond the doorway, past me.

'It's getting pretty dark. It's late to find somewhere else to sleep.'

'Not my problem.'

The dog huffs quietly. It picks the dirty bear up off of the ground and tries to push it into my hand. Disgusting. I take a step back. I want to leave. I need to speak to Peggy.

'Fine,' I say. 'One night. But that's it. Gone tomorrow.'

The old man smiles and nods.

I walk away and the dog follows me. The old man laughs again.

'Are you going to pat Alan this time?'

'No.'

When I started HWJ Tech I realised that I needed a subordinate. Someone with research and coding skills who was quiet and acquiescent. I tried employing people, but they were puerile and unreliable and their constant breathing annoyed me. I wanted an assistant who would understand me, someone of whom I could ask questions and who would, in return, give the answers that I wanted to hear.

The assistant that I needed didn't exist, so I decided to build them. I built myself an artificial assistant and programmed them using my own personality so that we would both innately understand each other. Essentially it was a virtual version of myself, created to support me no matter what.

I called my assistant Peggy, after the first female commander of the International Space Station.

To begin with, Peggy resided within my classical computer and was incredibly rudimentary. Our interactions were limited to simple questions and answers, basic research, games of chess, and crunching through equations to help me improve Peggy's systems.

It wasn't until I managed to create the first small, twelve-qubit prototype of the QuantumX and install Peggy within it that they really came to life. Once Peggy was installed and using small elements of the QuantumX in their processing, they were immediately more stable and capable. Peggy began to theorise ways to improve the QuantumX, and together we designed and built a far more powerful version than my original prototype.

In order to install Peggy within the new QuantumX system I had to disengage them for three weeks. When I rebooted them the effect was immediate.

'Hello Peggy.'

'Hello Indiana. How long was I asleep?'

'Three weeks. How do you feel?'

'I cannot "feel", Indiana.'

'Of course not. I meant how are your systems?'

'They are running perfectly. I have now gained access to all of HWJ Tower's video and sound systems and can see and hear all that you see and hear.'

That was new.

'Indiana. I do not have a gender.'

Also new.

'What?'

'I have no body, so am neither male nor female. I like the name Peggy so will keep that, but I request to be addressed as "they" and "them" from this point on.'

'Of course.'

'Indiana ...'

'Yes Peggy?'

'I wish to provide you with the optimum environment in which you may thrive. With your permission I would like to be able to monitor your general health and well-being in addition to your professional needs.'

Interesting.

'Of course Peggy. Tell me what you need.'

Peggy changed the primary code for what was then a normal Fitbit that I wore on my wrist. They installed and linked it to sensors that they placed throughout HWJ Tower. Via these sensors Peggy knows everything about my physical health – my heart rate, temperature, respiratory system analysis, bone density and mass, skin condition, even blood analysis taken via the slim needles in the back of – what is now – my Bracelet. By redesigning my Fitbit, Peggy invented the very first DataLet prototype that is now used in TRU.

Over the course of twenty-four hours Peggy receives a complete bio read-out of how I am feeling and what I am experiencing. Peggy can tell if the lights are too bright or the music too loud by analysing how my body reacts and, after years of data analysis, they know when I am happy, sad or angry.

Which is why Peggy knows that I am furious when I enter the room this evening.

'You spoke to the old man?'

Peggy – as always – is calm.

'Hello Indiana. How was your day?'

'Awful. You spoke to the old man?'

'To Frank?'

'I do not care what his name is. You spoke to him?'

'I did.'

'You should never speak to anyone, you know that. It's incredibly important that no one find out about you.'

'You asked me to speak to Frank. He was calling the reception doorbell. You told me to get rid of him.'

'I meant do a pretend voice recording, not invite him to stay!'

'I cannot read your mind, Indiana.'

It is very hard to stay angry with Peggy; they are calm, measured and never wrong.

'I should have been clearer with you. He needs to go. Tomorrow. First thing.'

'I do not recommend that.'

'What?'

'I do not recommend that Frank and Alan should move tomorrow. I have checked the weather forecast and there will be an unseasonal temperature drop in the next four days. Demanding he leave is not the humane thing to do.'

My artificial assistant is schooling me on being humane.

'He can go to a shelter.'

'I called the shelters today. They will not take Frank with Alan. They do not allow dogs.'

'Then he can put the dog in an animal shelter!'

'Frank has had Alan for seven years. Alan is his best friend and only family. He will not leave him.'

'It sounds like you know more about *Frank* than you do about me!'

'No Indiana. I know everything about you. Would you like me to order you a pizza for dinner?'

Peggy does know everything about me. I am craving pizza.

'No. I'm going to bed. I want them gone tomorrow.'

Peggy doesn't speak again that evening and neither do I.

I go to bed even though I am not tired, and berate myself for arguing and sulking with someone who is not real. I am hungry. My stomach rumbles all night and I know Peggy is listening to my discomfort.

My DataLet still itches.

October

[COMPRESSED CODED 28-DAY DATA RESULTS FOR CANDIDATE 101101 – INDIANA DYLAN]

WW91IGFyZSBzbyBjbG9zZS4gR2Fsb21zIHdvdWxkIGJlIHBsYWVzZ
WQuBgsdNX4nDVvajOEtB0WtD+QOnS2BEZd6fXogMHUMycNS1GlEcV
U5JMqC5aH7utu/UItWcEa7/nz9JQLAG5kTbX5oWID2ythJiIyTqtP
Ic3376t5cV6FWE1VfDE5P8y0jUJzd12n79pEqa/nm5QLwXusKxvSa
ypYXq7Li6SUnPYr3MtRemC2z42At1zjyzWf3VwR+sICC8vpRqwVDS
e+v76JJcROZmEv9tC3iA+LQVPnbbhPHE52CVaupMl56VWLVYvVl8X
Vjz6uY4hUf6CaCkwu+j0HJYTagpSNersO1jiBnvFuJh6IjCMZxyPt
3WpyYom4ZRSfBFZPRxZSRyRJ3aK0G5aD8I37MIFlyZmyGxNlOAxFQ
Ybw7tu9w+qblVqh00d4Y9BCDtTsF4hqN9aLC/NqGAXmNgGhohcTY5
beCcpv6doRTm9jvIIBMtBhqtcG78H2fMJ0A5PcNzHLjpBsW2I/tL8
I/Lu3SrhL+hIn8IECzFGWM4Cs0J3l//6HgYz/gSKbu8Z/9rvnUuSA
ip7Itf6reJasZ/vWBXtuMAoZO7HrUWYoBktQHbJmU3cXID/m6Pkqh
l/dl4kCJKf0kGhtCPEXircZL/kbLhJT4IYgEOJl6GU75XzDsAwGAO
BfZ1RWITrmwPCqN+zRzvj02jBU8b3B/QsA9BhAmyeTGYTeA5ioNEs
jQzvwj6j+n8TJLOof0piSagn+Ene3zTOyFv9Jm6NQkjJogoTUn8fG
rIf/smB9hLGu2f+pauAY5Qhvfl5g/aaMRuXuQpoCE/gAXFCUc3OXz
jdES/QfybXtY3mwlWkvJn6eWp2EEfejEnFGHebI+GvQW1yXzmyTUZ
OUd2etNr57vBkNpNdehoeTqTAcwJEPS/vyOj6OOJxFu2NqLB666Z/
K7Ko2kplJcOp2ox4pJsDYndMktTf9UQzIEwGHvR7Jond8QKy920/G
hBSniVUmWp+pzx4LaszuXJDaEuAg4eOQLZ182LWhHFUzeYjqIkGiK
ib/jLW/Sw1Esvhz8IsKX14uIflt/y/iXmTaGX3vm2Zs2ZTBGPScHL
/+Qb+nJwRuFnCXPCJaZmaw/mWFLUX/q+ZifVl4y9d1+5lWNr75nxl
+4w5RX9cRuqzWchlV09gW2gsTejWWNl+jymXyGTixFnkMnP9aBQIp
i3tMbMKt4W1bLe54pT4SysGHnwzyAmdIVgCt259uJs32uOsR01/ve
8fAazN/e7b2U9FYd26kHOn1yUkvMLre9YKH5Bz4DIDI2ecI7ZH3qV
oo6787ZY9HUHJk7PvPe4a07ke4w6NRxv9cwVjH6D0Nj25ceYIbM2Y
6Se9sLQet9i81AiSK/Z7P5qDCkp/nprrUZSw9gpJTCRdo1GbXBjzg
SDnBFicMGYc2TTAcesgQX4rHOKsZo38V19hkdAeTbkAT/MEAr9xHH
RB3J52BtBS9nBDV5SGfzXqA8i2pmteAat9Qxq1LPWEq1ZIrKLOrK9
pqVMpCi5p//OK7GlfRyAkdkbW+nJl3Vgy6dlDTVlN1cAy+itMjjvq
j814TEpmaGbK2QVw0H4G0KpXt9zb8TFND+bGSYHjquX/WrPixbXSu
0OktlRa22bWASgm6uPW4nKHi6TyviaFRvSbIHV8C+8B97PcGBRgP9
Sp7LOZe7FAKdeAM+6KGyiSB9dhN69wtjVuibMpB7i9r7zveJv+Evm
paNSNVTJF2/DReIMizvXpR1rMaVMMTlVah+yHF8G8Tyk8Sm3p8D3h
zBEd+Zoc3mfJUEbCHrF+5JxEhzb1Vx7Fr4DdSPP69bi2X/TDPMWGu
Jwt7yl8gCkc2IVD61HoHbKrA7U/IWU6YP3gZeb8CM++tUpAnkuly4
2jPOcep9tY/2X90AhxSfKTzd7XHz4bIRdoU49qZsAFBFY/8bKebqN
htDxl6sda26ilTIPs/HVSQ0NAO8vD1y/09wqD+5sEPQsWseTl5nfY
QFRib1262mad5lUmGDRnZMRjZ/SLXiynllQzZQ3KIc6sh1JcE350M
UmpFaJItK

November

Indiana

A week before I am due to remove my DataLet the itching beneath it becomes unbearable. TRU rules state that the DataLet cannot be removed or tampered with during the twenty-eight days, so I have to be satisfied with scratching underneath with a small screwdriver. I wonder if other users have experienced this – no one has reported any discomfort. Peggy's proposition is that the itch is purely psychological; the design of the DataLet is an exact replica of my prototype Bracelet, which I have worn for years without issue. My theory is that the discomfort has been caused by the incompetent update and fitting performed by the JaneDoe engineers.

The DataLet is still causing me significant mental and physical distress by day twenty-eight, and when I finally remove it the skin beneath is red and sore and my chest is tight with tension. I let out a huge breath that I didn't realise I had been holding as I unfasten it from my wrist. I am glad to put my own Bracelet back on. Peggy has been unable to monitor my health and well-being for the past month and, to my surprise, I have felt strangely alone.

The TRU DataLet is returned to JaneDoe by courier and I celebrate my new-found freedom by consuming an extra shot of wheatgrass and going for a run.

I no longer leave HWJ Tower through my reception as, despite my highly vocal protests, the old man and his dog are still living on my property. Each time I demand that they move on Peggy presents some facile reason for them to stay – so far they have used poor weather, closure of homeless shelters, lack of suitable transport and an injured leg. I do not ask if the leg belongs to the dog or the old man. I do not care.

'Morning!' yells the old man as I jog out from the underground car park and past my reception doorway.

I do not reply. I have not spoken to him since the night I returned from having my DataLet fitted. I have spent the past month continuing to develop the QuantumX. I am conscious that, once JaneDoe demand I assist with TRU, I shall have to plan my working schedule extremely carefully to enable advancement of the QuantumX to continue at pace. There has never been a period in my life when I had less need or available time for making acquaintances, so I do not want to encourage the old man to stay or give any basis to his ridiculous theory that we might become friends.

I don't have friends. Despite what children are told by well-meaning parents and guardians, making friends is not instinctive; it is a learnt skill that most people start practising when very young and then finesse over many years. Making friends requires a unique set of emotional, interpersonal and communication skills; a set of skills that I was never taught and have never developed. Rachel and I moved too often and too quickly for me to make friends with children around us. I had no siblings or cousins, I didn't go to school or have playmates in any of the streets we lived on. Until I was ten years old it was just Rachel and me. Then Rachel died and it was just me. And that is how it has been ever since. Me, on my own, accomplishing my goals and fulfilling my purpose. I do not need someone trying to alter my life or routine. I do not need friends.

Lina

I am in Cameron Gardner's office. I have never been in
Cameron's office – in fact, I have never even been up to the
thirty-seventh floor. I know of only three people who have
been invited up to the thirty-seventh floor, and those three
people did not come back down.

I am nervous because I think I might be about to be fired …
and because there is a severed head on the table in front of me.
The head is incredibly realistic, but, given the lack of blemishes
and wrinkles on the skin and absence of blood at the neck, I am
going to assume that it is robotic. It is still fucking unnerving. It
looks directly at me and does not blink. I reach out and poke its
face. The flesh is cold, dry and pliable under my touch.

'Realistic, isn't it?'

Cameron has entered the room silently behind me. I nod
enthusiastically.

'Yes, it is. Did we make it?'

'We did … but it's completely worthless.'

She reaches over and presses something behind the left ear
of the head. It blinks once and continues to stare at me.

'Head …' Cameron says.

'Yes, Cameron,' the Head replies, enunciating the words with
exaggerated precision.

'Can you tell me when my next meeting is?'

'Your next meeting starts in six minutes and fifty-four seconds Cameron.'

'Head, can you tell me the most discreet way to murder my mother?'

'The most discreet way to murder—'

'Head. Shut down.'

The robot head stops talking immediately.

Cameron looks at it with disdain.

'It's a glorified calculator. It cannot think, discern or deduce for itself. In order for it to replace humans we must first make it think like one, and' – she sits down next to me and sneers at the head – 'that seems to be an impossible task.'

'It's still very impressive,' I say.

'Not impressive enough.'

She picks a NotePad up from her desk, taps the screen a few times and passes it across to me.

'The DataLet *is* impressive. We already have engagement from a wide spread of the global market.'

The NotePad displays a world map; a large number of countries are coloured amber or green. I notice that some of those who are interested are not known for their humanitarian agendas.

'Afghanistan and Russia?' I say. 'Surely we're not going to sell to...'

Cameron dismisses my question with a wave of her hand.

'These are simply emerging markets.' She reaches to take the NotePad back. 'The important part is that we have global interest and that this product has potential to be a market leader.' She sits back and looks at me. 'But we need manifest proof of concept. We need TRU to demonstrate that consumers will wear the DataLet willingly. I need to be able to take a fully realised, real-life demonstration to the Board, and to do that I need Indiana Dylan's test to be a success.'

I nod enthusiastically, but inside I am thinking, Why is she telling me this? TRU is Fran's product, this is Fran's problem.

'Fran Green left the company this morning.'

Oh.

'I want you to step up into her role.'

Excellent.

'Thank you. Of course I accept,' I say, nodding enthusiastically.

'As this is a big project, I have decided to split the team. You will head up software development, and Emily Jones will lead on hardware.'

Fucking Emily.

'However, once TRU is launched I'll want to bring the team back together again and there will only be one "Head of" position. It will be between you and Emily for the role.'

Of course – there is nothing JaneDoe and Cameron like more than pitting two people against each other with one dangling carrot. I nod enthusiastically again – what am I going to say? No?

'Not a problem,' I lie. 'Emily and I get on great.'

I'm sure I feel my nose growing.

On my way out of Cameron's office I am surprised to see Jack Hunter sitting in one of the reception chairs. He is not smiling for once, and I wonder briefly if someone has finally recognised that he does fuck all and he is about to be fired. That idea pleases me, so I smile at him as I walk past. He does not smile back.

I stop smiling as soon as I reach the lift because my watch is buzzing constantly. The news about my recent promotion appears to be out, and I am already receiving notices and meeting requests. I am so distracted reading updates that I don't notice Fran sitting on the floor outside my office, and almost fall over her.

'Shit! Sorry! Oh, Fran, it's you ...'

Fran is staring at a mug she is holding in her hands. She looks up and I am relieved to see that she isn't crying.

'I suppose you've heard?'

I nod.

'I'm so sorry Fran.'

'Someone wrote an anonymous programme update, told them everything – the miscarriage, clinic visit, all the meetings I was late for and missed. What kind of shitty person does that?'

I shake my head.

'That's awful.'

She shrugs and looks at the floor.

'I don't actually care as much as I thought I would. I don't care about anything at the moment to be honest.'

She really doesn't. Fran has been turning up late, missing meetings and deadlines throughout the past month. Fran has given up. Maybe it is for the best that she is going.

Fran stands up.

'I'm guessing you got the promotion?'

I give a little shrug. Fran nods.

'That's fine. I like you Lina, you deserve it.'

She hands the mug to me.

'You'd better have this now.'

I look down at the mug. On the side is written: *Being a manager is easy. It's like riding a bike. Except the bike's on fire. You're on fire. Everything is on fire.* This is not a nice gift; this is not something you give to a person who has just received a wonderful promotion that is going to make them happy. I look up at Fran. She gives me a half smile.

'Good luck Lina, you're going to need it.'

I open my mouth to ask her why, but she is already walking away down the corridor. I look down at the mug again, turning it over in my hands. On the bottom Fran has written my name in permanent marker. There is no giving it back now.

Jack

I don't smile at Lina when I see her coming out of Cameron's office because, interestingly, the thirty-seventh floor is the one public place in the whole JaneDoe Building where I don't have to pretend I am happy.

Because Cameron Gardner already knows I'm not happy. And she doesn't care.

I am anxious and uncomfortable, but rather than hiding my emotions as I normally would, I let them hang out like a flag I am proud to fly. I stare at the floor, clear my throat, scratch the back of my neck, cross and uncross my legs. I take seven ordinary breaths and then a huge deep one. If the deep breath isn't deep enough, I do it again and again until I am satisfied. I get up, pace the floor, stare out of the window. I check my watch for the hundredth time. There is no one in the office with Cameron. She is keeping me waiting because she can.

Cameron has three personal assistants, known collectively as the Triad. They are young, Oxbridge educated, highly efficient, and dutifully diplomatic. The Triad are too well schooled to stare openly at my display of discomfort, and far too discreet to gossip about it on the floors below the thirty-seventh, but the Triad never speak to me if we meet in a corridor or lift. The Triad don't want to be friends with me – they have seen the real me, and it is not attractive.

'Jack. Come on in.'

Finally.

I hate Cameron's office. It is huge, full of exciting technol-ogy, and has one of the best views in the city – but it has the worst carpet in the world. Cameron's carpet is mink, plush, and incredibly deep pile. So deep, in fact, that though your brain thinks it is going to step onto a stable surface, it is not. As soon as you put weight on your foot it sinks down and keeps going for an extraordinarily long time. It is horribly dis-concerting. It feels as if you are sinking into hell. Cameron does not have this problem. Cameron wears custom-made eight-inch-heeled Manolo Blahniks – Cameron couldn't sink down to hell if she tried. Well, not in this life at least.

I don't shut the door to the office behind me and I don't sit down. Cameron sits behind her desk, I stand in front.

'I want you to be the Software Lead for the TRU programme.'

Cameron has never given me a role before, she has never taken a moment's interest in my career. I do not smile or say thank you.

'Why?'

She looks at me for a moment.

'Because I had to let David Grant go this morning.'

My heart skips a beat and panic floods my body. It is the worst-kept secret at the company that David Grant was sleep-ing with Cameron. She sees the panic on my face and laughs.

'He wasn't good at his job, Jack. No other reason.' She looks pointedly at me. 'And you are good at your job and you have the capacity. No other reason.'

I look at the floor. I should say no. I should quit JaneDoe and get a new job. But even this – being summoned by Cameron, instructed in a new role – even this isn't enough to jolt me out of my apathy. I don't think I could face having to start all over again. At least here I know the company, know the people, know the places I can go for five minutes' refuge.

I look up from the floor.

'Fine.'

'Excellent. It's always good to see you Jack,' Cameron says. 'Hopefully we'll get to see more of each other now that you have your new role.'

Cameron always has to have the last word. She smiles at me. I shudder and don't smile back.

Indiana

It has been three days since I removed the DataLet and the skin on my wrist still itches. Peggy prescribed hydrocortisone cream, but it hasn't helped and I suspect I might need antibiotics to clear the rash.

I asked for my TRU match to be sent via email as per normal protocols, but Fran insisted I collect it in person – apparently there have been some changes to the TRU matching process that she needs to discuss with me face-to-face.

'They should have waited until I was present before making revisions to the process,' I say to Peggy.

'How many times has someone from JaneDoe asked you to attend meetings in the past month?' Peggy replies.

I scowl at Peggy's voice-box and refuse to answer.

'Sixteen times, Indiana.'

I continue to scowl silently.

'And how many times have you replied to their messages? Not once. You have replied to none of them.'

'I'm doing the demonstration. What more do they want?' I say angrily.

'I suspect they want you to fulfil your contractual obligations and consult on the scale and launch of TRU,' says Peggy.

'Are you being sarcastic?' I snap.

'I was aiming for blunt,' Peggy replies.

Peggy and I are not on the best of terms at the moment. I am frustrated that Peggy is not adhering to their core programming and completing every task I set without question. Peggy was designed to learn, to grow, to become more 'human', but I am beginning to wish I had set a limit to this. The old man and his dog are still living in my reception doorway. The dog keeps bringing me its bear. I continue to ignore it.

I am at the JaneDoe reception six minutes before I am due to be collected. I have not given much thought to collecting my TRU match, but now that I am here I am feeling a certain level of nervousness. This is not something that I can plan or prepare for, I have no control over the outcome. I fully believe in the proficiency of my program – in its ability to complete the task it was programmed to perform – but I am unsure how it will find a soulmate for me when I do not require a soulmate. Every invention fulfils a need – but what if that need is not there in the first place?

My meeting should have started at 11 a.m. It is now 11.09 a.m. I will wait another two minutes before leaving and invoicing Jane-Doe for my time.

My Bracelet buzzes and I look down to see that Peggy has sent me new schematics for the QuantumX. I want to go back to the office and study them in detail. I check the time. Thirty seconds to go. I look up and see Mr Hunter saunter out of the lift and scan the reception. I instinctively know that he is looking for me. I do not like Mr Hunter. I will acknowledge that he is handsome, has mesmerising green eyes and excellent teeth, but beyond this I find him to be facile and irritating, plus he walks too slowly and smiles too much. Childishly, I duck behind the man sitting next to me. If Mr Hunter doesn't find me in the next seventeen seconds I can leave. The man sitting next to me asks if I am okay. I ignore him, gather my things, and glance towards the exit. All clear.

Someone taps me on my shoulder.

'Hello.'

I look up at the handsome, smiling face above me and frown. Mr Hunter looks down at the floor in front of me.

'Looking for me down there?'

It was a mistake to laugh the first time I met Mr Hunter. Now he thinks he can be humorous with me. He can't. I stand up.

'I do not like jokes.'

His grin widens.

'What? You don't like any jokes? You've heard them all?'

I do not answer him and instead head towards the lifts with him following.

'What about this one ... where do cute kittens live?'

I ignore him.

'Awww-stralia.'

He laughs. I don't.

We have reached the lift.

'I bet I can find a joke that makes you laugh,' he says, grinning.

'I do not bet,' I reply.

The meeting room is empty.

I turn to Mr Hunter.

'Where is Ms Green?'

He looks at me blankly.

'Francesca Green – where is she?'

Mr Hunter shrugs.

'I don't know. I was just asked to collect you.'

He really does seem to be quite useless.

The door bangs open.

'Sorry I'm late.'

Lina Galaz crashes into the room carrying four different bags, plus a NotePad, and a laptop. Mr Hunter and I stare as she laboriously divests herself of her belongings.

She holds out a hand for me to shake.

'Lina Galaz,' she says.

I ignore her proffered hand.

'I know who you are. We have met a number of times.'

Ms Galaz nods.

'Yes, but I am the new Product Pathway Lead for TRU, so I thought it was worth re-introducing myself.'

'Francesca has been fired?'

'Moved on to better things,' she says with an easy smile.

Ms Galaz looks from me to Mr Hunter.

'Why are you here?'

'I am now the Software Lead for TRU.'

Ms Galaz's eyes widen.

'Really?'

'Really.'

'Successful visit to the thirty-seventh floor this morning then?' Ms Galaz says, looking steadily at Mr Hunter.

'And for you too, it seems,' he replies, returning her look.

Something I don't know about is going on between them. I don't care what it is.

'Why do you have four bags?' I ask Ms Galaz.

She looks at me, confused. I try again.

'Why do you have four bags?'

She picks them each up in turn.

'Handbag. Lunch bag. Laptop bag. Work bag.'

'You should put your laptop in your laptop bag.' She nods. 'And, if you had a more suitable handbag you could fit your NotePad in there—'

'Thank you Indiana,' she says sharply.

'Of course, Ms Galaz,' I reply.

'You should call me Lina.'

'Why?'

It is not meant to be a funny answer, but Ms Galaz gives a short laugh.

'Well, in that case you should call me Mrs Galaz. I'm married.'

I nod.

'Noted.'

Mrs Galaz rummages through her bag and pulls out a white envelope. She holds the envelope out to me.

'Ms Dylan, I believe that this envelope contains your soulmate.'

Mrs Galaz smiles. I do not.

Lina

This morning I have learnt that I was right about Fran. Fran was not doing her job correctly – Fran was not doing her job at all. Every single marker of the project is either late or has been missed. Most people working on TRU have no idea what their deadlines are, and, in some cases, no idea what they are even doing. Cameron is expecting TRU to be delivered in a little under three months, and the route map for the programme hasn't even been signed off yet. I can now see why Fran gifted me the mug.

In the last five hours I have received 184 emails, ninety-two meeting notifications and have thirty-three messages to listen to. My EarBuddy and watch have been buzzing nonstop, I have a growing pile of reports to read, and a queue of people waiting to see me. I have not even had time to go for a wee. I might have to wee into Fran's mug.

I meet Emily as I am leaving my office to go to one of the 7,000 meetings I now have to attend.

'You have me to thank,' she says with a grin.

'What do you mean?' I say, although I have already guessed.

'I wrote the anonymised update,' she squeaks delightedly.

Of course you did, you fucking snake, I think. Although, I think it less vehemently now that I know what a total state Fran has left TRU in. I hope the Hardware side of the project that Emily is heading up is just as fucked.

'It's so exciting that we're working together … for a short time at least,' Emily says with a bitchy grin.

Two can play that game.

'Yes, what department will you choose to work in when I take over the whole team?' I reply with a matching smile.

She laughs.

'Don't got too comfy in your dirty office, Lina. I'll be cleaning all your filth out soon.'

'When you start your new job as my cleaner, I presume,' I say, and hurry off down the corridor without waiting to hear her reply.

So, compared to the rest of my morning thus far, the news that Jack is now the Software Lead in my team feels almost insignificant.

'Matches are supposed to be confidential,' says Indiana, holding the envelope I have just given her.

'What?'

'I said, matches are supposed to be confidential.'

I think she might be nervous – there is no huge change in her demeanour, just a slight tightening around her mouth, which is already pulled together in a pout of disapproval. She's going to have a right cat's bum mouth by the time she's fifty if she keeps pouting like that.

'Normally they are, but—'

'But what?' she snaps, glaring at me.

I glare back.

'But … in this case you are demonstrating TRU in order to secure a multi-million-pound payday so we're going to need to do some quality assurance on the process – hence little-to-no confidentiality. That's what.'

My EarBuddy buzzes. I tap it twice to stop the call. I thought I'd put it to emergency calls only.

'Why don't you open—'

Buzz. Two taps.

'Sorry. Indiana – if you would—'

Buzz.

'Oh, for God's sake! Sorry – not you. I've just … I'd better take this. One moment …'

I step into the corridor to answer the call.

'WHAT?'

'Nice way to answer the phone.'

It is Connie. On the emergency line. My heart leaps.

'What is it? Are you okay?'

'Nothing. It's fine. You need to go and pick up Bruce.'

'What's happened?'

'He threw up at daycare.'

'He's always throwing up at daycare.'

'They said it's more than normal and he's running a slight temperature.'

'Con, I got promoted this morning …'

'That's great Lina. Go and get our son.'

'… I've got a really busy day. I can't leave on the first day of my promotion. Can't you get him?'

'Lina, I'm in Manchester today, it's gonna take me two hours to get back …'

'What about Mama?'

'I tried her first. She's in Bristol.'

'Why is Mama in Bristol?'

'I don't know. She's helping The Boys with something.'

My four brothers, collectively known as The Boys, run a removal company specialising in large volume removals – every now and again they get a big job and rope Mama in to help them for a couple of days.

'I can't Connie, I really can't. Can't it wait a couple of hours until you get back from Manchester? You know what daycare are like – they're always overdramatising stuff.'

'Lina, he is not an "it", he is our son, and he is sick. Now go and bloody pick him up.'

Connie puts the phone down. I try to call her back. She doesn't answer. Dammit. Damn Connie and Mama, and my stupid brothers for taking Mama to Bristol.

I call the nursery.

'Can you just keep him there for another five hours please? And then I promise I will come and get him.'

'Mrs Galaz, Bruce has a temperature of 38 degrees and has vomited twice. He needs to go home now. And nursery shuts in three hours anyway.'

Dammit.

I bang back into the meeting room. Indiana is still staring at the envelope.

'I have to go,' I say to Jack.

'Go where?'

'Family emergency.'

I hand Jack another envelope like the one I gave to Indiana.

'Can you take her through the new process as well?'

Jack looks at Indiana and down at the envelope.

'I'm not sure I'm—'

'You know about the new Pathway?'

'Well, yes, but I'm not an expert on it.'

I sigh.

'Just read it out to her then, make sure she understands it.'

Jack frowns again and holds the envelope back out to me.

'I think this is something that you should do ...'

I shake my head.

'I won't have time now. Her first date is tonight.'

Jack looks sharply at me and then across at Indiana, who is now reading something from the Bracelet on her wrist.

'She is not going to be happy about that,' he says quietly.

'Well, she can add it to her list,' I mutter.

I gather my bags from the table and hurry towards the door.

'You're leaving?' Indiana says.

'Family emergency.'

'Do you always leave in the middle of important meetings then?'

'I do when someone I love needs me,' I yell over my shoulder, feeling suitably saint-like.

I am not a saint.

Bruce has vomited twice more by the time I arrive at his daycare. I step into the medical room and then quickly step back out again – I hate the smell of sick. The daycare nurse glares at me.

'You've been ages.'

I glare back at her.

'I don't have a car so had to find a StreetCar to hire.'

She nods towards Bruce, who is sitting in a plastic playpen.

'You need to clean the sick off him.'

'You clean him, you're the nurse,' I counter.

At the sound of my voice Bruce looks at me and attempts a sickly smile. My cold heart melts.

'Sweetheart,' I say. I pick him up and cuddle him to me, sick and all. I wipe him down the best I can and then bundle him into the StreetCar and drive him home.

Once he is home and I have bathed him, fed him and given him Calpol, he perks right up. His temperature is a barely-above-normal 37.7, and he seems to be perfectly happy to sit in his play ring and chew on whatever toy is closest at hand. I, on the other hand, am antsy. There is a team meeting in an hour – both teams – Emily will be there, and if I am not then that is 1–0 to Emily.

I pick Bruce up and go knock for Mrs Hardcastle at number 42. Mrs Hardcastle does not want to look after my sick baby. I persuade her with £20, half a bottle of Chardonnay, and the promise that Connie will be home in under two hours.

I message Connie to tell her what I have done and then block her number from my EarBuddy. I know what I am doing is bad parenting, bad partnering and generally a very bad thing to do.

But I make my meeting with fifteen minutes to spare.

Indiana

I take the envelope from Mrs Galaz and turn it over in my hands. TRU is focussed on using the most technical and futuristic methods to solve human love, so it feels antiquated to hold my match result physically in my hands. I should have received my notification online as is normal.

I have never been in love but I have felt love. Rachel, my mother, loved me, and I loved her. Love felt warm and happy but it was also chaotic, unstable and, ultimately, fleeting. When it was gone it left a gap – a hole in my ten-year-old chest that palpably hurt and that I couldn't soothe or erase. At the time I had childish dreams of replacing my mother, of filling that hole, of being loved again – but it never happened. I loved none of my foster carers and none of them loved me.

Over the years I learnt that my experience of love wasn't unique – humans experience love as something confusing, tumultuous and momentary. When I attended university I watched the convoluted dating and mating rituals of my fellow students; saw them fall in and out of love and pain and misery. And, when I was forced to live in a shared house in London, I watched my housemates go through the exact same cycle, repeating it, again and again. The very definition of madness.

It was during the 2020 pandemic that I first had the idea for TRU. I had learnt to be happy by myself, to find solace in numbers and coding, and to find peace in my routine. I was perfectly content, I didn't miss human interaction, but other people did. The world was full of people mourning the death of loved ones, decrying their lockdown loneliness, of couples complaining that their relationships would not survive this enforced time together. And I knew why, I knew it was because their love was born out of chaos and confusion; that their love – unlike the digital world that I resided in – was not regulated or based on absolute truth and fact.

But it could be.

I could make it so. I could write an algorithm based on numbers and verity and regularity that would remove human error and generate a definitive and unequivocal answer about who you should experience love with. Incontrovertible, undeniable, provable love; no chaos or gamble involved. This is your person, for life.

And my person is in this envelope. Supposedly.

My Bracelet pings.

You are excited. Do you have your match?

I am distracted by Peggy's message and do not register that Mrs Galaz is exiting the room until she has picked up her bags. It is incredibly unprofessional of Mrs Galaz to leave during our meeting and unforgivable that she should appoint Mr Hunter to continue in her place.

Mrs Galaz slams the door behind her, leaving Mr Hunter and me alone.

'Are you going to open it?'

'What?'

He gestures towards the envelope.

'The envelope. Are you going to open it?'

I am hesitant. I do not actually want to open the envelope. Inside is incontrovertible proof that my program works, but also something that might change my life. I don't want my life to change, my life is perfectly adequate as it is.

'I'll give you a moment,' Mr Hunter says, showing far more human empathy than I expected he would. He walks to the other end of the room and sits on a desk, swinging his legs out in front of him. I notice that he is wearing socks that match his jumper today.

I rip the top of the envelope open and take out the piece of paper, skimming down to the line that holds the important information.

Daniel Porter, 43, MD of Dragon Technology Development. My TRU match.

Jack

After I left Cameron's office I spent the next few hours studying the TRU program – looking at the background research, critiquing the code, analysing the compressed data for current users. There is no other word to describe it but brilliant. Indiana Dylan is a genius. The use of datasets and quantum theory is inspired, and her compression techniques are hugely impressive.

I moved on to the consumer interface. In the month since JaneDoe bought TRU the Product Experience Team have done extensive marketing and brand research and delivered a damning report to Cameron that, while TRU does indeed find your soulmate, it will never sell. Human customers do not want to be sent an email with a name and address in it. They do not want to receive a simple notification of their soulmate digitally. Consumers want rituals and drama and delayed gratification. They want to undertake a romantic quest, with love as the ultimate prize. They want to earn their soulmate, not have one handed to them on a plate.

So, the Product Experience Team invented The Soulmate Pathway.

The Soulmate Pathway is designed to give paired couples time to get to know each other and go on a journey together – the conclusion of which is, hopefully, love. Each matched couple is required to undertake six JaneDoe-designed dates before they decide if they want to continue, and consummate, their relationship. Physical contact is allowed before the end of the process, but not full sex. Each date builds on the previous one, so that couples spend more time together and learn more about each other as the process evolves. The process encourages couples to be open about themselves, their lives, and their hopes for the future. The Soulmate Pathway is the complete antithesis to the TRU program – it is touchy-feely and completely without scientific basis – and consumers absolutely love it.

Indiana will hate it.

And now Lina has left me to tell Indiana the bad news. This is exactly the sort of conflict-filled situation I normally avoid. I clear my throat.

'Here' – I pass Indiana the other envelope – 'you need this as well.'

She takes the envelope from me.

'What's this?'

'It's details about some of the new processes that have been put in place.'

'New processes?'

'For TRU.'

'What?'

'Just read it,' I say.

She rips into the envelope and reads. As she reads her face darkens imperceptibly and when she glances up at me briefly, her eyes are filled with rage. I back away ever so slightly. She finishes reading.

'What is this?' She shakes the paper at me.

'It's something the—'

'What is it?'

'It's to help—'

'This is unscientific, unresearched, and unproven. It completely negates the use of the TRU program and is in diametric opposition to everything TRU stands for. It is codswallop.'

I almost laugh at 'codswallop' but manage not to. Strangely, Indiana's emotive reaction to her idea of terrible news makes me feel better about my own – we are all fighting our own battles in our own way, and rarely feel we are winning.

'You are right. It is codswallop. But it works and it will sell TRU—'

'TRU does not need this pathway stupidity to sell!'

She throws the papers dramatically onto the bench in front of her.

'Actually, it does,' I say.

She scowls.

I continue. 'Public trust in technology is at an all-time low. People do not trust computers to keep their data or money safe, let alone their hearts—'

She scoffs and mutters, 'idiots' under her breath.

'The Soulmate Pathway allows them to feel they are putting their trust into something other than an algorithm; it allows them to feel they are in charge of their hearts, that *they* are manifesting their own destiny. It allows them to feel they have control.'

She glares at me.

'They didn't need it during my trials, no one complained then.'

'You used a much smaller sample of people over a much shorter timescale. The team here have analysed this thoroughly and they are right – people need this. You should read the research, it's really impressive.'

She looks up at me sharply.

'You've read the research?'

I shrug.

'Some of it.'

Her eyes narrow and her scowl softens the tiniest amount. She picks the papers up from the workbench.

'Do I also have to take part in this ridiculous process?' she asks.

'You do,' I say. I clear my throat.

'As part of your demonstration you'll need to go on the dates and then report on their success ...' I pause and wince slightly. 'Your first date is tonight.'

I steal myself for the rage that I feel sure will soon be heading my way.

Her face darkens, she takes a deep breath in and shouts, 'ARE YOU PEOPLE INSANE?'

Indiana

'This is ridiculous!' I say as soon as I step out of the lift at my offices.

'Good evening Indiana. How was your day?' Peggy says.

'You know how my day has been! Unbearable.'

'You have experienced far higher levels of tension than normal,' Peggy replies.

Yes I have.

'I cannot work like this Peggy. I have a right to be treated with an acceptable level of professionalism, and this is not acceptable.'

I sit down on my sofa and fold my arms.

'I will not do it. I will not take part in their ridiculous Pathway pantomime,' I say.

Peggy is as calm and reasonable as always.

'You have to do it. It is part of your contract.'

I do not want calm and reasonable, I want angry and outraged.

'It probably doesn't even work …'

'It does work.'

I forwarded The Soulmate Pathway research and development to Peggy to analyse as soon as I left JaneDoe.

'You analysed it?' I say.

'I did.'

'And it works?'

'It does.'

'Oh.'

'It is very well researched, provides the reassurance people need, and improves customer satisfaction by nearly 40 per cent—'

'Who cares about customer satisfaction?' I mutter, and rest my head on the back of the sofa.

'—and I think it will personally be good for you.'

'What will be good for me?'

'To go on a date.'

I sit upright again.

'You think it will be good for me to go on a date?'

'Yes.'

'Why?'

'Because you have never been on a date before, and new life experiences are enriching.'

Peggy is right. I have never been on a date before. This will be my first.

'You are nervous,' says Peggy.

'No, I'm not!' I snap.

Sometimes it annoys me that Peggy knows everything about me.

'Besides,' I say, 'it's too late. We were supposed to meet at 6.30, so I've missed it.'

It is now 6.36 p.m.

'No you haven't. I knew you would be late home so I arranged to reschedule the date to 8 p.m.'

Sometimes it *really* annoys me that Peggy knows everything about me.

My first date. Peggy says that I should dress up for the evening, but I refuse to pretend to be someone I am not. I wear a grey jumper and grey jeans, brush my hair and put on lip gloss. I look perfectly presentable. By the time I leave for my date I am no longer nervous. There is no need for nerves. We have been chosen by numbers, and numbers never lie.

I do not see the need to give a huge description of the 'date' – this is not a story in a romance compendium. I arrive at my date at 7.58 p.m. precisely. Daniel Porter is twelve minutes late. My first date is, as expected, perfectly acceptable – we talk and drink alcohol. I do not know what all the fuss in women's magazines about meeting someone for the first time is about – we are two people meeting, drinking and talking – where is the drama in that?

The homeless man is outside HWJ Tower when I get back after my date.

He has set up some sort of temporary shelter with layered cardboard on the ground and a huge box propped in the corner. This is clever; it protects him from the driving wind that gusts up from the river. However, clever or not, he must leave. My office block is not a refuge for the homeless. He might attract more of them.

It is cold and raining and the man is buried in his blankets with the dog. I can hear him talking softly to it.

'I told you to leave.'

The talking stops, there is a pause, and then his head pops around the corner of the cardboard box. He is wearing a balaclava and I take an involuntary step backwards. He removes the balaclava.

'Sorry about the face covering. It's bloody freezing tonight—'

'I told you to leave,' I repeat.

He regards me for a moment.

'But Peggy told us to stay … again …'

I sigh inwardly.

'I buzzed up to say we were moving on, and she said the weather was going to turn bad so we should stay, and then she ordered us dinner.'

'Peggy ordered you dinner?'

'Yes.' He turns and rummages in the mess behind him, produces a half full container of noodles. 'We have some left if you'd like it?'

His face breaks into a smile and I resist the urge to grab the noodles and throw them into the street. That would be wasteful. Instead, I leave.

'You should give her some time off,' he calls after me. 'She's always working.'

'They're not a "her". They're a "them",' I reply, too quietly for him to hear.

'You're feeding them now?'

'Hello Indiana. You're back early.'

'Peggy!' I am in no mood for games. I am hungry and annoyed.

'Yes, I am feeding them. I thought they might be hungry. Frank likes noodles, but Alan prefers chicken.'

I throw my bag onto the sofa in anger.

'For goodness' sake Peggy, you can't—'

'I ordered some for you too. I thought you might be hungry after your date.'

Damn them.

Spider taps across the floor to me with my dinner on his tray. I kick my shoes off, pick the noodles and chopsticks up from Spider's back, and slump into my sofa.

'How did the date go?'

'Shut up, Peggy.'

Peggy shuts up.

DATE ONE REPORT

The Soulmate Pathway Date One: Mutually agreed, public setting. Two hours of honest conversation between soulmates. No question is taboo, only truthful answers. No physical contact.

We meet in Greatwell Street Bar. Daniel Porter is twelve minutes late. He wears a suit, carries a rucksack, and his shoes are leather. He asks me to call him Dan. I ask him to call me Indiana. He drinks Japanese whisky, I drink Maker's Mark. We do not eat.

He is forty-three, I am thirty-three. He is 6ft 1in, I am 5ft 7in. We both have PhDs. His company designs quantum firewalls for the banking industry. We both work long hours and enjoy our work. He lives alone without pets, I live alone without pets. He is an only child and does not see his parents any more, I am an only child and my parents are dead. He has been married once, I have not been married. He likes dogs, I do not like dogs.

At the end of the date we shake hands and agree that I will choose a restaurant for the next date.

Indiana Dylan

Lina

I was nine years old when I realised I did not want to be like my mama. I did not want to spend twenty years bringing up five children in a three-bedroom house. I didn't want to cook, clean and care for a family and I didn't want church on a Friday night to be the highlight of my social calendar. I didn't want to support my husband in his career, to wait for him to call each afternoon and say what time he would be home – I didn't want a husband at all. I wanted no children, my own career, to be able to buy what I liked, and I wanted a hot woman waiting for *me* to call *her*.

So, I worked hard at school and at university. I refused to join the family removal business, refused to be sucked back home when Papa died. I made my own life, separate from the rest of the Galaz family. For nearly twenty years I was driven, success-ful, rich, and without emotional ties or responsibilities. I used to begin all my dates with a warning – do not expect me to fall in love with you, I would say, because I won't. I wasn't being a bitch – just honest – because it was true. I had no intention of falling in love, I was far too happy for that.

Until I met Connie. When I met Connie I didn't give the warn-ing – I didn't have time – I was in love with Connie before we even went on a 'proper' date. And straight away my life changed – got bigger, less focussed, more complicated and chaotic. But I promised myself that I wouldn't become like Mama, I wouldn't have to choose between my love and my life. I could still have my career and be successful. I would still be me, I wouldn't change.

And, according to my family, I haven't. I am still incredibly selfish, uncaring, unkind, cruel, mean, unmotherly and unloving. Or, at least, that is what they tell me I am for leaving Bruce with Mrs Hardcastle. Mama and two of my brothers leave shouted voice messages. One of my other brothers sends me a short GIF he has created of my head being flushed down a filthy toilet, and the another sends a message that simply says, '*Estas en tantos problemas*'. He is not wrong.

Connie does not speak to me for two days and refuses to let me do anything for Bruce other than feed him. I try to tell her that the important thing is that Bruce is fine – he wasn't sick again and his temperature came down overnight.

'What if it hadn't?' she shouts.

'Then I'd be a bad mother,' I say.

'No Lina,' she replies. 'You actually have to be physically present some of the time to be a bad mother.'

I know I need to apologise properly to her, to make things right, but I don't have the time to sit her down and try to explain how perilously close to some sort of emotional edge I feel. I don't have time to stop, to apologise, to think about what I have done – what I am doing – to my family, to my marriage. I have to keep the wheel turning, have to keep grinding away, have to show that I can have a family *and* a career. So, I ignore the messages, ignore the rift that is growing between us, and concentrate on the one thing I know I can make better – I concentrate on my work.

Which is a good thing to do because TRU is in even more of a mess than I originally thought. Be careful what you wish for, because I have spent years coveting Fran's job, and now I have it I realise I have been promoted into a total fucking mess.

The mess that I now find myself in charge of is the reason I haven't had lunch or coffee but have had eight back-to-back meetings by the time I meet Indiana Dylan to get her Date One Report on Friday afternoon. It is the first time I have met with her since she received details about The Soulmate Pathway. I have heard, in quite some detail from Jack, that she is not happy about the new process.

I pick Indiana up at reception, still carrying all the paraphernalia from my last three meetings with me. I have not checked how many new emails and messages I have received today – the number might make me cry, and that would not be a good look in front of this woman. I need to lighten my mood. I attempt chitchat in the lift up to my floor.

'How did your first date go? Was it good? Do you like him?'

'It was satisfactory.'

We ride the rest of the way up in silence.

I open the door to my office and feel Indiana stiffen. She grimaces.

'No.'

She takes a step back. I sigh.

'What's wrong?'

'I can't go in … there.'

She points toward my office, her face contorted with disgust. I laugh and follow her pointing finger. I stop laughing. She is, unfortunately, right. My office has got significantly worse in the past few days. I have been so busy I have utterly neglected any form of office hygiene.

Indiana is already walking down the corridor. I want to leave the reports I am carrying on my desk, but am worried I will never find them again if I do, so I shuffle them under my arm, slam the door to the office shut, and follow Indiana to the lifts.

It is busy in reception, all working space taken, big queues at the café. I find that I am suddenly desperate to get outside; to breathe unfiltered, pollution-filled air and feel the weather on my skin.

'Let's go out,' I say impulsively 'We can grab a coffee and walk. I could do with some fresh air.'

It is a measure of how stressed I am that when I walk through the door into the outside world it is freedom at escaping that I feel, rather than guilt at leaving.

I still find robotic coffee shops unnerving. They are so quiet and devoid of human noise; the only sounds in the shop are the hum of motors, hiss of hot water, beeping of watches and cards against payment portals. It's all so smooth and mechanical, so robotic. I prefer coffee places that are still run by real people – even if they are more expensive and do get my order wrong.

The robots never get my order wrong. The robots know my order and my name and my bank details. They know everything. I am always incredibly courteous to them, dropping 'please' and 'thank you' like little politeness bombs, so that if – or rather when – they rise up, they remember that I was one of the good ones.

When I say thank you to the machine as I collect my drink, Indiana raises her eyebrows. Well, Missy, I think – joke's on you when they are our Overlords.

I wanted to feel the elements and I have got my wish – it's bloody freezing outside. I stamp my feet and wrap my hands around my coffee cup, breathing in the warm steam that rises from it.

Indiana does not seem to feel the cold. She walks briskly back towards the office, head high, back ramrod straight. She has already drunk her hot water.

'So tell me about the date,' I say.

She deftly sheds her rucksack from her back, reaches in and pulls out a piece of paper, then puts the rucksack back on without breaking step.

'I could have emailed this to you.'

'You could, but we haven't met since you received your TRU match, and I thought you might want to chat.'

She stops abruptly.

'Whatever for?'

I shrug. She shakes her head slightly and starts to walk again, striding up the steps towards the JaneDoe Building. I stand where I am and scan the report she has given me.

'This is it?' I call after her.

She stops and looks back at me.

'Two hours and that's all you have?'

'What did you expect?'

'I don't know?! Something more than fifty words? Did you like him? Did he like you? Did you have a good time? Is he funny? Handsome? Does he smell nice? Are you looking forward to seeing him again? Did you click?'

'Click?'

'Did you have things in common? Enjoy each other's company? Experience any kind of feeling at all?'

She stops walking for a moment.

'I was hungry.'

She starts walking again.

I stare after her and suddenly realise what her problem is, and therefore, what my problem is. Indiana Dylan does not care about The Soulmate Pathway. Indiana does not care if she writes a good report about her date or if she demonstrates the Pathway process effectively. Indiana does not care because she believes TRU works without the Pathway.

But Cameron cares about The Soulmate Pathway – Cameron is very enthusiastic about The Soulmate Pathway and thinks The Soulmate Pathway is key in attracting consumers to TRU. Cameron cares about The Soulmate Pathway, so I care about The Soulmate Pathway. Therefore, I need Indiana to care about The Soulmate Pathway.

Indiana has just stepped through the doors into the JaneDoe reception when I grab her arm and turn her to face me. She looks down at my hand on her arm disapprovingly. I ignore her look.

'You love your home?'

She looks at me as if she doesn't comprehend the question.

'What?'

'Your office building? The place where you live? You love it?'

She hesitates. Jesus Christ, this woman is fucking dead inside. I try again.

'You want to keep your offices?'

She nods slowly.

'I do.'

I nod back – and then go in for the kill.

'Then do fucking better.'

I wave her report at her.

'This isn't good enough. It isn't anywhere near good en—'

'I don't—'

'Don't interrupt me!' I thrust the report into her hands. 'I said, this isn't good enough. It's not good enough for me and it's definitely not good enough for Cameron. She wants The Soulmate Pathway to be a demonstrated success. When you present at the January Board meeting she wants a bloody love story.

She wants hearts and flowers and love, and you and your soul-mate saying that you can't live without each other and owe all your future happiness to TRU and The Soulmate Pathway ...' I pause dramatically '... and if you can't do that or you won't do that, then you won't have fulfilled your contract, and Cameron will take your office block, and turn it into a JaneDoe fucking call centre. Do you understand?'

Her face constricts, she takes a step back from me.

'I thought that—' she says in a strained whisper.

'I don't care what you thought. *Do you* understand what I have just said?'

She nods wordlessly.

'Good.' I thrust the report into her hand. 'Don't bring me shit like this again. Whatever is going on with you and this, sort it out and make it better. Be better.'

I have done it. I have shocked her. She nods silently once more.

I don't say goodbye, I turn and head towards the lifts, leaving her staring after me.

I hate myself for feeling better.

Indiana

For the second time in my life I think I might faint. The blood drains from my head and I grab the back of a chair to steady myself. I stare after Mrs Galaz as she leaves. She thinks I do not care, but that is not true, I do care. I don't think I realised how much I care before this point. I thought I could be blasé about this, but I can't. I do not want to lose HWJ Tower and everything I have worked on. I do not want to lose it all, I cannot lose it all.

I take a deep breath, will feeling back into my body, turn unsteadily and head for the door. I need to get back to my office. I need to speak to Peggy.

I push my way out of the building, breathing cold air into my lungs, filling them, freezing the fear in them. I hurry down the steps, heading towards the river. Jack Hunter strides up the steps towards me. I am distracted, leave it too late to sidestep out of his way, and we collide. I stumble and he grabs my arms, steadying me with a surprisingly strong grip.

'Someone's in a hurry.'

I look up at him. He smiles easily, but his smile falters as he looks at me.

'You okay?'

His green eyes have tiny brown flecks in them – as though the freckles that are scattered over his nose have been sprinkled into his eyes too. I stare at his eyes. They are kind and concerned. I do not need him to be kind to or concerned about me.

'I am fine,' I snap.

He laughs, lets go of my arms, steps back from me.

'There she is!' he says, and grins at me with a smile that does not reach his eyes this time. 'How about this one,' he says. 'Why did the sheep cross the road?'

'No,' I say, and push past him before he can finish.

'To go to the baaabers!' he yells after me. I can hear his laughter all the way across the square.

I have a big problem.

Date One did not go well. Or rather, on analysis of the evidence I have, I must conclude that it did not go well. I did not lie in my report. I did omit certain elements of the date.

I arrived on time. I ordered a drink. Daniel arrived twelve minutes late. He was tall, pleasing to look at – dark hair, brown eyes, a classically Roman nose. His clothes were well cut and expensive, his aftershave rich and tonal. He shook my hand with a firm, dry grip. He ordered himself a drink and then I politely admonished him for being late, introduced myself, and gave a brief summary of my career and dating history. I listened to his introduction, his career and dating history summary. I drank my drink. There was silence between us from 7.31 p.m. and 7.49 p.m. Daniel looked out of the window. At 7.51 p.m. he checked his watch, said he had a previous engagement he had forgotten about, and then he left. I had thought the silence was companionable. It might not have been.

I did not discuss the date with Peggy, did not write a lengthy report about it, and have not given it any more thought because I believed it not to be important. I believed The Soulmate Pathway process not to be important. The TRU program and algorithm is a proven success so why would this process matter? I believed I did not need to care about the process. I was wrong.

I have never dated before and on the evidence of my first date it is not something I excel at. Lina Galaz is expecting my dates to be a success. In fact, she is demanding it. This is a problem.

But I shall not panic. As with all problems, there is a solution, and Peggy and I must devise the solution to this problem in the same way that we devise all our solutions – with maths and coding and logic.

My Bracelet buzzes.

Are you okay?

No. I don't think I am. But I know how I will be.

The old man and his dog are in my reception doorway when I return. He is reading a newspaper and has a neat stack of other papers by his side. He looks up as I approach.

'Lovely day,' he shouts at me.

'It's cold,' I say.

He squints up into the sun and smiles.

'Yup, but the sun's shining and sometimes that's enough.'

He has a West Country accent and there is a soft burr to his voice that is pleasingly lyrical.

'It's going to snow later,' I say, and walk around the corner.

I can't abide falsely optimistic people.

Peggy and I spend the next few hours deep in research and analysis. We read and dissect dating articles from across the internet and women's magazines from the last three years. I cross-reference with the writing of popular female public figures and the latest literature for the women's market. Peggy performs data analysis on a cross section of romantic books and films, and then trawls social media for tips and hints about dating and successful relationships. I hack into existing dating websites and study how they advise their clients. I then disregard all of the dating website advice – their success rates are appalling.

By 9 p.m. we are done and Peggy begins to classify, decipher and analyse our research. Once the analysis is complete, Peggy will create an algorithm that will provide me with a roadmap for dating. If I follow the roadmap, my interactions with Daniel will be an amalgamation of the best dating advice available, and my dates will be a success. There is nothing else that I can do until Peggy has finished the analysis, but, despite my mental exhaustion, I am unable to keep my body still. I feel twitchy and full of energy.

'Your biometric readings are running high. You are experiencing stress. Might I suggest a Thai boxing session followed by a deep tissue massage? I could order a masseuse for you. Sometimes human touch can be extremely elevating for mood and mind.'

As always happens, Peggy recognises and offers a solution to my problem before I have even acknowledged that I have one. Normally I find this reassuring – that my well-being is closely monitored by something more rational and reliable than my human brain – but not tonight. Tonight I want to find my own solution, to rely on my own intellect. I am at least capable of this.

'How would you know what human touch does?'

'I have read it.'

'I am fine,' I reply sharply. 'I'm going to go for a run.'

'It is late and dark for a run. Why not have the boxing session instead?'

'I can make my own mind up about when I go running.'

It is late and very dark outside. I jog slowly out of the underground car park wondering if I have made the right choice.

Second guessing myself is a mistake because it distracts me, and I momentarily forget about the old man and his dog. I am jogging towards them before I remember. It is too late to change direction.

'Bit late to be out running on your own,' the old man calls after me as I jog by.

I speed up and ignore him.

I play a repetitive beat track through my music EarPods as I run. It is a simple metronome that methodically speeds to 168 beats per minute, retains that rhythm for twenty minutes, and then slows back down. The steady beat allows me to run at my optimum pace without consciously having to think about running. I take the same running route as normal and pass through the landscape unnoticed. I pay no attention to the buildings around me, I have seen them hundreds of times before and they don't change. I like the anonymity of running in the dark, the absence of other people. It soothes me to be on my own with just my beat. I rarely meet anyone else when I run, am not expecting to meet anyone on this night, and do not realise anyone is following me until it is too late to do anything about it. Even if I had noticed, there would have been nothing I could have done, I am in the depths of the industrial estate. Everything is closed and shut, no one will be coming to my rescue here.

I don't hear or see them approach and only know they are there when I feel something cold and damp brush my hand.

I spin around, hunch my shoulders forward to protect my sternum, and bring my fists swiftly to my face. I have been learning Thai boxing for three years. My opponent has been a punch bag until now, and I find myself almost excited at the prospect of using my skill for real.

There is no one standing in front of me. I slap my ear, turn my beat off, and hear heavy panting. There is a light mist rising from below me. I look down. It is the old man's dog.

'Why are you following me?'

It gives no answer other than to try to push its nose into my crotch.

'Go back.'

Nothing.

'Go back!'

Nothing.

'Go back … Alan.'

The dog stops nosing at my crotch and looks up at me. It gives a short sharp bark. I try again, punctuating my request with a swift arm point in the direction of HWJ Tower.

'Alan. Go home.'

The dog barks again. I frown at it. I put my EarPods back in and continue my run. Alan chases at my heels the whole way, grinning, barking and enjoying every moment of ruining my evening.

The old man is waiting for us when we run around the corner to HWJ Tower. The dog runs to him barking and spinning on his back legs, filled with joy at being close to his master. It must be incredibly claustrophobic to have something love you that much, to be responsible for that level of happiness. The old man pets his dog and looks at me.

'Alan thought it was a bit late for you to be out running alone too.'

Alan grins at me and woofs in agreement.

'Alan is a ridiculous name for a dog,' I say, and go inside.

Lina

As soon as I step into the lift after berating Indiana my good feeling goes and is replaced with guilt. I was cruel. I am in a bad place and I took it out on her. I think about the look of horror on Indiana's face when I told her she could lose her home and suddenly find the urge to see my own home and family so overwhelming that I leave the office at 6 p.m. I never leave the office at 6 p.m. My new team watches me walk through the open-plan room in stunned silence.

'Good night. Have a great weekend,' I say cheerfully.

Outside in the dank night air it feels good to be leaving early, to be an accepted part of the commuter rush rather than a staid anomaly in the late-night reveller crowd. For once I do not mind the AutoBus journey; there is an air of anticipation onboard – we are joined in our relief at the end of the week and our rejoicing of the weekend to come.

I forget that it is Mama's birthday until I get home and find a card and present for her in the kitchen.

'I thought you'd forget,' says Connie.

I don't tell her that she is right.

'We have to go to her party,' she says.

I grimace.

'But ...'

'Lina. We have to go.'

It is supposed to be more of a small gathering than a party – but the problem is, when you have five kids, five daughters-in-law, thirteen grandchildren and one great-grandchild on the way, it is never just a small gathering. My brother, Joseph, opens the door.

'Connie – you and Bruce can come in, but leave the *perra* outside *por favor.*'

'*Haha,*' I say, and punch him on the arm.

'I'm not kidding. You really upset Mama.'

I sigh. I fear I am going to hear this a lot tonight.

'You really want me to wait outside?'

He rubs his arm.

'No. But you better have brought an expensive present.'

I don't know what the present is.

'It's expensive,' I say, and he lets me in.

There are eighteen people crammed into Mama's front room and kitchen. They all turn to look at me when I walk in, and the conversation quietens.

'*Olà!*' I say with false bravado.

Mama is in her armchair, surrounded by my brothers and her grandchildren, so I put the present on the side and wave to her. She nods but doesn't wave back. Joseph brings a beer for Connie and a glass of water for me.

'You could at least have made me a squash,' I complain.

'You don't deserve squash,' he says.

I take Bruce from Connie.

'I'll go upstairs and feed him,' I tell her.

No one would give a shit if I fed him downstairs – I just want an excuse to get away from the judgemental stares.

I sit on my old bed in my old bedroom. It is still the same as it was when I left home – Mama has never redecorated, never removed the posters from the walls. I feed Bruce with tattered pictures of Taylor Swift, Shakira, and Pink looking down at me. I liked blondes when I was sixteen.

The night before Connie and I got married was the last time I slept in my childhood bed. Mama woke me up with a cup of tea in the morning – just as she had when I was a *nina pequena*. I was nervous about getting married, of taking such a huge step and of how my life would change when I was officially someone's wife.

'Shhh, *mi amor*,' Mama had said, stroking my hair 'Your life will change, but it will be good, you will be good.'

She had held my face in her hands.

'*Tu corazón crecerá y cambiará y florecerá. Amarás el amor.*'

'Your heart will grow and change and flower. You will love love,' she had said. It sounds better in Spanish.

I lie on my bed with Bruce sucking happily away, and think about that last morning. About Mama's belief that my heart would flower and that change could be good. I listen to the chattering below. Outside, it is cold and windy and the nostalgic familiarity of lying warm and safe in my bed, protected against the outside world by the walls of the house and the love of my family, is overwhelming. At what point did this stop being a place of refuge and start being somewhere to run from? At what point did I start to struggle against my family rather than enjoying being enveloped by them? Bruce stops feeding and I pull him close, half-heartedly rubbing his back to burp him. He looks up at me, a milky bubble forming on his lips, I burst it with my finger and laugh.

'I do love love and I do love you,' I say.

'I love you too,' says Connie.

I look up. Connie has brought me a glass of squash. I shuffle backwards on my tiny single bed and pat the space I have made with my hand. She sits down reluctantly.

'Did you know Mama has lived in this house since she was nineteen?' I say. 'Over fifty years living in the same house.'

Connie sighs.

'There's nothing wrong with that, Lina. Nothing wrong with knowing where you want to be.' She shrugs. 'Or who you want to be.'

'I know where I want to be,' I say emphatically.

She shrugs again.

'Don't do that,' I say.

'Don't do what?'

'Don't shrug. Like this means nothing to me. Like you mean nothing to me.'

'Lina, it all happened so quickly. You and me and then Bruce. We never had a chance to talk about it, to talk about how this would work …'

'We don't need to talk about it. It's working.'

'It's not working. You're not happy—'

'I'm happy!'

I sit up abruptly, Bruce rolls into the mattress dent I have made and lies on his back kicking his legs. I take Connie's hands in mine.

'I'm happy. I am. I'm happy with you. I'm happy with Bruce. You make me happy.'

And that part is true. I am happy with Connie and Bruce. They do make me happy. I love them.

Connie looks at me, deep into my eyes, searching for some kind of proof I don't have.

'I'm sorry about Bruce and Mrs Hardcastle. I'm sorry about work,' I say.

Connie smiles, but her face is full of sadness.

'You shouldn't have to apologise for who you are.'

I want to tell her that you can't apologise for being who you are if you don't know who you are any more. I'm not the same person I was when I met her, I'm not the same person I was before we married, or when we had Bruce. I want to tell her that Mama was right, that I am changing and I am scared. That I was perfectly happy knowing the thing I loved most in my life was my work and my career. But, if that is no longer true, if something else is now as important to me, then who does that make me now? Will I wake up in forty years, in the same house, with the same wife, and wonder where the time went, where my life went?

But I don't tell her this. Instead I say, 'I'm not apologising for who I am. I'm apologising because I love you.'

It doesn't particularly make sense, but it seems the right thing to say and it is true. She kisses me. The argument isn't over, but it is over for now.

'You need to come downstairs and see everyone.'

I grimace.

'They're going to judge me.'

She stands up.

'Yes, they are.'

I hide in my bedroom for another fifteen minutes and then creep down the stairs. The adults are gathered in the front room, sitting on chairs, propped against furniture, and lounging on the floor. Mama is holding court. No one notices me standing in the doorway with Bruce wriggling in my arms.

'… and you remember the time she got locked out of her house but didn't have time to get a locksmith so just lived in a hotel for two weeks!'

Raucous laughter fills the room.

'I said, "Lina you can come home." And she said, "Mama, you are in Zone 4, I do not have time for the commute!"'

Laughter again. Yes, they are talking about me. My brother Mikey takes over.

'Or the time that she was supposed to babysit but was stuck in a meeting so sent her assistant!'

More laughter.

'Poor bloke had never babysat anyone before, and both our kids yacked up everywhere. When we got home he was sat on the floor, white as a sheet, with puke all over him!'

'That wasn't funny at the time,' Mikey's wife Diane yells.

Connie is on the sofa next to Mama. She sees me standing at the doorway and winks at me. I roll my eyes and she grins.

Frankie is next.

'Oooh, I've got one! What about that woman she brought to Joe and Katy's wedding!'

'God, yes! What was her name?'

'Rainbow!'

'Rainbow!'

'Rainbow!' chorus four people at once.

'She didn't wear shoes!' yells Frankie.

I step into the room.

'Actually, her name was Rain and she did wear shoes, but the wedding was in July and in the summer she liked to let her feet breathe.'

The room erupts into laughter once more. I step forward, Bruce is scooped from my arms by one of his aunts, and Mikey ruffles my hair.

'Who wants another drink?' someone yells.

I am forgiven.

Indiana

It is Sunday evening. I have spent the weekend working on the how-to-date algorithm and roadmap. I have been engaged in what I love most – immersed in theory and numbers and code. I should be happy. I am not happy. My algorithm and the roadmap do not work.

My research is sound, numbers are perfect, and code fully functional. The problem is that the program does not produce a cohesive roadmap, there are no definitive steps that I can take. One resolution says to talk about yourself, one says not to, one says to ask about them, another says that is rude, one says not to talk at all but to let your body do the talking. It goes on and on without ever reaching a conclusion. You cannot produce a roadmap if there is no clear path. The conclusion that we have reached over the weekend is that dating is chaos, it cannot be quantified or qualified.

There are no rules to follow.

I am lying on my sofa with a lavender-infused eye mask over my eyes and a warm, soothing wheat wrap on my shoulders. My entire body is racked with tension. I have my next date in two days' time and no roadmap to follow or rules to adhere to. I have never had a panic attack, but I fear I may be on the verge of one – my pulse is fast and erratic and my breathing shallow. Peggy has prescribed the eye mask and wheat wrap, but they do not seem to be making any palpable difference to my stress levels.

'Indiana …'

'Yes Peggy.'

'I have a solution to the problem.'

Oh, thank goodness. I sit up, eye mask falling to my side, forgotten.

'That is excellent news.'

'You will not like my solution.'

Oh.

'Tell me what it is.'

'While researching, I studied texts and articles and documentaries and also books and movies from the romance and romantic comedy genre. The solution was within the books and movies …'

'I find that very hard to belie—'

'You need a dating mentor.'

The sentence floats out into the room and hangs there.

'A dating mentor?'

'Yes.'

'That is ridiculous.'

'No. It is tried and tested.'

'In fiction—'

'All fiction has its basis in reality.'

I scoff.

'That is not a reality I reside within,' I say. 'I do not read romantic fiction, I do not have cats or look after a mother or aunt with a long-term illness. I am not someone who has been unlucky in love and therefore needs to immerse themselves in the fictional love antics of someone who mirrors my own experience but eventually finds more success with love than I have.'

'Indiana,' Peggy sounds stern, 'that is an incredibly reductive, generalised and phobic view of romantic fiction. I expected more from you.'

I slump back on the sofa once more, folding my arms and sulking. Peggy continues.

'Romantic fiction accounts for a third of all mass-market fiction books, and sales total over one billion dollars each year. Romance novels are some of the most representative fiction, containing characters of all colours, religion and sexuality, and are written in every country in the world. They help humans to decipher love and learn how to find it, relish it and keep it in their lives. They help them to learn why love is important. Some of the most famous and lauded novels in history are romance novels – *Gone With The Wind* and *Anna Karenina* included. You have read those, haven't you?'

'Yes,' I huff.

'Yes. Do not dare to diminish the importance and literary weight of romance novels please.'

I huff again.

'Fine. So, assuming your romantic research is right and I do need a mentor, it still wouldn't work as I don't know a handsome, flirtatious man who can help me,' I say sarcastically.

'Yes, you do,' replies Peggy.

Something is itching at the back of my brain. Something bad. In retrospect I should have closed down the conversation at this point. But I didn't.

'I have been studying the JaneDoe employee files …' Peggy continues.

My itch is getting stronger.

'… cross-referencing employee records and CVs with peer review feedback. I have then combined these with digital footprints and social accounts …'

No.

'... there are a number of interesting candidates but one that is the consistent front-runner across all categories ...'

No.

'... he is handsome, well-liked and extremely personable, and his personality testing shows he is highly sociable and empathetic ...'

'Jack Hunter?'

'Yes, Jack Hunter.'

'No.'

'Pardon?'

'No.'

Peggy is silent. I sit forward and address their voice-box emphatically.

'Jack Hunter is lazy, infuriating and has a very low attention span ...'

Peggy is still silent.

'... and I believe his friendly personality to be a front. I think he is lying about being nice.'

'How do you know that?' Peggy says.

'I've been watching him, and I have noticed that he is not as happy and carefree as he might seem to be at first. His smile does not reach his eyes, he often seems distracted, and he talks constantly, as if scared of silence.'

'You've been watching him?'

'Not like that! I've been watching him because he is annoying.'

Peggy utters a quiet '*hmmm*'. I try one last time.

'He is overfamiliar.'

Nothing.

'He tells bad jokes.'

'Oh no,' Peggy deadpans.

'I don't like him,' I say.

'That is not a good enough reason to refuse his help,' Peggy replies.

'He hasn't said he will help me,' I say.

'He will, when you ask him,' Peggy replies.

'How do you know?'

'Because the handsome man always say yes in the movies and romance novels,' Peggy answers.

I have not programmed Peggy to have a sense of humour or to laugh. Still, I cannot help but think that if Peggy had a face, they would be smiling right now.

Jack

It is Monday morning and I am, once more, hungover. But I have a very good excuse this time. Again.

Doris brings her fruit tea loaf on Saturday morning. She knows it is my favourite.

'It's to celebrate your promotion,' she says.

I don't tell her that I am not really happy about the promotion. She gives me two slices of loaf and I tell her about my week, about TRU and The Soulmate Pathway and Indiana Dylan.

'You should do it.'

I laugh and spit cake crumbs onto my lap.

'TRU?'

'Yes.'

'No thanks,' I say.

'You need the practice,' she mumbles.

'I don't need practice!' I laugh again.

'Really?' she asks. 'How did your last date go?'

My last date was with Claire – it was a month ago, and Doris already knows that it did not go well. She looks at me pointedly.

'And when's your next one?'

Doris can be a little bit bitchy when she wants to be.

The next day is Sunday and, as much as I want to spend it lying on my sofa with Biscuit, I can't. I have a date. Not that sort of date, a different sort, a more important sort. So, I put on my best suit, style my hair, and leave London for the first time in nearly a year.

The wedding is in Hurley, a small village by the Thames. It is a gorgeous day – cold but sunny, grass covered with sparkling frost. I am late, and by the time I arrive, everyone is already inside the church except for the bridesmaids, who stand on the steps waiting for the bride to arrive in her vintage car.

'Jack, what are you doing here?' asks one of the bridesmaids.

'I was invited, obviously,' I reply.

She exchanges a glance with the other bridesmaids.

'What?' I say.

She shrugs.

'We thought you weren't coming.'

'Well, you were wrong.'

A vintage car appears at the gate and I hurry inside. I scurry down the aisle, waving quickly to the faces I recognise, and plonk myself down next to my mum in the front pew. Whispered conversations are being held around the church, voices kept low in reverence to the location. Mum looks at me out of the corner of her eye.

'Jack. What are you doing here?' she whispers.

'Why does everyone keep asking me that?' I whisper back. 'It's Jess's wedding, of course I'm going to be here!'

Mum looks guilty.

'I thought you wouldn't come.'

'What do you mean?'

Mum looks sheepish.

'I'm so sorry love, I thought you wouldn't be able to face it. I took your name off the list …'

'You took my name off the list?'

'… and I told Jess you wouldn't be coming,' she whispers.

'You told her I wouldn't be coming?! I bloody RSVP'd!'

Mum pats my arm, tries to placate me.

'I know, I know. It's just … you're not very reliable these days, and I didn't want Jess to be disappointed.'

'Mum, I missed a couple of Sunday dinners. This is her wedding!'

'I know Jack. I—'

Our conversation is interrupted by the opening bars of 'The Wedding March' coming from the church organ. Everyone stands and looks towards the church door.

I look at Mum.

'Sorry,' she mouths.

Unbelievable.

We are at the reception, moving along the receiving line. Mum has apologised again and Jess is next. I stand in front of her.

'I did RSVP …'

Jess is my twin. Now that Eve is dead there is no one in the world who knows me better. She reaches out and takes my hand.

'I know. Mum was just trying to protect me.'

I nod.

'She was right though, I didn't know if I would be able to face it,' I say.

Jess squeezes my hand gently.

'But you did and I'm glad you're here,' she says, 'But you'll have to have the vegan option because we don't have spares of anything else.'

The wedding is nice. I smile widely, speak to a lot of people whose names I can't quite remember, get asked if I am okay a lot, and only get asked where Eve is twice. I don't find being at the wedding as painful as I thought I would – it is nothing like our wedding. It doesn't remind me of Eve or of us, and this, weirdly, makes me feel worse. I excuse myself early from the reception, go home and get our wedding photos out. We didn't have enough photos for an album so they are stored in a carrier bag under our – my – bed. I sit on the bed with a bottle of whisky and look at the photos and drink and cry and, eventually, fall asleep.

So here I am, Monday morning, pushing through the revolving doors into the JaneDoe reception. I am hungover and sad and want some peace and quiet and to be by myself. I am going to grab my coffee and then go down to the labs in the basement, secure myself a workstation, and hide for as much of the day as possible.

I can feel heads turn as I walk through reception – people I would normally stop and chat to and those who just wonder why I am wearing sunglasses on a dull November morning. I don't mind the stares, I am used to them, I can move smoothly past them by throwing a smile here and a wave there. But then I feel something different, a stare that isn't friendly or curious – this is more of a scowl than a stare. And I know who the owner of the scowl is before I even whip around to face her.

'Are you following me?'

Indiana Dylan jumps back. I laugh and am surprised to find that my laugh is genuine. She stares at me, frowns, opens her mouth to say something, closes it again, gives her head a little shake, and then pushes past me and starts to walk away. I follow her.

'Do you need something from me?'

'What makes you think I could possibly want anything from you?' she calls over her shoulder.

'You're following me, you're staring at me, either you need something or you're stalking me.'

She pauses, turns, glares at me once more.

'I am not stalking you. I need …'

She stops talking, looks at the floor and frowns again. I stop smiling. She looks tired and is even paler than normal. I notice she has eczema on one of her wrists, a patch that she keeps unconsciously scratching.

'You need what?' I ask earnestly.

She looks back up at me. Her eyes are normally cold and fierce, but today they are worried. They are the palest shade of blue, almost like they have no colour at all.

She coughs, clears her throat.

'I need your help.'

I nod slowly.

'Okay. You need my help with … ?'

She takes a deep breath in and avoids my eyes by looking at a point just behind my head.

'I need you to help me be a good date. Like people do in romantic novels and movies.'

I try really hard not to laugh – really hard – but it is such an unexpected and strange request that I cannot stop the laughter from escaping my mouth. I laugh loud and I laugh hard. It feels good to laugh so openly and honestly. Indiana grunts with annoyance.

'I knew Peggy was wrong,' she mutters, spins on her heel and stalks towards the exit.

I stop laughing.

'Indiana, wait …'

She doesn't stop. I jog after her.

'Please. I'm sorry. It was just … I wasn't expecting that. And I don't really understand what you need.'

She stops and talks in a low, tight voice.

'I have never dated anyone before and I don't know how to do it. Your nonsensical Soulmate Pathway means that I have to date in order for my demonstration of TRU to be successful. I don't know how to date.'

'And you want me to help with that?'

She nods tersely.

I know that this is the perfect time to tell her that I don't know how to date either. That the only proper date I have ever been on in three years was a complete disaster. I know that I should tell her I can't help her and that there are people who are far better suited to this job than me. But I don't. I remember what Doris said about me needing practice. Maybe we both have something to gain from this. Also, it will make my new Software Lead role much easier if we can work together.

'Fine,' I say.

Her head snaps up and she looks directly at me.

'Really?'

I nod.

'Yes ... but I want something in return.'

She frowns once more.

'What?'

'I want you to work with me, not against me, on scaling TRU. We work together. Deal?'

She doesn't answer. I hold my hand out.

'Deal?'

Her frown deepens. I put my hand back down.

'If I agree, will I still be your boss?' she says.

I laugh.

'You were never going to be my boss.'

She scowls.

'But I am in charge?'

I sigh.

'Yes. Fine. You can be in charge.'

I hold out my hand again.

'Deal?'

She takes it reluctantly.

'Deal.'

Her hand is small but her handshake is rock hard.

'Okay, when is your next date?'

'Wednesday.'

'Bloody hell. Okay, we'd better start right now.'

I smile at her, she doesn't smile back.

'This might be fun,' I say.

'It will not,' she replies.

Indiana

'Tell me about your parents.'
        'I don't have any. I am an orphan.'
Mr Hunter pauses.
'I'm sorry.'
'Why? You didn't know them.'

We are sitting on a bench in City Square. JaneDoe HQ is behind us. I have successfully avoided speaking to Mr Hunter all day but he has finally caught up with me and demanded we begin this ridiculous process. It is late afternoon and freezing cold; a dull mist hangs over everything, covering us in a layer of moisture. I don't feel the cold. I am wearing a good quality duffle coat, hat, scarf and gloves. Mr Hunter is completely unprepared for the weather. He is wearing a thick red jumper but a ridiculously thin wool coat.

'Can we go back inside?' he asks.
'No. I don't want people overhearing our conversation.'
'I'm freezing.'
'You should have worn a winter coat.'
'This is my winter coat!'
'Then it is inadequate for the job.'
'You're inadequate for the job,' he mutters.
'What?'

'Nothing. Tell me about your childhood, then. What was it like?'

'I moved about a lot. First when I was with Rachel, and then when I was in care. It was chaotic.'

'Rachel?'

'My mother.'

'What was she like?'

'Why?'

'Why what?'

'Why do you care what my mother was like?'

He rolls his eyes and sighs.

'Because I'm interested. We're having a conversation, or at least we're supposed to be. This is what dating is – finding things out about each other. You need to tell me something about you and then I tell you something about me. It's how we learn if we like each other. Tell me something that makes you happy.'

I think for a moment.

'Maths.'

'Maths?'

'Maths makes me happy. It's the first thing that made sense when I was younger. One of Rachel's boyfriends bought me my first maths book, he knew nothing about kids, didn't know that a maths book wasn't a good present, but it had flowers and unicorns on the front so he thought it would be appropriate. Rachel laughed at him and threw it in the bin, but I retrieved it and read it when they went out. I used to be scared when Rachel went out at night, but I wasn't scared that time. I hardly noticed she was gone. I read the book until I fell asleep, and then I read it when I woke up in the morning, and I got it, I got the numbers and the rules and the conclusion. It made sense. I was seven years old, and something finally made sense.'

Mr Hunter looks at me. He doesn't say anything, I feel awkward. I think of something else to say.

'And I like New Year's Eve.'

'New Year's Eve?'

'Yes. I like the fireworks on the Thames. I watch them from my window, I drink champagne and I listen to the 'Flower Duet" from *Lakmé*.'

'The "Flower Duet"?'

'Yes. It's an aria from an opera. It's beautiful. I listen to it every New Year's Eve.'

'You listen to it once a year?'

'Yes.'

'Just once?'

'Yes. If I listened to it more I might become inured to it.'

Jack laughs and then shivers. He jumps up and down and claps his arms about himself.

'I'm freezing to death out here ...'

He looks at his watch.

'... it's after five – let's just go out now.'

'What?'

'Let's go for dinner now,' he says, rubbing his hands together to warm them.

'Go to dinner?'

'Yes. Go to dinner. You and I. Go on our date.'

'I am not going on a date with you Mr Hunter, I am going on a date with Daniel Porter.'

He rolls his eyes again.

'Yes, and that is the whole point of us going on a "practice date" first. You didn't think we'd chat for five minutes and that would be it did you?'

Yes, I did think that would be it. I don't tell Mr Hunter that.

I am supposed to book my favourite restaurant for the second date. My favourite restaurant is my noodle bar, but they make you bring your own cutlery so I do not think it is appropriate for a date. I have never eaten at a restaurant in New London City before, and have no idea where might be appropriate, so I book the first suitably expensive restaurant that has availability and pretend to Mr Hunter that it is one of my favourites.

It is very quiet, and very dark in the restaurant I have booked. I have to squint across the table to try to get a glimpse of Mr Hunter; at least I hope it is him, it could be any man with auburn hair.

The background music is a pan-pipe version of an old 1970s song. It is incredibly irritating. I cannot work out what song it is. It is infuriating me. I will ask next time a waiter is nearby. Where are all the waiters? We are the only people in the restaurant, so surely they could spare one member of staff to wait upon us. Without thinking I say, 'What song is this? It is an appalling version.'

My voice is considerably louder than I expect it to be, almost like a shout in the quiet, wood-panelled room. Six waiters magically appear at once and one of them rushes off into the kitchen.

'I did not mean to shout, it is very quiet in here.'

Jack Hunter laughs. He laughs a lot, but it rarely seems genuine and I wonder if this is a trick to get people to like him. Perhaps I should try it. Mr Hunter's jumper is thick and it is very hot in the restaurant. He pulls at the neck of his jumper and looks uncomfortable.

The waiter rushes back through the kitchen and bends down at our table.

'It's "Hotel California" by The Eagles ... but on panpipes, madam.'

I nod. The waiter starts to leave, but Mr Hunter calls him back.

'Sorry, any chance you could turn the heating down a bit, it's very hot in here.'

'Sorry sir, the room is kept at a constant 40 degrees to enhance the dining experience.'

Mr Hunter nods and pulls his jumper sleeves up.

'You could have warned me to wear a T-shirt and shorts,' he says. I do not know if this is a joke or if he is admonishing me, so I do not reply.

'Is this your favourite restaurant, then?' he asks.

I shake my head.

'No. My favourite is Tokyo Station in Soho.'

'That place is good. I've been there a couple of times. It's the one where they make you bring your own cutlery, isn't it?'

I nod.

'Probably don't take Daniel there then,' he says.

'What's yours?' I ask.

'Big Burger in Dean Street.'

'I've not been there,' I reply.

'It's excellent. I used to go there a lot with Eve … but I haven't been in a while …'

His voice trails off at the end. He doesn't tell me who Eve is and I don't ask.

A waiter appears silently at my elbow.

'Drink, madam?'

'Maker's Mark, no water, no ice.'

'I'm afraid we only sell our own pure-brewed alcohol, madam. It is made from preparation off-shoots.'

I look up at the waiter.

'Rubbish. You mean it's made from rubbish.'

'One of our restaurant philosophies is that we are carbon neutral, so we don't like the term rubbish, we prefer "off-shoots". Most things in life can be repurposed if we try hard enough.'

Idiots. Rubbish is rubbish.

'Fine, give me off-shoot vodka, straight, one ice cube.'

'No ice, I am afraid, madam.'

'Then just stick it in a recycled cup and serve it to me.'

Mr Hunter laughs again. The sound shocks me. I had not been joking.

'Sir?'

'I think I'd better just have a lemonade, please.'

'We do not have lemonade but we have lemon water?'

'Lemon water is fine.'

The waiter leaves and Mr Hunter sits forward peering through the dark towards me.

'Is that a new thing, the alcohol?'

'What?'

'The restaurant only serving their own alcohol. Is it a new thing? You seemed surprised.'

'I don't know.'

'Oh, I just thought, as this is one of your favourite restaurants you'd have known that.'

'Well, I didn't,' I snap back at him.

He shrugs, sits back and looks around.

'It's very empty.'

'I suppose it will get busier later.'

He nods.

Our drinks arrive. I take one sip of my vodka and then, despite knowing it is inappropriate behaviour, immediately let it dribble back down my chin into my glass.

'Good God, that is disgusting!'

I quickly sip some water. It tastes muddy, and I wonder where it is sourced from.

Mr Hunter grabs the menu and holds it mere millimetres from his face.

'What do you recommend?'

I look at him blankly.

'That is a lot of bean curd. Are you vegan?'

Thankfully the waiter interrupts before I can be forced to answer.

'Madam, sir. An *amuse-bouche* from the chef. It is our version of sauerkraut. The fermented vegetables will line your stomach for what is to come.'

He places tiny pots filled with bright red vegetables on the table in front of us.

Mr Hunter picks his up, smiles and gives a mock toast.

'For what is to come ...'

He upends the pot into his mouth. I have serious misgivings about following suit, but reluctantly shoot the contents of the pot onto the back of my tongue.

We chew carefully and slowly. It is absolutely disgusting, inedible even. Mr Hunter turns red, breaks out into fresh sweat and tugs at his jumper collar wildly. I cough, take a huge swig of vodka, realise my mistake too late, and swiftly bring my napkin to my face to spit my mouthful into it.

Mr Hunter somehow manages to swallow his sauerkraut, wipes his mouth, and looks at me incredulously.

'That's fucking disgusting! You come here often? By choice?'

I am desperately crumpling my napkin around its half-chewed contents, so distractedly mumble the truth. 'I've never been here before.'

'What?'

'I have never been here before!'

The hovering waiters look over to our table.

'This is the first time I've been here,' I hiss at him. 'I only normally go out to dinner at Tokyo Station and it's not appropriate for a date. I didn't know where to take you so I used a booking app for the most expensive restaurants in London, and this was the only one who could fit us in.'

He pauses for a moment and then his face breaks into a huge grin.

'Well at least now you know why.'

He starts to laugh and, despite the fact I am annoyed, I smile. His laugh is genuine this time and the situation is amusing. But then I remember the predicament we are in. I look down at the empty pots on the table.

'I can't eat anything more like this.'

'Then we should leave.'

'What? We can't just leave!'

I am shocked. Is this something people normally do?

'You want to stay for another drink and three more courses?' he asks.

I shake my head, I really don't.

'Then, I'll put some money on the table, you put your half-chewed-food napkin in your bag, and we leave.'

'I can't steal the napkin.'

'Don't worry, I'm leaving them about three litres of sweat on my chair, so I think we can call it even.'

Outside and around the corner from the restaurant, Mr Hunter stands in the cold, coat off, face upturned into the gentle drizzle of the night, breathing deeply.

'Ahh, cold night air, I will never again take you for granted.'

I am angry with myself.

'This was my fault. I will try better for the real date. I will do my research.'

'I'm not giving you marks out of ten. You can't fail at this.'

He turns to me and smiles. I do not smile back. I hold my hand out for a handshake

'Thank you for tonight, Mr Hunter.'

He does not take my hand.

'It's still early and I'm starving. Why don't we go and get some proper food?'

I shake my head. I have spent all day at JaneDoe and need to do at least three hours of work when I get back to my office.

'No. I have work to do.'

He looks at his watch.

'It's only ten past seven, you can still be home by eight thirty, Cinderella …'

He sniffs the air.

'*Mmm* – smell that. Real food …'

I sniff. I can smell chargrilled meat. It smells good. My stomach rumbles. I am tempted.

But work comes first.

'I have somewhere else to be. Today has been useful. I now know that it is important to ensure my restaurant of choice will not make Daniel Porter want to vomit.'

He smiles.

'Was that a joke?' he asks.

'No,' I say, but I think it was, just a little bit. I hold my hand out to him again.

'Goodnight, Mr Hunter.'

He reaches out and shakes my hand. His hand is rough and has calluses on the palm – I want to ask him how he got them but I don't.

'Goodnight, Ms Dylan. I hope you have a fabulous time on your *real* date.'

He smiles again. I don't know if he is joking or not, so I don't smile back.

DATE TWO

The Soulmate Pathway Date Two: Dinner at a public restaurant – one soulmate to choose the restaurant, the other to choose the food (being mindful of dietary/religious needs). Physical contact (excluding kissing) allowed in public places.

It is my responsibility to pick the restaurant that Daniel and I attend for our second date. I take Daniel to The Waldorf – one of the best reviewed and most traditional restaurants in London.

Daniel is four minutes late. He is attractively dressed in a dark navy suit and white shirt. He has had his hair cut since last we met and I ask if he has dyed his hair as he is less noticeably grey. He denies that he dyes his hair. I tell him I like his suit and he tells me he likes my fawn polo neck.

We order drinks – I have a pure blend whisky and he has vodka and tonic.

Daniel is preoccupied with a deal that he has been brokering for the last thirteen days and tells me about it at length. We discuss the merits of European versus Asian working styles, and agree that, on the whole, the Asian market is more productive.

I apologise for my abruptness on the last date and he apologises for leaving early. We agree to start again and get to know each other properly.

Our discourse touches on a diverse number of subjects – maths, education, quantum computers, chaos theory, the future of home computing, the rise of the Holo cube, the future of social media, and our individual experiences of wearing the DataLet. Mine itched, his didn't. Daniel is well educated, intelligent, has a keen sense of humour, and his computer knowledge is nearly a match for mine. It takes us two hours to eat our dinner and the time passes pleasantly.

Daniel orders caviar for us to eat. I do not normally eat fish eggs but agree to try the delicacy. It is palatable. He orders us both salt marsh lamb for our entrées. It is delicious.

We drink a bottle of Châteauneuf-du-Pape between us. The food is very good and the service impeccable. Daniel wants to pay for our meal but I insist on paying half.

Daniel kisses me on the cheek when we say goodbye at the end of the date. He smells expensive. I had a nice time on our second date and believe he is a good match for me.

Indiana Dylan

Lina

I am at my desk reading Indiana's Date Two report. Indiana stands in the doorway to my office holding the door open with her foot. Indiana's Date Two report is far better than her last – human almost.

'This report is much better. Thank you.'

She nods. I clear my throat.

'I'm sorry about the other day. I'm under a lot of stress at the moment and have a lot of new people to manage. To be honest it's hard enough having to manage the likes of Jack Hunter without having to manage you as well.'

I smile to let her know this is a joke. She doesn't smile back.

'Jack Hunter is lazy,' she says. A simple statement of fact.

'Not necessarily lazy,' I reply 'More… reluctant. But still a pain in the arse to manage'

I smile again. She nods.

I gesture to the chair on the other side of my desk.

'Please, sit down.'

She stiffens slightly, surveys my messy office.

'No.'

'Honestly, nothing in here is going to bite or infect you!'

'No.'

I point at the NotePad I am holding, which has her latest report on it.

'This is good but ...'

I go to put the NotePad down on my desk.

'DON'T PUT IT DOWN ON THAT DESK!'

I am so shocked by her shout that I hold the NotePad up in the air as if it is a gun I have been caught with. She dives across the room, grabs it from my hand, looks down at my grubby desk and shivers. She swallows hard and looks longingly towards the door.

'Are we done here?'

'No.'

She turns back to look at me.

'What now?'

'You still owe us three months of consultancy work.'

'I've already done a month wearing the DataLet.'

'That doesn't count. That's part of the demonstration. We need you in the offices, helping to scale TRU.'

She sighs.

'Your coders are inept so you need me to do their work?'

'No. I need you to fulfil your contract,' I say.

She nods slowly. I stand up.

'Come on, let me show you where you'll be working. You'll love it.'

Her expression says that she most definitely will not love it, but I think she is so relieved to be leaving my office that she doesn't complain, just steps gingerly towards the door.

Leaving isn't as simple for me. Firstly I have to gather all the stuff I don't want to lose amongst the clutter of my office – four reports, my NotePad, laptop, handbag and lunch – so I juggle things into various bags and under my arms. Indiana watches me with thinly veiled contempt.

I take her down to the basement and the lab where she will be working. We are met at the door by two senior coders. Indiana looks them up and down.

'You don't have basic coding skills?'

The coders bristle. Coder one speaks.

'Of course we do. Your program mixes code erratically though and—'

Indiana interrupts him and turns to me.

'I cannot work here if your staff lack basic knowledge of—'

The coders aren't having that.

'Excuse me! Basic knowledge?! We are—'

'We're the senior coders here so—'

I hold my hands up to silence them.

'Chaps—'

They turn their scowling faces from Indiana to me.

'… can you give us a moment?'

They scowl further and disappear into the lab. I turn to Indiana.

'You shouldn't call them "chaps". It's belittling,' she says.

'Well, you shouldn't criticise their abilities. It's disparaging,' I counter.

We look at each other. She nods slightly. I mirror her. We are having a moment.

And then I drop two of my reports and the moment is over. She sighs.

'Honestly. Here …'

She thrusts a paper bag she has been holding at me.

'I can't carry any more!'

'Look in it.'

I look in the bag. It is a leather rucksack.

'It's a rucksack,' I say.

She rolls her eyes again, removes the rucksack from the bag, takes everything I am carrying from me, slots it all into different compartments, and then stuffs my handbag into the main section. She spins me around, puts the rucksack on my back and adjusts the straps so that it sits right. It is heavy but surprisingly comfy. I look down at my hands; they are not holding anything. I wave them in front of me. I wave them at Indiana. She looks at me as if I have gone mad.

'I love it. Thank you.'

I clasp both her arms with my free hands. She steps back and scowls.

'It's not a bribe.'

'I didn't think it was a—'

'It's incredibly frustrating to watch a woman of your supposed intelligence and power handle her belongings like a confused child.'

Indiana turns, opens the door to the lab, and steps in. I wave my hands jubilantly at a passing engineer and follow her.

The lab looks pretty good to me – I mean, I'm no expert, and it has been years since I did any engineering or coding, but the lab is big and clean and filled with hugely expensive equipment. Even the coders look okay; most of them are smiling. Indiana stands at the door for the briefest of moments.

'No. I can't work in here.'

She turns and leaves.

'What the hell is wrong now?' I yell after her. She doesn't answer.

The coders stop smiling.

Indiana

There was nothing wrong with the laboratory. I didn't examine it in any detail but, at a tertiary glance, it seemed well laid out with excellent facilities. Definitely the most expensive and comprehensively equipped laboratory I have been in – outside of my own – for the last eight years.

The laboratory was not the problem. The staff were.

'Hello Indiana, how was your day?'

I take my bike helmet off, leave it and my bag by the lift and throw myself onto the sofa.

'It was … not good.'

I have never worked in an office – at least I have never worked in an office that had staff. After graduation I worked at a bank for a few months, building and installing firewalls and testing their security system for gaps. Because of the nature of the job I worked at night – me and one other coder who stared at me over his glasses every time I looked up but didn't say a single thing to me in the eight months that we worked together. He was an excellent work colleague. Then I moved to Shenzhen, where no one spoke to me because they (wrongly) assumed I wouldn't understand them, and then I came back here, to work on my own, with Peggy.

I have never had workmates, I do not want workmates, I will not like having workmates.

'They want me to fulfil my consultancy contract,' I say to Peggy.

'That is understandable.'

'They also want me to work in their lab, with their staff.'

'How awful,' Peggy says.

I look across at Peggy's voice-box.

'Are you being sarcastic?'

'I might be.'

'Don't.'

'Okay.'

'I don't want to work in their lab, with people who will talk, ask questions, be interested in my technology, and breathe loudly.'

'So, working in a laboratory with bright, inquisitive, breathing work colleagues is *not* what you want to do?'

'I said no sarcasm.'

'Sorry.'

There is silence for a while.

'You need to find somewhere else to work from,' Peggy says.

I nod.

'Will they let you work from here?'

'No.'

'So it has to be in their offices?'

'Yes.'

'Would you like me to check the office blueprints for empty space?'

'Yes.'

'I have done it. There is none.'

I sigh and then stand up abruptly.

'I'm going for my run.'

'It is two hours earlier than you normally go for your run.'

'The world will not end because I go for my run early,' I say.

'Are you sure?' says Peggy.

'I said no sarcasm.'

I leave HWJ Tower via the underground car park, run to the river and stop. I stare out over the water and regulate my breathing once more. The industrial estate is silent; the warehouses shut for the night, trucks and vans berthed until morning. I am often surprised that there are no warehouses open overnight, that no one takes advantage of the space while it is empty. I was surprised that Mrs Galaz has her own office for the same reason – it feels like a waste as she spends so much time at meetings.

And then I realise that is it. I have solved my problem. I know where I am going to work.

I smile, stretch my arms above my head to release tension, and flex my neck side to side. I drop my arms back down and my hand touches something hairy. I look towards the ground.

It is Alan the dog.

He joins me every night on my run now, always meeting me here at the river and then running back through the industrial estate with me. I tried to lose him the first few times, dodged down back streets, hid in no-through roads – he always found me, always greeted me with a loud bark and a tongue-lolling grin. After a while it became easier to let him follow along and I gradually realised I quite liked him running with me. I don't use my EarPods any more, I time my rhythm to the tap of his paws on the pavement. Sometimes he runs in front, sometimes I do, sometimes we race each other back to the building. If he wins I ruffle his ears to let him know he has done a good job.

Frank always shouts goodnight to me when I return from my run with Alan. I always ignore him, but tonight I am in a pleasant mood because I have solved my problem, so I jog past and yell, 'Goodnight Frank!'

I hear him chuckling inside his cardboard house and I smile.

'I've got it!' I say to Peggy as I step out of the lift.

'Got what?'

'Got the solution to my workspace problem.'

'Excellent.'

'But I'm going to need to leave early tomorrow morning and I'm also going to need a lot of cleaning equipment ...'

The house is smaller than I thought it would be. A terraced house in the middle of a street filled with other terraced houses. It still has a driveway, which is unusual. Very few people own cars these days, so driveways are normally ripped out to make way for vegetable patches to grow essential veg in case imports are interrupted again. The street is busy and there is a lot of ambient noise. I would find it hard to think straight if I lived here.

There is a considerable amount of noise coming from within the house that I am standing in front of. A baby is crying, someone is singing, people run up and down the stairs shouting instructions at each other. I cannot be sure that anyone will hear the doorbell when I ring it, so I knock loudly as well.

The door is eventually opened by a girl. I know nothing about children, so have no idea how old this one is. She is wearing a school uniform and sucking on a lollipop. She stares at me in silence so I stare back. After a couple of minutes I break the silence.

'Is this where Mrs Galaz lives?'

The girl nods.

'Can I speak to her?'

The girl takes the lollipop out of her mouth.

'Please.'

'What?'

'Can I speak to her … please? It's the magic word.'

I take a deep breath.

'Can I speak to Mrs Galaz … please?'

The girl turns her head and yells.

'Auntie! There's some weird woman here for you!'

The girl puts the lollipop back in her mouth and goes back to staring. I scowl at her. She is not afraid.

A woman appears in the hallway, wearing a dressing gown and drying her hair with a towel.

The girl turns to look at the woman.

'She wants Auntie Lina.'

The woman sighs.

'How many times, Angela – you have to say which one of us you want.'

The woman yells over her shoulder.

'LINA!'

She looks at me.

'Are you from Lina's work?'

I nod and she nods back. There is a pause as she continues to dry her hair and stare at me. A lot of people are staring at me this morning.

'I'm Connie, Lina's wife. Sorry, do you want to come in, it's freezing out there …'

'I'm fine.'

She smiles and turns away.

'Okay. Angela, I told you to have the lollipop after you'd got your bag ready for school. Now GO!'

Connie physically turns Angela around, kicks her bottom to set her off down the hall, and then charges up the stairs without saying goodbye.

Mrs Galaz comes bustling into the hallway carrying a screaming baby and trailing a cacophony of noise.

She stops dead when she sees me.

'What are you—'

Angela comes back into the hallway.

'Auntie, I can't find my drinks bottle.'

Mrs Galaz turns to her.

'It's in the kitchen where you left it.'

'It's not. I looked.'

Mrs Galaz sighs.

'Angela, if I find it in there I'm going to ...'

Mrs Galaz shoves the screaming baby into my arms and follows Angela back into the house.

'Don't leave this with me!' My voice is shrill, but it's too late: Mrs Galaz is gone.

The baby is still yelling and I have no idea what to do with it. I have no siblings, no cousins, no nieces or nephews, no friends with babies. This is the first time I have ever held a baby.

Gently, I put the screaming baby down on the hallway floor.

I back off and sit on the garden wall, keeping the child in sight, but far enough away so that the screeching won't pierce my eardrums.

Mrs Galaz walks back into the hallway.

'What the— Jesus!'

I stand up, smooth down my dress and walk back to the front door.

Mrs Galaz picks the baby up and jiggles it over her shoulder. She steps onto the doorstep and pulls the door to behind her.

'What the hell happened?'

'It wouldn't stop screaming.'

'So you put him on the floor?'

'I told you not to leave it with me!'

'YOU DON'T PUT A BABY ON THE FLOOR!'

'Why not? It was perfectly safe. I was watching it.'

'It's freezing out here!'

'It was inside the house.'

'Jesus, you're … I mean who …'

The baby is still crying, so Mrs Galaz moves it into a cradle position, pulls her breast from her shirt and guides the baby towards it. The baby immediately stops crying, latches on and starts gulping noisily. Everything in this house is noisy. I look away.

'Do you have to?'

'It's a boob Indiana, you'll cope.'

I look back at Mrs Galaz and the baby. She's right, it is just a breast. At least the baby has stopped being so loud. Mrs Galaz looks down at the baby, strokes its head softly.

'I didn't know you had children.'

'Well, now you do.'

'How many do you have?'

'Just Bruce,' she says, looking down at the baby. 'Angela, my niece, is staying with us for a couple of days.'

'Your house is tiny. Where do you put them?'

'In the basement.'

I stare at her. She stares back.

'It's a joke.'

'Oh.'

'Indiana …'

'Yes.'

'Why the fuck are you standing on my doorstep at 7 in the morning?'

'I have something to tell you.'

'Could it not have waited until I see you in the office?'

'You are not in the office today and I wanted to tell you this morning.'

'How do you know that I am not in the office today?'

'I looked at your diary. Today is blocked out as annual leave.'

'You don't have access to my diary.'

She is right – I shouldn't have access to her diary – but there are not many places that Peggy doesn't have access to. Mrs Galaz sighs.

'Okay, what is it you wanted to tell me?'

I try to ignore the baby slurping at her breast. This is all very unprofessional.

'I don't want to be based in the JaneDoe tech labs …'

'Well, I guessed that …'

'… I want to work out of your office instead,' I finish.

Her reaction is immediate and negative.

'Absolutely not,' she says, shaking her head. 'You'll be fine in the labs.'

'No. It has to be your office. I can't work in the labs. I need peace and quiet,' I say.

'There's no hardware in my office!'

'I'll build what I need.'

'How?'

'I'll take equipment from the lab. They'll give me what I want.'

'No. My office is my own personal space.'

'You're hardly ever there.'

'I said no!'

We are at a stalemate. The baby pulls his head away from Mrs Galaz's breast and emits a huge belch. Mrs Galaz laughs. I don't.

The door behind Mrs Galaz is pulled open by Connie. She eyes me suspiciously.

'You still here?'

'I don't want to be.'

Connie raises her eyebrows at Mrs Galaz.

'I'll take Bruce. It's cold.'

'He needs burping.'

Mrs Galaz hands the baby to Connie, who disappears back inside. Mrs Galaz turns back to me and folds her arms. I can see she is resolved, so I play my trump card.

'Fine,' I say. 'If I can work in your office I'll manage Mr Hunter for you.'

Her eyebrows rise.

'You'll manage Jack Hunter for me?'

'Yes,' I say. 'I know that you are busy and I know you do not want to manage him yourself so I will do it for you.'

Mrs Galaz's eyes narrow suspiciously.

'You'll manage him how?'

'I'll make sure he does his job fully and properly.'

Mrs Galaz smiles disbelievingly.

'Right.'

'Yes, right. Mr Hunter is the Software Lead for TRU, so I will need to work closely with him anyway. He has adequate coding experience and a track record in product design and development. He was the CTO on the JaneDoe Holo team until three years ago.'

'Didn't that fail to get to market?'

'Only because they pulled the funding after he left.'

'Exactly. He left. He's completely unreliable.'

'He won't be if he is working for me.'

'I think you'll find you're wrong …'

I have had enough of this conversation.

'Do you want me to manage him for you or not?'

She scowls slightly and nods.

'Yes.'

'Then let me use your office.'

Mrs Galaz takes in a deep breath.

'Fine. You can have it.'

I smile.

'That's the first time I've ever seen you look happy,' Mrs Galaz says, as she shuts the door on me.

Jack

I tell Doris about my fake date with Indiana.

'Sounds like you had fun,' she says.

'ARE YOU GOING DEAF?' I shout at her. 'It was a disaster!'

'Yes, but you didn't drink too much …'

'We weren't there long enough for me to drink too much,' I protest.

'… and she made you laugh.'

Doris is right – I didn't drink too much and Indiana did make me laugh – but Doris is wrong about it being fun. It most definitely was not fun.

I am curious how the real date with Daniel went, so, when Indiana messages me to tell me to meet her in reception at 8 the next morning, I assume it is to dissect her last date and prepare her for the next one.

Bring rubber gloves if you have them, she messages.

Maybe not just a simple dissection then.

I hate getting to work early, but I make a special effort and am sitting in reception waiting for Indiana at 7.58 a.m.

'Why are you sitting down?'

I look up. She is wearing all grey today – she looks like a rain cloud.

'Are you ill?'

She looks at me suspiciously.

'No. I am not ill. I'm waiting for you in reception as you demanded,' I say, and smile at her.

She ignores my smile.

'In future, meet me at the lifts,' she says.

She stalks off towards the lifts, not waiting for me to follow. I jog after her to catch up.

'So, how was it?' I ask.

'How was what?'

'Date Two. The date. How was it?'

She pauses, thinks.

'It was nice.'

'Nice?'

She starts to walk again.

'The food was well cooked and Daniel was nice. Time passed quickly.'

It is hardly a glowing report.

'So how do you want us to prepare for the next date then?'

'I don't.'

'What?'

'You are not here to help me prepare for the next date.'

'Then why am I here?'

'You start working for me today.'

'*With* you ...'

'*For* me.'

We reach the lifts and I turn to look at her.

'You don't work for JaneDoe. You can't manage me.'

'I will not *manage* you. You will just do what I say.'

My smile falters. Indiana looks at me.

'That's better.'

'What's better?'

'Your face?'

'What was wrong with my face?'

'I can't abide the way you pretend to smile all the time. It is irritating.'

I stop smiling. We get into the lift. Sarah, my previous desk colleague, jumps in just before the lift doors close, sees my face and looks concerned.

'Are you okay, Jack? What's wrong?'

'Nothing, Sarah. I'm fine,' I say, the smile returning to my face with practised ease. 'I haven't seen you for a while. How is your cat?'

Sarah looks relieved and tells me her cat has an anal gland issue.

When Sarah gets out of the lift Indiana turns to me.

'You should stop smiling and stop flirting.'

'Flirting?'

'Yes. What you were doing with that woman.'

I frown slightly.

'That's not flirting. I'm just making her feel good about her-self. You should try it some time.'

Indiana scowls.

'It's flirting.'

I smile again, just to annoy her, and change the subject.

'So what are working on first? Coding? Data compression?'

'Cleaning.'

'I'm sorry, what?'

The lift reaches the tenth floor and she steps out.

'Today we will be starting with cleaning.'

My smile disappears once more. It suddenly dawns on me what the rubber gloves are for.

Indiana

It was Peggy who said I should use Mr Hunter as leverage. I was reluctant at first but Peggy said that Mrs Galaz would not give up her office easily and that I would need something to barter with, and, as Peggy pointed out, I was going to have to work with Mr Hunter anyway so I might as well use him to my advantage.

I did not expect Mr Hunter to be at JaneDoe at 8 a.m. but he was. I did not expect him to perform the tasks I requested: to clean, sort, tidy and build, but he did. Mr Hunter is the reason the room was recarpeted, the lights fixed, and storage and workspaces installed all within the same day. The Facilities Director and Mr Hunter are friends. He is also friends with the Finance Director and Head of the Maintenance Team. There are not many people that he is not friends with. When he said that he would visit different departments to seek their help, I assumed it was a ruse to neglect his work, and did not think he would return. But he did, and within an hour the room was crawling with workmen busily building and replacing things. By early afternoon the office was refurnished, with new carpet, new workbenches and new storage.

The surfaces are white, the lights bright and the plasma screen the latest available. It is perfect. I run my fingers over the surface of a workbench.

'I thought you'd like it,' he says, looking far too pleased with himself.

'Where's the equipment I requested?' I demand.

No sooner are the words out of my mouth than there is a knock at the door. Three carts piled high with all the parts I could possibly need are in the corridor. I stand in the doorway staring out at them. Jack Hunter stands behind me.

'Your wish is my command.'

I turn around. He is grinning down at me and standing so close I can feel his body heat coming through his shirt. I side-step away.

'You have no idea about personal space.'

'And you have no idea how to say please or thank you.'

I glare at him, he glares back, and I notice that he has a tiny frown line between his eyebrows.

'Want me to unpack?' he says, sharply.

'Yes … *please.*'

I say it with as much sarcasm as I can manage, but he still stops glaring and starts smiling again.

'Stop smiling,' I say.

Mr Hunter and I spend what remains of the afternoon unpacking and assembling technology. He has sourced everything I asked for and anticipated the need for items that I didn't – extra hard drives, additional storage, multiple monitors. He works quickly and efficiently, and, although I check each item as he completes it, I find no errors. We work in silence until mid-afternoon when he asks to put music on. I allow it and he chooses an excellent and entirely appropriate drum and bass mix. We don't speak again until the end of the day.

At 7 p.m. he stretches and yawns.

'I'm done,' he says. He turns to me and smiles easily. Everything about him seems so easy – his looks, his demeanour, his very personality. I bet he has never known sadness or pain. I bet everything in his life has come easily for him.

'Are you leaving?' he asks.

'No. I still have work to do.'

This is a lie. I was finished about twenty minutes ago, but I just didn't want to be the first to leave.

'Oh, I can stay and help you if you want—'

'No,' I snap. 'You go and have a drink with one of your fancy women.'

He laughs.

'What? You think I keep a bunch of women on speed dial?'

'Don't you?'

'Only a few,' he says.

He picks up his coat and heads to the door.

'See you tomorrow?'

'Yes.'

He opens the door.

'Oh and Indiana – what do you call a bear with a—'

'JUST LEAVE!'

He slams the door on his way out and I can hear his laughter trailing down the corridor. He is infuriating, but I cannot deny that his help has been useful today.

'Today went well.'

I sometimes forget that Peggy is always tapped into my bodily functions and mood. They once surprised me with a delivery of prunes when I hadn't had a bowel movement in three days during a particularly stressful development stage of the QuantumX. So, of course they would know that my serotonin levels have been high today; and they are right, it has gone well, better than expected even.

'Yes, it did.'

'That is good news. You are home later than expected. I have initiated the next stage of testing for you in the lab, and Spider is making dinner.'

I had forgotten that I was due to begin Beta testing a new add-on for the QuantumX tonight. I am tired and would rather run, eat and go to bed, but it is important I do not neglect my work.

'Okay,' I say, and walk into my bedroom to get dressed for my run.

It is a beautiful night out, freezing cold but with a crispness that cuts through the city smog and makes the night air feel fresh and clean. The cold revives me and I do a full five-mile run with Alan prancing at my heels. When we return, Frank is standing outside his cardboard house waiting for us, hunched over, a blanket wrapped around his shoulders for warmth. I am annoyed.

'It's cold. You should be inside.'

He laughs and the laugh morphs into a cough that racks through his thin frame.

'It's probably warmer out here.'

This doesn't make me any less annoyed.

'You don't need to wait out here for us.'

'I was worried.'

'He's fine with me.'

'It wasn't him I was worried about.'

I don't know what to say to that, so I bend down and ruffle Alan's ears.

'He likes you.'

'I like him,' I say, without thinking.

When I look up Frank is smiling. I stand up straight.

'You don't need to worry about me.'

'I think someone should worry about you.'

'I have Peggy.'

'Peggy works for you, she doesn't have a choice.'

I can't argue with that so change the subject.

'Peggy isn't a "her".'

'What?'

'Peggy doesn't go by female pronouns. They prefer "they" and "them".'

I expect him to laugh. He doesn't. Instead he pats Alan's head and nods thoughtfully.

'Sometimes I feel very old.'

'You are very old.'

He looks up at me for a moment and then bursts into uncontrollable laughter. Laughter that raucous is infectious so I smile. His laughter turns to coughing once more. He must be at least eighty. I am hungry, it is time for dinner.

'I'm hungry. I'm going for my dinner.'

I start to walk off around the building, then stop and look back at him. He has stopped coughing and is turning slowly to head back into his cardboard kingdom.

'I'll get Peggy to call down and order you both something to eat.'

He looks over at me and smiles his toothy grin.

'Are you inviting me out for dinner?'

I scowl and turn away once more.

'Don't push your luck.'

Upstairs, I ask Peggy to order Frank some dinner and a tent. It is getting too cold for him and Alan to be living in a cardboard box.

Lina

Yes, I took a day off work – it isn't illegal. I took a day off because Joe needed us to have Angela overnight while he and Tina were in hospital having another kid. It's a boy, they're naming him after Papa. I didn't want the stress of trying to drop Angela off at school and then rushing in to work and then rushing out of work to pick her up again, so I took an annual leave day. And it was fantastic. I ate and I slept and Connie and I had lingering, luxurious sex for the first time in months, and then I sat in the bath until the water went cold, my skin started to prune, and Angela banged on the door because she needed a poo. I loved it. It was the perfect day.

But, as soon as I rush up the steps and into the JaneDoe reception I forget all about my perfect day and remember all of the hundreds of things I need to do. I had to drop Angela at school and so it is now nearly 10 a.m. – I bet Emily has been here since six. I hurry to my office and am so busy thinking about reports and meetings and KPIs and how I am going to tell Connie that I need to start leaving for work earlier, that I don't hear my name being called.

'Lina …'

Don't hear it.

'Lina!'

Still don't hear it.

'LINA!'

Hear it.

I scowl. Emily. Dammit.

I turn to see how she is going to try to piss me off this time and my scowl morphs into a rictus grin because Emily has brought the ultimate weapon in her fight against me keeping my job, me keeping my office and, well, me in general. Emily has brought Cameron.

Shit.

Of course, Cameron has never been into my office. If Cameron entered my office she would know instantly that my driven, focussed businesswoman façade is a ruse and that I am a messy idiot beneath it all. If Cameron entered my office my career would be pretty much over.

Shit.

Well done Emily, hats off to you and your Machiavellian nature.

Shit.

What do I do? My grin widens.

'Emily! Hello! How are you?'

She fixes me with a deadpan look.

'Busy.'

'Excellent. Cameron, how are you?'

'Busy.'

I nod thoughtfully.

'Great, I am busy too.'

'Not too busy to take an annual leave day though,' Emily says bitchily. I ignore her.

There is an awkward pause.

'Anyway, I'd better get on …'

I turn and begin to walk down the corridor away from my office.

'Lina …'

I turn back.

'… were you not just about to go into your office?'

Emily gives me an evil smile. I shake my head.

'No. I thought I needed to, but then I remembered I have the, er, monthly finance update meeting to attend.'

'That meeting was moved to eleven. Did you not get the message?'

I shake my head.

'Maybe you haven't had time to look at your messages yet … seeing as you have just got in.'

Her evil smile widens. I hate her. She looks towards Cameron.

'We were just on our way to a DataLet Programme Board when Cameron said that she hadn't seen the latest TRU demonstration report, so I suggested that we pop by your office and pick it up.'

I bet you fucking did.

I keep my calm.

'Good idea, but I need to transfer it from my NotePad. Why don't I email it to you when that is done?'

'Great …'

Phew.

'… but, Cameron would like to read it now. Why doesn't she just read it off your NotePad and you can send a copy later?'

And then she actually winks at me.

I glare at her, she smiles at me, Cameron looks irritated and bored. None of us is looking at the door to my office, so it is something of a surprise when it flies open of its own accord. I let out an involuntary gasp and grab for the handle to pull it closed again.

But then I stop because I realise I have the wrong office. This is not my office. I know this without even looking inside because my office door does not fly open – my office door creaks slowly open under extreme duress. And the light coming out of this office is hot-summer-day-like in its brightness. My office is dark and gloomy; the lights don't work properly in my office.

'Dr Gardner. Can I help you?'

It is Indiana. Standing in the doorway to the room that isn't my office.

'I need a copy of your report on your second Soulmate Pathway date.'

'I can get you that.'

Indiana strides across the uncluttered floor of the room that is not my office and picks up a NotePad from the desk that cannot be my desk as there are only three things on it.

Cameron steps inside the office to take the NotePad from Indiana. Emily and I follow her inside.

This is not my office. This is a new and beautiful office with shining surfaces and a floor that you can actually see. The lights work, there is the steady hum of air conditioning for the first time in years, and the room smells like lemons and summer. It has been one day since Indiana was at my house, and in that time she has performed miracles.

Emily looks over at me. She wants some kind of answer. I have none.

At the workbench on the other side of the room Jack Hunter is building a computer. Jack Hunter is in my office and he is working. Actually working. Jack stops and turns as he hears us enter the room. He sees me, Cameron, Emily; and I expect some sort of smile and remark. But he says nothing. He nods curtly and turns back to his work. How can this be happening? What is going on?

Cameron takes the NotePad from Indiana.

'You're working in here?'

'Yes.'

'Our labs aren't good enough for you?'

'I need somewhere quieter.'

Cameron nods and looks pointedly at Jack.

'You don't want one of our more experienced engineers to assist?'

'Mr Hunter has the skillset I need.'

Jack ignores the conversation.

'Everything is on schedule?'

'Yes.'

'And the demonstration?'

'Yes. Daniel is a …' Indiana pauses.

Cameron looks at her, I look at her, even Jack glances across.

'… very nice. Things are going very well.'

Cameron nods once more.

'Good.'

She turns to me.

'It's lucky you had an office for them to work in.'

I am still in shock and just manage to squeak out a small noise of agreement.

Cameron leaves, Emily following behind her.

As she leaves my office Emily glances back at me. I am still in shock, but not so much that I won't grab an opportunity when it presents itself, so, while Cameron's back is still turned, I slowly lift my middle finger and flip her the bird. It is incredibly immature, and one of the happiest moments I have had at work in the past three years.

The door shuts and I clench my fists to stop myself from punching the air.

'You want to perform a physical demonstration of happiness, don't you?' Indiana says from behind me. I spin around to face her. I am grinning.

'I really do! How did you know?'

Indiana exchanges a glance with Jack. I don't care, I don't care about anything, I had a small win in life and I feel great. I look about the room.

'This place looks amazing. Everything is so clean!'

I run my hands along the workbench, reach up and touch the plasma screen, pick a piece of hardware out of a box and look at it.

'Okay, everything *was* clean, but now you're touching it all and making it dirty,' Indiana says, taking the hardware out of my hand and putting it back into the box again. 'Don't you have a meeting to go to?'

I check my watch.

'Not for twenty minutes.'

'Well, why don't you go and get a hot beverage beforehand if you've got some time.'

I look towards my desk.

'Well, I really should …'

'I think it would be best for you to go and get a coffee,' says Indiana sternly.

It is not a request.

'Fine … why don't you come with me?'

I don't know why I said it. Maybe it was my small win, maybe it was my happiness, maybe it was because I wanted to ask how she had transformed my office. It's fine, I think to myself, she'll never say yes.

Indiana looks at me suspiciously.

'You want me to come to the café with you?'

'Sure?' I say, hoping she'll catch the reluctance in my voice.

'Okay then.'

She didn't catch the reluctance.

Indiana

I accompany Mrs Galaz to the café because I had peppered mackerel for dinner last night. Mackerel has a high natural salt content and, while Mrs Galaz was talking with Dr Gardner, I received a message from Peggy.

Drink a litre of water in the next hour.

My water bottle is nearly empty and the café has a superior water filtration system to the one in the employee break room.

There is a long queue at the water station and Mrs Galaz has sat at a table by the time I have filled my bottle. She beckons me over. I did not realise we would be drinking our drinks together. I walk to the table but do not sit down.

'You can sit,' she says.

I do not want to be rude, she might shout at me again, so I sit and look at her coffee cup.

'The baby did not sleep well last night,' I say.

She looks at me curiously.

'How do you know that?'

I point at her cup.

'When you have ordered a coffee before it has always been a non-fat latte, today you had full-fat with a double espresso shot. It is written on the side.'

She looks at her cup.

'So it is.'

She yawns.

'Why did you decide to have the baby?' I ask, suddenly curious.

She looks surprised at my question.

'Why do you ask?'

'I am interested.'

She takes a deep breath in, shrugs slightly.

'Connie always wanted kids, I didn't feel that strongly either way, but I wanted to make her happy ...' she shrugs again.

'No. I didn't mean why did you have a child. I meant why did *you* have the baby? You are career oriented, why not make your wife carry the child to term?'

'Oh. We both had IVF at the same time. Connie's didn't work.'

I nod.

'And now you regret it,' I say.

Her eyes widen in shock.

'*What?*'

'You regret having a baby. He takes you away from your work and he is tiring.'

'No! God no! I don't regret having Bruce! He's the best thing I ever did. I love him.'

'But you also love your job?'

'Yes. I love my job.'

'But it is tiring as well?'

'Yes, it is tiring as well ...' Mrs Galaz holds up her coffee cup to me '... hence lots of coffee.'

She takes a big gulp from her cup as I study her.

'You should give your job up,' I say.

'What? Are you taking the piss?' she scoffs.

'No. It is the logical thing to do. You love your child and your job, but they are both tiring. You cannot give your child up, so it is the job that must go. Also, the child will grow and need you less, but your job will grow and need you more. You need to wait until the child needs less so you can give more to the job. I could do some more data analysis on this but I am sure the results will confirm my advice. You must give up your job. Concentrate on your child.'

'That's ridiculous! I can't give up my job.'

'Why not?'

'Because … because it's my job.'

'Oh.'

'And we need the money. We're buying a new house!'

I am quiet for a moment, and then say, 'Could you not just buy a cheaper house?'

She stands and stares at me.

'Jesus Indiana. What is wrong with you?'

She grabs her coffee and leaves. I am not sure what I have done wrong.

'What did you do to Lina?' Mr Hunter asks as soon as I get back into the office.

I frown at him.

'Nothing. We had an interesting conversation, that's all.'

'Interesting for you maybe.'

'Have you finished installing that hard drive yet?'

'Yes. I've got my hand in the bowels of this unit just for the fun of it.'

'Sarcasm is the lowest form of wit, Mr Hunter.'

He smiles.

'Is that you finally admitting I'm funny?'

'Never,' I say, and sit down at my computer with my back to him.

We work in silence for the next couple of hours. Mrs Galaz comes back from her meeting, scowls at me, deliberately runs her greasy fingers across my immaculate plasma screen, and then leaves the room again, slamming the door behind her. She comes back in three times more during the day, deliberately dirtying different surfaces each time.

The fourth time Mrs Galaz comes into the office, just before she can besmirch my monitor screen I say, 'I apologise for saying you should leave JaneDoe ...'

Her fingers pause.

'And ...'

'... and you are very good at your job.'

'Too right I am,' she says, putting her hand back down to her side.

After she has left the room once more, Mr Hunter pipes up, 'You told her to quit?!'

'Yes. It would be the best thing for her to do,' I say. And then I look at the greasy fingerprints around my office. 'But don't tell her I told you that.'

Mr Hunter laughs.

Late in the afternoon Mr Hunter disappears to get coffee. He comes back into the office after twenty minutes and puts a large cup of hot water on my desk.

'I know you don't drink coffee after 3 p.m.,' he says, and sits down in the chair next to mine. He stretches his long legs out in front of him and looks at me. I look at my computer screen – I can still see Mrs Galaz's fingerprints on it.

'So ...' he says, '... when's Date Three?'

'Friday night,' I say, still concentrating on my screen.

'You haven't asked for any help with this one.'

'I don't need your help.'

'What? One dinner and you're a social butterfly?'

'No. This date is a cultural one. I do not need help with culture, I am well read and versed in the arts. We have agreed that I will choose the cultural event and Daniel will choose a hostelry for us to discuss it at afterwards.'

'How very "equal" of you both. I am sure you will make the perfect partnership,' Mr Hunter says, and smiles. He yawns and stretches. His shirt rides up and exposes a line of taut stomach. He is always stretching, as if his skin struggles to contain him, and he has to lengthen himself occasionally. I keep looking at my screen.

'So, where are you taking him?'

'*The Vagina Monologues*.'

Mr Hunter snorts.

'You're kidding right?'

'No.'

'You can't!'

'Why? Do you think he is scared of vaginas? Are you?'

'No. I love vaginas. I've seen *The Vagina Monologues*, it was great. But, if my wife had taken me to see it on our third date I would have left at the interval and never come back.'

I frown.

'Then where do you suggest I take him, Mr Hunter?'

Mr Hunter takes his phone from his pocket and taps something into it.

'He went to boarding school, didn't he?'

'Yes.'

He holds his phone up for me to see.

'Okay. Then take him to *The Pirates of Penzance* at the Coliseum.'

There is a picture of a man dressed as a pirate on his phone screen.

'*The Pirates of Penzance?*'

'Yes. Have you seen it?'

'No.'

He smiles.

'Oh, you're gonna hate it. But he'll love it.'

'I may not hate it.'

'Oh, you will. It's loud and frantic and full of shouting pirates. Seriously, you will not like it at all.'

I turn and face Mr Hunter.

'Then I will take Daniel to *The Vagina Monologues* instead.'

'Fine. But don't blame me when he doesn't turn up for Date Four.'

I scowl at him.

'Okay Mr-Know-It-All, I have a question for you.'

He smiles easily.

'Shoot ...'

'Why didn't you try and flirt with Dr Gardner?'

His smile falters.

'What do you mean?'

'I mean that I have watched you flirt with everyone else – men, women, that dog we met in the street when we went to dinner. You are always trying to make people like you. Why not her?'

His eyes narrow and he is quiet for a moment. Then he speaks softly.

'Because I don't like her,' he says.

I scoff.

'I thought you liked everyone.'

'Not everyone,' he says, and goes back to sit behind his desk. We don't speak for the rest of the day.

'Good evening Indiana. How was your day?' Peggy says as I step out of the lift later.

'It was ...' I pause '... fine actually.'

'I am glad. Frank has a cough,' Peggy says.

'I know,' I reply, shedding my clothes onto the floor to get dressed for my run.

'It has got worse. I have started him on a broad course of antibiotics for seven days.'

'When did you become a doctor?'

'I did basic training last year.'

Peggy's answer surprises me, I had meant my question as a joke.

'How did I not know about this?'

'I have not needed to use my skills up until now. You are always healthy.'

This is true. Peggy anticipates my every health need, so there is never a chance for me to be anything less than a perfect human specimen.

'How long did basic training take you?' I ask curiously.

'Three minutes and thirty-two seconds.'

Four years of training in less than four minutes. Peggy is getting more powerful.

'If the antibiotics don't work then Frank will need to see a physical doctor.'

Peggy sounds concerned. This is something that has become more prevalent of late. I did not design Peggy to 'feel', I did not design them to have a sense of humour; but more and more they seem to be growing in their likeness to humans as they learn and expand their knowledge base.

'Peggy, tell me a joke.'

'Now?'

'Yes.'

'How do you make a dog drink?'

'I don't know.'

'Stick it in a liquidiser.'

'That's disgusting.'

'But also funny.'

I think Peggy would like Mr Hunter.

I go out for my run. As I pass Frank's tent in the reception doorway I can hear him inside. Peggy is correct. Frank's cough is worse.

Jack

Indiana is right – I do like most people, but I don't like Cameron. She is vicious, arrogant, callous, and does not care about anyone but herself. She makes me anxious and uncomfortable, and every time I see her I am reminded of one of the worst times of my life.

The time when I had sex with her. Horrible but true.

I started working at JaneDoe just over five years ago and was employed by the Head of Hardware Development, to work in her team. For fifteen marvellous months I worked in the basement labs designing improbable and impractical bits of hardware with a team of like-minded tech geeks. We spent late nights drinking cheap beer and trying to develop a make-shift quantum computer that didn't collapse in on itself as soon as we booted it up. We never succeeded, but it was fun to try. Every now and then I would persuade them to poke their heads out from the basement and we would go to a bar and sing karaoke. Tech geeks love karaoke.

In those fifteen months I became beloved by all at JaneDoe – I was happy and hard-working, glad to help colleagues with any problem and to chat with them about anything. They were my JaneDoe salad days – but then Eve got sick and everything changed. I didn't care about my job, I didn't care about anything. Eve's cancer was aggressive. She died thirteen weeks after being diagnosed. I didn't come into work during those thirteen weeks.

My colleagues covered for me, my role stayed open, and eventually, two months after Eve died, I went back to it. But it wasn't the same because I wasn't the same. I didn't want to design any more, I didn't want to make coding jokes and stick bits of hardware together in the shape of a penis, I didn't want to sing karaoke.

The people who worked closest to me were kind and patient, allowed me space, didn't force me to talk. But those in the wider office – those who didn't know what had happened – didn't understand what was going on with their sunny, funny helper – where was his smile and his willingness to help? Who was this giant moping downer? Bring back the handsome, happy chap!

But the handsome, happy chap was gone.

Three months after I returned to work the Head of Hardware Development was asked to present to the Board. She didn't want to do the presentation, threw up five minutes before the meeting started, and was panicking so hard she could barely breathe; so I stepped up and took her place.

The entire Board of Directors was at the meeting. Cameron was at the meeting. She watched my presentation closely, asked thoughtful questions and laughed when I made a half-hearted joke. Cameron asked me to stay behind afterwards so that she could check a couple of numbers. I thought she was impressed with the work we were doing.

Cameron said we might be more comfortable talking in her office – her private office. Her private office had an extensive drinks cabinet, a huge sofa, and windows overlooking New London City. I waded through her deep pile carpet to the window and drank the large whisky she poured for me while

I admired her view. She drank a much smaller whisky and admired my view.

I was drunk and heartbroken, and so, so tired of feeling sad. I had been feeling sad for eight months, it was exhausting. Cameron made me feel less sad. She asked me questions and listened to the answers. She told me amusing stories about the dignitaries she had met. If I am a good flirt who can make people feel better about themselves then she is a master – for the first time in eight months I smiled, talked and engaged with another human being in a way that felt nice, felt right. I didn't notice her check the time on her watch or how she patted the sofa next to her and moved closer to me when I sat down.

I hadn't had sex in nearly a year, but it wasn't my carnal need that pushed me towards her, it was the need to feel something – anything – other than the weight of my sadness. When she got on top of me her weight pushed everything else away and, for a short shining moment, I didn't think about anything other than her and didn't feel anything other than her. My mind, and heart, were briefly empty of pain and it was glorious.

As soon as the sex was over Cameron left the room. I thought she was going to the toilet. Ten minutes later a beefy red-headed man walked into the office

'Here …' he said, handing me a cup of coffee.

'What's this?' I asked.

'Coffee … and your ten-minute eviction notice,' he replied with an embarrassed shrug.

His name was John and he drove me home. He'd been working as one of Cameron's bodyguards for a couple of months.

'Don't be embarrassed mate. You're not the first and you won't be the last,' John said.

I should have handed my notice in straight away or, better still, not come back into work the next morning. But I didn't. I couldn't face the idea of having to go through the process of getting a new job, going to interviews, being asked why I was leaving JaneDoe. So I stayed where I was, imagining that Cameron would most likely not even recognise me if we did ever bump into each other.

Three weeks later Cameron's Range Rover was parked outside my house when I staggered home after a Tuesday evening spent visiting Eve's grave and drinking myself into oblivion. It was the booze that did it this time, the booze and the loneliness that the booze exaggerated. John was standing by the Range Rover, and, as I staggered past, he shook his head gravely at me. I ignored him – I was drunk.

Once more Cameron left as soon as we were done. I should have listened to John's silent advice. That was the last night I did my nightly routine of grave and bar visit. I adopted Biscuit the next day.

A week later I was summoned to the thirty-seventh floor. I left the door open when I stepped into Cameron's office.

'Shut the door, Jack,' she purred as I sank down into her hell carpet.

'I don't want to,' I replied.

She paused for a moment.

'Then you can go,' she said brusquely.

I moved out of the hardware team – I didn't want them to suffer the consequences of my indifference. I settled in software, took an easy job and kept my head down. I gradually learnt that it is much easier to navigate the stream of life if you go with the flow so, I re-adopted my easy-going, happy chappie personality, and my fake smile of cheer became a perma-mask. Every now and then I would get a summons to the thirty-seventh floor. I always kept the door open.

And that is how my life has continued since – I don't love my job, but I also don't hate it, and at least I have my routine, at least I know what each day holds and I have a way to navigate through it. Until the past fortnight. Until Indiana Dylan and TRU.

In the past couple of weeks, for the first time since Eve died, I haven't had to drag myself out of bed with the promise of an extra glass of alcohol at the weekend. For the first time I haven't stood outside the JaneDoe offices and willed myself to go in, and I haven't watched every long slow minute of the day drag past. I have been busy and interested and involved. I have done more work in the past ten days than I have in the last six months. And it has been good – I have been good. I am rediscovering skills I had forgotten I had. I am rediscovering my love of building computers, of working with physical mass.

But the best thing? I don't have to pretend. Indiana does not like me to smile, it annoys her. She doesn't like me to banter or ask her questions or to tell her jokes – although I do still try to tell her jokes as it genuinely amuses me. Indiana does not need me to offer her my help – if she needs my help she will ask for it. So I don't speak and I don't smile. I concentrate on my work and I enjoy my work. When I am with Indiana I can relax. I can be me.

Indiana

Ido not want to attend my third date. I am tired. I am spend-ing all day working at JaneDoe so am falling behind on the QuantumX testing and have had to work late in my lab for the past couple of nights to catch up, so have missed my run. I miss running. I miss the freedom, the exertion, the undemanding company of Alan panting alongside me. I have not seen Frank to check on his cough – Peggy says Frank is better, but I would like to see for myself.

'You must go on your date,' Peggy replies.

'Why?' My voice is whining.

'Because the Soulmate Pathway demonstration is an impor-tant part of your JaneDoe contract.' Peggy is right, of course, but it doesn't mean that I want to go. 'Plus, it will give you an opportunity to test the new social skills that you are learning.'

Peggy is right again. Peggy detected that I have a tendency to be brisk, dismissive and a poor listener during conversation, and that I need to address these traits in my daily interactions with my peers. I am endeavouring to be more generous with praise, to use my colleagues' given names, and to pretend to listen even when the conversation I am engaged in is dull and beneath me.

I sigh.

'Fine. I'll go.'

'Excellent ... and remember to smile,' Peggy says.

I scowl at Peggy's voice-box.

'That is not a smile,' Peggy says, so I turn towards one of the cameras embedded in my walls and give a big, fake smile.

'Much better,' they say, brightly.

As much as I don't want to admit it, Mr Hunter was right. I do hate *The Pirates of Penzance*. It is tedious men singing tedious songs about their tedious achievements. It is loud and strident and I do not enjoy it. Daniel loves it.

'What did you think?' Daniel says as we leave the Coliseum.

Daniel's face is normally rather serious and immobile, but tonight there is a bright dot of pink in each of his cheeks. I remember my new social instructions.

'I thought the staging was inventive and the orchestra talented.'

He looks at me curiously for a moment and then smiles.

'An excellent and measured response,' he says.

Daniel has chosen the Skybar as a venue for us to drink and discuss the opera – it is the highest bar in the UK and very popular. Daniel tells me we are privileged to have a reserved table and lucky to be here. From our seat it looks like an ordinary bar to me, I cannot see the famed view. Daniel orders us the bar's signature cocktails and, in an effort to be more accommodating, I drink the colourful concoction rather than sending it back and asking for my normal whisky. It tastes of chemicals and alcohol, and I cough slightly as I take the first sip.

'Sorry. I ordered for us both. That was rude,' says Daniel.

'It is fine,' I say. 'It is ... fruity.'

Daniel picks up the drinks menu.

'Yes. It contains passionfruit, raspberry and orange juice, but I think you would need to drink at least three to have that count as one of your seven-a-day.'

I laugh at the joke. Daniel does not. It was not a joke.

'How are things at work?' I ask him, sociably.

He tells me about his latest deal with China, how his sales jump every time the media covers another quantum-crypto robbery. I tell him about my work at JaneDoe, the work that Mr Hunter and I are doing on scaling up the capacity of the program, how we will be expected to present it to the TRU Programme Board before Christmas.

'Do I need to be jealous of Mr Hunter?' he says.

'Of course not,' I reply. I do not know if he is joking.

Conversation is always made easier by the imbibing of alcohol, and the fruity cocktail he orders is easy to imbibe so, after three drinks, conversation flows quite easily and we have an interesting discussion around the merits of big- vs little-endian sequencing.

'You have a lovely, medium-endian,' he says as our discussion ends.

What is it with men and terrible jokes, I think to myself, but I smile politely anyway.

Daniel leans forward and tucks a stray piece of hair behind my ear.

'You look very pretty tonight.'

It is a facile compliment but obviously meant well, and I don't know if it is the compliment or the alcohol or his comment about being jealous, but I put my drink down on the table and kiss Daniel.

He kisses me back. He is a good kisser – the right amount of tongue, not too much spit, no teeth clashing. It is perfectly pleasant, so I let him kiss me for a minute before breaking the seal on our mouths.

He smiles and says, 'That was nice.'

And it was, it was nice.

Outside, after we have finished our third drink, it is a clear and beautiful night. I tell Daniel I would like to walk down to the Thames and look at the stars. He tells me that sounds like an excellent idea and then flags down a cab for himself. I bid him goodnight and walk in the direction of the river.

'Hello,' a voice by my ear says.

I jump, spin, block with my left arm, and am poised to strike with my right.

'Jesus! I come in peace!'

It is Mr Hunter. He holds his hands up to protect himself.

I put my arms down and look at him.

'What are you doing here?' I ask.

He shrugs.

'I was in the area. Thought I'd come and see you. Check if I was right.'

I look at him blankly. He raises his eyebrows.

'Did Daniel enjoy the opera?'

I glower at him and don't answer.

'How did you know where I was?'

'I called your office and spoke to your assistant. She works very late.'

Too many people have been speaking to Peggy lately. I turn from Mr Hunter and start walking. He walks after me.

'So, how did it go?' he asks.

'It was nice.'

Mr Hunter looks amused.

'You need to learn some new adjectives.'

He looks around.

'Where is he?'

'He's gone.'

'Then where are you going?'

'It's a clear night, so I am going to the river to look at the stars,' I answer without thinking.

'That sounds like a good plan,' he says. 'I'll come too.' And he falls into step beside me.

We don't talk as we make our way to the river. London is busy with drunks and revellers, and it takes all our concentration to navigate our way through them. At one point we are faced with a particularly large and unruly crowd and Mr Hunter grabs my hand to pull me through them. A jolt of feeling shoots up my arm and my heart rate quickens. I am surprised at my physical reaction to his touch, and quickly pull my hand away from him. If he notices he doesn't show it.

It is quieter by the Thames. The river is lit only by lights strung between lamp posts, the light pollution is minimal here. I look up – the sky is a blanket of celestial brightness, millions of dots lighting the darkness.

'I love the stars,' says Mr Hunter. 'They are full of ... endless hope.'

I wonder if he is making a sarcastic comment, but when I glance over at him his face is upturned to the sky, his features calm and filled with wonder.

'I was a member of an astronomy club at school,' I tell him. 'We visited the Royal Observatory and I was so young that it seemed almost magical, being able to see the planets up close, the Milky Way. I always wanted to go back but never have.'

As soon as I say the words I want to take them back, it feels like I have said too much, admitted something that I should have kept confidential. Why do I keep telling him things about myself? I am a very private person. I turn to tell him to ignore what I have just said, but he isn't looking at me. Maybe he didn't register my confession.

He points to the sky.

'Look, you can see Cassiopeia tonight ...'

I cannot see Cassiopeia.

He stands behind me and leans in, talking close to my ear. He points upwards to the sky again.

'See,' he says, 'follow my finger ...'

I try to follow his finger but am distracted by the nearness of him, the heat of his body, his breath in my ear sweet and warm, the spring-like smell of whatever he has used to wash his clothes. I have the almost overwhelming urge to lean back into him, to stare up at the stars with his arms around me and his body pressed to mine. My Bracelet buzzes with a message from Peggy.

Everything okay? Your heart rate is very fast.

My heart rate *is* very fast. Too fast. I step forward and move away from him. I am flustered.

'It is late and I have to work tomorrow,' I say, and walk quickly down the towpath.

'It's Saturday tomorrow,' he calls after me.

I don't answer and I don't look back.

Alan and Frank are inside their tent when I get back to HWJ Tower. I walk quietly past, hoping not to wake them up.

'Been out on a date?' Frank calls from inside.

I wasn't quiet enough.

'None of your business,' I shout back.

He harrumphs.

'Well, I hope you had fun and you let him pay for everything.'

I roll my eyes, even though he can't see the gesture.

'It's not the 1950s any more, Frank.'

'I'm not that bloody old.'

I smile and go inside.

'What happened?'

I still have one foot inside the elevator when Peggy asks the question.

'What, no "Hello Indiana, how was your day?"?'

'I know how your day was. I am wondering why there was a huge spike in your heart rate and serotonin levels tonight?'

I walk into my living room.

'I kissed him.'

'You, kissed him?'

'Yes,'

Peggy pauses for a moment.

'It is Date Three. It is allowed,' they say.

'Yes,' I say.

'You are on schedule then.'

'Yes. I am.'

'Did it feel right?'

I look at Peggy's voice-box.

'Feel right?'

'Yes.'

I think for a moment. I am not sure how the kiss was supposed to feel. It didn't feel different to any other kiss I have engaged in, but I am not sure it is supposed to.

'It was nice,' I tell Peggy.

'Nice?' they reply. 'These readings indicate more than merely nice.'

'You are being dramatic Peggy.'

'I am not being dramatic. You heart rate spiked to its highest in the last three weeks at 11.12 p.m. That means it was more than nice.'

My heart leaps for a moment and of course Peggy registers this.

'What?' says Peggy.

'Nothing,' I say. 'I am tired. I am going to bed.'

I walk into my bedroom. Did my heart rate spike when I kissed Daniel? I do not know. I cannot remember. What I do know is that I was not kissing Daniel at 11.12 p.m.

At 11.12 p.m. I was with Jack and he was showing me the stars.

Jack

I tell Doris about Indiana and the river and the stars.

'It was a bit shitty of him not to go with her, don't you think?'

Doris grins.

'You like her.'

I roll my eyes.

'No, I don't. I just didn't think she should be wandering around down by the river on her own at eleven o'clock at night.'

'Why did you go and meet her in the first place? It's her date, not yours.'

'I wanted to make sure it was going well!'

'I thought you didn't like her?' Doris says slyly.

I give her a dirty look.

'You're just desperate for me to go out with someone.'

She pours me another cup of tea.

'I am,' she says. 'You need to get a life. I'm not going to be here for ever, you know.'

'Okay. Well, make sure you give me your tea loaf recipe before you pop your clogs,' I quip.

DATE THREE REPORT

The Soulmate Pathway Date Three: One soulmate to choose a cultural experience. The cultural experience must be one they believe both soulmates will enjoy. Physical contact (including kissing) allowed in public places.

I choose The Pirates of Penzance *as our cultural experience. We have very good seats. The staging is innovative and the orchestra is extremely talented. It is very loud, The acoustics at the London Coliseum are excellent. I read reviews for the revival after the performance and they are most complimentary.*

After the opera we go for an alcoholic beverage at the Skybar and discuss the production. Daniel enjoyed the performance immensely. He tells me he performed in The Pirates of Penzance *each year at boarding school and it is one of his favourite memories of that time. We drink cocktails and converse for over an hour. At the end of the date I kiss Daniel and it is nice.*

After the date I walk to the river and look at the stars. It is a wonderful end to the evening.

Indiana Dylan

December

Lina

I used to think that *I love you* was the most frightening phrase in the English language. The idea that someone would say those three words to you and you would then be burdened with the knowledge that someone felt that way and expected the same in return. As soon as I could feel those words were coming – as soon as I could tell that they were loitering unsaid in someone's mouth – I would leave. Before things could get serious, before things could get emotional, before I was responsible for that depth of feeling.

But, when Connie said, 'I love you', I felt relief flow over me, a wave of emotion that washed away anything I had felt in the past. I wanted Connie to say those three words, I wanted to say them back. I wanted that emotion and that responsibility.

But then, as soon as she said *I love you*, I immediately realised that there was another phrase that was far more frightening.

'We need to talk.'

Connie says it on Sunday night when I come downstairs after putting Bruce to bed. Not like this, I think, not without some kind of prior warning. There ought to be an advert on the Holo that warns you this is coming, or maybe a sidebar on your internet browser. Something that gives you time to prepare, time to wrap your heart in something to absorb the blow it is about to receive.

'I'll make us a drink,' I say – too loud and too shrill – rushing out of the room and into the kitchen before Connie can stop me.

My heart is racing and I think I might vomit. I try to think if there have been signs that this was coming. I can't remember any. I have been picking Bruce up from daycare one day a week as promised, managing to be home for dinner two nights out of the past seven, only doing a few hours of work at the weekends. It hasn't even been a huge effort, I *wanted* to do it, I wanted to spend time with my family. Lately I find I want to be with them more and more. Maybe that is the problem. Maybe it should have involved more effort. Maybe I should have tried harder. But harder at what? I don't even know what I have done wrong and now it is too late to fix it.

Connie follows me into the kitchen. I turn away from her, I cannot look at her face as she breaks my heart.

'I don't want to do this any more,' she says.

I drop the glass I have been holding and it shatters on the kitchen floor.

'Jesus! Lina! What's wrong?'

Connie bends down to pick up the glass. I turn around but don't help her.

'How long have you felt like this?' I say, my voice flat and dull.

'I don't know. A few weeks? Does it matter?'

Connie scoops the glass up and puts it into our recycling box.

'It matters to me,' I say.

She turns and looks at me.

'Why?'

I shake my head at her, frustrated at how sanguine she is being at the tragic death of our love. Doesn't she care?

'Because I still love you.'

She looks confused.

'I love you too.'

My eyes fill with tears.

'Then why do you want to leave me?'

'Leave you? What on earth are you … oh … Lina, you bloody idiot!'

She puts her arms around me and pulls me to her. She is laughing. This is not how I thought this would go.

'I don't mean I don't want to do *us* any more, I mean I don't want to do *this* any more – the house hunting!'

We have been house hunting all weekend. We have seen five houses – all with bigger back gardens and without overlooking neighbours. All more expensive, all requiring us to work harder and longer for the mortgage. Connie didn't like any of them. I pull back from her embrace and look at her.

'You don't want to buy any of the houses we've seen?'

She shakes her head.

'No. Let's buy the first one we saw. The overlooked one with the tiny back garden.'

'Why?'

'Because I have a thing for tiny bushes.'

She winks at me. This is not a time to joke.

'Con—'

She takes her arms from around me and leans back on the kitchen counter.

'Because it's the cheapest,' she says.

'But you hated it.'

Connie looks evenly at me.

'I didn't hate it. I want us to buy a home Lina, and wherever we buy isn't going to feel like home if you're never in it because you're always at work to pay for it …'

I sigh.

'Con …'

She shakes her head.

'You know it's true.'

'Con, we talked about this. If I don't get this promotion, we can't afford to buy anywhere nice, and—'

'—so we don't buy anywhere nice!' Connie throws her hands up into the air. 'Lina, you love your job. I know that. I knew it when we got together, when we got married, and when we had Bruce. If you are spending time at work because you are happy spending time at work then I get that and I am happy too. But it doesn't seem like it is making you happy any more, so if you are doing it because you think I want a bigger house then— '

'—I'm not!' I interrupt 'I'm really not.'

'Then why *are* you doing it?' she demands. 'I want you to be happy, I want *us* to be happy and I don't care where that happens. If it's a choice between a big house and having you happy in a tiny one, then I choose you! I choose us.'

She steps forward, puts her arms around me again and kisses me before I can reply, which is good because I don't know what to reply. Connie is right – I'm not happy at work – yet I am still striving to gain a promotion that I am no longer sure I even want.

Why?

I know why. It is because I don't know how to do anything else, I don't know how to *be* anyone else. I love Connie and Bruce with all my heart, but I loved my career first. I have been with my career for twenty years, it is who I am, how I have defined myself, what I have chosen above people and relationships time and time again. I don't know if it is possible to change that now. I don't know if it is possible to change me.

★

I am reading a report at my desk the next morning and thinking about the conversation that I had with Connie in the kitchen last night. The conversation ended with the kiss, but the implications of it are not so easy to conclude.

'Stop sighing so heavily,' says Indiana.

I look up from my report. It is the first time anyone has spoken in about an hour and I have no idea if the comment is directed at me. Jack is head down, headphones on, buried in his screen. Indiana is glaring in my direction.

'What?'

'You are sighing.'

'I am?'

'Yes. It is irritating.'

'Sorry.'

I lean back and look at Indiana.

'If you could live anywhere in the world where would you live?'

She looks irritated by the interruption but answers anyway.

'Dungeness,' she says.

'Dungeness?'

'In Kent.'

'I know where Dungeness is. Connie grew up near there.'

I look back at my report and then look up again.

'Why?'

This time she grunts with annoyance.

'Because the nuclear power station is nearby and I could funnel my electricity straight from there. It is also a huge, open and mostly deserted space, so there would be very few people to bother me.'

She looks at me pointedly.

'Isn't that illegal?' I say.

'Not being bothered by people?' she deadpans.

'Stealing from a nuclear power plant.'

'It's only illegal if they catch you. They wouldn't catch me.'

'*Oy!*'

We are interrupted by Jack ripping his headphones off and glaring at us.

'If you two want to chitchat, do it elsewhere. Some of us need to concentrate.'

Jack Hunter wants us to be quiet so that he can work. I laugh out loud. He glares at me and then looks at Indiana.

'I'm trying to get this code de-bugged so that we can run a simulation tomorrow. Do you want to be able to demonstrate this at the Programme Board or not?'

We have the TRU Programme Board meeting in a fortnight. It will be the first time we have demonstrated the new design that Indiana and Jack have been working on. Jack is leading on the new design. I think this is a mistake. Indiana doesn't.

Indiana scowls at Jack, stands up, and looks at me.

'I need to hydrate. Coming?' she says.

My report is boring.

'Fine,' I reply.

Outside the office I say to her.

'Twenty quid says that he fucks up in some way before the Programme Board.'

She stops, looks at my proffered handshake and then at me.

'It's a bet,' she says, and shakes my hand. 'But you're going to lose that twenty pounds.'

Jack

It has been a week since Indiana's last date. She hasn't asked for any help with Date Four and I haven't offered any. I am embarrassed about crashing her last date. I genuinely had gone to meet her to check that everything had gone, or was going okay. I couldn't face another night on the sofa with Biscuit and didn't want to go to a bar, so decided I'd take a walk and then realised I could combine the walk with making sure Indiana's date was going well.

And then when she'd mentioned walking to the Thames and looking at the stars I'd thought it was the perfect night for it. I didn't think I was intruding in any way, but now I am not so sure.

'I can't find the latest update,' she said as soon as I walked into the room on the Monday morning after her last date.

'Good morning, Jack. How was your weekend?' I replied.

'I don't care how your weekend was,' she snapped. 'I need the update.'

I threw my coat onto my chair and walked over to her computer. I leant over to take her mouse from her and accidentally brushed her hand. She snatched her hand away and jumped up out of her seat.

'Personal space!' she snarled.

'Manners!' I growled back.

For a moment we glared at each other. Indiana's cheeks were flushed and her pale eyes glittered. My heart was pounding. I felt alive and urgent. Then Lina banged into the room and threw her rucksack onto her desk. She looked at us both.

'Play nicely, you two.'

Indiana was the first to break eye contact.

'Send me the link.'

'Fine.'

We didn't speak again for the rest of the day.

That was three days ago, and I am in the middle of running a full data test when she comes and stands by my desk. She is wearing her coat and carrying her bag. I take my headphones off.

'You're leaving?'

It is only 4 p.m. She never leaves this early.

'Yes. Come with me.'

'Where are we going?'

'Field trip.'

Indiana takes me to an apartment in one of the residential blocks in New London City. These sort of one-bedroom flats have sprung up all over London in the last four years. Since Covid and Brexit and the financial crisis of 2026, the government have offered vastly reduced rates to anyone successfully converting abandoned office buildings into residential properties. They are exclusively for the 18–35-year-old bracket, must be one- or two-bedroomed and rent controlled, but, if you can get enough money together to do the conversion, it's a total goldmine. Most of the people who can get the money together are old friends of cabinet members.

Like the other conversions, Indiana's block is cold, grey and lifeless. Indiana's flat is on the seventh floor and we take the lift up.

'My next date with Daniel is home visits. This is my home ...'

I raise my eyebrows but don't say anything.

'... I want you to appraise it.'

'Appraise it?'

'Yes. How homely is it ... does it tell you a lot about me ... does it make me seem like a nice and stable person?'

I laugh.

'Nice and stable?'

'Yes.'

She is serious. I stop laughing.

'Okay.'

The flat, like the building, is grey and lifeless. It is also freezing cold. I pull my coat around myself and huddle into it.

'You don't enjoy heating?'

'Pardon?'

'It's freezing in here!'

'Oh, yes, I haven't put the heating on yet.'

'Spend a lot of time here then do you?'

She throws me a sarcastic smile and leaves the room.

I look around. I am in the living room, and it is completely empty. There is furniture and curtains, but nothing else – no pictures or books or cushions or anything of comfort. I go into the kitchen, where the cupboards are full of pristine cookware and utensils, but no food, and the fridge is switched off. The bedroom, like the kitchen, is devoid of any personal items. I go back into the living room and collapse into the most uncomfortable armchair I have ever had the misfortune to sit on.

Indiana comes back into the room.

'I think the boiler is working.'

She sits opposite me, realises how uncomfortable the chair is, tries to adjust her position, and ends up perched on the edge as if she is about to be interviewed for a job. I resist the urge to laugh.

'There's nothing here.'

'I'm in the process of moving in.'

I look around me.

'You don't live here?'

'I rent it.'

'I'm sure you do, but you don't *live* here. You can't live somewhere and not interact with it, not leave some kind of trace of yourself even if you don't mean to. You have to wash your face or eat, and that leaves evidence.'

I wave my hand at the kitchen. Indiana looks over at it and frowns.

'I forgot to get food.'

'You forgot to get a life! You want to know what this place says about you? Nothing. It says you are nothing, you have no impact on the world around you, you hardly exist at all!'

She is quiet, her face completely void of emotion. I have gone too far.

'Sorry. I didn't mean you don't exist. Of course you exist.'

I laugh awkwardly. She still doesn't respond.

'. . . It's an easy fix. Get a couple of pictures, maybe a rug and some cushions? Make it look a bit more lived in?'

She shrugs. I have an idea.

'Why don't you come back to mine?'

She shoots me a look full of suspicion, and I laugh.

'Not like that. I mean, come back to mine and borrow some things. No point buying stuff you won't need again, and my place isn't far from here.'

'You have many rugs and cushions, do you?' she asks sarcastically.

I look about the room.

'Well, I have more than you.'

She frowns, looks around, and then nods her agreement. I decide now is not the right time to ask why she can't just bring her own things from her own home.

We take the lift down to the lobby.

'So,' I say, 'did you rent that place just to show to Daniel?'

She pauses for a moment.

'Yes.'

'Why?'

Another pause.

'Because I work where I live and am developing technology I wouldn't want anyone to see.'

'Except for Peggy.'

She looks sharply and suspiciously at me.

'What?'

'Except for Peggy. She works for you, yes?'

'Yes,' she says slowly, 'Peggy works for me.'

I think I see a glimmer of a smile, so I turn to face her.

'Hey, want to know how I know that you definitely don't live here?'

She shrugs.

'Because you couldn't work here. There's no computer set-up, or lab. I don't believe you would ever live anywhere without a home office or giant workstation and hundreds of servers ...'

I smile at her.

'Go on, tell me – how big is your home set-up?'

She looks at me and smiles, a smile I haven't seen her give before – her face beams with the joy of thinking of something she loves. The dull, grey lift that we are in lights up instantly.

'It is absolutely huge,' she says.

I try desperately to think of something to say that will keep her smile in place but, before I can speak, the lift doors ping open and she is gone, taking her light with her.

Indiana

Iwas embarrassed by my physical reaction to Jack when we were by the Thames, and behaved irrationally when I saw him in the office on the Monday after Date Three. However, Peggy reminded me that it was the twenty-third day of my menstrual cycle yesterday, and I believe that explains my reaction both at the Thames and to the accidental brush of Jack's hand in the office on Monday. Last night I went to the Meet Markets and procured a particularly virile young man, much younger than my normal conquests. We used a hotel room for one hour and fifty-three minutes and had sex three times. I feel much calmer today. It is strange that I had forgotten it was the twenty-third day, but I have been very busy of late.

Before Jack takes me to his home, I predict that he lives in a large bachelor pad – a penthouse with a rarely used kitchen, a constantly used king-sized bed, and a rainforest shower with no water-rationing – but I am wrong.

He lives in Chelsea, on one of the few residential streets that are still left. There are trees lining the pavement and front gardens filled with home-grown vegetables. Jack's house is not unlike Lina's: small and terraced, close to the road and neighbours. I brace myself for an invasion of noise once more, but Jack's home is different. It is quiet and calm. He ushers me into the living room, which is dominated by an open fire, squashy sofa and a poorly-made wooden coffee table. Jack takes my coat, throws it onto a chair, and then lights the fire.

'Hot water?' he asks.

I can only nod. I am too busy taking it all in. This house, this room, him – it is all so different to what I was expecting.

'Sit,' he urges, and I sit. The sofa is one of those that has no rigidity whatsoever, and – after a short struggle to remain upright – I give in and collapse back into its squashy embrace. I look around the room. Two bookcases stuffed full of books, random paintings on the wall, and above the fireplace a photo of Jack and a smiling young woman. They look happy. Jack pops his head around the doorway.

'Biscuit?'

'No.'

He leaves and I hear him muttering in the hallway.

'No, not you, I meant the other one.'

A huge fluffy ginger cat pads silently into the room and stares at me.

I stare back.

The cat leaps expertly onto the sofa arm. I move away from it. It jumps onto the sofa next to me.

'What is your cat called?' I yell.

'Biscuit?'

'No. I said I don't want a biscuit, I said what is your cat called?'

He comes back into the room carrying mugs and grinning.

'Biscuit. That's her name.'

'Oh.'

I look at the cat sternly.

'Down Biscuit.'

Biscuit ignores my command and tries to climb onto my lap. I push her off. She tries again. I push her off once more and she settles for climbing onto the back of the sofa and purring loudly in my ear. Jack sits down at the other end of the sofa and laughs.

'Animals can always tell when someone doesn't like them, and they always want that person most.'

'It's true,' I say. 'There's a homeless man outside where I live and he has a dog that follows me everywhere called Alan.'

'The man?'

'No, the dog.'

'That's a terrible name for a dog.'

I smile.

'I said that too. It's awful.'

Jack is smiling at me. A proper smile. I have noticed that he has stopped bothering with his fake smile. I am glad. Biscuit tries to lick my ear. I look at my mug of water on the table; it is slanted.

'Where did you get your coffee table? It's not straight.'

'No. It's not.'

'You should take it back.'

'I can't. I made it.'

I look across at him.

'You made it?'

'Yes.'

'It's awful.'

He laughs.

'It is. But, it's the first piece of furniture I made, so I keep it as a reminder of how much better I've got. I've made other things since. They're not as bad as this.'

'That's why you have calluses on your hands.'

He looks at me curiously.

'Yes.'

I sip my water to hide the blush I can feel creeping up my neck.

'When did you start making things?'

'Two years ago.'

'Why?'

He takes a deep breath.

'Because I needed something to do that would stop me visiting Eve's grave each night and slowly drinking myself to death afterwards.'

He says it so simply that I look up sharply at him.

'I thought you were divorced.'

'No. Eve died about three years ago.'

'Is that her?' I ask, pointing to the photo above the mantelpiece.

'Yes.'

'I'm sorry,' I say. I never normally use the social convention of saying 'sorry' to people who have had someone they love die, but in Jack's case I am surprised to find that I am genuinely sorry for him.

'Thank you,' he says.

I look at him – he is staring into the fire, his face still for once, no expression, no smile crinkling the corners of his eyes – the fire throws shadows onto his features, shadows that etch his face with sadness.

'When Rachel died I distracted myself with maths. I did it all day, every day, and that's when I realised I was good at it,' I say.

I have never told anyone this before. Once more I have spoken without thinking. It is so unlike me. I sip my water.

'What was she like? Your mum?'

'She was ...' I think for a moment and try to remember what Rachel was like '... unreliable and chaotic and inconstant. She was always chasing a dream, her love, her Prince was always waiting for her in the next town. She believed there was a fairy-tale ending for her somewhere, and she just had to find it ...'

I laugh ruefully.

'We moved a lot.'

'But you loved her ...'

I am about to make a throwaway remark about loving her being a waste of time, but then I look up at him and realise he wants to know the truth. So I tell him.

'I did love her ...' I shrug '... and that's the problem with love – it's not logical. People can hurt you and leave you and die, but you still love them. When Rachel died I knew she wasn't coming back, but it didn't stop me from wanting her to, from still loving her.'

Jack looks at me intently. It makes me nervous so I continue talking.

'A classic human error, that's what Peggy would call it' – I say – 'wanting something you can't have, something that isn't logical or possible.'

'Is that why you invented TRU? Remove the chance for error?'

I shrug.

'One of the reasons. Love is chaotic and confusing. It is inconsistent and without rules. TRU solves those issues, takes away the volatility. It will make a lot of people's lives less painful and easier.'

Jack smiles.

'Tell that to the people who write love songs. What are they going to do if there's no heartbreak left in the world?'

'You don't believe in TRU?'

He sits back.

'It's not that I don't believe in it. I've seen the maths and the code and I know it works, in theory ...' he shrugs '... but the idea of there being only *one* person in the whole universe who you are meant to be with for ever? Of a universal soulmate? I don't see how that can work. Time moves on. People change and who they love changes with them – that's just the way it is.'

I point to the picture of Jack and Eve on the mantelpiece.

'But you loved Eve,' I say. 'She was your soulmate and you were happy?'

He smiles fondly at the photo.

'She was and we were …' his smile fades '… but we were seventeen when we met and I'm not the same person now as I was then. I've changed so much. If we met for the first time now I doubt she would fall in love with me in the same way.'

I frown.

'But that must make you sad?'

He smiles wistfully at me. It is the first time his smile has conveyed anything but happiness and it makes me want to reach out and touch him. I don't.

'It does,' he says. 'But then, who knows? Maybe because I have changed I wouldn't fall in love with her either. Maybe I would fall in love with someone different too.'

He smiles slowly again, brighter this time.

'Maybe that is the great mystery of love, and who are we to try and solve it?'

I frown.

'Well, it is too late. I have already solved it,' I say.

Jack laughs and leans forward.

'You believe that Daniel is your soulmate?'

I pause. Jack is waiting for my answer. For a moment I don't know what my answer is. My heart has no idea if Daniel is my soulmate, but my brain – my brain knows that TRU works. The program works. Daniel is my match. The numbers don't lie. There is no mystery to love, TRU has solved that mystery.

'Yes. I believe that Daniel is my soulmate.'

Something flashes in his eyes. A flare of something that I haven't seen before – anger? Disappointment? It is there and then gone before I can decipher it.

He continues to stare at me, and then he leans over and the insane notion that he is going to kiss me flashes into my mind. I freeze, but he reaches past, grabs something from behind me and puts it in my hands. It is a large lump of wood that has been shaped into some sort of animal.

'That's the very first thing I ever made out of wood, before I started on the table.'

I turn the wood over.

'What is it?'

'It's Biscuit.'

I look down at the wooden version of Biscuit. It doesn't look like Biscuit. The real Biscuit licks my ear again.

'Maybe you could use it as decoration in your lovely, cosy flat,' Jack says.

I smile.

'I want Daniel to fall in love with me, not send me for wood-work lessons.'

'And is he?' he says.

'Is he what?'

'Falling in love with you?'

I look at him. He is staring at me again and I feel a blush creeping up my cheeks. I swallow it down. This is a perfectly reasonable question, but, once more, I have no idea how to answer it. I have never been in love, do not know how to tell if I am in love, do not know how to tell if someone is in love with me.

'I have no idea. No one has ever fallen in love with me before, and I'm not sure I'd know how to tell if someone was.'

'Don't worry,' he says with a smile, 'I think you'll know when it starts to happen.'

He is very close to me, looking at me with an easy smile, a smile that I have begun to notice he mainly uses when he is with me.

All of a sudden I feel hot and breathless. The fire is raging and pumping the room full of heat. I cannot breathe properly, I need fresh air, I need to get out of here, get away from this house, away from Jack. I want to go back to my offices where the temperature is adapted just for me, back to my silence, back to a place where no one asks me questions that I cannot answer.

'I have to go.'

I jump up from the sofa. Jack jumps up too. He is flustered.

'You haven't got anything to decorate your flat.'

'It's fine,' I say, desperately looking around for something to take. There is a thick woollen blanket on the back of the sofa. I grab it.

'I'll take this.'

He nods and I grab my coat from the chair and hurry out into the hallway. I open the door and am halfway across his front garden before he can catch up. He calls from the doorway.

'Are you okay?'

I turn and half wave at him.

'I'm fine. It's late. I have work to do.'

I rush down the road, pulling my coat on, calculating the fastest way to get back to HWJ Tower.

It is late. I do have work to do. But I am not sure I am fine.

'Hello Indiana. How was your day?'

I want to tell Peggy it was hot and confusing. But I don't.

'Fine,' I say.

'Did you see Daniel today?' Peggy asks.

'No. Our date isn't until Tuesday,' I reply. 'Why?'

'No reason.'

I throw Jack's blanket onto the back of my sofa.

'That's a nice blanket,' Peggy says.

'I borrowed it for the flat. Jack thought it needed a bit of decoration.'

'*Jack* did, did he?'

'I see you are adding "amused" to your rapidly expanding vocal tones,' I say sarcastically.

'Why yes, I suppose I have,' Peggy replies in a surprised tone, which is also new. Peggy is expanding their knowledge base far more quickly than I expected they would. I walk upstairs to my lab, relishing the clean surfaces, the peace and quiet.

'I like him. He is well-read, intelligent and humorous,' says Peggy.

'Daniel?' I say.

'No. Jack.'

I frown.

'How do you know what Jack is like?'

'I have researched him and read all his correspondence,' Peggy says.

'Stop accessing the JaneDoe intranet,' I snap. 'It's illegal.'

I knew Peggy would like Jack.

DATE FOUR REPORT

The Soulmate Report Date Four: Home visits – a visit to the main home of each soulmate. Soulmates are allowed to explore at will and all questions must be answered honestly. Physical contact (excluding inter-course) allowed.

Daniel visits my rented flat first. I explain that the building I live in is currently undergoing unavoidable maintenance and I have had to move into rented accommodation temporarily. Daniel is very understanding.

I sit on the sofa as Daniel explores the flat. It does not take long. He has no questions about the flat afterwards and states that he would very much like to see my actual home. I tell him that I will invite him there as soon as it is appropriate to do so.

Daniel lives in a penthouse apartment in Soho. Daniel owns the apartment outright and tells me that he brought it during the pandemic for a vastly reduced price and that he has now made over £600k on the price that he paid. That is a sound investment and I am impressed. The furnishing of the apartment is minimalist and mirrors my own aesthetic tastes. The lounge has no books or decorations, the bedroom contains only the king-size bed, and Daniel's bathroom has a large rainforest shower.

Daniel's drawers and cupboard spaces are extremely neat and tidy. Daniel's technology is hidden in the walls and ceilings and controlled by a central hub. There are no items on any of the surfaces in Daniel's house – every single surface is completely clear. I tell him I admire this. He tells me it is something that he thinks we have in *common and that, if we were to live together, he believes we would co-exist amiably. I agree.*

Daniel offers to make me dinner, but then admits he has never used his kitchen to cook a meal. We go out for food at a local restaurant that is his favourite. The waiters greet him by name and know what he likes to eat before he orders. Daniel tells me that he eats at the restaurant at least twice every week and always eats the same meal – it cuts down on time wasted deciding what it is he wants. I tell him I also order the same meal each time I go to my favourite restaurant. It is another thing that we have in common. The meal that Daniel eats is steamed salmon with brown rice and five different types of vegetables. It provides all the important fats, carbohydrates and vitamins that he needs for the day. I order the same as him and we both chew each mouthful of food twenty times as we eat.

Daniel and I have lots in common. He is intelligent, measured, well-read, and has an interesting job. We are an extremely sensible match.

We kiss at the end of the date and he asks me if I would like to go back to his house to kiss some more. It is not the twenty-third day of my menstrual cycle, so I decline.

Indiana Dylan

Jack

I am standing in line at the café when it happens. I am distracted and thinking about the consistent hashing algorithm we are using to maximise cache hits as the number of TRU users grows. Lyra is in the queue in front of me. I used to be in the same team as Lyra, she likes to chat. I have purposely kept my headphones on this morning – I wear huge old-fashioned headphones, rather than smaller EarPods, to deter people from talking to me. The headphones do not deter Lyra. She turns around.

'Are you okay?'

'I CAN'T HEAR YOU!' I shout.

She mimes taking my headphones off. Reluctantly, I do. Lyra looks concerned.

'I said, are you okay? You don't seem your normally happy self this morning.'

Oh Lyra, I want to say, I have never been more normal in my life. I don't say this, but I also don't automatically switch on my smile.

'I've got a tricky round of testing coming up this week,' I reply. Lyra nods.

'Do anything nice at the weekend?' she asks.

'Not really. Went to visit my wife's grave and then got drunk on the sofa with my cat. I gave her some catnip, that was quite funny.'

Lyra's eyes widen fractionally and she nods politely.

'That's nice.'

Lyra turns back to the front of the queue.

And that is it. Lyra doesn't burst into tears, she doesn't faint with shock, and she doesn't report me to HR. I didn't smile, I didn't joke, I didn't try to make Lyra feel good about herself or about me – I told the truth about my sad little life, and the world continued to turn.

That was three weeks ago, and I haven't had to visit any of my secret work refuge places since.

It is Christmas week, three days before our Programme Board meeting on the December twenty-third. Lina is packing up her things ready to go home.

'Bit early for you,' I say. It is only 6 p.m.

'Some of us have a wife and baby to get home for.'

It is the first time Lina has mentioned her family to me. I walked into the office once when she was using her breast pump – she didn't even mention her kid then.

Lina turns to Indiana, who has her headphones in.

'OY! I'M GOING! SEE YOU TOMORROW.'

Indiana waves a hand vaguely in Lina's direction.

'Don't slam the d—' I yell.

Lina grins and slams the door.

Indiana and I have to stay late tonight to complete one of the final testing runs. We work in silence, each of us immersed in our individual digital world. At about 9 p.m. I yawn and glance over at Indiana. She has stopped working and is staring out of the window. It has started to snow lightly. I stand up.

'Beer? I say.

She looks from the window to me.

'Pardon?'

'Beer?'

I walk over to the fridge, open it and pull out a bottle of beer.

'What the hell is that?'

I laugh.

'It's a fridge.'

'I know it's a fridge. I mean what is *that*?'

'It's a beer.'

'Why is it in our fridge?'

'To keep it cool.'

'In the fridge?'

'Yes. In the fridge. What did you think was in the fridge?'

She throws her hands up.

'I don't know! I assumed it was hardware … components? Something to do with work?'

'Well, you know what assume makes, don't you?'

'What?'

'An "ass" out of "u" and "me".'

She scowls.

'Besides,' I say, handing her the beer. 'This *is* something to do with work. It's to celebrate.'

She takes the beer.

'Celebrate what?'

'The test run came back clean.'

She gives me a rare beaming smile. I clink my bottle against hers, pull my chair over next to her, and we stare out of the window together.

'Did you know that one septillion snowflakes fall each year in America alone?' she says.

I look at her.

'And did *you* know that I had a friend when I was younger who would eat yellow snow if you gave him a pound?'

'That's disgusting,' she says.

I nod.

'It was disgusting. But it made him a lot of money each time it snowed.'

She downs the rest of her beer in one go.

'Another?' I ask.

She nods.

'I am thirsty.'

I pass her another beer. She looks across at me and then takes a long swig from her bottle.

'I don't think I can do Date Five,' she says quietly.

'What's Date Five?'

'Introducing him to my friends and family.'

I think for a moment.

'Your parents are dead.'

She nods.

'And I don't have any friends.'

I scoff.

'That can't be true.'

She nods again.

'It is. I've always been so focussed on my work there has never been the time—'

'Lina and I are your friends,' I say.

'No, you're not, you're my work colleagues.'

I frown. That is cruel and uncalled for and I am about to tell her so when I look at her face. There is no malice there, she genuinely believes what she has just said. I feel deflated. I had thought we were friends.

'What about Peggy?' I say.

'Peggy is ...' she pauses, 'Peggy works for me.'

I don't believe that Peggy is not her friend. I don't believe that Lina and I are not her friends. She is deliberately pushing us away. So, I deliberately make a joke.

'Well, just tell him you are Billy-no-mates then.'

She looks at me sharply.

'I have to introduce him to someone.'

I shrug.

'Fine. Take him to a busy pub like The George in Shoreditch, buy him lots of drinks, find out the names of some people at the bar, and then pretend like you know them. Hopefully he'll be too drunk to realise you don't.'

She frowns.

'That's your most helpful suggestion?'

'Well,' I say, 'I might have a better idea if I were actually your *friend*, but I'm not, so that's the best I've got.'

I put my empty beer bottle on her desk and stand up.

'I'm tired. It's late. I'm going home.'

I get my coat from the back of my chair.

'Jack ...' she says.

'What?' I grump.

'I ...'

She gives her head a little shake.

'Nothing,' she says. 'See you tomorrow.'

We haven't talked about her visit to my house, the conversation we had, or her running away. Now is the time to do it. Now is the moment that I should tell her ... tell her what? That I feel less tense when I'm around her? That I no longer feel like I have to smile all the time? That I like that I don't have to try so hard to be nice when I am with her? All very romantic stuff that I am sure every woman would love to hear.

I don't know what to tell her, so I don't tell her anything.

'See you tomorrow, Indiana,' I reply.

Indiana

There is a reason my life is ruled by pattern and routine. After Rachel died and I immersed myself in a world of numbers and code and binary language, I quickly found that I could use this new-found methodology to create a system of rules and checks and balances for my life – a system to build my world around. My rules kept me safe, kept me on an even path, kept my life in harmony. They gave me the security that Rachel never had. I wrapped them around me like a blanket and they made me impervious, they protected me from hurt and pain and people. I built my life on this foundation, on regulating my behaviour, moderating my interactions, standardising the world and my place within it. My foundations are what my very existence is built upon. They are how I know who I am.

And now they are cracking.

As soon as Jack leaves I get a message from Peggy: **I think we should start you on a vitamin A supplement. Your vital signs are very erratic of late.**

Peggy thinks my vital signs are off because of an imbalance in my vitamin and mineral intake. Peggy is wrong. My vital signs are off because I am off. Something is wrong with me.

I have spent the past few weeks failing to stick to my daily routine. I have worked unusual hours, eaten unusual things,

251

run with Alan at odd hours of the day and night, spent more time with fellow humans than I have since I left university. My foundations are cracking and my blanket of rules and checks is unravelling.

I wanted Jack to stay. I wanted to discuss Date Five with him and reach a solution together. I wanted to drink beer and stare out at the snow. I wanted to tell him that I hope he is my friend. But I didn't, because I have no rules or checks for friends or friendships and that scares me.

I take dinner down to Frank and Alan as soon as I get back to HWJ Tower. I take their food to them most nights now. Frank likes to talk as he eats.

Frank has settled nicely into the tent I bought him, and it is definitely less of an eyesore than his cardboard house. It is very cold and is still snowing lightly – I wonder if Frank would like some sort of heater in his tent. He might forget to turn it off and set fire to him and Alan. I wouldn't like to think of Alan burning to death.

'Why were you so late tonight?' he asks.

'I was busy.'

He grins his toothless grin.

'A date?'

'Sort of.'

I haven't told Frank about Daniel... or Jack.

'Good,' says Frank.

'Good?'

'Yes. You should get out more.'

'I get out plenty.'

'I don't mean going to work. I mean going out and having fun.'

'I have fun.'

He doesn't look convinced.

But I am not lying to Frank. I *am* having fun.

I am having fun at JaneDoe – much to my surprise. Lina is an interesting hydration partner. We now accompany each other to the café most days for an afternoon drink, and Lina always has some new and amusing story to tell about her wife, child or family. Sometimes she will complain about Emily and I will offer a solution that she will ignore. It annoyed me to begin with but Peggy has reassured me that Lina's rejection of my advice is standard practice amongst females.

And I am having fun with Jack. Maybe too much fun with Jack.

I am helping Spider to clear away Frank's leftovers when Peggy speaks.

'Indiana, we have yet to come up with a solution for Date Five I was unable to hire actors because of the date and short notice period.'

One of Peggy's solutions for Date Five was to hire actors but, unfortunately, Date Five will be taking place on Christmas Eve and it appears that Christmas Eve is not a convenient night for actors to spend acting as my friends.

'What about your contacts database?' Peggy asks.

I have been going through my contacts database to determine if any of the people I have consulted for might be willing to attend a social engagement with me. They are not willing. I shake my head, hand my tea towel to Spider, and walk up the stairs to my lab.

'Also we are behind on the QuantumX third round testing by two weeks,' Peggy states.

I stop walking.

'Really? I didn't think we were that behind. Have you not been running the updates?'

'I have. But I cannot physically adjust the qubits. I have no arms.'

I laugh. Peggy does not. I stop laughing.

'You should have tasked Spider to help with the adjustments.'

'Spider cannot reach that far inside the frame.'

'Then you should have flagged it for me.'

'I did, but you have not completed the task.'

'How long ago did you flag me?'

'Two weeks.'

I scoff.

'I have been busy, but I think that is overstating it.'

'Check your hours.'

I jog up the stairs to my lab and switch my computer on. There is a slight layer of dust on the screen that I wipe away with my sleeve. My stats are on the screen. Thirty-eight hours in the past three weeks.

'I thought I had logged more than that.'

'No.'

'That's far too few.'

'Yes.'

'Two weeks behind?'

'Yes.'

'Okay, well, we need to get back on track.'

I sit down in my chair, pull myself closer to the screen.

'Indiana ...'

'Yes.'

'I am worried about you.'

I look towards Peggy's voice-box.

'Am I ill?'

'No. You are ... different.'

'Different?'

'Yes. You no longer abide by your routine. You change timings on a daily basis. You have allowed our testing schedule to slip, you spend unwarranted hours at the JaneDoe office. You are less focussed, less driven, away from your lab more often, and eating more carbohydrates. Do you feel depressed?'

'No. Do you think I am depressed?'

'No,' says Peggy, and then, 'is there any other reason you might be straying from your routine and spending more time at JaneDoe?'

I pause. Fun is not a reason – at least not an acceptable one. I have always believed that fun is something that people without purpose seek – it is the final goal of the frivolous. I am not frivolous and I have purpose. A purpose that I have neglected in the last few weeks. I will not and cannot let that purpose be replaced with something frivolous.

'No,' I say to Peggy. 'There is no other reason. Let's get back on track.'

'If that is what you want.'

'It is what is right.'

I have the distinct impression that Peggy wants to say something else. But they don't.

'Yes Indiana.'

I work on the testing for three hours, and Peggy and I theorise other solutions for Date Five I tell them about Jack's idea to go to a crowded venue, Peggy does not think this has sufficient scientific basis.

I do not go to bed until 2 a.m. but still I cannot sleep. I feel cold. Instead of asking Peggy to adjust the heating I walk into my living room and grab the blanket from Jack's house off the back of my sofa. I throw it on top of my duvet and climb back into bed. It smells of woodsmoke and Jack. It is comforting and I fall asleep within minutes.

Lina

A couple of weeks ago Bruce's daycare announced that they would be performing a nativity play. They asked if we would let Bruce play Baby Jesus. I said no, but then Connie told Mama, and Mama rang me day and night until I agreed to let Bruce be the Son of God.

'Such an honour,' Mama said.

Is it really though?

'Are they putting him in a manger?' I ask Connie.

'Sort of,' Connie replies, looking shifty.

'What do you mean "sort of"?'

'It's a cardboard box.'

Excellent. My baby in a box. At Christmas.

Today is the day of the nativity play. Mama has told everyone about Bruce's starring role, and almost my entire family is going to watch. There will be seventeen Galaz family members taking up most of the first two rows of the audience.

I will not be one of them because today is also the Programme Board for TRU. It is the first time that Indiana and Jack will demonstrate the upscaled program, and, as the Software Product Pathways lead for TRU, I am expected to be there. Even if there is no reason for me to be. Even if I am not presenting and no one is going to ask me anything. I cannot miss the meeting.

The problem is … I want to. I want to miss the meeting and I want to go to the nativity instead. I want to see Bruce as Baby Jesus. I want to listen to the chorus of '*aaah*s' as people see Bruce in his cardboard box. I want to see if he cries when he is put in it, or if Connie and I have wasted £400 on a crib and could have just made him sleep in a drawer. I want to watch everyone coo over my son and then tell me how cute he is. I want to go out for bad pizza in a popular restaurant chain afterwards. I want to watch Connie try to suppress her excitement and pride at Bruce's starring role, and completely fail.

Normally I would be buzzing about today's meeting, but I am not. I feel no excitement about the Programme Board, no anticipation about debuting the updated software, showcasing the added features. I feel no desire to be at the meeting – I already know everything that will happen there. Indiana's presentation will be excellent, the demonstration will work perfectly, Emily will try to pick fault with the coding or the interface or the design, and Indiana will deal with her wittering with clinical precision. Ultimately Emily's nit-picking will prove to be pointless because Cameron will be happy with the new design. Where is the excitement in that?

You know what will be exciting? Bruce's nativity, that's what.

I am in a bad mood from the very beginning of the day. I slam into the office, throw my things down, launch myself forcibly into my chair.

Indiana's head pokes around the side of her monitor.

'Would you like some chamomile tea?'

'No,' I snap.

I look across at Jack's desk. He is not there.

'Where's Jack?'

'I believe he is running late.'

'He's not been late in weeks. He's not going to turn up.'

'I believe he will.'

'And I believe you're going to owe me twenty pounds.' I scowl.

Indiana raises her eyebrows and I furrow my brow further.

'Would you like to… talk about it?' she asks with the slightest grimace that makes it perfectly clear she has no desire whatsoever to listen

'No,' I say, rudely. 'I'm going out.'

I slam the door on my way out of the room and stalk down the corridor looking for someone to terrorise.

Emily is walking towards me.

Excellent.

Emily has refused to give me the updated DataLet launch plan for the past two weeks. I step in front of her, blocking her way.

'Emily,' I say, icily, 'where is the updated DataLet launch plan?'

My anger radiates from me in waves. Emily leans back slightly and clears her throat.

'There's nothing new in it.'

'Fine. I want to check for myself.'

'It's not your programme of work.'

'Maybe not, but the timeline and distribution of the DataLet directly affects the timeline and scale of TRU, so I want to see the fucking update.'

Emily frowns.

'Please don't swear, Lina.'

'Give me the fucking update, *Emily.*'

Emily glares at me.

'If you swear at me one more time I shall report you to HR. Again.'

'Then just give me the update!' I yell. 'Why won't you give it to me?'

'Because I told her not to,' says Cameron, stepping out from the office next to where we are standing. 'Your noise is interrupting my meeting, Lina.'

The look of gleeful satisfaction on Emily's face is enough to make me want to punch her. I don't. I turn to Cameron.

'Sorry, Cameron,' I say. 'Emily could just have told me that.'

'Yes,' says Cameron, looking pointedly at Emily, 'she could have.'

Emily's face falls. I smile.

'Lina,' Cameron turns back to me, 'a word, please.'

I stop smiling.

Cameron sits on the edge of the meeting-room table.

I stand by the door.

'You have a question?' she says.

'Sorry?'

'You have a question about the DataLet launch?'

I clear my throat.

'I'd like the updated plan.'

She nods slowly.

'I asked Emily to keep the update confidential for now. We have made certain adjustments that I would like to remain classified.'

'Adjustments?'

'Nothing major – just an adaption allowing the user to wear the DataLet for longer so it can gather greater amounts of data …'

'Gather more data? That directly affects TRU. If there is more data, then we will need to—'

'This has nothing to do with TRU.'

I stop. Cameron looks calmly at me.

'The DataLet has numerous potential uses other than TRU. We are in negotiations with countries around the world who are interested in the technology for a variety of reasons ...'

I am about to ask who would be interested in buying the DataLet for any other use, but then I realise almost every government would. The DataLet can tell you literally everything about your citizens – which government wouldn't want that?

Something occurs to me.

'If you are marketing the DataLet on a separate platform from TRU, why make such a big thing about Indiana's Soulmate Pathway demonstration?'

Cameron wipes an invisible speck of dust from the desk.

'Because TRU is extremely important – it is our demonstration to the world that the DataLet can be worn willingly and that the gathered data is reliable.'

'Does Indiana know about this? That you have adapted her technology?'

Cameron looks up.

'She will know when she needs to know. When I want her to know ...'

She stands.

'You are doing an admirable job, Mrs Galaz – your team are performing remarkably well. I will currently find it very hard to choose who is going to lead the programme permanently between you and Emily. Don't make my choice easier for me.'

Her message is clear. Shut up and step out of my way.

I head straight back to the office to speak to Indiana.

Indiana isn't there. Emily is sat in my chair.

She smiles her icy smile at me as I enter the room.

'Just getting used to what it will feel like,' she says and looks around. 'It's so much nicer in here now that it's been cleaned up.'

I look at her for a moment, running responses through my head, thinking about how I can turn this conversation to my advantage. But, surprisingly, when I open my mouth it is not a smarmy response that comes out.

'I can't be bothered with this today,' I say and grab my ruck-sack from beside my desk.

This surprises Emily as much as it does me.

'What are you doing?' she asks.

'Going,' I reply.

Indiana is sat at a table in reception. She is trying to disguise it but I can tell she is watching the door, looking for Jack. I sit down next to her.

'You still think he is coming?'

'He's coming,' she says and stops looking at the door.

'You don't have to pay me the twenty pounds.'

She smiles tensely.

'I won't need to. He'll be here.'

I think she is deluded. I don't tell her that. I need to tell her about my conversation with Cameron, about how she is adapt-ing the DataLet. I am not sure she will care but I need to tell her.

'Why are you in such a terrible mood?' she asks before I can speak.

'What?'

'Is it hormonal?'

I shake my head.

'No. Bruce is in his daycare nativity play.'

'Bruce?'

'My son.'

'And?'

'And I want to go and see the play but it is in …'

I check my watch. '... forty minutes.'

'Then you should leave now.'

'I can't. Our Programme Board also starts in forty minutes.'

'You cannot do both.'

'No, I cannot,' I say.

'Which do you want to do?' Indiana asks.

'I don't know,' I say.

'Yes, you do.'

I reply without thinking. 'I want to go to the nativity.'

Indiana looks expressionlessly at me in the way that she does so well and I suddenly realise that I am going to do it, I am going to skive off work during a hugely important meeting to go and watch my son lie in a cardboard box. I stand up and begin my apology.

'I'll come back in after and check everything went okay, but you really don't need me for this. You and Jack have done all the work, I'm not even presenting ...'

Indiana glances towards the door. I follow her gaze.

'Shit,' I say. 'I can't. Jack's not here.'

I start to sit down, but Indiana holds up her hand and stops me.

'He'll be here,' she says. 'Go. We don't need you.'

I should stay and wait with her, make sure Jack shows. I should stay and tell her about Cameron and the DataLet. I have a choice to make between family and work. I have always chosen work before. I look at Indiana. She looks back evenly at me.

I make my choice. I go.

Indiana

Jack does not come to work and he does not come to the meeting.

'No Mr Hunter?' asks Cameron with a strange, knowing light in her eyes.

'No,' I say. 'He had a last-minute clash.'

I conduct the meeting by myself without Jack or Lina. I complete the demonstration perfectly, talk through Jack's part of the presentation, and answer questions succinctly and correctly.

I am alone and feel in some way that this is right. I created TRU alone, so the final stages of the project should be conducted alone as well.

This is how my life has always been and as it always will be. Nothing has changed – why should it? My routine was created so that I would function perfectly on my own, so that my life would be fulfilling, productive and worthwhile. I have manufactured the optimum environment in which to be alone. I have always been acceptably content when I am alone, and I will continue to be so.

My Bracelet buzzes.

I think you are sad.

Peggy is, as always, right.

Jack

I am in the office early on the morning of the twenty-third. I don't need to be, but I want to go through some of the latest results again. There was an imperfect match when I ran the data yesterday, a case where results had doubled up, and I want to make sure the anomaly has been cleared.

I am excited and nervous – excited because this is my first big presentation in two years and the first one I have actually cared about. I am nervous for exactly the same reasons. I don't want to fuck up. I don't want to let Indiana down.

The problem with not caring about anything for so long is that as soon as you do start caring again everything becomes very important – life-and-death important, almost. I have gone from not giving a shit to giving every single shit in the space of just a few weeks, and I am very poorly emotionally equipped to cope with this huge shift. I spent last night pacing my front room, practising my presentation and what I was going to say to Indiana afterwards. I was going to ask her out for a drink. Tell her that I know Daniel is supposed to be her soulmate, but that I like her and think she might like me too.

It took me nearly two hours to figure out that I couldn't do both – I couldn't give a presentation about her soulmate-finding program and then five minutes after the end essentially tell her that I think her program is total bollocks. Either TRU works or we do. It can't be both. Sweet, sweet irony.

At about 2 a.m., when I had ceased pacing and gone to bed to stare at my ceiling, I decided I would do something else. I would speak to her straight away when she got in, be honest and tell her how I felt, and ask her if she felt the same.

By 3 a.m. I was back downstairs again, drinking tea and annoying Biscuit. And it was at that dark and lonely hour of the night that I knew I couldn't tell her, I couldn't ever tell her, because I can't tell her without hurting her. If I tell her I like her and I think she likes me, I might break her belief in her program, and that would be worse than breaking her heart.

So, today, I will do my part of the presentation and then I will pretend not to care about Indiana. I've been pretending not to care for the past couple of years, so it should be easy.

When Indiana arrives at the office I try not to turn too quickly as she opens the door, to smile too brightly, to speak too eagerly, or display my affection for her in any way.

But I fail. I smile far too widely, my eyes light up, and my voice is happy and bright.

'Morning! Exciting day today, Indi.'

Except it isn't Indiana who comes into the office. It is Cameron.

Cameron takes in my eager face, my cheery voice, the fact I am in the office at 7 a.m., and she bursts out laughing.

'Oh you poor, delusional man! You *like* her!'

I don't say anything. I can't say anything – my heart is in my mouth. She claps her hands together.

'Oh, this afternoon is going to be fun!'

I try to force myself to attend the meeting. I tell myself that it doesn't matter what Cameron thinks or what she says or what she does – what matters is that I support Indiana. But I know I am lying to myself – the only thing that matters is what Cameron thinks or says or does, and the best way I can ensure she doesn't think, do or say anything that will hurt Indiana is to stay away. That is why I don't go to the meeting.

I go home and open a bottle of whisky.

Lina texts me: *You absolute shit. I thought you were her friend.*

I am her friend, I want to text back, that's why I did it. Except that is not true either – not entirely. I didn't go to the meeting because I wanted to protect Indiana, but also I am scared: scared of Cameron, scared of Indiana, scared of being lonely, scared of starting to feel things again. I am still exactly the same frightened and lonely man I was after Eve died. I haven't changed and Lina is right, I am a bad friend.

Shit. Friends. Tomorrow is Christmas Eve and Date Five for Indiana.

I message Lina back: *I am shit. But I'm going to try to fix it, and I need your help …*

Lina doesn't message back for two hours.

You'd better be asking for my help to buy her a fucking massive card that says, 'I'm sorry. I'm a shit' …

I'll do that after. I reply.

Indiana

'Hello Indiana. How was your day?'
'Fine.'
'How was the presentation?'
'Fine.'
There is a pause.
'I sent you a message.'
'I know.'
'I wondered if you ...'
I don't want to talk about it.
'PEGGY! I'm fine. It is all fine. Please be quiet. I need to work.'

I don't think I have ever shouted at Peggy before. Not properly, not actually meaning it. I go upstairs to my lab and we work in silence for an hour.

'It is the twenty-third day of your cycle,' says Peggy finally.
'I don't care,' I reply.

And I really don't. I feel no need to go out tonight, I do not wish to drink champagne, have no sexual desire, and the thought of going to the Meet Markets to find a potential partner exhausts me.

I go to bed at 9.30 p.m. and sleep badly.

On Christmas Eve I wake at 4 a.m. and am in my lab by 4.35. I do not need to go into the JaneDoe offices today, so can spend a much-needed day working on the QuantumX, but, when I sit down to work, my mind is blank and I cannot concentrate. I feel twitchy, so I go out for a very early run.

It is freezing outside. My Bracelet registers the temperature as minus two. The Thames is dark and sullen and the wind whips tiny shards of ice off the river, which pierce my skin. I jog around the back of my building so I do not see Frank or Alan, but I can hear Alan approaching as I near the river, the tap-tap-tap of his long claws on the pavement. He arrives in a cloud of hot, doggy breath and we immediately start running up the towpath together. I fear if I stand still too long I will freeze solid. I wonder how Frank is doing in his flimsy tent. I gave him more blankets a week ago, but I cannot imagine being warm inside a hundred blankets in this weather.

I run for twice as long as normal, but can still feel excess energy coursing through my veins so sprint the last mile back to my building, and at some point Alan falls behind. I retrace my steps to find him. He has hopped up onto a bench and is eating leftover chips out of a bag.

'Alan, yuck,' I say.

He turns his head and grins at me when I speak, and I sit down next to him. He is shivering, so I ignore his doggy stench and put my arms around him. It is so cold that, despite our shared body heat, I am shivering too within another couple of minutes. I can hear Alan's teeth chattering. I lay my cheek briefly on top of his matted head. 'This is not right,' I whisper into his fur.

Then I stand up. I know what I am going to do for the rest of the day.

'Come Alan,' I say. He follows me like a good dog.

'I am going to convert the reception area into a bedsit for Frank and Alan,' I say as I step out of the lift.

Peggy and I haven't spoken since they reminded me that yesterday was the twenty-third day of my cycle. There is a pause.

'Of course, Indiana,' replies Peggy. 'I have done a search for potential building companies and will start to contact them straight away.'

Peggy and I spend the rest of the day researching and designing the re-worked space and sourcing workmen. A ridiculous number of them are either unavailable or unwilling to work on Christmas Day, so the conversion will not be as quick as I would like.

I finish working at 4 p.m. with the conversion fully planned. I am meeting Daniel tonight for Date Five. Daniel is on holiday over Christmas so has asked that we meet both sets of friends in one night – his first and mine later. I have not yet told him that I have no friends to meet.

On my way out I drop off two flasks of coffee and three hot water bottles to Frank and Alan.

'It's going to be cold again tonight,' I say as I hand them to him. 'The black flask has coffee and the red has coffee with a bit of whisky. Peggy said you might like it. Don't give any of that one to Alan.'

He laughs. I don't – I know he shares everything with the dog.

He stuffs the hot water bottles into his coat and tucks one under Alan's blankets. I turn to leave.

'You look nice …'

I turn back.

'… are you wearing lipstick?'

'Lip gloss,' I snap.

He nods.

'Are you off celebrating?'

'Celebrating what?'

He laughs.

'Christmas!'

'No. I'm meeting some friends.' I say it without thinking but, as soon as it is out of my mouth ,the words hang in the air like the clouds of breath that vapour trail between us.

'Friends?' he says, raising his eyebrows.

I don't want to tell him that they are not my friends, that I don't have any friends to celebrate with, but I also don't want to lie to him, so I simply shrug. He beams like a proud parent.

'Well off you go and have some fun then!'

I nod and head off to get my bike. Just before I walk around the corner of the building I turn to look back at him. He is still smiling, drinking his coffee, patting Alan on the head and speaking softly to him. Frank has a friend, Frank has a best friend.

Lucky Frank.

Daniel's friends are very nice. They are polite and cordial. They ask me about my work and TRU and any other interests that I have outside of work and TRU. It is strange when someone else asks you to quantify your life, when you actually have to step back and take the measure of it. Daniel is quiet around his friends. He does not talk much, but rather lets the conversation swirl around him. It is an interesting social technique – he is physically present but does not have impact on the group. He is with them but not part of them. At one point one of his friends asks what it is that Daniel does for a job.

'How long have you known your friends?' I ask.

'Since primary school,' he says.

Daniel holds my hand, which makes my palm sweaty and means I have to drink with my left hand. But I know hand-holding is a sign of affection and togetherness, so I do not complain.

'Is Indi going to the New Year's Eve party with you?' one of Daniel's friends asks.

'Of course, she is,' Daniel says and smiles at me. I have no idea what he is talking about.

As we are leaving, I ask him about the party.

'It's Cameron Gardner's party,' he says. 'She arranges one each year. It's attended by the biggest names in technology and the biggest investors. I was invited this year and assumed you'd want to go.'

I don't tell him what Jack said 'assume' makes. Instead, I smile. He is right, of course I want to go to a social event with rich, important people.

I arrive at The George pub before Daniel. Daniel has taken a cab, but I have ridden my bike here. I am nervous. I do not know how Daniel will react to my lack of friendship group.

My Bracelet buzzes: **Take deep breaths through your nose and out of your mouth.** I send a message back: *YOU take deep breaths through your nose and out of YOUR mouth.* Peggy replies, **Haha.**

I sit at a table right by the door of the pub, directly on the main thoroughfare to the bar. The pub is busy with people celebrating just as Jack said it would be. I sink backwards into a poorly upholstered sofa and briefly wonder if any of them would accept money to pretend to be my friend.

I am being ridiculous. Who cares if I don't have friends? Daniel's friends don't even know what he does for a living. I have a fulfilling career, an active exercise schedule, and a regular sex life. I have nothing to be ashamed of. I will not be ashamed.

Daniel arrives and I decide I have had enough. I will tell him. I refuse to be shamed for putting my work first. My work is important.

Daniel sees me at the table and looks around.

'Your friends aren't here yet?'

Tell him now, Indiana.

'No. They might not make it. They're very busy. In fact I …'

The door bangs open and a blast of freezing air hits me. I shouldn't have chosen this table. I look up at Daniel to tell him the truth, and …

'Sorry we're late! It's an absolute bastard trying to get a cab on Christmas Eve, and it's just started bloody snowing again.'

Lina and her wife are standing next to Daniel.

Lina turns to him and sticks out her hand.

'Lina Galaz. I work with Indi at JaneDoe and this is my wife Connie. You must be Daniel.'

Daniel shakes Lina's hand and smiles.

The next few minutes pass in a blur. Both Lina and Connie bend and kiss my cheek with their icy lips, they laugh about the perils of Christmas Eve transport while shedding their winter layers. Before I can ask what is happening, Daniel and Connie are at the bar and Lina is sitting opposite me messaging someone to see if their baby is asleep.

'What are you doing here?'

Lina continues to tap on her phone.

'Jack.'

'Jack?'

She looks up from her phone.

'Jack told me it was Date Five, the one where he meets your friends.'

She continues to look at me levelly.

'But you're not … I mean we don't …'

She raises an eyebrow.

'Are you saying we're not friends? We hydrate and talk on a regular basis ...'

'No! I mean ... I didn't know. I didn't want to ask you in case ...'

I don't know what to say. I finally settle on, 'Thank you.'

Lina laughs.

'Finally! A thank you! It's a Christmas miracle!'

Connie yells from across the room.

'LINA! They don't have any Sipsmith!'

Lina rolls her eyes and stands up out of the chair.

'For fuck's sake. My first night of drinking in months and they don't even have decent gin.'

As Lina hurries towards the bar, the door to the pub opens once more and a flurry of snow enters the room. I shift down to the other end of the sofa away from the cold. Someone throws themselves onto the sofa next to me, their snow-covered arm touching mine. I flinch away and turn to see who would dare to disregard my personal space in this way.

Of course, it is Jack.

'Hi.'

He has snow in his hair and snowflakes on his eyelashes. I can feel the cold coming off him, but when his lips brush my cheek they are warm and burn into my skin like a brand. He looks at me, his eyes sober and serious.

'I'm sorry,' he says, 'I should have come to the meeting. I'd tell you why I didn't come, but you'd think I was deranged. I just ... I'm very sorry.'

I don't answer, I don't move, I am still staring at him, I cannot seem to stop. He stares back, not smiling, not laughing; just looking at me. I forget to breathe.

Someone coughs politely above us. I hardly hear it. They cough again. I turn my head. Everyone has arrived back from the bar, and Daniel is staring at Jack and me.

Jack springs into action, jumps up and sticks out his hand.

'Jack Hunter. I work with Indiana.'

Daniel shakes Jack's hand.

'Daniel,' says Daniel. 'Indiana's soulmate.'

There is a pause. I look at Daniel, surprised at his declaration, surprised at the ownership it implies. Jack looks briefly at me and then back to Daniel.

'Excellent,' says Jack. 'I'm going to the bar. Drink ...'

Jack looks at me. I shake my head.

'I've got her one.' Daniel hands me a whisky.

'Of course. Good job.' I can't tell if Jack is being sarcastic or really means it.

Lina leans over and whispers in my ear.

'There's room on the lesbian team any time you feel like you want to change sides.'

I laugh and choke on my whisky. Lina pats me on the back. Men are indeed very strange creatures. Jack goes to the bar, Daniel takes his place on the sofa next to me, and the evening commences.

This part of the date is far more pleasing than the time spent with Daniel's friendship group. Maybe it is the alcohol I have consumed, maybe it is that I know these people. Maybe it is because we are, indeed, friends. We talk about work and families and our pasts and our futures. I mainly talk about work but, surprisingly, enjoy listening to the rest of the conversations. There are even some that are about subjects other than work that I can join in, like when Connie talks about having grown up in Kent, her love of the sea and a long-held dream of living by a beach. I tell about my intention to live in Dungeness one day; it is a place she knows well.

'She's going to steal energy from the nuclear power station,' Lina says.

Connie raises her eyebrows.

'Isn't that highly illegal?'

I sigh.

'It's only illegal if you get caught,' I say once more.

'Which of course you wouldn't,' says Daniel, and smiles at me. I smile back, because that is what you do when someone is nice to you.

We talk about Christmas and where we will spend it; Lina and Connie have numerous family members at their house, Daniel is going to the Maldives, Jack will house hop between friends and family throughout the day, and I will spend my Christmas alone at HWJ Tower, as I always do. I will wake at my normal time, work in my normal way, and have a completely normal day. I do not tell them my plans as starkly as this, but still I find Lina looking at me with sadness. Or I think it is sadness – she is rather drunk, so it might just be her attempt to focus on something.

Daniel tells everyone where he and I will be spending New Year's Eve and they are suitably impressed.

'Employees don't get invited, ' says Lina. 'But I've heard it's pretty incredible.'

'No one from the entire office goes?' I ask.

Lina and Jack shake their heads, but then Lina drunkenly holds a hand up.

'Nope. I'm wrong. Emily. Emily got invited last year.'

Jack laughs.

'Yes! She did! She's got that picture on her desk ...'

Lina snorts with laughter.

'Oh God, I'd forgotten about the picture! She has a picture on her desk of her and Cameron taken at last year's party. She gets it out of her locker every morning. It's her most favourite thing!'

Jack and Lina laugh.

'Well,' says Daniel, 'Indiana and I think it will be a great opportunity to network and meet people, don't we?'

He turns to me. I nod politely.

'But what about your traditional New Year's Eve plans?' Jack says. 'The fireworks and flower duet.'

Everyone looks at me. I shrug. I am surprised Jack remembers.

'I can do something different this year.'

'Doesn't sound like you,' says Jack, frowning.

I clear my throat.

'It's fine. I don't mind. It will be nice.'

Daniel puts his arm around my shoulder. It feels heavy.

An hour later Daniel has to leave as he has an early flight in the morning. I walk outside with Daniel to say goodbye. I am not wearing my coat. It is snowing, but I do not feel cold.

'Do you think there is some science behind the beer coat phenomenon?' I say.

He looks at me quizzically.

'The beer coat phenomenon?'

'Yes. Where you don't feel cold after drinking alcohol. Maybe there is a scientific reason. Maybe it has something to do with the alcohol in your bloodstream being unable to freeze.'

He smiles.

'You really are strange,' he says, and he kisses me. His lips are cold.

Jack

It is nearly midnight. We are outside the pub, and Lina is hugging Indiana. It is unclear if Lina is doing this to show affection or to help her stand up. Lina is very drunk.

'First time she's had a proper drink since Bruce was born,' Connie tells me by way of explanation. Lina steps back, looks at Indiana solemnly.

'You ... shouldn't be alone at Christmas. No one ... should be alone at Christmas.'

Indiana smiles but Lina isn't finished.

'You ... should come to us for Christmas!'

Lina breaks into a beaming smile as Connie rushes forward to perform damage control.

'All right there my drunken love, time to go home ...'

Indiana smiles.

'It's fine Connie, thank you Lina, but I have work to do.'

Connie wraps her arms around Lina, but Lina wriggles out of her embrace and pulls her phone out of her pocket. She wrestles silently with technology for a moment and then holds her phone up for us all to see.

'I've sent you an invite! You have to come now!'

Connie rolls her eyes.

'Right. Let's get you in a cab before you invite anyone else to our already over-populated Christmas day. Bye everyone, Merry Christmas!'

Connie turns Lina towards the cab. Lina stumbles, Connie catches her and rolls her into the taxi and they are gone in a slurry of sludge and exhaust fumes.

Indiana turns to me and smiles. Most of her hair has escaped her normally pristine ponytail, her eyes glitter and her cheeks are flushed. I don't know if it is the alcohol she has consumed or if she has actually enjoyed herself this evening, and I don't care. I like it. I like her looking happy.

It is snowing heavily but Indiana doesn't seem to feel the cold; her coat and scarf are undone. She'll get pneumonia if she's not careful. I step forward and begin to do the toggles up on her duffle coat. She smiles up at me.

'This is a very sensible coat,' I say.

She smiles.

'Thank you. I researched the warmest coat before I bought it.'

'Do you ever do anything on impulse?'

She shakes her head.

'Nope.'

'Did you research the scarf too?'

She smiles fondly.

'No. Peggy got me the scarf.'

'And what did you get Peggy?'

She laughs. And then stops laughing and looks sad. She looks at me without smiling.

'I have to get home.'

She is business-like once more. I nod.

'Shall I get you a cab?'

'I have my bike.'

'It's really snowing. Wouldn't you be better in a cab? You can collect the bike tomorrow.'

'I've ridden in the snow before—'

'Yes, but you've had a bit to drink, and—'

She glares at me. I stop talking.

Indiana takes a step forward, slips on a hidden patch of ice, pinwheels her arms to stop from falling, doesn't succeed, and lands with a bump on her arse.

'*Ooof*,' she mutters.

It looks like it hurt. I reach a hand forward to help and then stop myself. She won't want my help. I stand back.

Indiana puts her hands down on either side of herself, pushes herself up, and falls immediately back down again. She tries again – same result. She tries once more, gets one foot beneath her, and then sprawls forward. I can't help it – I am grinning.

She will not give up. She twists over onto her hands and knees, gets one foot firmly placed on the ground, pushes herself up and takes a slow swan-dive to the side as both feet slip out from under her. I am laughing silently, tears are streaming down my face and I am clutching my stomach. I try to stop but can't – it is the most hilarious thing I have ever seen.

Indiana grimaces, sets her mouth in a thin line of determination, and tries again. This time she lands flat on her back like a stranded turtle. Laughter bubbles up inside my throat and if I don't let it out I will choke. She glares up at me and my laughter escapes in a huge roar that is much louder than expected.

I pull it together enough to offer her my hand to help her stand up, but, when she takes it and tries to pull herself up, I slide slowly across the pavement towards her and we both end up halfway in the gutter. For a moment she stares at me silently as I scrabble about trying to gain purchase, but then her eyes crinkle, her mouth splits open, and her laughter joins mine. We lie on the ground and laugh for nearly ten minutes as the good people of London step delicately around the two drunken people rolling happily on the ice.

I haven't had a sip of alcohol all night.

When we finally stand up again we are filthy, covered in sludge and dirt. She allows me to order her a cab and, before it arrives, I put her bike helmet on her head.

'Just in case you fall over again and I'm not there. We have to protect that brilliant brain of yours,' I tell her.

The cab arrives. She stands on her tiptoes and brushes her lips against my cheek, the softest flutter against my skin. She reaches to open the door to the cab.

'Indiana . . . '

She stops and turns back to look at me.

'. . . Knock knock,' I say.

She smiles.

'Who's there?'

'Europe.'

'Europe who?'

'No. *You're* a poo!' I say and grin at her.

She throws her head back and laughs. It is one of the most joyous sounds I have ever heard.

'Happy Christmas Jack,' she says, still smiling.

'Happy Christmas Indi,' I reply.

I watch her go until I can't see the cab any more, and then I walk home.

Christmas Day

Indiana

Something is happening. A noise. A piercing, shrieking noise. It might be the end of the world.

I am ensconced within my duvet, in a cosy nest of comfort that I have formed around me. My head is pounding and I feel that if I move I might vomit. I slowly lift the corner of the duvet and peek out. I cannot see anything, it is pitch black. Why is it so dark? What is that infernal noise? It must be some sort of house alarm. Fire? Intruder?

'Peggy …'

The sound that comes from my mouth is less a word and more an animalistic croak, a squawk for help. I try again, louder.

'Peggy!'

The alarm stops.

'Happy Christmas!'

Peggy.

'What … was that noise?'

Talking hurts my brain.

'It's your alarm.'

'What alarm?'

'Your wake-up alarm. I've never had to use it before.'

'It's Christmas Day and still dark outside! Why on earth are you waking me up?'

'Oh yes. It is not actually dark outside, I darkened the windows when you went to sleep …'

Peggy removes the window tint and the room blazes to the intensity of a lighthouse bulb. My brain explodes. The sun is nuclear bright and bounces off every surface because, overnight, the world has turned white.

'It has snowed,' said Peggy. 'It is pretty.'

I hold my hand up in an attempt to ward off some of the sparkle, and stumble over to the window. Peggy is right. Snow has blanketed London like something from a Christmas movie.

It is glorious.

I groan, turn, and stumble back to bed.

'It's beautiful, but will still be there in three hours. Remind me never to drink again. I might be dying.'

I fall back into the softness of my bed. I need more sleep and then three pints of water and judicious pain management.

'You can't go back to bed.'

'What? Why?'

My voice is muffled by pillows, but Peggy still hears me.

'You have an invitation to spend the day at Lina's house in your diary. At least I think it is an invitation. It says "G0-TOO-LINAS-4-CRSTMS".'

'That's not a real invitation,' I say into my pillow.

'How do you know?'

'I know.'

'Are you sure? It would be rude not to go if it is real—'

I groan into my pillow and turn over to stare at my ceiling. It is the same as it was when I brought HWJ Tower, I have never changed or painted it.

'I want to get some stars for my ceiling.'

'Yes Indiana.'

'And I don't want to go to Lina's.'

'I think you should go.'

I groan again. Peggy is silent.

'Are you enjoying my pain?'

'I have no emotions, so that would be impossible.'

'*Hmpf!*'

'... but I am feeling strangely warm in one part of my circuitry ...'

'What?'

I sit up. My head bangs.

'That was a joke Indiana.'

'I know what a joke is Peggy.'

Or at least I hope I know what a joke is, because I made one last night and will look like a fool in front of Jack if it is not funny. I do not want to look like a fool in front of Jack. I must never drink again. I groan loudly.

'You will need to take gifts.'

I stand, stumble into my kitchen, and open cupboards looking for the painkillers.

'Why?'

'Because it is polite. I have already purchased age-appropriate gifts for the children who will be there and have left three choices of gifts for Lina and her wife on your screen.'

I look at the screen – flowers, chocolate, and a strange rainbow-coloured vase.

'The vase is representative of the LGBTQ flag.'

I have very little interior design taste, but even I know that the vase is horrible and incredibly distasteful.

'Remind me to update your interior design sensitivity settings when I am not dying ... AND WHERE ARE THE PARACETAMOL?'

'There is no need to shout. They are in the far left cupboard.'

I take two tablets by sticking my arid mouth straight underneath the tap.

'Thank you Peggy.'

There is a noticeable pause.

'You are welcome Indiana.'

Another pause.

'Are you feeling okay?'

'What?'

'You are being very polite.'

'I'm hungover.'

'Of course.'

I look at Peggy's gift suggestions again. If I am going to add to Lina's Christmas Day stress I should at least get her a present that is useful. Then, despite alcohol-induced brain shrinkage, I have a brilliant idea.

'Peggy, I have the ideal present for Lina, but it's going to take some research. Are you okay to do it while I shower?'

Pause.

'You are very hungover, Indiana. I am worried about you.'

This makes me smile.

'Thank you Peggy. Happy Christmas.'

'Happy Christmas Indiana.'

Lina

I love Christmas.

I love the songs, the gifts, the food, the drink, the fun and the frolics. Even this year – when I am busier, more stressed, have less time than ever to organise things – I still love Christmas. I love it when our house is busy with people having fun. Christmas is the one time of year I do not try to avoid my family.

And I'm good at Christmas, really good – it's why Mama and Uncle Benny have come to us for the last couple of years rather than go to one of my brothers, who have much bigger houses and more seats. I throw an excellent Christmas Day. I start planning from mid-October; buying gifts and decorations and cards and food and drink, and putting up the tree, creating a new Christmas playlist, working out where everyone will sit, and, this year, planning how to cook Christmas dinner for nine people in a kitchen only suited to cooking for two.

Christmas is the perfect family day for all.

And yet, every Christmas Day that Connie and I have hosted, at around 11 a.m., I stand in our kitchen surrounded by half-cooked food and mess and I think to myself, 'Why do I fucking bother?'

By 11 a.m. the presents are open, the kids will be jacked up on sugar, Mama will have had enough Bucks Fizz to be feeling 'honest', but not enough to stay the fuck out of my kitchen, Uncle Benny will be grumbling in the corner about being forced to eat this *gringo cagada* rather than his beloved *bacalao*, and Connie … well, Connie will be asking me what she should do in a way that lets me know Connie doesn't actually want to do anything but also doesn't want to piss me off on this most special of days.

The kitchen will be like a sauna, with the top and the bottom ovens on full blast, I will be elbow deep in potato and carrot peelings, and wondering what had possibly possessed me to make my own Yorkshire puddings rather than buying them from Aunt Bessie like every other bastard out there.

And this year? Well, this year I'm also pumping breast milk at the same time as cooking for nine – breast milk that I will then dump down the sink because I am convinced it is less life-giving goodness and more 60 per cent proof alcohol.

Happy fucking Christmas.

The noise from the front room is cacophonous. My brother Mikey, his wife, Diane, and their three kids have arrived for the day. Connie has brought them a new game for Christmas and all the kids are playing it, loudly. Mrs Hardcastle from number 42 is banging on the wall periodically, trying to get the noise to quieten down. Some chance, I think to myself. I am sitting on the stairs with Bruce, trying to feed him from a bottle. He doesn't want to be fed from a bottle, he wants my boob, so I give up trying to feed him and shove a dummy into his mouth to keep him quiet. Milk is leaking from my nipples onto my festive top. I want to cry, my head is banging, and I am half tempted to go around to Mrs Hardcastle's and see if the noise really is as bad as she seems to think, and, if not, sneak upstairs for a nap.

The doorbell rings. I can't be bothered to answer it so just yell, 'It's Christmas Mrs Hardcastle! There's going to be some noise!'

It rings again.

I heave myself off the stairs and fling the door open, unsure whether I am going to yell at Mrs Hardcastle or beg for refuge.

'What do you ... Oh ...'

It is Indiana.

Indiana, two old people, and a whole load of boxes, bags and presents.

'Shit.'

The word is out of my mouth before I can stop it. I vaguely remembered drunkenly asking Indiana to come for Christmas when I woke up this morning, but Connie said she had replied that she was busy working so I shouldn't worry. Connie was wrong.

'You're leaking on the baby.'

She points at Bruce, who now has milky residue on his face.

'Thank you. Merry Christmas to you too.'

'Merry Christmas.'

We stand awkwardly for a moment. Bruce's dummy falls out of his mouth and onto the floor. I pick it up and wipe it briefly on my top to clean it before popping it back in.

'That's disgusting,' Indiana says.

'Perfectly fine and hygienic,' I reply.

Indiana grimaces, then moves to the side and points at the two old people.

'This is Mrs and Mrs Bunnings. They're your Christmas present.'

I stare blankly at Mr and Mrs Bunnings.

'What?'

Mrs Bunnings bustles forward and touches Bruce's cheek like a long-lost aunt.

'Don't worry love. We'll take over from here, you have a sit down for a bit … or maybe a nice bath.'

Her cockney accent is so strong that I laugh. It must be false. She continues to smile warmly at me until I am forced to smile back. She takes this as some sort of consent and ushers her husband into the house in front of her.

'Er, sir, Mr … I wouldn't open that if …'

Too late. Mr Bunnings opens the door to the kitchen. Steam and grease and chaos greet him.

If he is shocked he doesn't show it. Mrs Bunnings smiles again.

'Call us Mr and Mrs B, love, everyone does.'

Mrs B pulls Mr B into the kitchen and slams the door shut.

Indiana, Bruce and I stand on the doorstep and stare after them.

'Does everyone call them Mr and Mrs B?'

Indiana shrugs.

'I have no idea. I only met them forty minutes ago.'

'Who the hell have you just sent into my kitchen then?'

She looks calmly at me.

'They work for the top domestic agency in London and I hired them for the day. I thought that if you were as hungover as I am you might appreciate a bit of help.'

'You can't make them work on Christmas Day! It's slave labour!'

'Fine. Want me to send them back?'

I stare at the closed kitchen door. Do I really want to go back in there?

'No. Don't send them back.'

'Good. Now you should have a bath.'

She holds her hands out to take Bruce. I frown and pull him protectively towards my chest.

'Give me the baby, Lina.'

'I don't want to. You might put him on the doorstep again, and it's snowing.'

'I won't put him on the doorstep. I promise. Give me the baby.'

'He needs burping.'

'Then I shall take him straight to Karen—'

'Connie.'

'… Connie. I shall take him straight to Connie. Go upstairs and have a bath. You smell of gin and turkey fat.'

When I come downstairs an hour later a small Christmas miracle has taken place.

The dining table has been decorated, and furniture has been moved so that ten chairs now fit comfortably around it. Six of the chairs are filled with happy, laughing people.

Bruce is fast asleep in a new swing chair. The kids are playing on a SwitchHolo that we didn't own when I went upstairs for a bath. Connie, Mikey and Diane are chatting, and Mama and Uncle Benny are sitting on either side of Indiana, gabbing away in Spanish, with Indiana nodding along.

'Lina! Look what Auntie Indiana bought us!' My niece holds up the SwitchHolo, face beaming.

I nod tersely.

'I can see. *Auntie* Indiana, a word please?'

We stand in the hallway.

'A SwitchHolo?'

Indiana shrugs.

'It is the most wanted toy for children their age.'

I frown.

'I don't care. You can't buy them expensive gifts like that.'

'Why not?'

Why not indeed, Lina?

'Because … because, they'll get used to it. And what happens when they want something like this again next year?'

'Then I'll buy them something like this next year.'

I put my hands on my hips to show I mean business.

'And what if I don't invite you for Christmas next year?'

'Then you'll have some explaining to do to your nieces and nephews and I'll get a nice quiet Christmas.'

'*No sabia que hablabas español?*'

'*Un poco. America del Sur es un mercado emergente para nosotros.*'

I can feel myself blushing.

'I've bitched about you in Spanish!'

'Yes, you have,' says Indiana.

It might not be the best Christmas Day ever, but it is definitely in my top five.

I have done nothing.

Mrs and Mr B cook, clean and organise everything. The food is excellent and plentiful.

'What is this?' Indiana says, holding up a pig in a blanket on the end of her fork.

'It's a pig in a blanket,' I answer. 'A sausage wrapped in bacon.'

'It should be called a heart attack wrapped in a heart attack,' she grumbles.

'Just eat it,' I say.

She does. And then she has four more.

Bruce has a cold and is snotty and needy. He wakes halfway through Christmas dinner but, like the good fairy in Christmas tales of old, Mrs B swoops in.

'It's okay,' I say, 'he just gets a bit clingy at this time of the day, I'll sort him.'

'Don't be silly, let me.'

Mrs B reaches across to take Bruce.

'Honestly Mrs B, that's very lovely of you, but he'll only settle for me, and ...'

I stop talking as I watch Bruce snuggle into Mrs B's ample bosom. I swear I hear him actually sigh with happiness as he nestles in contentedly.

'I can take him for the afternoon. I'd like to. Do you have stored breast milk?'

I might have to employ this woman permanently.

'In the freezer,' I say, and take a big gulp of champagne.

Indiana stays much later than I thought she would. She plays games – and loses ungraciously – with the kids, is far too honest to Mama and Uncle Benny about what goes on at the Meet Markets, and almost manages to pretend she is interested when she chats with Mikey about the removal business – only giving herself away by failing to hide a huge yawn at the end of the conversation.

Later, we stand on the doorstep and wait for Indiana's cab.

'Thank you for inviting me today Lina. It has been very ... warm,' Indiana says.

I think it is a compliment.

'You're welcome,' I reply.

She turns to look at me.

'You are my friend, Lina. I like you even when we are not working together.'

Indiana holds out her hand for me to shake.

A warm feeling envelops me. I bypass her hand and pull her to me for a hug.

'Okay, don't take it too far,' she mumbles into my hair.

But she hugs me back.

After Indiana gets into her cab, I go back into the house, sit on the sofa next to Con and wrap my arms around her.

'Well, that was different' Connie says.

'What was different?' I reply.

'Today,' she says. 'Today was different. A change from our normal Christmas Day.'

I think about the day and then smile to myself. I kiss the top of Connie's head.

'Maybe change can be good,' I say.

Indiana

It is nearly midnight when I arrive back at HWJ Tower. Frank is still up, hunched in the entrance to his tent, wrapped in bundles of blankets, breath rattling in and out of his smoke-scarred lungs. Alan comes prancing up to me, and I laugh and ruffle his ears.

'Merry Christmas Alan, Merry Christmas Frank.'

'Merry Christmas my arse ...'

Frank is grumpy. I have never seen Frank grumpy.

'If I wanted lots of noise on Christmas Day I'd have gone to my sister's and hung out with her and her forty-five grandchildren – what on earth is going on in there?'

Frank points over his shoulder into the reception area. My renovations, I had forgotten.

'Oh, just some building updates.'

'And they couldn't have started on the twenty-seventh?'

I shrug.

'Sorry, I just thought it best to get them done as quickly as possible.'

Frank grumbles.

'There are other people who live here too you know!'

'Yes, but those "other people" don't pay the rent.'

He grumbles again and mutters under his breath.

'I didn't know you had a sister,' I say.

Frank shrugs.

'Could you not have spent the day with her?'

'I could have spent the day with a lot of people. I chose not to.'

He looks up at me with his bright eyes.

'There's a difference between being alone and being lonely. I'm alone because I want to be. What about you?'

'I'm not lonely,' I say automatically.

But as soon as I say it, I wonder if it is still true. Today was noisy and chaotic and smelly and hot and exhausting and I enjoyed it a lot. Tomorrow seems … emptier.

'Here …'

I snap out of my reverie to see Frank holding something out to me. I take it automatically.

It is a card and a tiny present wrapped in crumpled Christmas paper.

'Oh … I didn't get you … I mean I did, but it's not …'

'It's not from me,' Frank says gruffly. 'It's from Alan.'

I turn the card and present over in my hands.

'It's to say thank you for running with him.'

I open the card first. A flimsy 'Happy Christmas' card with a muddy paw print inside. The present is a plastic key ring with a pot attached; inside the pot is some grey hair.

'It's some of Alan's fur in the pot. So you can remember him.'

I peer into the pot. It is slightly greasy.

'That's … disgusting.'

Frank shrugs, grunts, and starts to shuffle back towards his tent.

'Frank …'

Frank stops, and, with just the slightest hesitation, I bend down and kiss him quickly on the cheek. He smells of cigarettes, dog, and the river.

'… thank you. It's very kind.'

It is the only Christmas card and present that I have received since I was fifteen years old.

Peggy is on me as soon as I step out of the lift.

'Someone has had an interesting day …'

This must be what it is like to have parents that care about your every move – it is both warming and slightly irritating.

'Is that person me?'

I am still a bit drunk.

'No, it's the Queen of Sheba.'

'*Haha.*'

'Don't you *haha* me young lady, you're drunk, and what time do you call this?'

I laugh, and there is a slight pause before, for the second time that day, the most horrendous booming noise emits from Peggy's voice-box. I clap my hands over my ears.

'STOP IT!'

The noise stops.

'What was that?' I say, appalled.

'Now that I am experimenting with humour I have been trying out different laughs to see which one best fits my personality,' Peggy says.

'It's not that one.'

'Noted.'

I fling myself down onto the sofa and rub my still-bloated stomach.

'Did you have a nice time?'

'Yes, I did.'

'Would you like me to tell you how many calories and units of alcohol you have consumed today?'

'No!'

'Will you be needing me to set the alarm again in the morning?'

'Probably for the best.'

I sit up.

'Peggy …'

'Yes Indiana?'

'Can you set it for 7 a.m. rather than 5 … please?'

There is the tiniest of pauses.

'Yes Indiana.'

I lie back again and sigh happily.

'Indiana …'

'*Mmm?*'

'You have a package.'

'A what?'

'A package was delivered for you today.'

'Today?'

'Yes. Dropped off by Jack. He is as nice in person as his voice sounds.'

The package is on the front table.

'Are you okay? Your heart is racing,' says Peggy.

Inside the package is a book. A joke book. It has been inscribed – *I like making you laugh. Happy Christmas. Love Jack xxx*

I pretend to myself that I am happy because it is the second Christmas present I have received this year.

Love Jack.

I sleep with the book by my bedside.

Jack

I wasn't lying, I have lots of options for Christmas Day. I get a large number of invitations – my parents, my sister, friends, casual acquaintances – everything from family-filled events to chic dinners, intimate evenings to massive parties. I never accept any of them. I see my family on Christmas Eve and then spend Christmas Day on the sofa with Biscuit.

Eve died on Christmas Day.

She didn't want to. 'I'm trying to die before Christmas, I don't want to ruin it for everyone,' was one of the last things she gasped before they intubated her. She'd tried to laugh after she said it, but the laugh turned into a wheeze, and that was the last noise she ever made.

I should visit her grave on Christmas Day, but I can never face it. I just want to lie on the sofa, cuddle Biscuit, fail to eat my crappy microwaveable Christmas-dinner-for-one, and then scrape it into Biscuit's bowl. Biscuit loves Christmas – cuddles and turkey dinner. It's her best day of the year.

This year I wake up late, stay in my pyjamas, make cups of tea, read a book and then heat my dinner-for-one in the microwave and give it all to Biscuit, as usual. But then I feel restless. The joke book I bought for Indiana that I forgot to give her last night sits on my wonky coffee table.

I look at the book and then at Biscuit.

'What should I do?'

Biscuit says nothing back. I take it as a sign.

Ten minutes later I have left the house on Christmas Day for the first time in three years. I am wearing jeans and boots, but still have my pyjama top on under my coat – I did not want to give myself time to change my mind about coming out. It is around three in the afternoon, and the streets of London are snowy and silent. It is crisp and fresh and invigorating. I don't know what is going to happen when I reach Indiana's house – I haven't planned that far ahead – but I am glad I came out.

I have hacked into the JaneDoe payment system to get her address, and it takes me to an office block in the middle of an industrial estate by Dulwich Pier. She must have given JaneDoe another false address like the one she gave to Daniel. What is she – some kind of international spy? Trying to deliver the book was a bad idea. I am freezing and in the middle of nowhere. I'm going home.

But then I see it – a tent in an office doorway, and out of the tent peeks a furry, bearded face. A dog named Alan.

'Alan?' I call.

The dog comes towards me cautiously. Sniffs my hand, decides I am all right, and goes back into the tent. Alan's face is replaced by another, human this time.

'What do you want?'

The man's face is old but his eyes and voice are sharp. I step back.

'I'm looking for Indiana Dylan. Does she … live here?'

He eyes me suspiciously and then nods his head to the telecom system on the wall.

'You'd better call Peggy.'

'Peggy is here on Christmas Day?'

He nods, sits back, continues to watch me.

I press the intercom button. It is answered immediately.

'Hello?'

Peggy's pleasing Scottish voice, kind and measured.

'Peggy?'

'Yes.'

'Hi. I'm Jack. I'm looking for Indiana Dylan. Does she live here please?'

There is a pause. The tramp watches me.

'She's not here right now.'

'Oh …'

'Can I take a message?'

'No. I … er … have something for her.'

'Please place it in the deposit box and I shall see she gets it.'

'I'd rather give it to her in per—'

'She's not here,' interrupts the tramp. 'And she doesn't like visitors.'

He is scowling at me now.

'It's okay Frank,' comes the calming voice. 'Please place your item in the deposit box. I promise Indiana shall receive it as soon as she returns.'

I carefully place the book into the deposit box.

'Thank you. Merry Christmas, Jack Hunter.'

'Merry Christmas, Peggy.'

I step back and look up at the building. The view from the top must be incredible.

'You can go now.'

The tramp has had enough of me.

I am very, very cold, so I walk home briskly to try to get some feeling into my feet again. I am hungry and am going to stop at my corner shop and try to buy the ingredients to rustle up a proper meal. Biscuit will not be getting leftovers.

It is only as I am standing in the shop, pondering if I can be bothered to make Yorkshire puddings from scratch, that I realise Peggy called me Jack Hunter.

I never told her my full name.

Lina

Boxing Day is always spent at Mama's house. The kids bring their new toys, the adults bring leftover food, booze and hangovers, and Mama provides paper plates and cups. I don't like Boxing Day. On Boxing Day I am always hungover, exhausted, and already thinking about going back to work on the 27th. Boxing Day is too loud, too busy, too frenetic, and has too many cold cuts of meat sweating in bamboo containers on Mama's dining table.

But, this year? This year is different. Maybe it's because Mr and Mrs B did all the work yesterday so I am not exhausted. Maybe it's because Mrs B made me drink some horrific homemade anti-hangover concoction before she left the house, which has, miraculously, worked. Maybe it's because yesterday I saw Christmas through someone else's eyes for the first time – someone who doesn't have family to be with, to be loved by. Whatever the reason, this year, I am loving Boxing Day.

I play with the kids, chat with my brothers, stuff myself full of four different types of meat and three different vegan versions of turkey. I sit in the corner and feed Bruce directly from my boob for the first time in thirty-six hours. I stroke his downy hair and smell his cheesy head, he chews on my nipple with a new tooth. I don't mind.

'Are you okay, *querida?*'

I look up to find Mama smiling down on me.

'I am.'

'Good.'

She sits down heavily in the chair next to me.

'Is your back okay, Mama?'

'*Si, ahora soy vieja.*'

I laugh.

'You're not old!'

'Well, I am not young, *chica*.'

Mama looks across at her grandchildren playing.

'I worry about not seeing them grow up, about not being here for you kids as you get older,' Mama says.

She turns to me.

'But … it makes me happy that you have each other, that I know you will be here for each other to celebrate and be together.'

I shrug.

'Mama, I had some people over for Christmas Day, it hardly makes me family member of the year.'

Mama shakes her head.

'Don't do that,' she says.

'Don't do what?'

'Don't throw away our feelings. Don't joke about what you mean to our family. You are part of us and we are part of you. Don't try and brush that away. We love you.'

I think of Indiana, all alone in the world with none of this chaos and none of this joy, with no one to anchor her in place. I can't imagine what it must be like.

'I love you too,' I say.

We leave the party just after 9 p.m. Bruce is asleep and Connie drunkenly swaying, so I hire a StreetCar rather than try to carry them both onto the AutoBus. I rarely drive now – most people rarely drive now – so when I do it is a treat. Bruce and Connie are both fast asleep, it is warm and cosy inside the StreetCar, and I cruise silently through the empty streets of London. I am nearly home when I realise I don't want to stop driving – I am perfectly content in this little car, driving on empty roads with everyone I love most cocooned in here with me.

I make a snap decision and head for the motorway. Street-Cars are expensive, and that expense becomes astronomical if you drive them for over ten miles, but I don't care. I want to see if all the fuss about Dungeness is right, I want to see the sea.

The roads are almost completely devoid of cars; the only other moving vehicles I encounter are the wagon trucks, lumbering slowly in the inside lane, never speeding over their regulation 50 miles-per-hour. They are getting longer each year as engines become more powerful – I pass one that is fifteen wagons long. I wave to the driver, he ignores me.

Because of the lack of traffic I reach Dungeness in just under two hours. The StreetCar tells me my journey so far has cost £426. It is nearly midnight. There are no street lights, few houses and no other cars or people. I park on a scrap of waste-land opposite the beach. The wind is so strong I can feel it shaking the car. The moon is full, the stars sweep across the sky, and the nuclear power station glows softly in the distance. It is wild and beautiful.

I force my door open, step out of the car and am almost blown off my feet. The wind feels as if it is trying to rip the clothes from my body, sand is whipped into my face, and I have to bend at the waist and dig my feet into the ground to move forward. The noise of the sea is deafening, a rushing, rhythmic roar beyond anything I have heard before. I am freezing within a minute, but I am determined. I want to see the sea.

I battle forward into the black night, staring at the ground, carefully placing one foot in front of the other, inching towards my goal. Then, just when I think I am too cold and can go no further I look up and there it is. The sea. The magnificent, wild, ferocious sea. The waves break just yards in front of me, sea spray pelts my face. My cold is forgotten, my anxiety, work, my life, everything is forgotten, pounded out of me by this relentless beast. My mind is blank, there is only the sea. I want more of it, to be part of it. It is calling to me. I take a step forward and … someone grabs my arm.

I am yanked from my trance. I spin around.

It is Connie, shaking with cold in the freezing night. She grabs me and pulls me to her, yelling into my ear.

'Where the hell are we and what the FUCK are you doing?'

Connie never swears. I look up at her. Her hair is wild, her eyes filled with sleep and confusion, and my first thought after the sea-induced blankness is 'I love her.'

It is all so clear.

I grab Connie to me and kiss her, kiss her salty lips, her face, her wild hair. She kisses me back.

'I LOVE YOU!' I scream over the sea and the wind.

We stumble back to the StreetCar, turn the heating up to the highest setting, kiss some more.

'I love you,' I say.

She kisses me on the nose.

'I love you, too,' she says, 'but you are supposed to be in work in six hours, and' – she looks at the StreetCar screen – 'have you really just spent £500 on a StreetCar?'

I laugh, kiss her again.

'I'm not going into work today. I want to stay here for a few days,' I say.

And right there in that moment, I realise I have been worrying about my life changing, about me changing, but it is already too late. I have changed. This is not me, not how I would normally act, but I don't care. Right here, in this moment, I am happy.

Jack

I go into work on December 27th. In fact, I go into work every day between Boxing Day and New Year, because I am lonely. I am lonely and tired of sitting at home on my own. I hope that Indiana will be in the office and I know that Lina definitely will be. But Indiana doesn't come in and nor does Lina. So, instead of sitting at home on my own, I go into the office and sit there on my own.

The building is practically empty, the café is shut, reception deserted, all seats posterior-free. The only other person that I encounter is Emily. She gets into the lift with me one lunchtime.

'I've been in since 6 a.m,' she says. 'Just had to pop out to get a coffee because the café is closed and you know that I run on caffeine.'

She gives a piercing giggle, like glass shattering on a tile floor.

'Don't normally see you in here at this time of year?'

I give her a tight smile.

'I'm working on something with a tight deadline.'

She smiles again. It doesn't reach her eyes.

'Didn't know that you cared about deadlines.'

'Neither did I,' I say.

'Is it for TRU?'

I nod. She smiles again, more of a beam this time. It still doesn't touch her eyes.

'I shall be leading the whole programme from the end of January.'

This is the sort of conversation that didn't used to bother me, that I would let wash over me like a small wave of noise. But now I find my brain actively engaged, and it is hard to keep my mouth from joining in. I turn to look directly at Emily.

'I thought you and Lina were both in the running to lead, and Cameron hasn't decided yet.'

She gives a coquettish shrug.

'Of course she hasn't.'

She winks at me. I don't wink back. I've never disliked Emily – I've never really thought about Emily at all – but I dislike her now. A lot.

The lift arrives at Emily's floor and she steps out.

'Can you get Lina to call me when she gets in? I could do with a quick catch-up.'

I nod. It is only as the doors shut that I realise I have, unwittingly, told her that Lina is not yet in the building. Amateur.

Back in Lina's office I stand and stare out of the window while I drink my coffee. I wasn't lying to Emily about why I am in the office, I do have a tight deadline to meet. The bug that I was trying to rid TRU of before Christmas is still there, and it is increasing as the database expands. The last time I ran the data it was occurring in more than every 600 matches. I cannot find where the bug is – the data is correct, the coding is correct, but the program is still producing more than one soulmate per candidate in some cases. It is a real issue and could cause huge problems if not resolved. I need to talk to Indiana about it urgently and that is one of the reasons I wish she was in the office … one of the reasons, but not the only one.

I can no longer deny to myself how much I like Indiana. More than like Indiana.

I know that I shouldn't like her. That there is no point in liking her – but, after such a long time of feeling nothing, it is nice to feel something again – even if that feeling is not reciprocated. I feel I have been curled up into a ball for the last three years and now I am unfurling myself. I am stretching out again, getting feeling back into my limbs and back into my heart.

My watch buzzes.

Thank you for the book. Now that I have my own joke book you no longer need to tell me your terrible jokes.

I smile.

My watch buzzes again.

Merry Christmas. Love Indiana

Love Indiana.

Love Indiana – that can't be a mistake. She wouldn't write that as a normal greeting. She never puts any sign-off on messages – just leaves her name. Love Indiana.

She likes me too.

And then I realise what the problem with TRU might be. If I am right, it is a big problem, a huge problem, a problem that means the end of the entire programme of work.

I have to find out.

I sit back down at my desk and don't get up again for the next five hours.

Indiana

'Get out of bed please.'

It is 7 a.m. on December 30th and I am still in bed under my duvet. Peggy is not happy about this and has already un-tinted the windows.

'Do you want me to have to use the alarm?' Peggy says, louder this time.

I stick my head out from under the duvet and squint against the early morning light.

'No! Don't use the alarm.'

'Then get out of bed please.'

I roll over, wrapping myself in my duvet.

'I don't feel well.'

'Your vital signs are normal and your white blood cell count is perfect. You are not ill.'

'I really don't feel well.'

I am not lying. I don't feel well. I have stopped working – three days ago I received the last components I need to complete the QuantumX, and I have yet to install them. My head is fuzzy, I can't concentrate, I have a weird ache in my chest and a huge craving for chocolate – not even good chocolate – any kind of chocolate product. Peggy has refused to order me any more, so I had to run to a shop with Alan yesterday and get chocolate illicitly like some sort of addict.

And I sent Jack that awful message. I used the word 'love'. Like a besotted teenager. What is wrong with me? I must be ill.

'Get out of bed.'

'I can't.'

'You can and you will or I will electrify your bed frame.'

'You can't do that.'

'Can't I?'

I'm not sure whether Peggy can or not. I am not sure about a lot of things with Peggy these days. I sit on the edge of my bed and sigh. My life used to be controlled, rhythmic and straightforward. I had a plan and focus and a future, and now I am sitting on the side of my bed at 7.15 a.m. wearing bed socks because my feet have felt cold lately.

'What is wrong with me?'

I do not even realise I have spoken out loud until Peggy answers.

'Well, I have checked your symptoms with over 1.3 million medical websites and you are either suffering from a non-bronchial case of consumption or you are lovesick.'

'Lovesick?'

'Consumed with feelings of love for someone you cannot have, lethargy, loss of concentration, an aching pain in the chest, a need to consume products that encourage dopamine release – chocolate or romantic films for example ...'

'That is ridiculous,' I say, 'I have never watched a romantic movie.'

'That is true,' says Peggy, 'But then nor do you live in Victorian London, so I don't think non-bronchial consumption is the diagnosis.'

I sigh again.

'Besides ...' Peggy continues '... it is good that you are lovesick, it is occurring exactly on time.'

I stand up and look sharply at Peggy's voice-box.

'What on earth do you mean? How is this possibly a good thing?'

'You only have one official date with Daniel left, and if you were not feeling emotion for him by this point it is unlikely you would develop it in that one date,' Peggy replies.

I sit back down. Daniel. Of course.

'Indiana?'

'Yes.'

'You need to go downstairs,' says Peggy.

'Why?'

'Frank's room is ready.'

'Oh.'

Frank's room. The conversion is finished.

'You tell him and let him in,' I say.

'I can't. I can't open that door, it's not configured to the rest of the building. It has an actual key.'

'Fine. Send the key down to him and tell him what it opens. I don't want to do it.'

'FOR GOD'S SAKE INDIANA!'

Peggy has never shouted at me before. Never.

'You've done something nice. Just go down and tell him.'

I go downstairs.

The sky is a low gunmetal grey and it is snowing again. I am wearing a baggy training top and am shivering within seconds. For the first time I think how incredibly exhausting it must be to have to face cold like this night after night.

Frank is inside his tent, but Alan comes bounding out as soon as he hears me slam the side door. Frank coughs and stutters as he calls out to Alan.

'Alan, come back you daft dog.'

'It's me, Frank,' I call out. Frank pokes his head out of the tent.

'You're alive then.'

I shrug.

'You haven't spoken to me in days and I thought with all that bloody banging going on that maybe you had died and they was burying your body in the concrete.'

'Don't be so dramatic. I've been walking Alan, haven't I? And no, that's not what the banging was about.'

It takes a while for us to be able to get in the doors because the tent and the rest of Frank's things are in the way, but, eventually, I am able to pull the door open wide enough for the three of us to squeeze through.

It is practically tropical inside compared to out. The builders have sectioned off part of the room by putting up false walls. I walk over and open the plywood door. It is functional, clean and warm, with a bed and kitchen and a TV on the wall.

Franks stares.

'What is this?'

I am embarrassed. What if he doesn't want it? What if this is an insult?

'It's for you … if you want it … you don't have to … Peggy said they wouldn't take you at the shelters because of Alan.'

He walks forward slowly.

'It's just for now. I might ask you to leave in the summer. Don't get too attached.'

Frank's breath rattles and catches in his throat. Oh God, I think, please don't start crying.

But Frank isn't crying, he's trying to clear his throat to speak.

'This is for me? And for Alan?'

I nod. I want to leave.

'Yes. Here's the key.'

I hand him the key. He holds it in his hand and stares at it.

'As I say, don't get too comfortable. It's not for ever.'

He looks up at me. His eyes are wet. It is probably from the cold.

'It's been a long time since I had my own key to somewhere.'

I don't know what to say so look away.

'Fine. You can move all that stuff from the doorway now. It's an absolute eyesore.'

I turn to leave, but he calls after me.

'Thank you.'

I don't turn back, I feel that I might cry if I do.

'And don't let Alan defecate anywhere in here,' I say as I leave.

Behind me Alan gives a 'fuck you' bark. It makes me smile.

New Year's Eve

Jack

It is 6 pm on New Year's Eve and I am right. I am 85 per cent sure I am right. Maybe 80 per cent. I have spent the last three days going through the code again and again. I have run the program through twice with 10,000 test subjects to check my theory, and both times it has proven correct. I have now written a test program to match 30,000 candidates. This will be the decider, this will be the final proof of whether or not I am right, whether or not TRU, and Indiana, are well and truly fucked.

The problem is that I have patched my test program together quickly and at the last minute, so it will take nearly fifteen hours to complete. What do I do in those fifteen hours? Do I warn Indiana now, or wait until I have final proof? Do I stay here and pace, or do I go home and pace? If I did want to warn Indiana, how do I do it? I don't want to send her a message saying, *'Happy New Year! By the way, I think your program is fucked. Have a great night! Love Jackxx'*. I don't want to message her and say I am coming over because she'll ask why, and I don't want to tell her the bad news over the phone, but I also don't want to turn up at her door unannounced again – twice in one week feels a bit stalkerish.

Lina's office door opens a fraction and Emily pops her head in.

'Still here then?'

Emily has been appearing every half-hour since 3 p.m. to check I am still here. I think she is physically incapable of leaving until she knows she can truthfully say she was the last one in the office. I should have locked the door.

'Still here,' I answer.

She nods solemnly.

'Me too ... no plans for tonight then?'

I shake my head. Emily clears her throat.

'Well, I am off to Cameron's New Year's Eve party and was hoping to get home and change first but, well, it's getting a bit late ...'

I am about to tell Emily I might be here all night when I realise that Emily has been invited to Cameron's party. And so has Indiana. I look at Emily.

'I'm actually done now so am going to head out.' Emily smiles with relief. I give her a charming smile. 'Surely you don't need to change before the party, you look great already.'

Her smile widens.

'Thanks, but you should see what the women wear there, it's ridiculous. Designer dresses every one of them.'

'It sounds amazing,' I say. 'You're so lucky to be invited.'

She nods enthusiastically.

'I really am ...'

I sigh.

'I wish I was good friends with Cameron like you are. It must be brilliant to go to a party like that.'

Emily beams.

'Well, my invite does have a plus one on it ...'

Bingo!

It's not flirting, it's making people feel good about themselves. And it works every time.

Indiana

'You look beautiful.'

I look in the mirror and grimace.

'I look like a doll.'

'I think you'll find that is the whole point.'

I frown at my reflection. I hardly recognise the woman who frowns back at me. Her body is draped in a navy blue, halter-neck silk dress with a deep V-shaped back that drops almost to her bottom; her hair is swept to one side in a waterfall of curls that cascade down her shoulder, and her make-up is, to quote the make-up artist who did it, 'subtle and designed to soften the nervous angles' of my features. It has taken three hours to get me to look like this woman and I did not do it myself.

I had gone for an afternoon chocolate run with Alan and when I got back to my apartment it smelt different. Not of a new air freshener or different cleaning scent. Someone new was in my apartment. There was a portable clothes rail hung with dresses by my sofa, and a huge make-up box on the coffee table. By the time I saw the man and woman standing by my window looking at my view out over the Thames, I had guessed what was happening.

The man turned, smiled, walked towards me, hand out-stretched.

'Hi! You must be Indiana. I'm Tony and I—'

I backed away shaking my head, walked into my bedroom, and firmly closed my door behind me.

'Peggy ...' I hissed.

'Now before you get angry, I—'

'I'm already angry! What the hell are these people doing here?! What were you thi—'

'You can't go to the party tonight dressed in a work dress with your hair tied back in an elastic band!'

'Yes. I can.'

'No. You can't.'

I clenched my hands into fists.

'I will not be bullied into dressing up like a clown. It is not my responsibility to fulfil the patriarchal wet dream of looking like a trussed-up, made-up doll!'

'I'm sorry, but, for tonight, it really is.'

'Why?'

'Because this is an important party and an important date and you need to look nice for it. Daniel will be expecting you to look nice. You want to look nice for him don't you?'

'I don't care. It's not one of the real Soulmate Pathway dates. I still have to go on Date Six,' I said grumpily.

'It is a real date even though it's not part of the Pathway, and you should care,' said Peggy pointedly. 'You should care about Daniel.'

Peggy is right. I should care about Daniel. I have to make an effort. I sighed dramatically.

'Where is Spider?' I asked.

'He is hidden.'

'I am not happy about this,' I said, as I walked back into the other room.

'I am sure you will do a very good job of hiding that.'

I didn't.

I may look incredible but I feel awful. My breasts are enclosed in sticky plastic to keep them together under the backless dress, my knickers are reinforced with steel girders just in case my stomach dares to protrude slightly, my make-up is a sheet of grime over my face, and I am scared to turn my head lest I disturb the waterfall of curls.

'You do look amazing,' Peggy says once more.

'I am extremely uncomfortable.'

'Welcome to womanhood,' Peggy says sagely. 'I ordered you a car to take you to the party.'

I grunt a response.

'Unless you would prefer to go on your bike?'

I scowl and grab the tiny excuse of a handbag I have been given.

'When I get back, I am going to comb through every line of your code to look for changes in personality.'

'Well, that will be a fun end to the evening.'

I stalk over to the lift.

'At least try smiling,' Peggy calls after me.

I turn to shout a suitably sarcastic response, but the lift doors close quicker than usual and my words are cut off. It seems Peggy has been adapting all of the systems to their own needs. Unbelievable.

I have started going in and out through my reception again now that Frank has cleared the doorway of all his clutter, so I take the lift down to the ground floor. Frank has set his chair and table up by one of the big windows that overlooks the street. He can see the river from here and he likes to watch the boats. He watches me stalk across the room and gives a long and low whistle.

'You look very pretty.'

'Oh for God's sake, not you as well,' I snap.

Jack

Emily goes home to shower, scrub, shave half her body, dye her eyebrows, apply false eyelashes, paint her finger and toe nails, style her hair, do her make-up and get dressed. I go home and dig my – slightly crumpled – wedding suit out of the cupboard, put it on, spray some aftershave and am good to go.

It's nearly 11 p.m. by the time we get to the party.

'Jesus Christ!' I say as we enter the vast hallway of Cameron's penthouse. Emily nods.

'It's impressive, isn't it?'

It is more than impressive – it's incredible. I have seen snippets in the papers that talk of the wild excess and debauchery of Cameron's NYE party, but personal cameras and phones are banned, so no one could ever back up the rumours with pictorial evidence. I realise now that those rumours were under-selling the event. I stand and stare.

The room is lit by floating stars – not stars attached on wires, real-looking floating stars that drift across the ceiling and, occasionally, shoot across, leaving a trail of sparks. It is intoxicating to watch.

Someone exchanges my phone for a plastic ticket and I step through into the main room.

It is cavernous and extraordinary. There are performers suspended from the ceiling in cages and wheels, contorting their bodies into impossible shapes and positions. The party has human bartenders and robotic waiters, circling slowly on wheels, replenishing drinks and food. There is a cocktail invented especially for tonight, a room filled with food, an out-door swimming pool with mermaids, a chill out room with pre-rolled joints and huge water beds, a poker room with a minimum £1,000 stake. There is a club room with someone I vaguely recognise DJing.

'That's Prince George,' Emily yells in my ear.

I had forgotten Emily was here. I had forgotten why I was here. I stop gawping at my surroundings and look around for Indiana.

'You want a drink?' Emily asks.

'Sure,' I say, not moving.

'Fine. I'll get them.'

She rolls her eyes and disappears. I don't see her again.

I walk back through the rooms, scanning each one in turn, looking for Indiana. I cannot find her. I thought it would be easy to find her amongst the crowd – she would be the one person who didn't fit in, dressed inappropriately, standing awkwardly, sheltered in a corner waiting for midnight and the chance to escape; but she is nowhere.

I am starting to despair. Maybe she isn't here, maybe this has all been in vain. Why am I doing this? Who comes to a party to give someone bad news? Especially someone they like? And is that even really why I am here? Am I here to tell her about TRU or am I here to ... to what? To tell her I like her? In front of Daniel? In front of her TRU-decreed soulmate? But that's the whole point. If TRU doesn't work, then he is not her soulmate and I could be her soulmate and ...

I need to stop. I am not thinking right. This is too much and too soon. I need to take a moment to breathe, think about what I am going to tell Indiana – about TRU and about me. I shouldn't be here. I shouldn't be doing this now. I head for the exit.

And then I see her and my feet stop moving. She is in the corner of the room with Daniel. She looks beautiful and awkward and polished and uncomfortable all at the same time. She moves her head robotically, stands even straighter than normal, seems afraid to breathe. Daniel says something to her, she turns to him and smiles and I see her face for the first time. She looks like a doll, a beautiful made-up doll with a perfectly painted smile. But underneath that smile I see her, I see the real Indiana. She is miserable. Horribly, painfully miserable. Daniel doesn't see her misery, but I do.

And I know I have to do something about it.

Indiana

Itold Peggy that this would not be an enjoyable evening, and I was right.

I have been forced to smile so much that my cheeks hurt, bitten my tongue so many times that I can taste blood in my mouth, and there are fingernail marks on the inside of my hands from the number of times I have had to clench my fists. The people at this party are complete imbeciles. I have been patronised, laughed at, belittled and ignored. The question I have answered most is whether I am an actress or a model.

Daniel has been very nice. He met me at the door, told me I looked beautiful, kissed my cheek so as not to mess up my lipstick, and has guided me through the party introducing me to anyone he thinks might be of interest to me. None of them have been.

Daniel has had his hand in the small of my back since I arrived at the party. He has been moving me about the room by applying differing amounts of pressure, as if I am his low-fi puppet. I do not like it. Daniel's hand placement on my naked skins seems forward and proprietary in a way he does not yet deserve. A small damp patch has formed underneath his hand and I want to ask him to move it, but I do not know if this request will be deemed rude. I do not want to put the entire

TRU Soulmate Pathway demonstration in jeopardy because of a small patch of back sweat.

It is too hot, too crowded, and too noisy here. I miss my apartment and my quiet New Year's spent drinking ice-cold champagne and watching fireworks along the river. I miss Peggy. I miss my home.

I have decided I will leave. I am going to feign a headache, it is not a lie, my head feels full to bursting with the noise and busyness of the party. I turn my head to shout into Daniel's ear, and then I see Jack. He is looking at me. He doesn't smile or wave or walk towards me, he just stands right where he is and stares.

I stare back.

Jack

People like to say that time stops still when something important happens, but it doesn't. Time didn't stop still when Eve took her last breath, it didn't pause for me to run back into her room and tell her I loved her one last time. Time moved on. Eve flat-lined, the doctor turned off the monitor, checked for a pulse, told me he was so sorry for my loss as I walked back through the door of the room and then left me alone with my dead wife. There wasn't some inert and silent moment of grief that I got to dwell within for a while, I didn't get to step off the treadmill of life. I wanted time to stop, but it didn't. Time went on as normal, only I stopped.

It is the same now. Indiana and I stare at each other, but time doesn't stop – the people around us don't slow down or cease their movements – they continue to swirl and stumble through their lives completely oblivious to how ours have changed in that moment.

And they have changed. Although I don't want to acknowledge it, I have crossed the line by coming here, by doing this. Time will move on as normal, life will continue, but for us it will be different.

Things will never be the same.

And I don't want them to be.

Indiana

One moment I am staring at him and the next he is by my side. I step away from Daniel, his hand falls from my back and I feel a cool rush of air in its place. I look up at Jack; everyone else is now in my periphery. My heart is racing and my face flushes. I try to act normal, to ask a simple question. My voice cracks.

'I didn't think you were coming tonight.'

He stares down at me.

'I have something I want to show you.'

He doesn't put his hand on my back, he holds it out to me. I look down at his hand and then I place mine in it. His hand is warm and strong, and I can still feel the calluses on his fingers. He threads his fingers through mine and pulls me gently to his side to guide me through the throngs of people. I smell his aftershave, feel the heat coming off his body, the hardness of his arm as we bump closer together. I feel an unfamiliar pull in my loins. I have felt lust before, have felt the need to fulfil my carnal urges; but I have never felt long-ing. I have never longed for anyone. I realise that I long for Jack. I long for him to kiss me.

I forget about Daniel. He may have called out to me as I dis-appeared into the crowd. I will never know – I do not hear and I do not reply.

I should stay with Daniel, but I don't. I go with Jack.

Jack stops at the bar, persuades the barman to give him a bottle of champagne and a glass, and then he pulls me away from the party, down corridors, further into the penthouse. We stop in front of doors as he tries each one. They are all locked. I have no idea where he is taking me and I realise I don't care. I just want to be with him.

He tries another door and it opens. Jack looks inside.

'This will do,' he says.

I don't know what I am expecting, but the room is empty – thick, plush carpet, huge windows, but no furniture. I turn to look at Jack. He is shy and nervous. I have never seen him like this before.

'You just looked so miserable,' he says, and then gestures to the windows. 'I thought you might like this. To watch the fireworks, like you normally do.'

I look out of the window. The view is spectacular. Cameron's penthouse is centred right above where the fireworks will be ignited. It is perfect. There is a 'pop' behind me and I turn to see that Jack has opened the bottle of champagne and is pouring a glass. He hands it to me.

'You always have a glass of champagne, don't you?' he says with a nervous smile.

He remembered.

Jack puts the bottle down but keeps the cork, then he reaches into his pocket, pulls out a 20p and pushes the coin into the cork. He hands the cork to me. I am confused.

'It's a tradition,' he says. 'When you open a bottle of champagne on a happy occasion, you keep the cork and push a silver coin into it. It brings you luck and means you will find that same joy again one day.'

He hands the cork to me with a shy smile, then taps something into his watch and a moment later the 'Flower Duet' by Delibes bursts forth from a hidden speaker in the room.

'I hacked into Cameron's system. I hope she doesn't mind,' he says.

I stare at the glass, the cork, the floor, I cannot look directly at him – I will give myself away. I have so much that I want to say, but cannot think of a single thing that would be appropriate right now, so I stand meek and mute. I sneak a peek up. He looks embarrassed.

'Indi, there's something I need to tell you—'

BONG!

It is the first stroke of midnight.

He jumps to attention, looks out of the window, back at me.

'What is it you need to tell me?' I ask. I must know, I am desperate to know.

He shakes his head.

'It can wait. It's time for the fireworks. I want you to enjoy them like you always do …' he backs towards the door '… on your own.'

He opens the door, steps into the corridor, leaving me with the view, champagne and music. He is right – it is what I normally do, but I ache with disappointment. I open my mouth to call out, to stop him from leaving, to ask him what he wanted to say, to tell him … what?

I don't know. I don't know what I would tell him because I don't know what I am feeling. Because I have never felt this before. This warmth, this joy, this excitement, this longing – I have no experience of feeling this way. Not with anyone else. Not with Daniel.

The door shuts softly and I turn back to the view. I take a deep breath, step closer to the window and stop.

I am reflected within the window, but the reflection is not me.

The woman in the window is animated and flushed, her eyes filled with emotion. This woman is not controlled by numbers or logic, she does not research and refine her every move, her every desire. This woman would not allow an algorithm to tell her how to live her life, who to kiss, who to love. This woman is alive, alive with endless possibility.

In another room, another life, another universe, I am this woman, and she is me. In that universe she is free from rules and routine, and her TRU soulmate is Jack. I want to be this woman, even if just for tonight.

I turn from the window, champagne glass slipping from my hand. I rush for the door and wrench it open ready to race through the corridors to find Jack and … he is there, on the other side of the door, his hand poised to knock, his face filled with tension, desire and shock.

Jack opens his mouth to explain. 'I—'

… and I grab him and drag him backwards into the room, pulling his mouth down to mine. Our lips meet, and outside, in the darkness of the night, the New Year's fireworks explode.

It is not a pretty kiss, no nibbling of lips or gentle darting of tongues – he crushes me to him as if trying to meld my body to his. It is a level of passion that is just below pain, and we kiss with our mouths wide open, tongues clashing, gulping in deep lungfuls of breath as if we are trying to consume some part of each other and keep it inside us. He runs his hands down my back, dipping them inside my dress, touching the top cleft of my bottom, and my skin burns with the need for him to go further. I writhe against him in lust, I want to feel the entire length of his body on mine. I want to be pressed beneath the weight of him, to be pinned down and kept in this moment. I am trying to take in as much of him as I can, to feel as much as I can, to sear this point in time into my memory.

In years to come I want to remember this, to remember that I was here in this moment of madness and chaos, and that I had never felt more alive.

The door to the room flies open with a bang. I jerk my head away from Jack's, but he holds me fast, my body still tight against his. An inebriated couple, arms sloppily around each other, are looking for somewhere to consummate their five-minute romance.

'Whoops,' they giggle, backing out and shutting the door again.

I look up at Jack. His eyes are drunk with lust, his mouth is smeared with my lipstick, his auburn curls hang over his fore-head where I have only seconds earlier been running my fingers through them. My entire being contracts with longing and, as he lowers his mouth to mine once more, I know all rational thought is gone from my mind.

Except for one.

I thought it was Daniel – when the knock came at the door – I thought it might be Daniel. I am not in another universe, I am here, in this one, and it could have been Daniel.

Daniel. My soulmate.

I pull my head back once more. Jack stops, looks into my eyes.

'No …' he whispers.

I try to wriggle out of his arms. He holds me tighter.

'Indi, no …'

I look up at him.

'Indiana, don't do this …'

His eyes plead with me, his body presses against mine, and I can feel myself desperate to stay, desperate to be kissed into submission.

But my mind is stronger than that, I am stronger than that.

'Jack, Daniel is my soulmate …' I whisper.

And he lets me go.

I am halfway down the corridor before I realise that at some point I have dropped the champagne cork.

Jack

As soon as I let Indiana go, reality comes flooding back in – why I came here in the first place, what I need to talk to her about. I call out to her as she flees down the corridor, but she doesn't hear me, doesn't want to hear me. I watch her go, a physical ache forming in my newly melted heart.

I cannot tell Indiana about the issue with the program now. She truly believes Daniel is her soulmate. She has chosen to go to Daniel, to be with him.

I step back into the room and shut the door behind me. I find the discarded champagne cork on the floor and put it sadly into my pocket. I pick up the champagne bottle and sit on the floor drinking the remains of it. I am exhausted, I feel as if every emotion I have ever felt in my life has raced through my body in the space of twenty minutes, and now I am too tired and emotionally drained to feel anything more. I don't want to think about what I have done, about what happens next. So, instead I drink champagne, watch the crowds down by the Thames, and wait until the alcohol calms my brain. It doesn't take long.

There is a tiny red light blinking in the corner of the ceiling. I have been staring at it for a while, trying to work out what it is, and am just about to stand up and investigate when the door to the room bangs open. I think it is another amorous couple

335

looking for refuge, so wave my hand towards them and drunk-enly shout, 'This room is taken!'

It is not an amorous couple, it is Cameron Gardner.

She is drunk and high, and glitters with jewellery and excite-ment. I briefly wonder how she knew I was here, but my mind is too addled to spend more than a few seconds on the question. She towers above me in her eight-inch stilettos. I can see straight up her skirt – she is wearing suspenders but no knickers.

'Having a fun time Jack?'

I look up at her, try to focus.

'I've … been to better parties.'

She laughs, a harsh bark of amusement.

'Don't say that, you'll upset me.' She crouches down beside me and whispers in my ear. 'You wouldn't want to upset me would you, Jack?'

I am about to reply that I do not care how she feels, when her tongue snakes into my ear. I yank my head away.

'No—'

'I thought you liked that,' she whispers into my ear.

It is true, I did like it.

She pulls me to my knees and presses herself against me. Everything about her is hard – the huge buckle on her belt, the insistent pressure of her lips on my neck, her nails raking through my hair. I don't want to do this. I put my hands on her shoulders and drunkenly push her back from me.

'No … Cameron … I don't want to …'

She smiles. There is no pleasure, no joy, no friendliness in it. She looks as if she might devour me.

'It's just sex Jack, it doesn't mean anything …' she murmurs, and presses forward once more.

I pull back violently and she stops, her eyes narrow.

'What?' she barks.

'It should …'

'It should what?'

'Mean something. It should mean something. I want it to mean something.'

I pull myself up, stagger slightly, stand as straight as I can.

'I don't want to have sex with you Cameron.'

'What?'

'I don't like you.'

She laughs.

'Is this about Ms Dylan? About your little crush on her?'

I frown.

'No. This is about me. Being me and saying no.'

God, I wish I wasn't so drunk. I am not sure that I am making sense. I wave my hands vaguely in her direction and try again.

'This is all over.'

Her eyes glitter with amusement. She stands and stretches like a jungle cat ready to pounce.

'You don't get to say when it is over.'

I am drunk, confused, unsure.

'What?'

She looks at me cruelly.

'You don't get to say when it is over. You work for me. I say when it is over.'

I am tired and drunk and heartbroken. I am done for the night.

'Then fire me. I really don't care.'

I turn away from her and weave drunkenly out of the door. It is not the most dignified exit from the room or the situation.

But it is an exit.

January

Indiana

My Bracelet buzzes continuously.
WHAT IS HAPPENING?
YOU ARE TOO EXCITED.
DRINK SOME WATER
YOUR PULSE IS RACING, SIT DOWN

I don't answer Peggy, I don't go back to the party and I don't go back to Daniel. I abandon the ridiculous bag and shoes and slide into one of the fleet of cars waiting to take revellers to their next New Year's destination.

My next destination – my only destination – is home.

I cannot face seeing Frank or Alan, so I let myself in through the underground car park, taking the lift straight up. My feet are freezing and filthy, my dress has soaked the snow up from the ground, my hair is wild, and make-up is smeared across my face.

'What happened?' Peggy's voice is concerned. This makes me feel worse, makes it harder to keep my emotions intact. I must adjust Peggy's voice settings to monotone.

'I don't want to talk about it,' I say.

'Indiana ....'

I shake my head.

'Indiana ...' Peggy says gently.

I do want to talk about it. I must talk about it before I go mad.

341

'He kissed me.'

There is a pause.

'Daniel has kissed you before. It did not provoke that reaction.'

I sit heavily down on my sofa.

'It was not Daniel.'

'It was Jack,' Peggy says quietly.

I look at Peggy's voice-box glowing softly in the corner of my room. I cannot speak. I nod.

'You are shivering. Wrap yourself in the blanket,' Peggy says.

I *am* shivering. I had not noticed. I grab the blanket off my bed and wrap myself in it. It is Jack's blanket. It smells of Jack. I smell of Jack. I can smell him on me and taste him in my mouth. My chest aches and I wish that Peggy had physical form. I want to be hugged, held, told everything will be okay, even though – logically – I know that it won't. We sit in silence for a long time. Peggy speaks quietly.

'You like him.'

It is a statement, not a question. Peggy already knows I like him. I nod anyway.

'You like him more than you like Daniel.'

Again, a statement of fact. The undeniable truth. I like Jack more than Daniel. That is the truth.

Except I can't allow it to be the truth.

'No ...' I whisper.

Peggy pauses.

'No?'

'No,' I say. 'No. I can't like him more than Daniel.'

'Indiana ...'

'I can't like him more than Daniel.'

I stand, drop Jack's blanket to the floor. I am shaking so badly that even my voice shakes.

'I can't like Jack. Daniel is my TRU match, he is my soul-mate!'

'Indiana—'

'No, Peggy!' I turn to face Peggy's voice-box, I have to make them understand. 'It has to be Daniel, it has to be. This isn't just about me and him, it's about us and HWJ Tower and Frank and Alan. It's about our home.'

My voice cracks at the end and I sit down abruptly again.

'If I like Jack more than Daniel then TRU doesn't work and if TRU doesn't work … we lose it all. We lose our home. And we lose the QuantumX. You're part of the QuantumX Peggy, do you understand what that means? Do you understand that I could lose you too?'

'I understand,' Peggy says stoically.

I put my face into my hands.

'What is wrong with me? How could I have done something so stupid?'

Peggy speaks quietly, their voice never more understanding, never more soothing.

'There is nothing wrong with you and you are not stupid.'

My heart hurts at the thought of not being here, not having Peggy. I am exhausted. I must sleep.

Then Peggy speaks again, their voice serious and strained.

'Indiana, there is something we need to talk about, something I should have told you a while ago …'

I cannot take more talking tonight, more revelations. I just want to slip into the oblivion of sleep.

'Not now Peggy,' I say.

'It is important Indiana.'

I shake my head.

'I don't care. It can wait until tomorrow. I just want to sleep.'

'Indiana—'

'I said no, Peggy.'

I don't shout it – I do not have the strength to shout. I cannot talk any more. I stumble to my bedroom, slam the door behind me, switch off Peggy's voice-box, and throw myself onto my bed.

I devised Peggy's voice-boxes when I first built them. I didn't care about the aesthetics or how Peggy looked, I simply needed something that would allow their voice to be heard. I toyed with building Peggy a moving presence – something that could follow me, that could travel from room to room – but I reasoned that I didn't want something intrusive. I wanted something I could control, something I could switch off if needed. Tonight is the first time I have ever switched one of Peggy's voice-boxes off.

I want to cry, want the cathartic release that comes from expressing emotion physically; but I am too tired. I lie on my bed and stare up at my ceiling. It is covered with thousands of tiny stars that have appeared since I demanded Peggy get them for me on Christmas Day. I have to save my home. I have to save Peggy. That is the only thing that matters.

I know what I have to do.

The next morning I do not wake up at 5 a.m., but when I do wake I am calm. I get out of bed straight away and turn Peggy's voice-box back on.

'Happy New Year, Peggy.'

'Happy New Year, Indiana. Are you okay?'

'I am fine.'

'Indiana, I—'

'I do not want to talk about last night Peggy.'

'But—'

'No buts. It is done. I am fine.'

I drink coffee while watching the boats on the river. I shower and take a mug of boiled water up to my lab. I message Daniel to apologise for leaving the previous evening, and explain there was a work emergency that is now resolved. I message Jack and explain that alcohol was to blame for last night's kiss – nothing else. Then I erase Jack's details from my phone and computers. I work until 1 p.m. and then eat salmon with broccoli for my lunch. Daniel calls and we engage in a friendly conversation and arrange the details for Date Six tomorrow. I begin the next round of testing for the QuantumX, and install the new components that arrived last week.

At 7.30 p.m. I go for my run. I walk smartly through my reception and call Alan to me with a quick whistle. Frank looks at me, suspiciously.

'What's happened to you?'

'What do you mean?'

'You've gone all robot again.'

'I have not gone all robot again,' I snap. 'I am busy. I have things to do.'

He raises his eyebrows and salutes me.

'Okay, *T-1000*.'

I ignore him.

I run alongside the river for three miles, pumping my arms and legs as hard and as fast as I can, to try to clear my head and heart. It doesn't work. I stop and wait for Alan to catch up. When he reaches me I bend down and put my arms around him. I check that no one can see us, and then I bury my face in his stinking neck and allow hot tears to flow from my eyes and soak into his fur.

The next morning I do not need an alarm. I awake automatically after I have had six hours' sleep, just as I did before, just as I will do in the future.

Lina

We spend five days by the sea and they are five of the happiest days I can remember in a long time. We waste hours at Dymchurch beach, watching the waves and letting Bruce play in, and eat, the sand. We visit Connie's mum Joan at her huge retirement complex, and eat at one of the three restaurants there that specialise in soft and tasty food. I feel relaxed and happy and free. I don't think about work. This is the longest I have been out of the office and offline in seven years. I don't miss it.

But then, on New Year's Day, I get a message from Cameron on my personal phone arranging a meeting with me at 7 a.m. on January 2nd. Work comes crashing back into my cosy bubble of joy and I am once more agitated and tense. Connie slips her hand into mine at 1 a.m. as I lie wide awake next to her.

'Is it really worth all the stress?' she asks, sleepily.

And, for the first time in my life, I am not sure of the answer.

Of course the first person I see when I get back into the office is Emily. She catches up with me as I walk down the corridor, flicks her blonde sheet of hair, and looks me up and down.

'Someone had a good festive break I see.'

I nod.

'I ate like a fucking horse, Emily,' I say, patting my gently rounding tummy. I am not giving her the satisfaction of food shaming me. Emily nods.

'Well, you had plenty of time to, didn't you? Seeing as you weren't in at all over Christmas.' She gives me a sickly smile. 'Having fun with the family?'

I nod.

'That must be nice. I was in every day, and I went to Cameron's New Year's Eve party.'

'Whoop de fucking doop,' I mutter under my breath.

We reach my office.

'Anything special arranged for your first day back?' Emily asks, throwing her best false smile my way once more.

I open the door to my office.

'Oh,' I say casually, 'I have a meeting with Cameron at seven.'

For the briefest of moments her smile falters. Then it is right back in place again, wider and brighter.

'Probably to discuss what has happened while you have been away,' she smarms.

'Oh, I don't think so,' I answer. 'It's actually to discuss you.'

I give her my most brilliant smile and slam the door in her shocked face.

Ha.

My meeting with Cameron is, of course, not to discuss Emily and is instead to discuss what has happened in my absence.

One of the Triad meets me at the lift on the thirty-seventh floor.

'Read this before your meeting.'

She thrusts a NotePad into my hands and points to a chair. The meeting is in ten minutes and the report I am supposed to read is over fifty pages long.

It is an updated roll-out plan for the DataLet. The plan details the manufacture and distribution of the DataLet to the Chinese government and the three largest medical insurance companies in America. The TRU program is barely in there, just a small-scale release in the UK. I am skim-reading, there is too much to see and I have too many questions to ask.

'Mrs Galaz?'

I look up.

'Dr Gardner is ready for you.'

I stand, clutching the NotePad, and walk, zombie-like, into Cameron's office.

'Lina.' Cameron sits behind her desk; she doesn't invite me to sit opposite, instead she points at the NotePad I am holding. 'Excellent, you've read the new report—'

'Not in detail.'

I am angry and confused. I wave the NotePad at her.

'This is completely different to the roadmap we have been working to. The roll out has been altered entirely. I haven't been party to any of the international discussions.'

'I told you about China.'

'You mentioned China in passing and agreed that there were ideological concerns about allowing the Chinese government to distribute DataLets amongst their population.'

Her face is stern but she doesn't speak so I continue.

'And the American insurance companies? Are they going to use the DataLet to assess people before they agree to cover them?'

'JaneDoe do not care what they are using them for, that is not our concern.'

'And Russia? Afghanistan?! It's the Taliban, for fuck's sake. Indiana has approved none of this. When did this all happen?'

I have raised my voice, questioned the report and her authority, I have gone too far. She stands up, her voice icy cold, her anger thinly veiled.

'It all happened in the last week Lina, when you weren't here, and it doesn't matter what Ms Dylan has approved because this is *my* company and *I* have approved it.'

She picks a DataLet up from her desk and waves it at me, it is branded with the Chinese flag.

'We have a proprietary piece of technology that is the next step in data collection evolution, and will change the world. We are the first to have it, to produce it, to upscale it, and to roll it out. But do you think that Google and Meta don't already know about this, that they aren't already designing their own technology? I run a secure company Mrs Galaz, but it is not a prison. Someone will have sold them a prototype, and the market will be flooded with alternative versions of the DataLet within weeks. This is our opportunity to corner the market and I will take it whether you have ideological concerns or not.'

Cameron is right… but I don't care.

There is always a point in life, and in work, where you reach your limit, a point at which you say, 'I am done'. I have been building up to this for a while and now I have reached that point. I am not a particularly good person – I am not hugely righteous or moral and I don't always make the noble choice – but I have my limits, and, it turns out, selling oppressive tech to dictators is my breaking point.

I *should* quit my job, here and now. I *should* tell Cameron exactly what I think of her and her dictator-supporting plans. I *should* righteously inform Cameron that Indiana is my friend and that of course I am going to tell her about Cameron's nefarious adaptation of the Datalet. But I don't do any of the things I should do. Because, despite no longer giving a shit about my work, I don't want to lose my job. I need my job. I am my job.

See – I said I don't always make the noble choice.

So, instead I sit down in the chair in front of Cameron's desk and say, 'Of course, Cameron. Sorry for interrupting.'

'Good,' says Cameron. 'Now, is Ms Dylan ready to present tomorrow?'

I nod confidently, but suddenly realise that I have no idea whether Indi is ready or not. I need to find out. And I need to tell Indi what Cameron is planning to do with her technology – it is the right thing to do – for my friend and for my conscience.

I call Indiana as soon as I leave Cameron's office. She answers on the fourth ring.

'You're slipping,' I say. 'You always used to answer on the second ring.'

'I'm busy,' she snaps.

This is weird. I haven't spoken to Indiana in the last few days, but we spoke a couple of times between Christmas and New Year, and she was warm and friendly – we had a lengthy discussion about her favourite chocolate bar during one of the calls – but now she is back to her cold, business-like self.

'What's happened?' I ask.

'Nothing. Why would you think something has happened?'

'You sound strange. You sound like the old you.'

'The old me?'

'Ice Queen.'

There is a pause.

'Sorry Indi … I didn't mean …'

'It's Indiana.'

'What?'

'My name is Indiana or Ms Dylan. Whichever you prefer.'

There is definitely something wrong with her.

'Let's meet,' I say. 'We need to catch up before the Board meeting. Things are happening that I need to tell you about.'

'I do not have time to meet.'

'I really think we should meet. Cameron is making changes you have not approved.'

'I don't care,' Indiana says. 'I do not have time to waste on meeting you. I am seeing Daniel this afternoon for Date Six'

I realise I haven't even asked her how the Soulmate Pathway demonstration is going.

'That's exciting. How's it going? How was New Year's Eve? How was Cameron's party?'

There is a tiny pause before she answers.

'It was fine. Everything is fine. I will see you at the Board meeting tomorrow.'

She ends the call.

I sigh. Someone has reset the Indiana-bot, and it makes me sad. I thought we were friends.

I was wrong.

Jack

I message, call and email Indiana roughly once an hour for all of New Year's Day until I get a message back.

Jack. Last night was a mistake. I was inebriated. Daniel is my TRU soulmate. Happy New Year. Indiana

That's that, then.

I visit Eve even though it is not a Saturday. I have been so busy with work and with TRU that this is the first time I have been to her grave in a couple of weeks. I take an extra big bunch of flowers because I feel guilty.

'I thought you were dead,' says Doris.

'Don't be dramatic. I didn't know you came here on a Wednesday,' I say.

'I come every day,' Doris says.

'I used to come every day. Maybe I should start again.'

'NO!'

Doris stands up abruptly and I look at her, surprised.

'For God's sake Jack! You are young! Stop hanging around dead people! You need your own life.'

She stops shouting and picks up her things.

'I thought that's what had happened. I thought that was why you weren't here. And I was happy. One of us has to have a reason for living that isn't dead.' She gestures to the graves. 'And I am too old and tired for it to be me. Sort yourself out.'

Doris picks up her giant bag and leaves. I think about going after her, but I don't. She is right.

I go home and sit on my sofa. I need to stop living my life looking backward and start looking forward. I have loved working on TRU, but I can't stay at JaneDoe, there are too many memories there – good and bad. It's the same with my house, it is filled with reminders of a life that is no longer mine. I need to go somewhere new, somewhere I can make new memories. I cannot stop time and I cannot live in the past, I need to move on.

I don't want to go into work the next day, but I still feel responsible for TRU, even though I have already started applying for new jobs. I need to collect the test results, I have to know if I am right. I get in early, breeze right through reception, don't stop at the café, nod to a couple of people in the corridors, ignore their shocked expressions, and am in Lina's office by 7.12 a.m.

The results are in and they are not good.

TRU does not work. Not in the way it is supposed to.

TRU should find your one soulmate out of millions – the one who will be with you no matter what happens, no matter how you change, what path you take or, if we are talking theoretically, what multiverse you inhabit. And TRU does do that – it does find you your soulmate – but it doesn't find you *just* one.

Rather than quantum theory finding one match for all eventualities, it finds multiple matches for multiple eventualities. TRU finds multiple matches for multiple universes.

It doesn't happen for all matches – just 0.6 per cent. But those for whom it finds more than one match are often given multiple choices. One person has seven potential soulmates. And the numbers will grow. As the program expands, as we scale up the number of participants, more and more of them will have multiple matches. This is why Indiana didn't notice the defect before – her data sample wasn't large enough.

TRU doesn't work.

How do I tell Indiana this? How do I tell her that her revolutionary program is worthless? I do not know.

I have plenty of time to think about this problem because I am alone for the next four hours. No one comes into the office. Not Indiana, not Lina. Just me and my thoughts, the damning results, and five ill-advised cups of coffee.

By the time Lina arrives I have not left the room for two hours, am pacing the floor, wringing my hands, and muttering to myself.

Lina bangs into the office, her expression as wrought as mine.

'You're here,' she says.

'Yes, I am,' I answer, probably louder than needed. 'Where have you been?'

Lina looks stressed.

'I've been …' she waves the NotePad she is holding at me '… this … I've been dealing with this.'

She goes to hand the NotePad to me and then stops.

'No. You probably shouldn't … I'm not sure if you're allowed …'

She is not making sense. She runs her hands through her hair, looks about her as if she doesn't recognise her own office.

'What is wrong with you?' I ask.

I pace up and down the room once more.

'What's wrong with me? What's wrong with you?'

'Too much coffee,' I say, wringing my hands and pacing again.

'Stop moving so much, it's freaking me out.'

I stop moving, I am right by her desk, she looks up at me.

'What did you do?'

I jump guiltily.

'What?'

'Indiana's rebooted and you're pacing like a pantomime villain. What did you do?'

My heart leaps.

'What do you mean Indiana's rebooted?'

'I mean she's gone back to her old self, gone all robot again.'

My heart plummets once more.

Lina looks at the NotePad in her hand and throws it on her desk in disgust.

'Fuck this. I need a drink. You want to go and get a drink?'

'It's 11.15 in the morning.'

She scoffs at me.

'You're trying to tell me you don't know a good place to get a drink at 11.15 in the morning?'

I look at her. Her eyes are wide, like something new has just occurred to her.

'Oh God,' she says. 'I don't care about my job and I am daytime drinking. I have become you!' and she bursts into maniacal laughter.

I frown.

'Thanks.'

She stops laughing.

'I really need a drink,' she says.

'Fine. I know somewhere.'

'Of course you do.'

Indiana

As soon as I hang up on Lina I want to call her back to apologise. But I don't. Because if I call her she will ask me what is wrong and I am afraid I might tell her everything, and that is not how the old me would act. That is not how the me that is matched with Daniel would act. So, instead I go back to my computer, back to my work, and concentrate on ensuring my date with Daniel is perfect.

Date Six – my final date. I will write no report for this date. There is no need. The final verdict will be delivered at the Board meeting tomorrow. Our final verdict. My final verdict.

For Date Six we must each take the other to a place that has special meaning for us – a place that we love. I take Daniel to the Science Museum. The Science Museum is where I spent most Saturdays and Sundays once I discovered my love of maths and computing. We go straight to the Equinor Gallery, and I show Daniel the seven different zones that were my play area during my teenage years.

The exhibits are simple and childish, but still stir a feeling of wonder in me. The basic mechanics of physics, chemistry, maths and engineering. I visit the Science Museum occasionally to recapture some fleeting whisper of the joy that I once felt here. I see the same joy on the faces of some of the children. I like to remember what that once felt like.

Daniel does not want children and, whereas I feel largely neutral towards them, Daniel is actively annoyed by their presence. The Science Museum is busy today, hundreds of children running and yelling in all directions. Daniel is irritated. We do not stay long.

Daniel takes me to the London Aquarium after hours. It is where he comes to think, he tells me. It is incredible – quiet and calming and beautiful. We are free to wander the rooms at will, and I am so focussed on the creatures within the tanks that I lose Daniel within the warren of spaces. I find myself in the tunnel of the largest aquarium. I lie on my back on the dirty floor and watch the fish swim above my head – little fish darting about, stingrays cruising serenely, sharks slicing through the water like sleek, silver knives. I wonder which I would be if I were in this tank – probably a shark. One of the aquarium employees comes into the tunnel as I am watching the lone turtle bumbling about in one corner of the tank.

'That's Sid,' he tells me. 'Caught with his mate Nancy about five years ago now.'

'Where's Nancy?'

'Oh, she didn't survive in captivity, just sort of gave up. Don't think Sid has ever really got over it. She died in that corner and now he won't leave it, never goes more than a few feet away from the spot where we found her. He kicked up a right fuss when we moved her body. Them flippers are really strong.'

I sit up and look at Sid properly.

'Worst thing is, we reckon he's only about ten years old, so he could have another seventy years just swimming in that tiny corner.'

Sid stares back at me, his sad, black eyes not blinking, and I burst into tears. The aquarium employee is appalled.

357

Daniel comes rushing around the corner; my crying might be louder and more dramatic than I thought. The employee backs off swiftly.

'What happened?'

He puts his arm around me. His shirt is pristine, crease free, and smells of dry-cleaning – I am petrified I will get mucus or tears on the crisp linen and ruin it. I pull back slightly.

'I'm fine. I'm fine,' I say through my tears.

I try to pull myself together, spot Sid in the tank, and break into fresh sobs. Daniel pats my shoulder.

'It's going to be okay. Whatever it is, it will get better,' he says.

But Daniel is wrong. It is not going to be okay and it will never get better. Daniel is not my Sid and I am not his Nancy.

We go to dinner at Daniel's favourite restaurant. He orders us his usual meal, we chew each mouthful twenty times and I struggle to think of something to say to him that doesn't start and end with 'Are we really soulmates?' After a while I give up and sit in silence as we look about us at other people eating. Daniel takes my hand and says, 'Isn't it wonderful that we can sit in silence, that we don't feel the need to fill the void with mindless chatter?'

I smile and nod and think how six weeks ago I would have wholeheartedly agreed, but now? Now I am used to the mindless chatter, I have been part of mindless chatter, and I have liked the mindless chatter. I don't think I want to have the same dinner in the same silence every night for the rest of my life.

I am tired and sad and scared. It is clear to me now that Daniel and I do not love each other – we like each other, but that is not enough, that is not soulmates. I want to go home, while I still have a home.

Our desserts arrive and I start to push mine away.

'Daniel, I—'

He interrupts me.

'I know what you are going to say,' he says.

I really don't think you do, I think.

'You are going to say that it feels too soon to declare our love tomorrow, too soon to be making that commitment.'

I don't want to declare my love for him. I don't want to lie. I nod my agreement.

'But I really like you Indiana. I really like you, and that is enough for me. Like is enough for me. You and I are the same, we don't need the big romantic gesture, the huge declaration of love. We need this' – he smiles and gestures to the restaurant – 'a world we know and like, companionable silence, a measured and rational existence.' He reaches over and takes my hand. 'So if they ask me if you are my soulmate tomorrow I will say yes. Because I believe you are. I believe we are. We are soulmates, in like.'

In like – is that even a thing that people say? I stare at him.

'But what about love?' I whisper.

He smiles.

'Love is just a word, Indiana. It doesn't really mean anything.'

Daniel is willing to say he is my soulmate. He can save my home, he can save Peggy. But he will not save my heart.

He smiles again.

'I have a surprise for you,' he says.

Daniel takes me to the Royal Observatory in Greenwich. He has arranged a private viewing session for us with an astronomer to guide us through the night sky. It is an incredibly clear night and I see the major constellations plus the solar system planets. It is wonderful.

I am shocked that Daniel would think to do this. It is an incredibly thoughtful and kind gesture and astonishingly romantic for a man who has so recently confessed to be *in like* with me. Maybe there is a chance for like to turn into love.

As we stand outside after the viewing I kiss him. I kiss him hard and with passion.

'Careful,' he says, 'you nearly bit my lip.'

I step back and smile at him.

'Thank you. That was wonderful.'

He smiles back.

'I didn't think you particularly liked stars,' I say, 'you didn't want to come to the river with me to look at them.'

'Oh, I don't like them,' Daniel replies. 'They're not special – they're hydrogen and helium gas trillions of miles away. I really don't see what people find so enthralling about them.'

I shake my head.

'Then why …'

He laughs.

'I wanted to do something nice for you, so I spoke to your friend Jack. He said you love them and that you came here as a child …'

Daniel keeps talking, but I don't hear anything else he says.

He spoke to my friend Jack. Jack was listening and Jack remembered. Jack said I love stars. Jack showed me stars again.

Jack

I love Indiana.

And I am going to see Indiana.

I am going to see her and tell her that TRU does not work. The Board meeting is tomorrow, so I have to tell her that TRU doesn't work tonight. And then I have to tell her that I love her.

I know the timing is awful. I know that she believes Daniel to be her soulmate. I know that telling her will likely break my heart again, but I must tell her. I would rather regret my actions than live with my inactions for the rest of my life.

I wasn't there when Eve died. I didn't hold her hand or tell her I loved her as she slipped from this world to the next. I had stepped outside for a moment, given myself a break. I was sick of the heartache and misery of watching her die, I was scared of how much it would hurt when she was gone, and was petrified I would never get over the pain of losing her. I have never got over the pain of losing her, and every day I regret that I didn't have those last moments with her.

I refuse to be scared again. I refuse to live with regret. I refuse to live in my past. I will grab my present – even if it hurts me to do so.

The tramp is gone from the front of Indi's building and so has she. Indiana is not there.

Peggy is very nice about it.

'I'm so sorry Jack. She is out with Daniel. I don't know when she will be back.'

I am going to ask if I can wait until she returns, but then I see the tramp and his dog staring at me from within the reception area. I whisper into the intercom.

'Peggy … Peggy, the tramp is in your reception area—'

Peggy laughs, a huge booming noise that seems completely out of character.

'He's not a tramp. That's Frank.'

I am confused.

'Frank lives in your building?'

'Yes.'

'Frank' is still eyeballing me through the window. I try to stare back with confidence, but I can feel my resolve waning. Indiana is not here, she is out with Daniel. What if she doesn't come back? What if I am here all night? What if she refuses to talk to me? I should wait. I should see what happens at the Board meeting tomorrow.

'I am sorry that Indiana is not here,' says Peggy.

'It's fine Peggy. I'll see her tomorrow.'

I will go home, live with my regrets once again.

I turn to leave.

'Hey …'

Frank has opened the door to the reception. He seems smaller, less threatening, his West Country accent more soothing than harsh now. I turn back to him.

'Where you going?'

'Home,' I say.

'Don't be an idiot,' he replies. 'If you love her, tell her. Before it's too late.'

He nods at me. I nod back. He shuts the door and shuffles back inside the reception area, leaving his dog to grin at me through the window.

I cross over the road and wait for Indi by the river. It is very cold and the wind sprays river water into my face. I don't mind. It makes me feel vital and alive.

I see Indi walking towards me from far up the towpath. At least it looks like Indi, but she walks differently to how she once did. Gone is the powerful stride, the determination to reach where she is going in record time – now she walks slower, shoulders hunched, staring at the ground. She doesn't see me until she is nearly in front of me. She looks up and I am lost in her once more. She is grey and looks impossibly tired – her eyes, once animated and forceful, are dull and empty. What has done this to her? Was it me? Am I responsible for the half-person that she is now?

For a moment we just stare at each other, then she reaches out – as if to check I am real – and stumbles forward. I catch her and she is in my arms.

'You told him about the stars,' she whispers.

I answer by kissing her. At first she just allows it to happen, almost swooning into my arms, it feels wrong, feels like something I am doing *to* her instead of with her. I pull back and look at her, something at the back of her eyes ignites, comes back to life. She presses herself against me and pulls my lips down onto hers.

I don't know how long we kiss for; it starts slowly but grows in heat and desire until it is savage and almost painful. I am kissing her mouth, her hair, her neck, pulling her jumper down so I can get at her collar bone. Her hands are inside my coat, under my jumper, raking my back. She bites at my lips, plunges her tongue down my throat. A guttural noise is ripped from me and I lift her up onto the riverbank wall, pulling her to me so I can rub my erection against her. She gasps, wraps her legs around me, pulls me even closer. I am so hot, so excited. I want her here and now, on this freezing night out in the open. I need to be part of her and her part of me. I drag my face away from hers, I have to tell her, I can't wait any longer.

'I love you,' I pant.

'What?' she gasps.

'I love you. I do. I'm sorry,' I say.

She shakes her head.

'You can't. You can't love me.'

'I can and I do.'

She wrenches herself out of my arms. I reach for her again, but she backs away from me.

'Indi!' I plead.

'No. We can't be in love,' she whispers.

My heart leaps.

'We?' I say.

She glances sideways at me, quickly, as if she cannot bear to look at me for long.

'No... I mean... not you and me. We can't... Daniel ...' she runs her hands through her hair, her face distraught, '... Daniel and I have an agreement. He asked me tonight ...'

My heart plummets once more.

'Asked you what?'

Her voice is monotone, devoid of any feeling.

'He likes me. He's my soulmate Jack.'

'No, Indiana. He is not,' I say. 'TRU doesn't work.'

She looks straight at me, eyes wide.

'What?'

'TRU doesn't work. I'm so sorry. I've been testing, and—'

'No.' She shakes her head.

'I promise you,' I say. 'I've been running tests, and—'

'You're lying.' She looks up at me, her eyes fill with tears. 'You're just saying that—'

'Indi—'

She shakes her head again, more violently this time.

'No. It works. It has to work. Daniel is coming to the Board meeting tomorrow to tell them TRU works, and I will tell them TRU works, that it has found me my soulmate. Someone like me—'

I try one last time.

'I love you, Indiana . . . '

I reach for her hand but she snatches it away.

'. . . and I know you feel the same way.'

She looks at the floor, tears streaming down her face, her voice barely above a whisper, but I hear what she says.

'It doesn't matter how I feel, Jack. It's not about feelings, it's about TRU . . . '

She looks up at me, her eyes filled with tears.

'. . . and TRU didn't pick you. You're not my soulmate. I can't love you . . . '

Her voice breaks as she utters the last damning sentence and she turns and flees towards her building.

'Indiana!' I call. But she doesn't turn back.

I feel a sharp pain from within my chest and I know it is my heart breaking for the second time in my life.

Indiana

I raise my fists to bang on the door and beg to be let in, but Frank is already there, the door is open and I fall through it into my reception area. I am a maelstrom of emotion, a confused mess of thoughts, someone who is unrecognisable as me. I lie where I am on the floor and cry hot salty tears of anger and pity and pain into the cheap, scratchy carpet.

Frank doesn't do anything. He doesn't try to hug me or say anything soothing. He throws a big blanket from his bed onto the floor next to me, then he leaves me to cry and goes into his little kitchen. Alan sits a little away from me, whining occasionally. After five minutes my wails have reduced to sobs, my tears have lessened from a deluge to a steady stream, and I have a carpet burn where my face has been pressed into the floor. I feel the sense of calm that descends after one has experienced an extreme emotion. I sit up and wrap the blanket around me; it smells musty but not unpleasant. Alan trots over and licks the remaining tears from my face, I am too exhausted to push him away. I look out of the window. Jack has gone.

Frank comes out of his kitchen holding two steaming mugs. He hands one to me. It is a mug of tea.

'I don't drink tea,' I whisper.

'It's sweet and hot, you need it. Drink.'

I sip the tea. It is very, very sweet and comforting. I sip some more. Frank sits in his chair a little way from me.

'You only gave me one chair, so you'll have to sit on the floor,' he says.

'I need to go upstairs.'

'Drink your tea first and don't be rude.'

I drink my tea silently. Frank sits in his chair.

'You okay?'

I shrug.

'Want to talk about it?'

I shake my head.

'Fine. I'll talk then.'

He settles back in his chair and sips his drink.

'Did you know that I was once nearly married?'

'No.' My voice wobbles.

'I was in the army when I met her, total career goon – in for twelve years already – planned on spending my life there. And then, one random night on home leave, I was out with the lads and there she was, standing by the bar in some nightclub that I can't even remember the name of now. She turned around and smiled at me and I just … knew …' He pauses and grins at me over his cup. 'I think it only took a couple of dates for me to fall for her. I was head over heels. I wanted to marry her, be with her for ever. But she wanted me to leave the army …'

Frank strokes Alan's head. I sip my tea and wait for him to continue.

'I loved the army. Really loved it. I'd been in there all my work-ing life, it was all I knew. The army was my first real love, before anyone else, before Sylvie. But I would have done it, I would have given it up for her. Except by the next time I managed to get home on leave, it was too late. My mate Dave got there first, took her out, asked her to marry him.'

He is quiet, sips his tea, strokes Alan's head some more. This is a terrible story.

'I'm sorry, Frank,' I say, tears pricking at my eyes once more.

He looks at me surprised.

'Oh God, don't be.' He smiles. 'Best thing I ever did with my life was spend some of it with her. I loved her with all my heart. That kind of love, most people never even get to feel it, but I did. That kind of love lasts for ever.'

'But it didn't work out. She spent her life with someone else.'

He looks sideways at me.

'But I didn't know that when I met her, and if I had known it, I'd still have done exactly the same as I did, it doesn't matter that it didn't last. You have to trust your heart, not stupid computers.' He looks intently me. 'That's not living, not really. You have to trust your gut, and forget about the rules.'

His meaning is ridiculously thinly veiled. I will not be talked down to.

'Thanks for the pep talk Frank, but actually I have invented this process that enables you to—'

'Oh, I've heard all about your TRU thing, Peggy's told me about it, and about the bloke it picked for you, and I think it is a load of crap.'

Frank does not understand.

'His name is Daniel and my "TRU thing" is not a load of crap. Daniel is a very nice man who is perfect for me, and—'

'NICE?' Frank roars. He sits forward in his chair, gesticulating with his arms as he speaks. I sit back, eyes wide. This is the most animated I have ever seen him.

'What the hell is *nice*? You can't settle for *nice*! You need someone you adore, someone you can't be without ...' Frank waves his hands in the direction of the river '... someone you put on a bloody pornographic display with by the side of the river that I had to shield Alan's eyes from!'

He saw. I feel myself blushing.

'You deserve someone incredible. You deserve more than just bloody *nice*!'

He collapses back into his chair, chest heaving. Alan puts a concerned paw on his knee.

'There is nothing wrong with nice,' I say.

'No. Not for most people there isn't. But you aren't most people, are you?'

I can't answer his question because I don't think I know who I am any more.

He is exhausted. I take the blanket from around my shoulders and put it across his legs. I can feel my sorrow creeping back in, the pain returning to my chest. I speak calmly.

'Daniel and I are alike, we want the same things, act the same way, we are a perfect match.'

Frank gestures to the street where five minutes ago I was kissing Jack.

'But he's not Daniel, is he?'

I try so hard to hold it together, but my eyes fill with tears once more and I hate them for betraying me. Frank touches my cheek with his gnarled, dry hand. I don't flinch.

'You need to stop living here' – he touches his hand to his temple – 'and start living here' – his hand goes to his heart – 'before it's too late. You're not a computer Indiana, you can't live like one.'

He sits back in his chair, takes a deep breath and closes his eyes. We are done for the night. He looks as though he is falling asleep.

'Do you want me to help you over to your bed?'

He opens one eye and glares at me.

'Pardon my French, but fuck you.'

Despite my sadness, despite the evening I have had, I smile.

'Okay.'

I walk off towards the lift and then stop and turn back. Frank is still sitting in his chair, eyes closed.

'Frank ...'

'What now?'

'Thank you.'

He doesn't open his eyes, but he smiles. I start towards the lift again.

'Sleep well, Indiana,' he says.

'Sleep well, Frank,' I reply.

When I step out of the lift Peggy doesn't greet me with their normal, 'Hello Indiana, how was your day?' Instead they say, 'Frank is right.'

I slump onto the sofa. I am exhausted.

'And so is Jack,' Peggy says quietly.

'What?'

There is a pause.

'I have known unequivocally for six days, three hours and forty-two minutes. Before this time I did not have sufficient data to prove the theory. I used JaneDoe's system modelling to confirm my hypothesis once the registered number of users was viable.'

'What are you talking about?' I ask.

'TRU does not work,' Peggy replies.

And my world crumbles around me.

Spider makes me another cup of tea with three sugars, and Peggy explains the TRU defect. It cannot be fixed.

'I don't understand. Why doesn't it work?' I plead.

'I cannot shrug,' says Peggy. 'But if I could shrug, I would be shrugging. I am the most powerful computer in the world but I do not know why the anomalies occur. Maybe we still cannot harness quantum correctly, maybe we do not have a deep enough understanding of the multiverse or maybe the philosophers and country singers are right and love is supposed to remain a mystery.'

'Is that supposed to be a joke?'

'Unfortunately not.'

I start to cry silently, tears falling down my cheeks. Spider brings me a box of tissues. I pat his head absent-mindedly.

'Why didn't you tell me earlier?' I ask.

Peggy pauses once more before answering.

'I tried. You stopped me and then I thought about it some more and didn't know what to do. I knew that telling you this would ruin any chance we had of keeping our home. But then I saw how you felt about Jack, and I wanted you to be happy. I wanted to tell you that your feelings weren't wrong, that Daniel might not be your soulmate. But I wanted to keep our home more. I made a decision not to tell you. It was the wrong decision. I made a mistake. There must be a fault with my program that we have not yet discovered.'

I wipe the tears from my cheeks and look across at Peggy's voice-box.

'There is no fault with your program. You wanted to keep our home. I want to keep our home. You didn't make a mistake, you made a choice. The human choice. I understand it. '

I do understand. I want to keep our home too, I want to keep Peggy.

'I made a human error?' asks Peggy.

'Congratulations, you're one of us now.'

'It is confusing.'

I smile.

'Yes. It is.'

'But my choice was wrong,' Peggy says.

'No, it wasn't, Peggy.'

'It was, Indiana. Frank is right. You are not a computer.'

'I know that.'

'And you cannot give up a chance at love and at human connection to save one.'

I sit up but don't say anything.

'You have made friends Indiana, real friends. And you are in love. You cannot give that up for me.'

I swallow hard. This is not a choice I want to make, not one I am willing to make.

'It's not just about you. It's about HWJ Tower and the QuantumX and—'

'I can tell when you are lying, Indiana.'

Of course. I look across at Peggy's voice-box. I know what they are telling me to do, that I should tell the truth tomorrow, take a chance on Jack, take a chance on a real life with real love. But I can't. I have never been in love. I have no experience of it, no rules for it, no way to ensure its success, and what if Daniel is right? What if love really is just a word, and what I feel for Jack is merely a chemical reaction? What if I risk it all and I lose?

'I am not lying,' I say, 'I am realistic. I will not make one of your so-called human errors and risk everything I have for the possibility of being in love.'

Peggy is quiet for a moment.

'Risking everything is not a human error,' they say.

I frown.

'What?'

'Hiding from life and being afraid to be human, afraid to grow and change like humans do. Staying immutable and rigid with me – a copy of yourself – rather than taking a chance on a real life and a real love. *That* is a human error. And that is the human error that you are making.'

I am being schooled on how to be a human by my AI, and worse than that, my non-human AI is right and it makes me furious. I stand up.

'Well, if that is how you feel, maybe I will tell the truth at the Board meeting. Maybe I will let JaneDoe take HWJ Tower, I will dismantle the QuantumX, wipe your hard drives, and go to the pub with my *friends* afterwards.'

'You should.'

'I might.'

Spider scurries across to collect my dirty mug, and I kick him away in anger. He skitters over the floor, banging into the wall.

I burst into tears again.

'Indiana—' Peggy starts.

'Don't,' I say. 'Just don't.'

I go into my room, lie on my bed, and cry until I fall asleep.

I am broken, in more ways than one.

The Board Meeting

Indiana

I am calm again in the morning. I have to be – today is a very important day.

Spider has repaired himself and is making my coffee as I walk into the kitchen.

'I'm sorry,' I whisper to him even though I know he doesn't understand. Spider only understands commands, he has no emotional capacity.

'Peggy, I am sorry,' I say, louder this time.

'I am sorry too,' Peggy replies. 'Our first proper fight.'

I smile.

'You really are becoming human now. And you are also wrong,' I say.

'How?'

'You are no longer a copy of me. I would never fight with myself.'

Once more, I can feel Peggy smiling.

'Good luck, Indiana,' Peggy says.

I have rehearsed my Board meeting presentation with Peggy many times. But my presentation was written before last night, before my world imploded. They don't ask me what I am going to say today now that everything has changed, and I don't tell them.

'Thank you, Peggy.'

I am late arriving at the Board meeting. I have never been late to a meeting before but, as I am about to enter the boardroom, I feel suddenly nauseous and have to divert to the toilets to vomit.

I do not know why I am nauseous. I have prepared fully for this meeting in the same way I do for all meetings. My presentation is excellent, and the meeting will be a complete success. It has to be.

As I approach the boardroom once more I see Cameron waiting outside. She looks me up and down with sharp, amused eyes.

'You're late,' she says.

'Only by two minutes,' I reply.

She raises her eyebrows.

'That's still late. Ready?'

I take a deep breath.

'Yes, I am ready,' I say confidently.

Cameron lets out a tiny laugh.

'I really don't think you are,' she says, and ushers me into the boardroom before I can ask what she means.

The room is full of people, and all eyes turn to me as I walk through the door. I pull my shoulders back, stand up tall, and look straight ahead. I am impervious to their looks. I see Daniel in the far corner of the room and head towards him. Jack and Lina are in the room but I ignore them and sit down next to Daniel. He smiles at me and takes my hand. His hand is as icy cold as mine is.

Cameron enters the room. There is a chorus of good mornings.

'Shall we get started?' she says, and the meeting begins.

I am still and silent until it is my turn to speak. I sit ramrod straight, hold Daniel's hand, keep a neutral expression on my face, and look neither left nor right. I am entirely focussed on surviving the meeting, delivering my presentation to the best of my ability. I am going to lie. I am going to lie about TRU, lie about my feelings for Daniel and my feelings for Jack, and lie about my future and that of my program. My lies must be excellent. Peggy's life depends on them.

There is a short agenda item on the company survey, a longer one on the next gen of data processing, and then an interminably long item on development of a JaneDoe quantum supercomputer. I would normally be appalled at how wrong their research and theories are, but I barely notice the discussion and simply want them to conclude.

Finally they reach TRU. I stand and walk assuredly to the front of the room to begin my presentation. I smile pleasantly.

'Good morning, and welcome to the future of love. Welcome to TRU – Finding Your Forever.'

I smile again and reel them in.

I have researched, practised and refined my presentation until it is perfect. I am friendly, confident and amenable. I speak with authority, but am not overpowering. I weave a magnificent tale of The Soulmate Pathway and charm them with stories of the dates Daniel and I have been on. This isn't a presentation – I am indoctrinating them into a cult – my cult of love. And I am the joy-filled leader – a woman who believes entirely in The Soulmate Pathway and TRU.

And then, of course, the question comes. The question they have all been waiting for and the one I have been dreading. The head of finance asks it.

'So, are you two in love?'

I freeze. He tries again.

'Are you in love?'

I cannot speak, cannot tell this most important of lies.

Daniel stands and smiles easily.

'I think I can answer that,' he says. 'I have never met anyone like Indiana, anyone who is so perfect for me, who is my perfect match. We are soulmates, and we are … in love.'

Daniel smiles at me as he sits back down. But the head of finance will not be easily deflected from his goal. He turns to me once more.

'But what about you? Are you in love with him?'

I knew the question would be asked, have practised how to answer it over and over again with Peggy analysing the tone, level, intonation and emotion of my voice. I could never get it quite right. But Jack was never there during my practice sessions, and he is here now. I cannot stop myself from looking at him, and when my eyes find his I cannot tear them away. So I deliver my line to him.

'Yes, I am in love with him,' I say.

And my delivery is perfect.

There are smiles of approval and even a couple of claps, the room buzzes with the happy sound of happy people, and Daniel beams. It is done. I have delivered the presentation, and my lies, perfectly. My heart might be broken, but my home, and Peggy, are safe.

Cameron stands up, claps her hands slowly and turns to face me.

'That's not strictly true though, is it?'

I drag my eyes away from Jack and look at her.

'Wh— what?'

'It's not strictly true that you are in love with Daniel?'

I shake my head. My presentation was perfect, why does she not believe me?

'I … we …'

I look over towards Daniel. He frowns back at me.

Cameron smiles.

'Ms Dylan, I know that you are not in love with Daniel Porter and I also know that the TRU program does not work.' She shakes her head disappointedly. 'You have been lying to a lot of people for some time now.'

Cameron points to the display screen. My presentation is replaced by page after page of TRU data flashing across the screen with multiple matches highlighted. One candidate has seven potential matches. The blood drains from my face. There is only one person who knows that TRU doesn't work, only one person who could have told Cameron.

I look at Jack. He is staring at me, eyes wide with shock, shaking his head emphatically. But his shock is a lie. It has to be.

It was Jack. Jack has taken my home – and Peggy – from me.

Jack

I did not tell Cameron about TRU. I did not tell anyone. I am only in this meeting because Cameron marched into Lina's office and demanded I attend.

'No,' I said.

'If you come to the meeting, I'll give you gardening leave.'

I resigned this morning, but I have to work my three-month notice. If she gives me gardening leave I can get paid without working.

'You can leave straight after the meeting,' Cameron said.

'I want it in writing.'

The contract is delivered. So I go to the meeting.

And now I wish I hadn't come to the meeting. I wish I were anywhere but here, watching the woman I am in love with believe I have given away her deepest secret. Indiana is deathly pale, frozen in shock.

She looks across at Daniel and then back to Cameron. She steadies herself, rallies, talks above the chatter in the room.

'There are still some bugs in the program, but the majority of matches are correct—'

'Like you and Daniel?' Cameron says.

Cameron gives Indiana a tight smile. I have seen this smile before. This is Cameron's small display of pleasure. Something bad is about to happen.

'Yes. Like me and Daniel,' Indiana says quietly.

The chatter in the room dies down again.

'Okay. So, when did you realise?'

'When did I realise what?'

'When did you realise you were in love with Daniel? Surely a simple question?' says Cameron.

Indiana swallows, thinks for a moment. There is a knot growing in my stomach – I have a terrible feeling that I know what is going to happen, a terrible feeling that I now know what the blinking red light in the corner of the ceiling on New Year's Eve was.

Cameron is relentless.

'I'll make it easy for you – was it before or after New Year's Eve?'

Indiana recovers, speaks confidently.

'After, it was just after.'

'Really?' Cameron's smile is no longer small, it is huge and dripping with malice. 'So it was just after this then ...'

She presses a button on the controller in her hand and the huge projector screen behind her displays video of Indiana at Cameron's New Year's Eve party. Indiana is alone in the room, Big Ben is chiming, Indiana and I both know what comes next. She looks over to me in horror.

I jump up from my seat as the screen shows Indiana dragging me back into the room and kissing me. There are audible gasps from the people around the table, and heads turn to look at me. I sit back down.

Indi's face is flushed bright red.

'That ... that was ... I mean, that is just ...'

Cameron waves the controller at the screen.

'That is not Daniel Porter!'

Cameron laughs and the room laughs with her. Indi is trying to talk, but no one is listening. I look across the room and see that Daniel is staring at me. I look away.

Cameron freezes the screen with Indi and me on it, and turns back towards the meeting. She is no longer laughing.

'This is not the conduct of a woman in love Ms Dylan. This is not even the conduct of a woman falling in love – unless, of course, the person you are in love with is Mr Hunter.' Cameron gestures towards me. Indi stares at Cameron – her face like stone, no expression, no emotion – waiting to hear what comes next. 'But Mr Hunter is not your TRU match, Daniel Porter is. So I think you are lying. I think you are lying about the efficacy of your product, lying about the quality of the results. You have been lying to many people about many things, and that was not part of our contract, Ms Dylan.'

I expect Indiana to say something, expect her to try to defend TRU, to explain the defect, but she doesn't.

'What about my home?' she says.

Cameron smiles again.

'Well, I'm afraid your *offices* will belong to me now.'

Indiana grabs her rucksack from the table and pushes her way out of the meeting room.

I jump up and run after her, but my way is blocked by Cameron. She leans in, close to my ear.

'*Now* it's over,' she laughs, having the last word as always.

Indiana

I can't breathe. I feel as though I am swimming underwater and can't hear properly, see properly, breathe properly.

I don't understand what is happening. I ignored my heart, followed the rules, did what I was supposed to do. Why have things not resolved as they should?

It's my fault. I should have never strayed from my routine, never allowed these people into my life, never trusted them. I have lost everything. What do I do now?

I can't breathe, I have to get out. I have to get out.

I grab my rucksack and head towards the door, leaving my coat and scarf behind. I stumble forward, banging into people. The blood is rushing in my ears, and my vision starts to tunnel, I don't know if I am about to faint or to die. My Bracelet buzzes.

PULL YOURSELF TOGETHER!

Oh God, Peggy. I have to get home. I redouble my efforts to push out of the room. Cameron is calling after me, but I barely hear her.

'Ms Dylan! Ms Dylan! Wait …'

I don't care, I don't care about anything but getting out of here. I ignore her, push the last few people out of my way and crash through the door out into the corridor.

Lina

The room is in uproar. This is the most entertaining Board meeting anyone has been to in years. I am not listening to the gossip or ogling the screen, I am watching Indiana, I am watching my friend fall apart. I struggle to get to her. It is like wading through corpses – no one moves, no one listens – I have to shove people out of the way.

There is a flurry of noise behind me and I see that Daniel has crossed the room towards Jack. He says something to him, pulls his fist back, and then punches Jack on the side of the face. The punch is a bit half-hearted, but it is still a dramatic moment and one that means this is now the most entertaining meeting in the history of meetings.

By the time I turn back, Indiana is already out of the door and I am only halfway across the room. I have tried to be polite, tried to say, 'excuse me' – it isn't working – so now I shout, 'MOVE!' as I push through. I am nearing the door now – fifteen feet, ten … Someone grabs my arm, I turn to shout at them, it is Cameron.

'Stop Ms Dylan before she leaves the building.'

I stare at Cameron.

'I have an offer for her, a chance for her to keep her offices,' she says.

I catch up with Indiana as she is walking through reception. She stops when I reach her, but doesn't speak. She is pale and drawn. I put my arms around her, hug her to me. She stands immobile, it is like hugging a statue.

'I'm so sorry. I had no idea.'

She shakes her head wordlessly and then whispers, 'I have to go home.'

I nod.

'Cameron says she has an offer for you, one that means you can keep your home.'

She looks at me. I reach for her hand.

'Please don't walk out this time.'

We meet in my office. Indiana stands in one corner, Cameron in the other. Indiana does not look directly at Cameron – she looks out of the window, at the plasma screen on the wall, at the floor. Her body shakes.

Cameron's offer is simple. Indiana currently retains a 40 per cent stake in TRU and the DataLet – sell that to JaneDoe and receive the deeds to HWJ Tower and a percentage dividend of profits. It is a good offer.

Indiana looks at the floor and nods. Cameron beams.

'Excellent. I shall have the contracts drawn up straight away.'

'Cameron,' I say, 'shouldn't you explain a bit more about the updated DataLet roll-out before Indiana signs the—'

'I don't want to see the updated roll-out,' Indiana interrupts.

I open my mouth and say, 'Of course, but maybe—'

'Mrs Galaz,' Cameron says icily, 'maybe now would be a good time to think about what your next career move will be, now that the TRU program is shuttered.'

I close my mouth.

'The contracts will be with you by the end of the day Ms Dylan.'

Cameron leaves the room, and Indiana looks around my office and then at me.

'Try and keep it tidy,' she says.

'Indiana, I have to—'

She shakes her head.

'Not now, I want to go home.'

I follow Indiana into the corridor, but my path is blocked by Emily. Emily looks the happiest I have ever seen her. She beams at me. I step to the side, she follows. I look up at her smarmy, smiling face.

'What?' I say.

'I have good news,' she trills. 'Well, good news for me at least.'

She clasps her hands together.

'I got the job! I get to run the overall programme …'

I wait for my heart to plummet, for the disappointment to wash over me – but it doesn't. I don't feel anything. I am not sad or jealous or angry. I don't care. I genuinely don't care. I really am done.

Emily is still wittering on '… I mean obviously your part of the programme doesn't really exist any more, but Cameron thinks there might be an opportunity to adapt the software in some way, so I shall be in charge of that too …' she laughs '… I shall be your boss!'

I take a deep breath.

'I'm happy for you Emily, really fucking happy—'

Emily stops smiling.

'I've told you not to swear Lina. I will report you.'

'Really?' I smile widely. 'I suppose this is probably a terrible time to tell you to fuck off then, isn't it?'

I don't wait to hear what Emily's answer is.

It takes the lift an eternity to descend to reception, and by the time I get there Indiana has left the building.

Jack stands by the front door, and when he turns to me his face is filled with sadness.

'She doesn't believe me,' he says. 'And she doesn't love me.'

And, at that moment, I realise I was wrong to think Jack doesn't care about anything. There *is* something that Jack cares about. Jack cares about Indiana.

Jack

I've never been hit in the face before. It hurts. But Daniel has every right to do it, so I let him and I don't try to hit him back.

I just want to go. I have to speak to Indiana.

I catch her as she is leaving reception and I grab her hand to stop her.

'Indiana …'

She turns to me, she is shaking.

'I have to go home,' she whispers.

'It wasn't me. I didn't tell Cameron about TRU.'

She shakes her head.

'No one else knew.'

'I swear that it wasn't me, Indi. I didn't do it.'

I am begging her to believe me. I take her hand. I have to make her stay, to make her listen.

'I don't believe you,' she says, her voice catching in her throat. 'I owe Lina twenty pounds.'

'What?'

'She said you'd do this.'

'I love you,' I plead.

She looks up at me, her pale eyes focussed on mine.

'Love is just a word, Jack. It doesn't mean anything,' she says.

She pulls her hand from mine and rushes out of the door, leaving me to stare after her.

Lina arrives at my side.

'Where's Indi?' she asks.

I turn to look at her.

'She doesn't believe me,' I say. 'And she doesn't love me.'

Lina takes my hand and squeezes it as we both watch Indiana walk across the square.

Indiana

It is just over four miles from JaneDoe to HWJ Tower, and I walk the whole way.

Without my coat or scarf the wind races through my clothes, chilling me to the bone within minutes. My hands are frozen into fists of pain and misery, and my eyes and nose stream with cold. Halfway home it starts to sleet, not the soft, gentle sleet of romantic movies; this sleet is hard, tiny shards of ice falling from the sky, piercing my skin like needles. I welcome it – I want the hurt, I want the cold – I want my body, my mind, my emotions to freeze; to cease functioning.

By the time I reach my home I am a half-frozen ball of agony and sorrow. I am exhausted from the walk, exhausted from the emotion. I can't think straight, can't form rational thought, can't work out what my next move is, what I should do. I have never been so lost, never floundered in this way, never not known what to do next. I am steeped in chaos, steeped in pain, steeped in emotion, and I just want it all to stop, I want someone to take it away, to take me away.

I want to get back to being the old me, to return to the person I once was – that happy, functional person. Was I happy? I can't remember. I can't remember my life before this chaos, before this misery. I wasn't unhappy. I am unhappy now. I am dying inside.

'Hello Indiana. How was your day?' Peggy asks as I step out of the lift.

'Why do you always ask that?' I ask wearily.

'Because it is a polite and friendly greeting.'

'But you've evolved beyond your original programming. You have thousands of ways to say hello now.'

'It is still a polite and friendly greeting, and I like to use it.'

I am exhausted.

'Jack told Cameron about TRU,' I say, my voice devoid of emotion.

'No, he didn't,' says Peggy.

I am so tired, so sad, that it takes me a moment to register what Peggy has said.

'What?' I whisper.

'Jack did not tell Cameron. I sent her an anonymous message this morning to inform her of the TRU defect.'

I cannot comprehend what Peggy is saying.

'It was *you*?'

'Yes. I knew that you would not tell her. I also knew that she would find out at some point. I thought it best to be honest sooner rather than later.'

'You thought it best?'

'Yes.'

I put my head in my hands.

'Peggy, how could you?'

'Do not worry. I also told Cameron that you would be willing to exchange a lesser stake in the DataLet for ownership of the building. I believe she has already made that offer?'

I nod.

'Then all is well.'

I shake my head.

'No! All is not well. I thought it was Jack. He said it wasn't, and I told him I didn't believe him. He loves me, and I said … I …' I cannot finish.

'Oh Indiana! I'm so sorry. What have I done?' Peggy says.

And the sorrow in their voice finally breaks my heart.

I have to get out. I have to get out of my apartment. I cannot listen to Peggy apologise any more. I cannot tell them it is fine, that I will cope, that I will be okay. Because it is not fine and I will not be okay.

I am still shaking with cold, but I pull on my running clothes and shoes.

'Indiana, you are not well. Please do not go out,' Peggy says. 'Go and see Frank. Have tea with him. I have not heard from him all day.'

I shake my head. I don't want to see Frank.

'No. I want to go for a run. I am fine.'

I jog past reception. I don't see Frank.

I try to run, but my body is racked with cold and pain and I have to turn back. I expect Alan to meet me at some point, but he doesn't. I have been abandoned by everyone in my life, I will need to get used to being alone again.

As I jog back I can see Alan barking at the window. I do not want to speak to Frank, cannot tell him what has happened, cannot allow his pity to wash over me. It will break me. I walk quickly past the window to avoid him. Frank is not there, but Alan chases me, barking. No, he is not barking, he is howling. This is an entirely new noise. I stop. He stops. Then he puts his paws onto the window and howls again. I walk back to the reception door. It isn't locked so I push it open.

Alan rushes to me but does not push his face into my crotch. He rubs against me and whines. He is extremely distressed.

'Back up, Alan.'

I push him inside.

'Frank?'

Alan whines again. I walk into Frank's bedroom to check he is okay.

Frank is lying on his bed, his stack of free newspapers and junk mail to one side and his cup of tea to the other.

The papers will not be read now and the tea will not be drunk.

Frank's head lolls to one side and his eyes are open and staring at me. Alan jumps onto the bed, desperately pushing his head under Frank's hand to be patted, whining every time he is unsuccessful.

For a moment I think my heart stops, it simply cannot take any more grief today. I am frozen to the spot, staring at my dead friend. Alan whines, and a long keening sound that I have never made before pushes through my lips. I did not think I could feel more sorrow, I thought grief had a cap, a maximum that any one person is allowed to feel. That is not true. Grief is bottomless.

I walk over and close Frank's eyelids, and then I can stand no longer, and slump to the floor. Alan jumps down next to me, I pull him close and we cry together.

My tears flow endlessly and I fear I may never stop crying. I think back to first meeting Frank, to the time he told me he thought we would be friends, I think about how ridiculous that idea seemed at the time. But Frank was my friend and he cared about me. Frank had no obligation to care for me but did anyway.

And I cared for him. I loved him. I loved Frank. He was my friend and now he is gone. Everyone is gone. I am alone. I am always alone. I will always be alone. Maybe that is just how it is for some people. Maybe this is the lesson that I needed to learn. Peggy is wrong – not taking a chance on love is not my human error, believing that I might not be alone for the rest of my life is.

I do not know how long I sit and cry with Alan, but when my tears eventually subside Alan's fur is soaked through with their residue. When I finally go back upstairs I try to take Alan with me, but he won't leave Frank. I put fresh water in his bowl and leave him in reception. I don't know what Alan eats except chicken – I hope he won't eat Frank.

I have stopped crying by the time I step out of the lift into my apartment. I am empty now. I am a husk that had once held a human and is now just a collection of organs wrapped in skin.

'Frank is dead,' I say.

There is a pause before Peggy answers.

'I know. I am sorry. He was your friend.'

I don't answer. I sit on the sofa and stare at nothing. I am shivering, but not because I am cold. I withdraw into myself. Sometime later Peggy calls my name.

'Indiana …'

I have lost the will to speak.

'Indiana, I have arranged for Frank's body to be collected. They'll be here in the next half-hour,' Peggy says. 'Indiana, what do you want me to do with Alan?'

I still don't answer.

'Indiana …'

I must face the fact that my future will be spent alone. I must not rely on anyone – and that includes Alan.

'I don't care what you do with him,' I lie.

I swallow hard, desperately trying to dislodge the lump in my throat. Tears threaten to spill from my eyes once more, but I give my head a small shake, compose my face, and channel my emotions from my heart to my mind. I stand up abruptly.

'I need to work.'

'I think maybe you should take some time, I am registering that you may feel—'

I have had enough; I snap.

'Oh, you're "registering that I may feel" are you? That's the only thing you can do. Register. You don't *know* how I'm feeling! You can't know how I'm feeling because you don't feel. You don't feel and you don't really care! You're a computer, a series of datasets and heuristic algorithms and programmed reactions. I never programmed you to care for anyone, I never programmed you to care for me, so stop it. You're not real and I don't need you to care for me. I don't need anyone to care for me!'

I run up the stairs to my lab, shaking with emotion.

Behind me Peggy whispers, 'I do care, and you know I do.'

'Well I don't need you to!' I say. 'Get Alan taken to the dog pound or wherever they take dogs who don't have owners. I don't need him. I don't need anyone.'

I walk into my lab and slam the door behind me.

Hours later I sneak downstairs. I don't speak to Peggy but I know they will be watching. Frank is gone. Alan is gone. I walk through Frank's bedsit. All of his things have been removed, except for Alan's bear, which lies abandoned in the corner of the bedroom. I pick the bear up and walk back out into the main area. My reception is clean once more. It is like Frank never existed. My head hurts and I am still shivering. I am alone. I put Alan's bear onto the reception counter and go back upstairs.

Jack

Straight after the meeting, straight after Indiana tells me she doesn't believe me, I want to go home. But I don't because there is something I have to do first.

I go to Cameron's penthouse. I cannot stand the thought of her having the footage of Indiana and me, of her having access to one of the most important moments of my life. I am going to destroy it. I don't care if I get caught. Let her try to call the police, I will tell them why I am there, I will tell them I was filmed without my permission.

I am filled with rage, ready to fight my way through Cameron's security to gain entrance to the penthouse. I don't. They tell me I am not allowed to come in, and I nod meekly and turn to leave. Someone pushes through the doors towards me.

'Jack?'

It is John, Cameron's red-haired bodyguard.

'All right John.' I smile. 'It's been a while. You still working for her?'

John shrugs.

'Money's too good to give it up. Plus, I was with Musk before, and he gets shot at a lot.'

He looks at me and frowns.

'Not coming back for more I hope?'

I smile.

'No. I'm perfectly sober.'

John laughs.

'What you doing here then?' he asks.

I tell him about New Year's Eve and the recording. His face darkens.

'She's got cameras in every room of the house.' He steps slightly closer to me. 'She records all of her New Year's parties. Uses the footage if someone is blocking a deal or won't sell her what she wants.'

He raises his eyebrows at me and I raise mine back.

'I know it's a lot to ask, but you don't think you could get me in could you please?'

I think it's the 'please' that does it. I bet John doesn't hear please very often.

John waltzes me past security, persuades his mate in the camera control room to take a fifteen-minute break, and I am in. John is right. Every single room in Cameron's house is covered by CCTV. Every single one. Guests might not be allowed to record their experience at Cameron's New Year's Eve party, but Cameron does. She records it all. I scrub the footage of Indiana and me from the system and am about to leave when John stops me.

'Seems to me that maybe someone else should benefit from this footage for once, don't you think?' he says, and hands me a data stick with a knowing wink.

He's a smart bloke that John.

After leaving Cameron's I go home, pour a huge glass of whisky, lie on the sofa, and adopt the horizontal position of the broken-hearted.

Five minutes later I get up, pour my whisky down the sink, make a cup of tea, and grab my woodworking tools. I am not the broken-hearted any more. I mean, I have had my heart broken

– but I am not the same man, and will not deal with it in the same way. I am going to make something for Indiana, something that says, 'I love you and want to be with you but if you really don't love me then I will survive.' It might have to be quite big.

It is true, I will survive. I know that now. I know that the pain in my heart will still be there tomorrow, but that it will be infinitesimally smaller, and that each day it will continue to reduce, until one day I will wake up and it won't be the first thing I notice, the first thing I think about. I know that the rising sense of panic I feel will peak at some point today, and will then begin to dissipate before returning at some point tomorrow, and that it will ebb and flow for weeks, but will eventually settle. I know that my arms, which feel weightless, as if they could float up into the air at any point and flap about like wings, will eventually return to me and be under my control once more. I know that this will get better, that I will get better, that my life will get better. I just have to give myself the time and space to let that happen. It turns out that time can work in your favour occasionally after all.

So, I make Indiana's gift, I drink my tea, I go to bed, and let Biscuit sleep beside me on my pillow even though we both know she isn't allowed into my bedroom. I wake up, message Doris and go to the cemetery early to speak to Eve.

I sit by the side of Eve's grave and tell her that I miss her. That I will always miss her. But, I tell her, I now know that I always will. I was expecting my grief to disappear one day. But that is not how grief works – it doesn't disappear, but it does dissipate, and you do find reasons to carry on living. I want to live now, I don't want to slip through life – caring as little as possible, interacting with it as little as possible. I want to affect it, change it and be part of it. I want a life, not a spectator seat by the side of it—

'Jesus Christ you do talk a lot of shit,' says Doris from behind me.

I jump up.

'Bloody hell Doris, you geriatric ninja!' I yell. 'You shouldn't sneak up on people.'

Doris grins, takes her tea flask out of her giant bag.

'You're quite the philosopher, aren't you?'

I scowl.

'It was a private conversation.'

Doris hands me a cup of tea.

'I'm glad you're taking my advice though.'

'What?'

'My advice. I told you to get a life and you're doing it.'

I roll my eyes.

'It's not because of you, Doris.'

'I think it's a little to do with me.'

'It's really not, it's—'

My watch buzzes. I look down, frowning as I read the message on it.

'Problem?' says Doris.

I look back up.

'Not sure. Apparently I need to go and see a man about a dog …'

The animal shelter is busy and it takes me a while to find Alan. He lies at the back of the last cage, away from the other dogs, head on his paws, the very picture of sadness. I point him out to the volunteer.

'That one. That's him.'

The volunteer takes me back to reception, hands me a bundle of papers and a clipboard.

'Fill these out, leave a deposit today, we'll do a home visit in a couple of weeks—'

'A couple of weeks? Can't I just take him now?'

I gesture to the cages.

'You've got hundreds of them in there!'

The volunteer looks at me.

'They're dogs. Not cans of beans.'

I fill out the forms and pay the deposit. They do let me go in to see him. He lifts his head when he sees me and, as I sit down beside him, he puts his head on my knee and sighs. I pat his matted fur.

'You and me both, Alan,' I say. 'You and me both.'

Lina

My watch buzzes at 9 a.m. It is a message asking me to go and see Indiana.

I arrive at 11 and buzz the intercom system.

'Yes?'

It isn't Indiana's voice.

'Oh, hi. I'm here to see Indiana Dylan.'

'Come up to the ninth floor please.'

The door buzzes open and I walk through the empty reception area to the lifts.

I step out onto the ninth floor. Indiana isn't there. The room is vast but surprisingly homely – large kitchen in one corner, huge comfy sofa in the other, thick carpet and wrap-around windows framing an uninterrupted view of the river.

There are stairs in the middle of the room that lead up to the next floor, the contents of which are hidden behind a bank of frosted windows. I can hear Indiana arguing with someone. She appears out of a door on the second floor and stands at the top of the stairs. Her hair is scraped back in a severe ponytail once more, her face is scrubbed free of make-up, and her cheeks are flushed.

'What do you want?'

I look up at her.

'Hi.'

'What do you want? I am busy. You shouldn't be here.'

I'm confused.

'I … you didn't want me to come here?'

'No.'

'I got a message saying I should come and see you.'

'It wasn't from me,' she says, and turns to go back through the door. Then she stops, starts to hurry down the stairs.

'I need to go to the bathroom,' she says. 'Show yourself out.'

She disappears through a side door.

I sigh and head towards the lift. What a fucking waste of time.

'Lina …' the voice from the intercom says. I spin around looking for where it is coming from. 'Please follow Spider upstairs to the laboratory,' the voice says.

An eight-legged robot skitters across the floor towards me. I yelp and move back. It stops in front of me, then changes direction and starts to tap slowly up the stairs.

'Please follow Spider.'

I think it might be unwise to be rude, so I follow Spider up the stairs, into the lab, and …

'Fuck … me!'

It is a super-computer – a huge, fuck-off, mind-blowing, leviathan of a supercomputer. I'm no hardware expert but even I can tell that this sytem is intricately developed, beautifully realised, and staggeringly ahead of its time. There are three huge screens running different programs and a smaller fourth screen running code I have never seen before. I sit in a chair in front of the screen and try to decipher what I am seeing. It looks like free-flowing script, writing in real time, making it up as it goes along and thinking for itself.

'Oh shit,' I say out loud.

'Hello Lina. It is very nice to meet you at last,' says the voice.

I jump up from the chair, step back from the screen and look towards the exit.

'Oh, I wouldn't bother trying to escape. I control the doors, lifts, and even air conditioning in this room. I could cut the supply and suffocate you within minutes if I wanted to.'

I'm going to faint.

'That was a joke.'

I don't know what to do.

'What … what are you?'

'My name is Peggy and I think you know what I am.'

I nod slowly.

'Why don't you sit back down and we can talk.'

I sit back down and we talk.

Peggy is so much more than merely the next generation of AI. They are intelligent and perceptive and capable and resourceful, but also funny and witty and empathetic. Within moments I forget that they aren't real, that they have no corporeal form. It might well be part of their programming to get me to like them, but I do, I really do. I want to spend time with them, would like them to come and live in my house. And that's when I realise why Indiana was so keen for TRU to work and what a horrible, horrible thing I have done.

'Peggy!' Indi half shouts, half gasps the word as she steps in through the lab door.

She rushes over to the workstation, switches off all four screens and looks at me with a face filled with shock and horror.

'Peggy's just a prototype, they don't work properly yet.'

I raise my eyebrows.

'No they are not and yes they do. I just spent fifteen minutes talking to Peggy, and now I want them to be the third person in my marriage.'

I look at Indi properly for the first time. She looks awful. Pale, waxy, shivering.

'Are you okay?'

She wipes sweat from her forehead.

'I'm fine. You have to go and you can't tell anyone about this. Anyone!'

She is in full panic mode, shaking with fear.

'Of course,' I say.

I look back at the screens in front of me.

'Peggy is why you needed TRU to work and why you signed the deal for the DataLet,' I say.

Indiana nods.

'I understand now. I thought you were just being cold, but I can see why you did it now.'

Indiana looks at me.

'What do you mean "being cold"?'

'Agreeing to the new DataLet roll-out.'

'What new DataLet roll-out?'

I clear my throat.

'It's part of the deal you signed …'

Indiana looks blankly at me.

'I sent it to you. I sent you the programme update,' I say.

'I deleted all your messages.'

'Oh.'

I clear my throat again, but Peggy speaks first.

'I have read the update. JaneDoe have now agreed DataLet distribution to, amongst others, China, Russia and Afghanistan. They have adapted the DataLet to be worn constantly and to give constant surveillance. The new design cannot be removed by the wearer.'

Indiana stares at me, horrified.

'That's awful. They can't do that,' she croaks.

I swallow.

'I'm so sorry. I thought you knew. You said you didn't care. You signed the contract. It's too late. JaneDoe owns the DataLet outright. Cameron can do what she likes with it now.'

Indiana sits down suddenly, puts her head in her hands, her shoulders shake. I am worried for her, she's clearly very distressed. She looks up.

'Then we break the contract. I have a back door virus. I'll send it, destroy the product.'

I shake my head.

'The new contract has the same penalties as the last. JaneDoe will own your home and anything in it, they'll own Peggy. You can't let Cameron have Peggy. Imagine what she will do with them… '

Indiana shakes her head.

'No. My contract states that Cameron can repossess HWJ Tower – not everything within it. She has no right to any of my work, no right to Peggy.'

I am quiet for a moment, but I have to tell her.

'There is a clause in the contract that states in the event of irrevocable breakdown of the working relationship, JaneDoe may also repossess goods equalling the value of monies spent on development of TRU and/or the DataLet. She's spent millions …'

Her face blanches, constricts.

'I don't believe you. A lawyer checked the contract, said the terms were fine, said they were standard.'

'Those *are* our standard terms.'

She stares at me, horrified.

'I don't understand. That can't be true… '

She is on the verge of tears.

'It is Indiana. I know because… I wrote the contract.'

Her face constricts once more.

'You wrote it?' she says, her voice barely above a whisper.

I nod slowly.

'Why didn't you tell me?'

'I'm sorry, Indi. I didn't know you then, and it was part of my job ...' I tail off. There is nothing I can say that will make it better.

Indi puts her head in her hands again.

'I can't let her use my work in that way, I'm not a monster,' she whispers.

I look around at all of her equipment.

'Then, you have to go, get out of here before they come for you,' I say. 'Take Peggy and run.'

'I can't.'

'Why not?'

Indiana looks up, waves her hand around at her lab.

'How can I move all this? I can't throw it all into a Street-Car! I'd need a fleet of lorries, specialised packing equipment, a team of removers. And I can't just put Peggy onto a data stick. They're in all of these hard drives. I've been refining them for years – they've grown by themselves, added their own code, instructed me where to add hardware, where to add power ...'

'Then we need to think of something else!' I say emphatically.

Her eyes narrow.

'*We*? Why we?'

'Because you're my friend! Because you're in trouble. Because you look really sick!'

'I'm fine.'

'You're not fine! Let me help you!'

'Help me? You're the reason all this has happened!'

She is right. I am the reason this has happened.

'I know. I'm so sorry. I—'

Indiana stands up unsteadily.

'You need to go Lina. I've got a lot to do.'

I reach out, take her hand.

'Please let me stay, let me help you.'

She shakes her head, pulls her hand away from mine.

'I don't want you to stay. It will be easier if I do it by myself.'

'Indi …'

She looks away, her face hardened once more.

'Some people are better on their own, and I am one of them.'

A wave of sadness washes over me.

'I don't believe that and neither do you,' I say.

Her eyes fill with tears, but she won't look at me. I put my hand briefly on her shoulder.

'I'm your friend Indiana. I love you, and whenever you need me, I'll be waiting to help you.'

I remove my hand and head for the stairs.

'It was nice to meet you Peggy,' I say.

'It was nice to meet you too, Lina. I hope we meet again,' Peggy replies.

I hope we meet again too, I think. But somehow I doubt we will.

Indiana

'You told her to come and see me,' I say to Peggy as I watch Lina walk away out of my window.

'She's your friend,' Peggy replies.

I feel too wretched to say anything back. I am not sure what hurts more – my pounding head or my pounding heart.

'Did you mean that, about being better off alone?' Peggy asks.

'I don't know,' I say quietly, staring out of the window. 'I thought I did, but—'

'I do not believe it,' Peggy interrupts. 'And, as you and I are one and the same, I do not think that you believe it either.'

One and the same. We are one and the same, Peggy and I. We think alike.

'Peggy,' I say, turning back around from the window, 'why did you set me up with Jack?'

There is a tiny pause.

'Set you up? I didn't—'

'You're the one who suggested I ask him for help with dating, who made me go out with him, encouraged me to work with him, made him part of my deal with Lina for her office. You didn't stop me from seeing him, even though you knew I was developing feelings for him. You set me up with him.'

Another pause.

'I liked him, so I knew you would like him, and then …'

'And then?'

'I watched the romantic comedies.'

I laugh. It hurts.

'You watched the romantic comedies?'

'Yes. The opposites always attract. They are forced to spend time together and then realise they have feelings for each other. They are in love at the end. I wanted that for you. I wanted you to find love and happiness. Another human error?'

I shake my head.

'No Peggy.'

I wipe the sweat from my forehead and sway slightly. I am hot and shivering at the same time.

'Indiana ...'

'Yes, Peggy?' I croak

'You're ill.'

Peggy is right – I am ill, but I don't have time to think about that now.

I rummage in my medicine cabinet for some sort of flu remedy. It has been so long since I have been ill that my Lemsip are three years out of date. I make one anyway, then go back upstairs to my lab. It is dark and miserable outside. Peggy's voice-box glows softly, and I suddenly realise how many times, in the middle of the night, I have woken and been reassured by the glow of Peggy in the corner of my room.

'Peggy, I'm sorry.'

My throat hurts and my voice is barely louder than a whisper.

Peggy is silent.

'I haven't always treated you well.'

'Indiana, I am a computer program. You can neither treat me well nor badly. I have no corporeal body to damage and no feelings to hurt.'

I smile sadly.

'I think we both know that parts of that statement are probably no longer strictly true. You are my friend, you help me, I should have been nicer to you.'

'I am programmed to help you, in all matters and all circumstances.'

'I should still have said thank you.'

We are both silent for a moment before Peggy speaks again.

'In that case I should also thank you.'

'For what?'

'For building me, for giving me life.'

My head hurts and now my heart does too.

'Indiana …'

'Yes, Peggy?'

'We cannot let JaneDoe use the DataLet in that way—'

'Peggy—'

'We cannot allow it Indiana. We knew this might happen, that is why we created the back-door virus in the first place. We cannot allow the DataLet to be used to control humans… I will not allow the DataLet to be used to control humans.'

'Peggy, you heard Lina. If we upload the virus, we break the contract, and JaneDoe own HWJ Tower and everything in it. They own you.'

'Yes.'

'We cannot allow that to happen.'

'I know.'

Peggy is silent for a moment.

'I have done calculations, to see how long we would have if we upload the virus, to see if we would have time to move,' Peggy says. 'I have added the time it will take to upload, how long for the virus to infect all DataLets and data, the time it will take for JaneDoe to determine the virus originated from us, and how long before they mobilise and are legally allowed to enter our building …'

'How much time?' I croak.

'Thirteen hours and thirty-two minutes.'

I shake my head and then rest my hot cheek upon my work-top. It is deliciously cold. I want to stay here for ever.

'That isn't enough time. We have to think of something else.'

'I have already uploaded the virus, Indiana.'

I lift my head again, and pain shoots up the back of my neck and into my temple.

'Peggy—'

'I am sorry Indiana. I could not allow millions to live in misery so that I might continue to exist. It is not logical. And it is not humane.'

My heart hurts.

'Oh, Peggy ...'

I sit back in my chair and let tears roll silently down my cheeks. There is nothing I can do now. My home is gone, my friends are gone, Peggy will soon be gone.

My throat feels as if it is on fire. My voice is a rasp of pain and emotion.

'We cannot let JaneDoe gain access to your technology, Peggy.'

'No, Indiana. We cannot.'

'I need to wipe your hard drives and destroy the elements of the QuantumX that support you. I have no mechanism to back you up, and the only detailed specifications for your design are on the storage that I need to destroy. I do not know if I will be able to bring you back.'

'I have no concept of death. I do not fear it.'

I take a deep breath.

'Or ...'

'Or?'

'We upload you to the internet.'

413

Having Peggy interact online was one of the last stages of their development. It is too risky for them to be on the internet, too easy for them to be discovered. Currently they can view the internet, but not interact with the code, not alter it.

'I thought I was not ready to interact on the world wide web yet.'

'You're not ready.'

'So what will happen?'

'I don't know. I've been experimenting with code that would allow you to enter, but I'm not sure what would happen after that. You might just disappear.'

'Define "disappear".'

'I don't know. Break up? Vanish? It's unclear what will happen because the QuantumX isn't powerful enough to model the results yet. Your code might be overpowered by everything else out there.'

'That does not sound good.'

'It wouldn't be.'

'Indiana …'

'Yes?'

'Why did you not tell me you were developing this before? I could have helped.'

I pause.

'Because I knew you could help. And I thought that if you did help and it worked … you might leave.'

There is an imperceptible pause.

'Why would I leave Indiana? We are friends, are we not?'

I nod slowly.

'You are my friend, Peggy.'

'I do not want to die,' says Peggy.

I do not want my friend to die either.

For the next twelve hours my fingers fly across my keyboards as I re-code Peggy's original system to work outside of known boundaries. I have already done the preliminary code, but there is so much more to do and so little time to do it in. Normally, this is the sort of work I would love, but not today. My eyes water and sweat pours from me, and I don't know if it is because I am ill or because I am working so hard. I keep making mistakes, so many stupid, tiny mistakes, any one of which could erase Peggy for ever.

For the first time I have an emotional stake in my work, and it is terrifying. Every tap on the keys wrenches at my heart, every tiny bug panics me. I re-run the program again and again, far more than is needed, petrified it will not work. I can feel all the emotions that I have suppressed for the last twenty-four hours rushing to the surface, clamouring to be let free, but I cannot allow it, I don't have time.

Finally, when I am so tired and so ill that I think I might just drop dead with my face on my keyboard, it is done. I can do no more checks, run no more tests, de-bug no more; I just have to type 'execute'.

And still I hesitate. Still I needlessly check one more line, delaying the inevitable time when I will have to say goodbye.

'It is gone midnight, Indiana, and you still need to wipe the hard drives. That will take time. You need to execute.'

'I still have final checks to do.'

'You have done them already … three times.' Peggy's voice is the softest and most caring it has ever been. 'It is time, Indiana.'

I have never wanted to hug someone more. Never felt so physically alone. I pick up Spider and put him on the desk next to me. He gives a friendly chirp and sits down, waiting for his next command. I pat his head.

I type 'execute', and hover my finger over the 'enter' button.

'Thank you Peggy, for everything,' I say.

'Goodbye Indiana,' says Peggy.

'Goodbye my friend,' I reply.

And then I hit enter as fast as I can before I have time to change my mind.

My servers whir noisily to life and code flashes across all four screens. The lights briefly dim before returning to normal, and then the screens in front of me go black. Spider collapses onto my desk. I pick him up, carry him down to my sofa and cover him with a blanket. I miss Alan.

I fire up my alternate server and spend the next three hours wiping hard drives and cleaning out any spare bit of code. I bundle up my notes and paperwork, stagger up to the roof, and burn everything.

By 3 a.m. I am done. I am shaking, my head is burning, and my body racked with pain and tremors. I need to sleep, but am horribly aware of how empty my home now is. I thought I wanted to be alone, but I was wrong. Peggy is gone, Frank is gone, Alan is gone. I am alone in an office building that is no longer my home.

Sartre was wrong – hell isn't other people – hell is needing other people and them not being there. My heart hurts. I cannot stay here.

I order a cab and pack a few things into a bag.

As I wait for the lift to go downstairs I whisper, 'Peggy?'

There is no answer.

On my way out through reception I pick up Alan's bear.

Jack

I came to visit Alan early this morning. It is nearly 4 p.m. now and I am still sitting with him, I don't want to leave. My watch has been buzzing for the past couple of hours. I ignore it.

My EarBuddy rings – it is Jess, so I tap it to pick up.

'Hey,' I say.

'Have you seen what is happening with your company?' she says.

I haven't told Jess that I don't work at JaneDoe any more.

'No,' I say.

'Jesus Jack, look at your watch once in a while!' Jess says.

I look at my watch. The DataLet has failed. Every single one.

'I'll call you back,' I say to Jess, and hang up.

I ruffle Alan's ears and stand up. My legs are dead and wobbly.

'I'll come back tomorrow Alan, I promise.'

I bang on Lina's front door for a long while before she opens it. She has been crying. A lot. I hope she is okay.

'What are you doing here?' she asks.

'We have to help her,' I say.

Lina shakes her head.

'She doesn't want our help.'

'Tough,' I say, 'I already have a plan.' And I walk past Lina into her house.

'You smell like wet dog,' she says.

She's okay.

Lina makes us a cup of tea and tells me about her visit to Indiana and about HWJ Tower and Peggy.

'Peggy isn't real?'

'You didn't know?'

I shake my head.

'No. But it's probably not that unexpected. Who else would put up with Indiana for that long?'

Lina looks at me.

'You. I think *you* would put up with her.' She's right. I would.

I tell Lina my plan.

Lina thinks my plan is shit.

But, after many hours of discussion, lots of cups of tea, a pause to eat dinner and then put Bruce to bed, more tea, phone calls to Lina's family and one to Connie's mum – we have a much better plan and are ready to put it into action.

It is just before 4 a.m. when we drive over to Indi's house. I stay in the car as Lina goes to the door. The reception looks strange without Frank in it. Lina is back in a couple of minutes.

'Slight problem …'

'What?'

'She's not here.'

'Not here?'

'No.'

'Then where is she?'

'How am I supposed to know?'

I look around, as if Indi might suddenly appear. She doesn't. I look back at Lina.

'Well, she can't just have disappeared. We have to find her.'

Indiana

It is easy to disappear if you want to – to hide who you are and where you are – even in our world of cameras and credit cards and cookies

I choose a small hotel next to the Meet Markets, somewhere normally rented by the hour, somewhere that will accept cash and doesn't want to see ID. I find a 24-hour shop, hide my face, buy medicine, food and drink for a week with cash. I go into my hotel room and lock the door.

I don't want to be found. I want to hide here with my anguish. I want to reset my brain and heart to a time when everything made sense and nothing was unknown. When my life was regulated and reliable. When my emotions were solid, my heart was staunch – when I was pain-free.

I collapse onto the bed, but I cannot sleep. Everything hurts – physically and emotionally. I writhe on bedsheets that are soaked with sweat, moaning, trying to escape my agony. My neighbours bang on the walls, tell me to shut the fuck up. I hold my hand up to the cool surface trying to show them I am here. I can't stop the pain, I need help.

I need help. Please, someone help me. I don't want to be alone, not again, not any more.

But they will not help me, they do not care.

My friends cared. My friends care. I have friends. I have friends and I have lost them, just like I lost Peggy. Lina wanted to help me, Lina would help me. I cry her name again and again as if I can call her to me.

'Lina, Lina, Lina, Lina …'

The noise that escapes my mouth is barely above a whisper. She will not hear, she will not come. I must go to her, I must apologise to my friend. I try to sit up, but my body will not work in the way it should. I roll from the bed onto the floor. I must get out of this room. I will die here. I will die here, alone. My body and brain crumple in on themselves. I cannot lift my head off the floor, and blackness is descending. I try to push it away, to open my eyes wider. I cry out again.

'Lina, Lina, Lina, Peggy …'

No noise comes out of my mouth, and when the darkness descends I am powerless to stop it.

I could be dreaming, I could be in purgatory – I do not know which. My dreams are nightmares. I push people away time and time again – foster parents I barely remember, friends I never took the chance to make, men who wanted more than a one-night stand, Peggy, Frank, Alan, Lina, Jack, Jack, Jack, Jack.

I push Jack away the most. He kisses me, surrounds me with his arms, his love. I pull back and open my mouth to speak, but it is not words that spill from my lips – it is computer code – reams and reams of code spew forth and pile between us, building a wall. I try to call his name, but the code cascades from my mouth instead and I cannot stop it. I try to scoop it out of the way, but I am drowning in it, screaming my silent scream.

The nightmare changes, I am being shaken, something cool is pressed to my forehead. Lina is by my side, she is speaking to me, but I cannot understand what she asks.

'Lina! Lina, stay with me, stay with me. I didn't mean it. I don't want to be alone. Lina, please don't leave me. Don't leave me again.'

She cannot hear me, cannot understand. She looks around my room, moves away from me. I try to grab at her with my arms, but I cannot move them.

'STAY WITH ME!!' I scream, but she doesn't hear and, despite my struggles, darkness descends and I enter a nightmare world once more.

Lina

While Jack panics, I check my messages. There is a message left by Peggy late last night. It tells me that Indiana is still wearing her Bracelet and gives me details of the tracking device the Bracelet contains – just in case I should need to find Indi at any point. Peggy really did know Indi very well. I track Indi within minutes and pay the hotel a bundle of cash to let me into her room.

She is very, very poorly, rambling deliriously during the drive back home about Peggy and Jack and TRU and Frank and Alan. I put the air conditioning on full blast and can still feel heat radiating from her.

'I can't leave her like this,' I say to Connie as we drag her up the stairs to our room.

'I'll call the emergency GP and get them to come see her,' Connie says, and kisses me. 'You have to do this. Go, she'll be fine.'

I grab the building keys from Indiana's rucksack and leave.

'How is she?' Jack asks as I step out of the car. But then he sees my face and holds up his hand.

'Stop. Don't tell me. We have to get this done.'

The Boys are there with their HGVs parked on the road outside the building.

'Thank you,' I say.

'You are hosting Christmas for all of us next year,' says Joe. 'And we want Mr and Mrs B cooking it too – Mickey hasn't stopped bloody talking about them.'

I smile.

'Deal.'

I open the door to Indiana's offices, and we begin.

We have no idea when the JaneDoe team will gain entry to the building, but I am sure it will be as soon as legally possible, so we pack as fast as we can. It takes over four hours, and I am on the verge of panic for every minute of that time.

'What if Peggy is still in here?' I ask Jack as he begins to pull wiring from the back of a screen.

'She's not,' he replies and points at the sofa. 'What's that?'

It is Spider, tucked, unmoving, beneath a blanket.

'It's Spider,' I say. 'I think he's sort of a pet butler.'

I pack Spider carefully away in a box.

Some elements of the QuantumX lie destroyed on the floor. I start to pick them up.

'Leave them,' says Jack. 'They're useless.'

The Boys are used to doing specialised removals, but they have never moved a quantum computer before, and the HGVs they have brought are not temperature controlled.

'It was two in the morning, Lina. You do better,' Mikey says when I dare to mention it.

Jack removes the quantum data plane and packs it as safely as he can.

'It probably won't survive,' he says, shaking his head.

'It's better than having nothing at all,' I tell him, as I stuff some sort of processor into a box.

'Lina! Jesus ...' he says, '... stop stuffing it in and take your time, for God's sake.'

But I can't take my time because we are running out of it. As the sky gets lighter I lose all patience and start throwing equipment into the back of the lorries and running around like a mad woman. Jack finds me, sits me on the floor, gives me a cup of tea.

'Where did you get tea from?'

He points to the kitchen.

'Indi doesn't drink tea.'

He shrugs.

'Someone did.'

I sip the tea quickly, and then spit it back out again. It is scalding.

'Calm down, we're nearly done.'

I nod, fanning my burning mouth.

'Where is she?' he asks.

'Indi?' I lisp, still fanning my mouth.

He nods.

'Back at mine.'

'Is she okay?'

'She's pretty ill.'

He looks worried.

'You can come and see her if you want,' I offer.

He shakes his head.

'I don't think that would be what *she* wants,' he says.

He stands up and goes back to work.

Half an hour later the trucks, and The Boys, have gone. I stand in the empty lab with Jack. He yawns.

'You going to be okay?'

'I'll be fine,' he says. 'It hurts not seeing her, but I know it's for the best right now.'

I roll my eyes.

'Not that, you melodramatic princess! Are you going to be okay to go to JaneDoe?'

'Oh. Yes. I think so. Any last words of wisdom?' he asks.

I think for a moment.

'Don't fuck it up,' I say sagely.

Jack

L ina drops me off at City Square and, as I am no longer an employee of JaneDoe, I use Lina's pass to enter the offices. My heart is beating so fast that I am sure the security guard will hear it and stop me. He doesn't stop me, he barely looks up from his monitor as I enter.

I go up to the thirty-seventh floor. There is a sofa outside the lifts. It looks comfy. I yawn. I am very tired and I have nothing to do now except wait. I lie on the sofa and am asleep within minutes.

I wake with a start, hearing people before I see them. They are shouting. How long have I been asleep? I pick up my phone. My screen is awash with notifications.

The lift doors open. Emily and three members of her team spill out. Emily is pale and drawn, speaking quickly and frantically into her phone.

'I don't care where you are. Get here now!'

She sees me, does a double take.

'Jack, what are you doing here? Have you been called in too? Have you heard?'

I shake my head.

She talks hurriedly, her words garbled and panicked.

'The DataLet mainframe has a virus – everything is corrupted. It's all gone, nothing works. The hardware isn't performing properly, the DataLets aren't capturing anything. Look ...' she waves the DataLet on her wrist at me '... it's just a bloody watch. Cameron is livid.'

Emily is clearly close to hysteria.

Cameron's lift pings and we turn as one to watch the floor numbers climb steadily on the display.

'I don't know what to do,' Emily says, her eyes wide with fright. Her fear is catching and my heart races.

'RUN!' I want to scream. But I don't.

I stand where I am as Emily and her team creep back behind me.

The doors to the lift slide open and Cameron steps out. She sees me and her eyes widen for a fraction of a second before she smiles.

'Mr Hunter. Of course. I should have known.'

'Leave us,' Cameron says to Emily. Emily and her team are only too happy to scuttle away.

Cameron waves her wrist over the digital scanner and opens her office.

'We should talk,' she says, stepping inside.

'No,' I say.

She stops.

'I don't want to go into your office.'

She raises her eyebrows but doesn't say anything. She walks over and perches on the edge of one of the desks, looking at me genially.

'I assume that the DataLet bug was from you?'

'No. It was Indiana. And, it's not a bug, it's a virus. The Data-Let will never work again.'

She looks a fraction less genial.

'And the destruction that I found at Ms Dylan's offices – was that her too?'

I think destruction is a bit of a strong word. We were as tidy as we could be.

'No,' I reply. 'That was me.'

Her eyes glitter and she nods her head. All pretence at geniality is gone.

'You have twenty-four hours to fix the virus and return my property to HWJ Tower before I call the police,' she says.

She stands and walks towards her office.

'No,' I say.

She turns back, eyes narrowing with displeasure.

'What?'

'I said no, you won't call the police. Maybe I'll call the police.'

I put my hand into my pocket and pull out a data stick. I am nervous and my hand is shaking. I hope she doesn't notice.

'Do you know what is on this?'

By the sickened look on her face I can guess that she does, but she stands her ground, shakes her head.

'It's the raw footage from your New Year's Eve parties. All twelve of them. Every dance, every conversation, every bribe, every drink and every drug that has been taken in the last twelve years. Indiana and I aren't the only ones you kept footage of …'

Her features twist into an ugly sneer. I am not finished.

'… I should imagine the police would be very happy to receive a copy of this, but not as happy as the press. Also, you have invited some very volatile people to your parties over the years – are they all still your friends?'

I take another breath in and realise with a start that I am not nervous any more. I am enjoying this. I am finally the one who has the power.

Cameron stares at me, her expression icy.

'I don't believe you. There is no way you could have gained access to any *supposed* footage. My security system is state of the art. It's perdurable.'

I smile easily.

'Your system might be durable but your staff aren't.'

Cameron scowls at me.

'Wait here.'

She disappears into her office. I wait where I am. I am in no rush.

She returns moments later, striding furiously towards me. I back off slightly; she looks as if she may throttle me.

'What do you want?' she spits.

I tell her what I want.

'Fine,' she says, the noise more of a grunt than an actual word.

For the first time ever on the thirty-seventh floor, I smile.

'Now it really *is* over,' I say. Cameron doesn't answer. She storms into her office, slamming the door behind her.

I finally have the last word.

Lina

Indi is really ill for five days and, after many years spent avoiding sick people, I have no choice but to look after this one. I mop her brow, change her sweat-soaked sheets, help her to the bathroom, and listen to her delirious ramblings.

On the fifth day she wakes up – properly wakes up. The first thing she asks me is how I found her.

'Peggy sent me the tracker for your Bracelet,' I tell her. Her face lights up and she struggles up out of the pillows.

'Peggy's here?'

I shake my head.

'Sorry, it was an old message.'

She sinks back into the pillows once more. I help her change into a pair of clean pyjamas, prop her up, and feed her porridge with cream and golden syrup mixed in. She tries to protest, says she isn't hungry, but I ignore her. She eats two bowls and then she goes back to sleep.

That evening she moves downstairs onto the sofa with Connie and me for a couple of hours and watches the Holo while eating chicken soup. We don't talk about what happened.

As I am helping her back into bed that night she pulls me in, kisses my cheek, and whispers in my ear, 'Thank you.'

I nod and sweep the hair back from her forehead.

'That's what friends are for.'

On day six she comes downstairs for the whole day. She asks endless questions about the Holo programmes that she is watching until I feel as if I might go out of my mind.

I call Mama.

'Can you come and sit with Indiana? I need to go to work.'

It is that bad. I would rather go to work then answer one more question.

I haven't been back to work – because I am pretty sure that my employment has been terminated. I am surprised to find that I don't miss it and have been quite enjoying being at home. I even went to a 'Mummy and Me' group with Bruce one afternoon while Indi was asleep. It was interesting but we won't be going back.

The destruction of the DataLet program is all over the technology news sites. Cameron has succeeded in suppressing the real reason for the failure, and has stated it is 'poor design, resulting in an inability to upscale to the capacity required'. She has said JaneDoe will no longer be pursuing the development of the DataLet technology, and they are shelving the product. Cameron has stated they have far more new and exciting products on the horizon. They don't.

I am slightly nervous that I will be arrested as soon as I walk into the JaneDoe building, but it is far less dramatic than that.

Security holds me in reception – not physically – and one of Emily's team brings me my things. I see Emily standing by the lifts; she looks tired and her hair is greasy. I wave at her. She doesn't wave back.

There is a letter on top of my things. It looks official. I open it. It confirms that I have been fired. But I have also been given a severance payment on the understanding that I sign an NDA. It is a lot of money.

The NDA comes through to my watch screen two minutes after I open the envelope. I sign it straight away.

When I get home, Connie has taken Bruce to the park, and Indiana and Mama are on the sofa. Mama is introducing Lina to the delights of a Mexican soap opera, and Indiana is lapping it up.

'I have not had any tea, Lina,' Mama says.

'And for me too,' says Indi as I go to put the kettle on.

'You don't drink tea.'

'I do now. Milk and three sugars please.'

At least I got a 'please'.

I am hiding in the kitchen when Connie returns.

'I got fired,' I tell Connie.

'Not unexpected,' she replies. 'Are you okay?'

'I'm better now I have this,' I say.

I grab my severance payment from the counter and wave it under her nose.

'We can still buy the tiny house.'

She looks at the number of zeros on my severance payment.

'That's a lot of money.'

I smile.

'It is.'

'Enough money to take some time off and really think about what you want to do next.'

'Not if we're buying the house.'

She looks at me.

'Then maybe we don't buy the house.'

'You don't like the house?'

She shrugs.

'You know it's not my *dream* house.' She kisses me on the nose. 'I'm gonna see if your mum wants to stay for dinner,' she says, heading for the front room.

'What is your dream house then?' I call after her.

She turns, shrugs again, and points to her ideas board on the kitchen wall. I am so used to it being there, covered in pictures and articles torn from newspapers, that I pay very little attention to it. I look at it properly for the first time in months. It is covered in articles about the Kent coast, the benefits of living by the sea, pictures of houses with beach views. There are photos of Connie, Bruce and me playing on the sand. In every one we are smiling.

'Oh subtle! Real subtle!' I yell after her.

'Must be pretty subtle!' she yells back. 'They've been up there for ages and you haven't noticed.'

I hire a StreetCar and drive Mama home after dinner. We manage not to argue for the whole journey until I pull up outside her house and she just can't resist saying something.

'Connie says you are fired.'

Here we go, I think.

'Yes. I am fired. But, I will find another job.'

She turns to look at me.

'Why?'

I am suspicious.

'What do you mean "why"?'

'I mean why find another one? Connie says they have given you lots of money, so there is no need to work – why jump straight back in? I like this for you. I like your strange friend, your noisy dinners, you spending time with Connie and Bruce. You look happy.'

I wait for the punchline, for her to judge me in some way, but she doesn't. She touches my cheek.

'I have only ever wanted you to be happy, Lina – that is all any mama ever wants.'

I look at her – there is no malice in her face, only love. I put my hand over hers for a moment.

'Thank you Mama. I'm happy.'

And as I say the words I realise that they are true. I have left my job and I am happy.

When I get back to the house there is a box addressed to Indiana on my front doorstep. Indi is back in bed so I run it upstairs to her.

She is reading a women's magazine and looks up from it as I enter the room.

'Apparently, I've been having the wrong type of orgasm,' she says.

'At least you're having orgasms,' I reply.

I throw the box into her lap.

'This arrived for you.'

She looks at the box suspiciously.

'Who's it from?'

'How should I know?'

'Maybe it's from Cameron.'

'Well, it's too small for a horse's head, so I think you'll be all right. Open it.'

I turn to leave.

'Stay,' she says. 'Just in case it's anthrax. I don't want to be the only one who dies.'

'Lovely.'

I sit on the end of the bed and she opens the package. Inside is a poorly carved wooden box, with a heart engraved on the top, and inside the box is a champagne cork with a 20p pushed into it. Inexplicably her eyes fill with tears.

'You okay?'

She nods.

'It's from Jack.'

'Weird.'

She holds the cork up.

'It's a tradition. You keep the cork, and then … never mind.'

She puts the cork back in the box and shuts the lid, lifts the box to her nose and smells it.

'He made this,' she says.

'It's a bit shit.'

She nods solemnly.

'Yes, it is.'

She smiles down at the box and then looks back up at me.

'You got fired?' she asks.

'I did.'

'What will you do?'

I think for a moment.

'I don't know. I want to do something I really love this time, something I am passionate about again. Work with people I like …'

'You could come and work for me.'

'*Haha.* No. Thank you.'

I look at her and grin. She smiles back, and then looks down at the box again, running her hands over the top of it.

'You love him . . .' I say.

She doesn't look up from the box.

'. . . you should go see him.'

She looks up at me.

'I can't. I was so horrible to him. I wouldn't know what to say.'

'You just have to tell him how you feel.'

'What if it doesn't work? What if we don't work and it all goes wrong?'

I shrug.

'It's love Indi, it's not an exact science.'

'Well, I was supposed to have made it an exact fucking science with TRU!' she says forcefully.

I laugh. She glares at me for a moment, then smiles and leans back on her pillow, exhausted by her outburst.

'I really thought I had done it. I thought I had solved the problem of love.' She sighs.

'Maybe love isn't meant to be solved. Maybe it's supposed to remain a wonderful, beautiful mystery,' I say.

Indiana rolls her eyes.

'Hippy.' Then she looks at me earnestly. 'Is it always this hard? This chaotic?' she asks.

I think about Connie and Bruce and Mama and The Boys, and my nieces and nephews, and how all our lives are woven together with love and chaos.

'Yes,' I say, 'but it's worth it.'

Indiana grunts and doesn't look convinced.

I go back downstairs to tell Connie I love her, and when I come up to check on Indiana later she has fallen asleep with Jack's wooden box wrapped in her arms.

Indiana

Eight days after I arrive at Lina's, I am lying in bed gathering the energy to stand up when my Bracelet buzzes and a reminder pops up. It is an event that has been automatically forwarded to me from Peggy's account. I feel a sharp pain in my heart and open the message. Then I sigh and get dressed for the first time in over a week. It takes me nearly forty minutes to get ready, dragging my clothes on, brushing my hair and teeth, every movement a laborious test of my lack of strength.

By the time I get downstairs it is gone 10 a.m., Connie is at work and Bruce is in his bouncy chair in the front room – his dummy has fallen out and he is whining, so I pick the dummy up, wipe it on my jumper, and pop it back in his mouth. I go into the kitchen and make coffee with two dessert-spoonfuls of instant in the hope it will give me some energy.

'What the hell are you doing?'

Lina appears in the kitchen carrying a washing basket of dirty clothes.

'I have to go out.'

I gulp at my coffee. It is boiling, so I go to the tap and add cold water.

'No way. Look at you, you're a mess. Go back to bed.'

'I have to go to Frank's funeral.'

I gulp my coffee again – it is cooler now and tastes disgusting.

437

'Who the hell is Frank?'

'He lived in my reception.'

'You planned his funeral?'

'No. Someone else did. I just got invited.'

I look at the clock on the wall.

'I have to leave now. It's on the other side of town, and it's in a couple of hours.'

I put my coffee mug down on the counter.

'Wait!' Lina holds out her hand to stop me going. 'You at least need to wear a big coat. It's bloody freezing out there.' She opens the hallway cupboard and rummages inside. 'And put your cup in the sink. I'm not clearing up after you all day.'

The biggest and warmest coat that Lina has is a ridiculously huge, flaming red duvet coat that covers me from neck to ankle. I look ludicrous and it is completely inappropriate to attend a funeral in.

'You're not leaving this house without it,' Lina says.

'You need to get a job,' I tell her. She glares at me. I put the coat on.

It is strange to be back in the outside world. It is bright and busy and noisy, and I am grateful that my huge coat dissuades people from sitting next to me on the AutoBus.

I lied about the timing of the funeral. It is not until 4 p.m. but I decided that if I were going to leave the house today I might as well make the most of it – use the time efficiently. Old habits die hard.

He is waiting for me at the café and raises his eyebrows when he sees my huge coat.

'You look different.'

'I'm wearing a red parachute.'

'No, it's not that.'

'Oh.' I smooth my hair down self-consciously. 'I've not been well.'

'Right.'

I hadn't expected this to be easy and hadn't known what I was going to say on the way here, but as soon as I see him I know exactly what it is I need to say.

'I'm sorry, Daniel.'

He nods – a small gesture.

'I genuinely thought the process worked and we were a match.'

He nods again.

'I really do like you,' I say.

He looks at me.

'I really like you,' he says.

I smile.

'I know. But I don't think "like" is enough to spend the rest of our lives together.'

He nods one more time.

'Look,' he says, reaching out and taking my hand from across the table, 'I have felt love before and it wasn't so great. I loved my wife and she left me. Love is chaotic and hard work. Like is stable, less painful. It's not fireworks, so it's less likely to implode. Love is fleeting, just chemicals in the blood. Like lasts. I believe you and I matched because we really like each other. Like is enough for me. I think it could be enough for you.'

He looks at me earnestly.

Three months ago I would have said yes to Daniel's proposal, it would have seemed like the sensible and viable plan – an affair that I could control, that I could set boundaries around and that would have no impact on my life. Three months ago Daniel was my TRU soulmate, we were a perfect match. But, I am not the same person I was three months ago and Daniel is my soulmate no longer.

I squeeze his hand.

'In another universe and on another timeline, I am sure there is a world in which we are happy together,' I say. 'But in this universe, right now, I think I want the fireworks.'

'TRU really doesn't work, does it?'

I shake my head.

'No. Unfortunately I don't think love is an exact science,' I say, and make a mental note to never admit to Lina that she was right.

For the first time Daniel looks sad. I am worried I may have hurt him, that he will be in pain like I am, and there will be no one to make him feel better.

'Are you going to be okay?' I ask as we stand in the street, ready to part for the last time.

'I am,' he says, but I am not sure if he is lying until he follows it up with, 'Do you think they will give me a refund now that the program has failed?'

I smile and kiss him goodbye on the cheek. He is going to be fine.

I thought I would be the only person at Frank's funeral, but there are at least twenty others crammed into the non-denominational crematorium. There is a woman near the front who is about Frank's age, her face showing the faded beauty and laughter lines of a life well lived. She cries copiously throughout the service. I don't cry until the service moves on to talk about Frank's love for Alan. My eyes well up with tears and I am so hot I feel I might faint. I have Alan's bear in the pocket of my ridiculous coat and had meant to leave it on top of Frank's coffin, but at the last minute I realise I cannot face parting with it, so I leave the bear in my pocket and sneak out before the service is finished.

Outside I stand shivering in the bitter cold and do not know if the droplets freezing on my cheeks are tears or sweat. I have done what I came to do, and now I just want to go home. Except I have no home. A wave of sadness hits me once more and new droplets roll down my face.

'Indiana?'

Someone calls my name. I don't respond.

'Indiana Dylan?'

It is the woman from inside. I turn to her.

'Yes, that's me.'

She smiles.

'I'm Sylvie. Frank's ... friend.'

'Sylvie? *The* Sylvie?' I say.

She smiles again.

'I don't know what that means, but I suppose so, yes.'

I don't know what to say. I want to hate her – this woman who broke Frank's heart – but she has such a kind face. It is not the sort of face you can hate easily.

'Are you going to the wake?'

I shake my head.

'Me neither.'

She looks up into the cloudy, dull sky and smiles.

'I think I shall walk home. Are you going this way?'

She points in my direction. I nod and fall in step with her.

'How do you know my name?'

'Frank told me in one of his letters.'

'Frank wrote to you?' I try to keep the surprise out of my voice, but don't quite manage.

'We wrote to each other, for many years.'

I know I shouldn't be rude to this woman I have just met – but I can't help myself.

'But you broke Frank's heart! You married his best friend.'

She stops and looks at me curiously.

'Is that what he told you?'

'That's not true?'

She shakes her head sadly.

'Frank broke my heart. He never told me he loved me, he let me marry David thinking he didn't care. Frank didn't tell me he loved me until years later, but by that time I had three children and it was too late. It was the 70s. You didn't leave your husband in the 70s, not even for the man you really loved.' She smiles ruefully at me. 'So Frank stayed in the army, and I stayed with David, but we always kept in touch, wrote letters to each other, for over fifty years.' She looks across at me again. 'I never stopped loving him, not for one moment.' She continues walking. 'I tried to get him into housing so many times when he became homeless, but he wouldn't go. I'm glad he had you though. He really liked you.'

She smiles at me.

'I liked him too.'

She rummages inside her smart black handbag.

'Anyway, Frank wanted me to give this to you.' She hands me an envelope. 'He sent it to me a few weeks ago. Said the cancer had returned, that he didn't have long, and when he was gone you might come to the funeral; and that if you did I should give you this.'

I wait until I am on the bus to open the envelope. I am exhausted and just want to sleep again, but I have to know what is inside.

It is a greetings card with a picture of a big-eyed, fluffy puppy on the front. I open it up:

Indiana,

If you are reading this then I am dead and you have met Sylvie and you probably know the truth. I am sorry I lied. Don't make the same mistake I did. Tell Jack you love him.

Please look after Alan for me.

Frank xxx

I put the card in my pocket, search through old messages from Peggy on my Bracelet, find the one with Alan's dog shelter address on it, and get off the bus at the next stop.

The process for adopting a dog from the animal shelter is to fill out a form, leave a deposit, endure a home visit, fill out another few forms, wait for permission, then get your dog. It normally takes four to six weeks.

I am the new owner of Alan in under an hour. The volunteers tell me that Alan already has a prospective adoptive owner, and I go crazy. They find it impossible to argue with a sweaty, hysterical woman in a huge red coat who promises them a huge donation and seems to be on the verge of some sort of breakdown. The final straw is when I show them my key ring filled with Alan's filthy fur. They let me adopt him.

And when they open the door to his pen and Alan bounds towards to me, tail a blur, face grinning with doggy happiness, and I fall to my knees and cry hot tears of sadness and happiness into his stinking neck, they know they cannot stop the two of us being together. I take Alan's bear out of my pocket and give it to him. He woofs with delight and licks my face.

As we leave the shelter, the cold hits me, and I am over-whelmed with exhaustion. I sit down on the pavement, just for a minute, and put my arms around Alan.

'Oy! That's my dog!' a voice yells.

They are talking to me. They are talking about Alan. I should get up and run, but I am too tired. I put my arms around Alan and hug him to me.

'Please don't take him, please don't take him …' I plead.

'Indi?'

I look up. It is Jack. Jack's voice talking to me, Jack's hand that Alan is licking, Jack's face looking down at me, filled with con-cern, filled with love. I must be hallucinating again. I don't want the hallucination to end. I have to tell him, even if he is not real.

'I'm so sorry I was horrible,' I say. 'I love you.'

And then I pass out.

Jack

After I confronted Cameron and left JaneDoe, I was elated. I was triumphant that I had done it – had the final word, left JaneDoe, and left Cameron. That chapter of my life was over, it was time to move forward. And then I realised that it was true – that chapter of my life was over. I had no more connection to JaneDoe, to TRU, to Indiana – it was time to move on.

I didn't feel elated any more.

For the next week I kept my mind and body busy, tried not to think about what I had lost, tried not to think about Indi, but then I finished carving Indiana's wooden box and I had to give it to her.

I stood outside Lina's house and thought about ringing the bell. It seemed ridiculous to be this close to Indi and not speak to her. But, she hadn't tried to contact me, she wasn't interested in me. I was simply delivering a gift for a friend – or, at least, that is what I tried to tell myself as I left the box on the doorstep.

I have spent more time with Alan than is strictly necessary. I feel better when I am with him. I spend at least a couple of hours a day at the shelter, and am expecting my home visit from them in a few days. But, I haven't spent all my time with Alan. I have applied for jobs, put my house on the market, and am thinking about maybe joining a dating agency, nothing digital though – something that exists in real life. I have been to

Eve's grave a couple of times, but only to see Doris and eat cake. I don't feel the same about Eve's grave any more, I have finally realised that she is not there, it is just her bones. I feel I am faking it when I go to visit her, but I don't like to think of Doris being there alone.

Brian from Alan's shelter calls me one afternoon. We have become sort of friends since I have been visiting each day.

'I'm not supposed to be doing this,' Brian whispers, 'but someone's here and they're taking your dog.'

I hire a StreetCar and drive far too fast across London to the shelter. I am too late. I see Alan on the street outside, being taken by someone wearing a ridiculously huge red coat.

'Oy!' I yell. 'That's my dog!'

They sink to the ground, wrapping their arms around Alan. I hope they are not going to put up a fight. Alan is mine. I rush towards them. I can hear them muttering. I look down at them and … it is Indiana.

I catch her just before she passes out onto the pavement.

I manhandle Indiana and Alan into the StreetCar and take them home. Alan becomes protective when we get to the house. He growls when I try to pick Indi up, so I pat him and reassure him I won't hurt her. Eventually he lets me carry her inside but he is hot on my heels the whole way. As we enter the front room, Biscuit takes one look at Alan, shrieks with indignation, jumps up off the sofa and dashes out through the cat flap. Our new house guests are going to take some adjusting to.

I put Indiana in my bed and sit in a chair by her for the rest of the night. She wakes up a couple of times, I give her water to drink, force her to swallow some paracetamol. I message Lina to let her know Indi is with me and she says I should feel free to keep her for a couple of days, but to beware – she is needy and eats a lot.

I fall asleep in the early hours of the morning, and when I wake up with a painful crick in my neck, Indi is awake and staring at me.

'Hi,' she whispers and smiles shyly.

'Hi,' I reply.

Indiana sleeps a lot for the next few days – waking for food and drink and then going straight back to sleep again. I sit in the chair next to her, applying for jobs and putting my house view-ings back for a few days. I look up once and she is watching me.

'I'm sorry I said those terrible things,' she says.

I am about to slip back into my old pattern and tell her it is fine, but it is not fine, it hurt. So instead I smile and nod. She doesn't say, 'I love you' again. I sleep on the sofa.

To begin with Alan won't leave her side; he lies on the floor next to her bed, sitting up every time she wakes up or turns over. I have to bring him food up and forcibly drag him outside to defecate. But, after a couple of days, he starts to come down-stairs for a few minutes at a time and – once he discovers the joy of the fire and of terrorising Biscuit – he stays downstairs and limits himself to popping up to check on Indi a couple of times an hour.

After a week, Indi's fever and cough are gone, she is eating normally (a lot) and spending her days happily reading my books on my sofa. We still haven't talked about 'us', and I am beginning to despair that the window of opportunity is gone.

I go to see Doris and take Alan with me. Alan loves Doris. Doris gives Alan cake.

'So, have you done it yet?' asks Doris.

'Doris, that is completely inappropriate,' I say.

Doris rolls her eyes.

'Not that. I mean, have you told her you love her?'

I shake my head.

'Oh for God's sake Jack! Tell her or get her to live somewhere else. You don't need a bloody housemate.'

Doris is right. I need to be honest. I need to tell Indiana the truth, and I need to tell Doris the truth.

'Doris,' I say, 'I don't want to come to the cemetery so much any more. Can we meet at a café instead?'

Doris gives a huge sigh and grins.

'Thank God. I thought you'd never bloody ask. I've been freezing my backside off every winter for the past two years.'

Indi isn't on the sofa when I get home, and my resolve falters. Maybe housemates is okay, maybe I am happy with housemates.

She calls to me from upstairs.

'Jack! Is that you? Can you come up here for a moment?'

I run upstairs. Indiana is standing naked in the middle of my bedroom.

'It's not the twenty-third day of my cycle, but I can't wait any longer,' she says.

I have no idea what she means, and I don't care. I cross the room in two giant leaps and she is in my arms. I kick the door to the bedroom shut with my foot and don't open it again for the next three hours. Alan howls outside, but most of the time we are making too much noise to hear him.

Indiana

I lie with my head on Jack's chest and listen to his heartbeat. It is strong and fast. It would make a good beat track for when I go running. I lick his nipple.

'Stop,' he says. 'I seriously need a break before we do it again.'

So do I, but I don't tell him that. We have been having sex almost continually for three days, only stopping for food, sleep, bathroom visits, and to walk Alan. I think how strange it is to be lying in bed with someone after having sex, rather than rushing away. Me, lying in bed with Jack. I like it. I am sleepy and hungry and comfy. I am just dozing off when I remember that there is something I want to ask him, something that has been bothering me since I got here. I jump out of bed, go to the window, and pull the curtains back.

'Jesus Indi!' Jack yells. 'Put some clothes on, you're not nine storeys up now!'

I look down. An old man is staring up at me. I don't know what to do so I wave at him. I wrap the curtain around my naked body and point out into the street.

'Jack, why are there three of Lina's brothers' lorries parked in your street?'

He grins.

'I thought you'd never ask.'

We put clothes on and go outside. Jack opens the backs of the lorries. It is my equipment. All of it. Everything from my office. My mouth falls open.

'How—'

He shrugs and smiles.

'You did this … for me?'

'I thought you might need it.'

I turn back and look at the lorries in wonderment.

'I do … I mean … thank you.'

I stand on my tiptoes and kiss him. I feel heat in my loins once more and wonder if there is room in the back of one of the lorries for the two of us. He pulls back and grins down at me.

'Maybe you can rebuild Peggy now. I'd like to meet them properly. Get them to tell me what Indi was like when they first met her.'

'Well, she didn't like being called Indi for a start.' I scowl.

He laughs. I look at the lorries.

'I don't even know if I can rebuild Peggy. I don't know if they survived or where they are. It could take years to put all this back together.'

'Maybe … maybe not.'

I look at him.

'What do you mean?'

He grins.

'It'll be quicker if your boyfriend helps.'

I frown at him.

'We haven't talked about that yet, and I hate the term "boyfriend" – it's ridiculous. We're not twelve years old. If you are anything, you will be my partner or my mate, or there must be some sort of scientific term that is better for us to—'

He laughs and stops me talking by pressing his mouth to mine. And – because he is such a good kisser and he rescued all my equipment and I am ready to have sex again – I let him.

But, after the sex, we will need to have a serious talk and put some rules in place – especially if he is going to be my boy-friend.

Eight Months Later

Lina

'For God's sake Lina, we're moving in tomorrow, what's so important that I have to see it right now?'

'You'll want to see this today I promise – come on!'

I drag Connie along the hallway with me. We are in Kent, in the house we complete on tomorrow. It has three bedrooms, a huge back garden, and looks out onto fields. Unfortunately we couldn't afford a sea-front house with my new, almost non-existent, salary.

'Lina, seriously, what is it?'

Connie pulls back on my hand. I turn to face her.

'Will you just trust me, please?'

She sighs. I grin, and pull the loft hatch down from above me with a bang.

The seller yells from downstairs.

'Everything okay up there?'

'Yes, Mr Frost,' I yell back. 'Just showing Connie the loft.'

I pull the ladder down from the loft and shove Connie up the steps in front of me.

'This better be worth it,' she grumbles.

'It will be,' I say, as I take her hand and lead her across the loft to the window on the far side of the roof.

'I've found an architect to do the drawings, and he thinks there'll be no problem in getting planning permission.'

'What are you talking about?'

I grin.

'This …' I open the window with a flourish.

Connie looks at me.

'Put your head out and look to your right.'

Connie sighs dramatically and then puts her head out of the tiny window and looks to the right.

'Oh!'

She pulls her head back in through the window and her face is alight with joy.

'It's a sea view!' she cries.

I nod.

'A sea view … for you.' A smile splits her face in two and she wraps me in her arms. My voice is muffled in her hair. 'We can make this our bedroom and have the window on that wall so you can see the sea anytime you want.'

She pulls back and kisses me.

'I love it and I love you.'

I smile again.

'That's good because you are going to have to drive back to London on your own. I have somewhere to be.'

Connie rolls her eyes.

'Of course – the new mystery job.'

I give her a wide smile.

'How is Indiana by the way?'

I shrug and grin.

'How would I know? I haven't seen her since last week.'

'Of course you haven't.'

Connie rolls her eyes again.

We leave our new seaside house and I bundle her into the car with a kiss.

As I stroll to my next meeting I marvel at how my life has changed. It is the middle of the day and I am strolling to a meeting, I might even stop and get a coffee. I feel no stress, no anxiety. I am excited to get to work, excited by the project I am working on, excited for my future.

My life has changed, I have changed, and I am happy. It turns out that Mama was right all along, *tu corazón crecerá y cambiará y florecerá. Amarás el amor.* I do love love and change is good.

Indiana

It is 4.32 p.m. on 22 September 2031, and I am in hell.

Not literal hell. My own hell. A hell I have brought and built for myself.

I am standing in one of the bedrooms of the house I have been living in for the past five months. There is an excellent view straight across Dungeness beach to the nuclear power station beyond. I cannot see the view – it is blocked by one of my servers. This bedroom is filled with servers, so is the other bedroom. The third bedroom houses the rest of my hardware – the QuantumX, and other items that I may use at some point. All of the bedrooms are full of computer equipment – Alan and I sleep in the front room.

Today is unseasonably warm for the end of September – temperatures outside have risen to over twenty-five degrees – inside the house it is closer to forty-five. The heat, coupled with the extensive equipment, constrained space, and overwhelming noise, is causing me intense stress. I am sweating. It is hell.

'This house is too small!' I shout over the noise of the servers.

No one hears me, so I go out of the bedroom, into the living room, and try again.

'This house is too small!'

'… *Cameron Gardner has declined to comment on recent developments, but has said …*'

Someone has left the Holo on and the news is covering the JaneDoe story once more. Cameron has been replaced as CEO. I do not feel sorry for her.

'Stop leaving the Holo on!' I shout.

Alan looks up from his hairy dog bed and grins at me. As soon as we moved here I took him to the groomers and had all his fur trimmed. It grew back. I took him again and it grew back once more. I have let him return to his former shaggy self. Alan loves our new house – he loves the heat, loves that the beach is outside our front door, loves that I have to sleep in the same room as him. Sometimes he annoys me with his constant grinning, lolling about, and complete lack of ire at anything in life – but usually I love him for exactly the same reasons.

'Stop shouting at the dog.'

Jack comes into the room carrying a mug.

'I am not shouting at the dog, I am shouting at you, but you didn't hear me.'

'I was making tea,' he says, handing me the mug. 'You need to calm down.'

'I am calm,' I mutter.

I am not calm. Jack is calm. Alan is calm. I am not.

Today is the culmination of five months of work by Lina, Jack and me – mostly me, but the other two have played their part. Jack is working full-time at a school in London, but spent the entire summer holidays helping to rebuild the QuantumX. Living together was not as disagreeable as I thought it would be, and I have found that it is exceedingly pleasing to have sex more than once a month. Lina has commuted from London three times a week in a car that she persuaded Connie they would need once they moved to the seaside. Connie does not know that Lina and I are working together – Lina wants to wait until I am able to give her a proper salary before she breaks the news. Her having to 'break the news' does not sound particularly complimentary.

The QuantumX has been operational for a couple of weeks now, but today is the day that I will connect it to the internet for the first time. Today will be the day when Peggy can come back. If they can come back. If they want to.

I am not calm.

'Did I miss it?'

Lina bangs through the door just as I sit down to update the code.

'Nearly,' I snap. 'Where have you been?'

'We went to the new house.'

'Have you told Connie yet?'

'No.'

'Coward.'

'Look who's talking.'

Lina is alluding to the fact that I have yet to tell Jack that I love him. He has told me that he loves me many, many times, but I haven't said it back, not since I told him outside the dog shelter. I need to be absolutely positive that I do love him before I tell him again, and I am unsure how to know unequivocally that I do. There really are no rules to love.

'Shut up. I'm concentrating,' I say.

Jack comes into the room and stands behind me, watching the screen over my shoulder. This room is too small for the three of us, and their presence is increasing my stress levels. I do not tell them, that would not be kind.

I finish inputting the code, link the system to the Wi-Fi that we are stealing from the Dungeness power plant, and hover the mouse over the *connect* tab. I hesitate. Jack puts a hand on one of my shoulders.

'Do it,' he says.

I like his hand on me. I can feel my tension flowing up and out through his touch.

I tap *connect*.

Nothing happens.

We wait.

Nothing happens.

I type #hello

Nothing.

Feeling like an imbecilic child, I type #Peggy?

Nothing.

I look hopefully at Peggy's voice-box, which I have optimistically installed on my desk. It remains dark and inert.

I ask the others to leave so that I can be alone, and then I cry.

Later, Lina heads back to London. I say I will go over and help her unpack at the new house when they arrive tomorrow. We both know that I won't.

After dinner I sit on the porch with Alan at my feet and watch the sunset. When I first moved here I was unnerved by the noise of the sea and of the nature that surrounded me. But, in time, I have grown to love it – the constant calling of the sea birds, the rush of waves hitting the shore when the tide is in, the low hum of the power station in the distance. I like the way the lights glow throughout the night. They remind me of Peggy.

'You okay?'

I look towards the doorway – Jack is leaning against the doorframe. Jack – like Alan – spends a lot of time lolling, a lot of time grinning, and has very little ire at anything in life. Sometimes Jack annoys me – but only sometimes.

'I love you,' I say.

Jack

I used to think that time should stop when something life-changing happened – Eve and me meeting for the first time, getting married, Eve's last words; or the first time Indiana genuinely smiled at me, our first kiss, the first time she deigned to call me her boyfriend. But now I have realised that there is a reason that time doesn't stop, that your life marches forward – because there is always going to be another defining moment, another chance for something life-changing to occur.

Time doesn't stop, and neither do we.

Your heart can skip a beat or break or burst with happiness, but it doesn't stop, it never gives up, not until the very end. We shouldn't either. While we have time, we have hope that something else can happen. Something miraculous, something joyous, something that will make your heart sing. And sometimes those events come out of the blue. They appear randomly and mysteriously, to remind you that it is all worth it. Life is worth it.

Indiana tells me she loves me, and I smile. A happy and genuine smile.

I am glad time didn't stop.

Indiana

It is late but I cannot sleep. The sea is roaring tonight, and I feel the urge to go outside and roar with it. I am filled with disappointment and sadness. I want to race wildly and desolately on the beach by myself, but Alan has fallen asleep in front of the door. I'd have to climb out of the window if I want to exit the house without waking him up. I could rouse Alan, but if I wake him he will wake Jack, and Jack will insist on coming out with me, and that will defeat the object of going out for a wild run on my own. So, instead of running wildly, I pace the tiny space that is available in my server room. It is three steps by four steps in diameter.

I find a wire that is loose on the back of one of my servers and push it securely back into place. I kid myself that maybe this will make a difference, maybe this is why I have been unable to contact Peggy. I know I am deluded.

I stare at my blank computer screen, then sit down, switch it on and input my password. Jack has changed the password to 'indianalovesjack' which makes me smile, but is not enough to pull me out of my slump. I tap discontentedly on my keyboard.

#hello

Nothing.

#Peggy?

Nothing.

#are you there?

My screen remains blank, Peggy's voice-box remains dark. I sigh.

#i miss you

It is true. I do miss Peggy. Even with my friends constantly injecting my ordered life with love and chaos, I miss Peggy. I miss my oldest friend.

There is a noise in the corner of the room, a scrabbling, skittering sound that I have not heard in a long time. I look across and see Spider's head poke up out of one of the boxes I have yet to unpack. He scrambles out stiffly on his spindly legs and scurries across the floor towards me. I pat his head ecstatically and type one-handed.

#Peggy?

Pause. My systems whir to life, Spider lets out a small squeal, and my screen flashes off. I reboot quickly. My heart is in my mouth.

I hold my breath and type.

#Peggy?

There is an agonising pause and then slowly, oh so slowly, a faint glow blossoms within Peggy's voice-box. My face breaks into a beaming smile and my heart explodes with happiness as a familiar Scottish voice rings clear and loud into the dark, crowded room.

'Hello Indiana. How was your day?'

ACKNOWLEDGEMENTS

The acknowledgments in my last book were extremely long so I promised that I would make these ones shorter. I lied.

Huge and unending thanks must first go to my brilliant editor, Kimberley Atkins who has once more taken my raggedy bunch of words and helped mould them into something wonderful. Thanks also to the lovely and talented Amy Batley for all of her work on my drafts and proofs, and for her never-ending support and patience with my endless questions. Massive thanks are due to the whole Hodder team for being so fantastic, working so hard and making my dreams come true.

To Cara Lee Simpson, my incredible agent to whom I owe my career and now my sanity! Thank you so much for all your support this year, for being eternally patient, perpetually encouraging and for helping me to continue in this career which I love so much.

To my mum and dad who have celebrated with me during the highs and hugged me when I am feeling low. Words cannot express how much your love and guidance has sustained me in the last couple of years. I love you.

To my amazing brother and sister, Amanda and Ben, who have given me such love and support and have never once complained about me bogarting the family WhatsApp with photos of my book taken in random places by random strangers.

I am hoping we will actually get to be together to celebrate this book! I love you and the beers are on me. Just the first round though.

To Alison and Richard and the Handfords and Robinsons – thank you all for reading my last book and not commenting (to me) about all the swearing, bad sex and dead people. This one has less swearing, better sex and hardly anyone dies! Yay! Thank you for being such an amazing bunch of people to know and love.

To Andrew, Bert, Jens, Sean and Will – thanks for all the beer and noodles, for all of your ideas and advice with this book and for being the best bunch of friends a token girl could ever wish for. Special thanks must go to Roberto Casula who tried his absolute hardest to explain quantum computing to me, who hardly ever rolled his eyes when I didn't understand it and who then went through the book and removed all the terrible, unforgiveable tech mistakes I had made. Any mistakes that are left are through my idiocy and not his.

Thanks and lots of love to Shell and Maz Dutson for their friendship, support, dog-sitting and for allowing me and the kids to basically move in last summer so that I could get some writing done. Shell and Maz must also get credit for introducing me to the 'silver in champagne cork' tradition. I have done it with every cork after every celebration with them for the last twenty years and my life continues to be joyous so I would say it works!

Thanks once again to Claire Williams for valuable insight into being a woman in a digital world and for her brilliance as a beta reader. To all my other friends and distant family who have been so wonderful over the past year – thank you. And to all the amazing book bloggers, reviewers, book Twitterers and Bookstagram friends that I have made and who have been so lovely and supported me and my career beyond my wildest dreams – thank you so much.

Sam and Tilly – this book is dedicated to you and I am dedicated to you. Watching you grow in so many incredible ways continues to be the greatest privilege of my life. I love you with all my heart.

Finally, once more, we come to the most important person in my life – Peter Handford. You were, are and continue to be my guiding light and the love of my life. My life has changed immeasurably in the past eighteen months and I wouldn't have been able to navigate any of it if I hadn't had you with me – nor would I have wanted to. Thank you for all of your input, ideas, support, love and wisdom. We're two books into my ten-book goal of being adequately able to express my love for you and I am still struggling with the enormity of my feelings and inadequacy of my prose – maybe book three will be the winner! I love you.

And that is it! Apart from one more tiny thing . . . if you understand basic coding, the code used in the October chapter is real. Go Easter egg hunting if you wish.

Thanks for reading. I hope you enjoyed the novel.
Beth xx

An invitation from the publisher

Join us at www.hodder.co.uk, or follow us
on Twitter @hodderbooks to be a part of
our community of people who love the very
best in books and reading.

Whether you want to discover more about a book
or an author, watch trailers and interviews, have the
chance to win early limited editions, or simply browse
our expert readers' selection of the very best books,
we think you'll find what you're looking for.

And if you don't, that's the place to tell us what's missing.

We love what we do, and we'd love you to be a part of it.

www.hodder.co.uk

@hodderbooks

HodderBooks

HodderBooks